By Anne Perry

Featuring William Monk

The Face of a Stranger
A Dangerous Mourning
Defend and Betray
A Sudden, Fearful Death
The Sins of the Wolf
Cain His Brother
Weighed in the Balance
The Silent Cry
A Breach of Promise
The Twisted Root
Slaves of Obsession
Funeral in Blue
Death of a Stranger
The Shifting Tide
Dark Assassin
Execution Dock
Acceptable Loss
A Sunless Sea
Blind Justice
Blood on the Water

Featuring Charlotte and Thomas Pitt

The Cater Street Hangman
Callander Square
Paragon Walk
Resurrection Row
Bluegate Fields
Rutland Place
Death in the Devil's Acre
Cardington Crescent
Silence in Hanover Close
Bethlehem Road
Farriers' Lane
Hyde Park Headsman
Traitors Gate
Pentecost Alley
Ashworth Hall
Brunswick Gardens
Bedford Square
Half Moon Street
The Whitechapel Conspiracy
Southampton Row
Seven Dials
Long Spoon Lane
Buckingham Palace Gardens
Treason at Lisson Grove
Dorchester Terrace
Midnight at Marble Arch
Death on Blackheath

BLOOD ON THE WATER

ANNE PERRY

BLOOD ON THE WATER

A William Monk Novel

BALLANTINE BOOKS • NEW YORK

Blood on the Water is a work of fiction. Names, characters, places, and incidents are the products of the author's imagination or are used fictitiously. Any resemblance to actual events, locales, or persons, living or dead, is entirely coincidental.

Copyright © 2014 by Anne Perry

All rights reserved.

Published in the United States by Ballantine Books, an imprint of Random House, a division of Random House LLC, a Penguin Random House Company, New York.

BALLANTINE and the HOUSE colophon are registered trademarks of Random House LLC.

ISBN 978-0-345-54843-6
eBook ISBN 978-0-345-54844-3

Printed in the United States of America on acid-free paper

www.ballantinebooks.com

2 4 6 8 9 7 5 3 1

First Edition

Book design by Karin Batten

To Victoria Zackheim,
for her unfailing friendship.

BLOOD ON THE WATER

CHAPTER

1

Monk leaned forward, resting on his oar for a moment as he stared across the water at the Pool of London. Ships from every country on earth lay at anchor, riding lights swaying in the dusk wind. The sun was low in the early summer sky and streaks of red flared across the west.

Behind him, at the other oar, Orme rested also. He was a quiet man who had worked on the river all his life.

"Good sight, eh, sir?" he said, his wind-burned face creased in satisfaction. "I reckon there ain't none like it in the world."

Monk smiled. For Orme that was an emotional—and lengthy—speech. "I think you're right," he agreed.

In unison they bent to their oars again. There was a pleasure boat a hundred yards or so in front of them, and they could hear the music and the laughter echoing from the lantern-strung decks, even from this distance. The boat had probably been out most of the day, perhaps as far as Gravesend on the estuary. It was perfect weather for it.

Some young men were playing around, mock fighting—too close to the rail, Monk thought. They ought to be more careful. The Thames current was deceptively swift, and the water filthy.

A few other small boats dotted the water close by, one within yards of the pleasure boat.

Monk frowned as a man on the deck shouted loudly and waved his arms, running towards the railing as if he would jump over it.

Then suddenly there was a shattering roar and a great gout of flame leaped from the bow. Debris shot high into the air and the column of light seared Monk's eyes. Instinctively he ducked as the shock wave struck, and pieces of wood and metal pelted into the water around him and Orme with deafening splashes. As one, they grasped the oars and fought to steady the boat in the turbulence that washed out from the stricken vessel.

There seemed to be bodies everywhere, people thrashing in the water, shouting above the din.

Monk was speechless, his chest almost too tight to draw breath. Without a word, he and Orme dug the oars in deep to race into the nightmare, shoulders bent, muscles straining, oblivious of everything but the horror.

Even as they rowed, the gaping hole in what was left of the bow was swallowed in water; and, huge paddles still turning, the boat plunged beneath the surface.

Within minutes they reached the first body: a man floating face up, eyes wide and sightless. They tried to lift him before realizing that both his legs were gone, bloody stumps half obscured in the filth of the river. He was beyond their help. Monk's stomach clenched as he let the corpse fall back into the water.

The second victim they found was a woman, her huge skirts already sodden and dragging her down. It took all Monk's strength to heave her aboard and Orme's very considerable skill to keep the boat steady. She was barely conscious, but there were too many others sinking fast to take the time to revive her. All they could do was put her as gently as possible face downward so the water she spewed did not drown her.

They worked in perfect synchronization, bending, lifting, keeping the boat from capsizing as it swung and tipped with their movement, and the clutching of desperate hands as white faces upturned in the gloom. It seemed few in the water could swim, and those who could were losing strength fast. Monk reached for one swimmer and felt fingers like iron digging into his flesh as he heaved him aboard.

He and Orme were both soaked to the skin, muscles aching, arms bruised. Monk's heart beat in his throat as if it would choke him. He could not do enough, not nearly enough.

It was only minutes after the explosion when the last of the boat slid into the dark river and disappeared. There was nothing left but the cries, the debris, and the bodies—some motionless, some still fighting to stay above the water.

Other boats were coming. A ferry was less than forty feet away. As it swung around and the men reached over to pull people from the water, the fading sunlight momentarily illuminated a picture and a name painted on the stern. A barge was making its way slowly, dragged against the current as it came closer. The bargee was bending and reaching out to help those closest to him. A small coal freighter was flinging barrels and scrap wood overboard; anything that anyone in the water could clutch on to to help them float before their imprisoning clothes dragged them, still screaming, under.

Monk and Orme had heaved six exhausted people out of the water, but that was all they dared carry. Sick with misery, they had to beat off others whose weight would have sunk the boat. Monk had to forcibly push one man away from the gunwales with the blade of his oar, afraid that he would overturn the boat in his frantic attempt to climb aboard.

They pulled for the shore, hearing the repeated thanks of the survivors who were huddled together, trying to assist one another in the body of the boat, holding up those barely conscious. Men on the banks were wading as far as they could, roped together, stretching out to lift and help.

Monk and Orme went back out again into the near darkness, directed now as much by cries as by sight. They pulled several more people out of the water, and rowed them ashore.

Monk lost all track of time. He was wet to the skin and so cold he was shaking, yet he and Orme could not give up. If there was even one person still alive in that black water, then they must find him or her.

It seemed every man in the River Police was here with them, and all manner of others joined in, united in their horror and grief. The banks were lined with people offering aid. Some pushed mugs of hot tea and whisky into freezing hands, helping the rescued to hold on and drink. Others had blankets; some even had their own spare, dry clothes.

The moon was high in the sky when Monk and Orme finally moored the boat and climbed wearily up the steps from the river to the level dockside, acknowledging in a glance that they had done all they could. The wind had risen and scythed across the open stretch in front of the Wapping Police Station, which was their headquarters.

Monk hunched into his coat instinctively but it was pointless when everything he wore was soaking wet. He increased his pace. Weary as he was, the cold was worse. He could hardly feel his feet and all his bones ached. The palms of his hands were blistered so he could barely move them.

He reached the door with Orme a step behind him. Inside, the woodstove was lit. The air was blessedly warm.

Sergeant Jackson came bustling toward them immediately, attending to Monk first, as rank demanded.

"You'd better get them clothes off, sir. We got plenty o' dry ones in the cupboard. Not your taste, sir, bein' a bit of a dandy like you are. But dry's all that matters now, or you'll catch your death. Beggin' yer pardon, sir, but you look like hell!"

Monk was shaking so hard his teeth were chattering and it was beyond his control to stop. "I thought hell was supposed to be hot!" he said with an attempt at a smile.

"No, sir, cold an' wet. Ask any seaman, 'e'll tell you," Jackson replied. He turned to Orme. "You too, Mr. Orme. You don't look no better. When you come out I'll 'ave an 'ot mug o' tea for yer wi' a good dash o' whisky in it."

"A very good dash, if you please," Monk added. He wanted the fire of it to take the edge off the horror inside him, the pity and guilt he felt for those he had not saved. He sat down and let the warmth of the fire wrap around him like a blanket, for a moment obliterating everything else.

Jackson did not say anything, but bustled about preparing the tea. He had spent all his life on the river, like Orme. He had seen other tragedies before, but nothing like this. He had been there all evening organizing men and boats, and answering desperate questions as well as he could.

Twenty minutes later, skin toweled hard enough to hurt, in clean, dry clothes, but still conscious of the stench of the river on his skin and in his hair, Monk sat near the stove and sipped his tea. It was piping hot, and at least half whisky. Orme was in the chair beside him, and Jackson was fussing over the next men to come in.

"That explosion," Orme said grimly, pulling a face as the tea burned his mouth, "couldn't have been the boiler. The explosion came from the bow, nowhere near the engines. So what the devil was it?"

"Can't see any other way it could've been an accident," Monk said. "That only leaves sabotage."

Orme scowled. "Why, sir? What kind of a madman would blow up a pleasure boat? It doesn't make any sense."

Monk thought about it for several moments. He was exhausted. Few ideas made sense. Why would anyone intentionally sink a pleasure boat? There was no cargo to steal or destroy, only people to kill. Was it an enmity against the owners of the boat? A business rivalry or vendetta? Or perhaps a grudge against some guests on the boat? Was it political? Or even an act of war by some insane foreign power or a group of anarchists?

"I don't know yet. Perhaps someone who hates Britain," Monk said finally. "There are a few of those." He finished the last of his tea and stood up, stumbling a little but quickly regaining his balance.

The door swung open and Hooper came in. He was a tall, loose-limbed man and was shedding water with every step. His face was haggard with grief. He didn't say a word, but folded himself up into one of the chairs as Jackson stood up to fetch him tea.

"We'd better go and speak to the survivors," Monk said quietly to Orme. "Somebody must have seen something. Big question is—did whoever did it escape, or did they intend to go down with the boat?" He put his hand on Hooper's shoulder for a moment. Words between them were unnecessary.

Orme set his mug down. "God help us, we really are talking about madness, aren't we?"

Monk did not bother to answer. He walked out into the night, his face cold again after the warmth of the room. In the clear sky moonlight spread a silver path across the river and the dark debris floating on its surface. He shivered at the thought that the boats still out there were only picking up bodies now, although most of the dead would be trapped in the wreck, settling into mud on the riverbed.

As he moved across the open space toward the dockside he thought of what he must do, and dreaded it. But it was inescapably his job. He was Commander of the Thames River Police. Any crime on the river was his responsibility, and this was the worst incident in living memory. There must have been the best part of two hundred people on the boat. The bereaved would be numerous. At the moment the whole tragedy seemed chaotic, senseless. Where could he begin?

Coleman, one of his own men, approached him in the dark. Monk could hardly see his face, but his voice when he spoke was rough-edged, only just in control.

"Looks like we saved about fifty, sir. Got most of them here on the north bank." He coughed, his throat tight. "Put 'em anywhere we can.

You could start with that warehouse over there, Stillman's. A lot of survivors there and they're making room for more, if there are any. All sorts 'ave come with blankets, clothes, tea, whisky, anything that can help." He coughed again. "Got half a dozen sent to hospital, too, but I can't see how they'll make it. That water's like to poison you even if you don't drown in it."

"Thank you, Coleman." Monk nodded and walked on. The warehouse was close. He needed to put his emotions aside and concentrate on the questions he had to ask and the answers he needed to know to begin to make sense of this.

He picked his way between the boxes, kegs, and bales outside in the warehouse yard. He went up the step to the cracks of light he could see around the door.

Inside, the warehouse was lit by bull's-eye lanterns, and there were a dozen or so people lying on the floor wrapped in blankets. Several women were ministering to them with hot drinks and towels, in some cases rubbing their arms and legs, all the time talking to them gently. Only a few glanced up at Monk's entry. He did not look like a policeman; he was exhausted, unshaven, and dressed in ill-fitting waterman's clothes.

"My name is Monk," he introduced himself to a woman carrying towels and bandages. "River Police. We need to find out what happened. Which of these people can I speak to?" he asked.

"Does it have to be now?" the woman said sharply. Her face was gray with fatigue, eyes red-rimmed. There were stains of dirt and blood down the front of her dress.

"Yes," he said quietly. "Before they forget."

Another, older, woman rose to her feet from where she had been helping a man sip a hot drink. She was strongly built, her clothes so worn they were faded in patches where the pattern had been rubbed off the cloth. In the yellow light of the lantern her face suggested not only weariness but disgust.

"It's unlikely they'll forget!" she said between her teeth. "They will probably relive it the rest of their lives!"

"None of us will forget the horror," Monk answered her quietly. "But it wasn't an accident. I need to know who did this, and for that I need details only they can provide."

"Find whoever built the damn boat!" she retorted bitterly, turning away from him and towards a man cradling a broken arm.

Monk put his hand on her arm, holding her firmly. He felt her tense and then pull against him. "It was an explosion," he said between his teeth. "The whole bow blew out; there was a hole in it you could drive a coach and four through."

She turned back to him, her eyes wide. "Who told you that?"

"No one. I was on the river, a hundred yards away. I saw it."

The woman crossed herself, as if to ward off an unimaginable evil. "Don't keep 'em long," was the only thing she said.

Slowly Monk went with her from one to another of them, helping her to hold them up, to keep the blankets around them. He refilled cups and mugs with tea and as much whisky as he dared, all the while gaining the halting accounts of what little they knew. There were few facts to be had. Everyone agreed that there had been no warning. One moment they were laughing and talking, listening to the music, watching the lights, flirting, telling jokes. The next there was a deafening noise. Some found themselves in the water almost immediately. Others recalled scrambling across the deck and jumping as the whole boat seemed to heave them off.

Most of them had tales of how they were rescued, the despair as the water washed over them, then the feeling of relief as hands grasped theirs, all but wrenching their arms from the sockets as they were pulled upward, gasping and trying to stammer their gratitude. Others had clung onto wreckage for what seemed like ages until a barge or a ferry made its third or fourth rescue journey.

One man in a torn shirt broke down and wept. He had been on the deck with his wife. The very first shock of the explosion had separated them and he had not seen her again. Monk wanted to offer him some hope, but even before he spoke the words he cringed at how meaningless they were. After all, how would he have felt had it been his own wife, Hester?

If Hester had drowned then he would wish he had too. Melodramatic? Perhaps. But he could not even imagine the pain of never seeing her again, or touching her, never being able to speak to her, hear her footsteps in the house. Never sharing anything more with her.

He gripped the man's hand and let him weep, holding on to him as if he, too, were drowning.

All the survivors he spoke to were men, except one. It was more than just greater physical strength that had saved the men rather than the women. It was the complete inability of the women to fight free of the heavy, wet skirts wrapped around them.

From all of the survivors, the story was the same. They could offer no details that could help make sense of the explosion; just the horror of what they had experienced, the darkness and cold and fear that they would die in the water. By dawn there was nothing else to ask, nothing to hear. Monk went back to the station at Wapping to snatch an hour or two of sleep, and to send a message to Hester that he was unhurt.

He found Orme standing before the potbellied stove warming himself as if he, too, had just come in. He straightened up as soon as Monk entered, and moved a little to one side to make room for him.

"Learn anything useful?" Monk asked.

Orme huddled further into his jacket, which was pulled up around his ears.

"No, sir, nothing as I didn't expect—poor devils. All on deck when it exploded. Everyone agrees it was in the bow. Just blew the whole thing off, but we knew that. Took in water like a scoop."

"No one saw anybody acting strangely?" Monk persisted. He did not look at Orme's face. He did not want to see the emotion in it. Only two days ago he had been celebrating the birth of his first granddaughter, wanting to share his happiness with everyone. Now his voice was hoarse, as if his throat hurt.

"No, sir. Too busy having fun, dancing, joking, doing what people do on a cruise." He took a long breath.

"No one from below deck?" Monk asked. They must keep talking; silence would be worse.

"Not that I saw," Orme answered. "Apparently there was some kind of fancy party going on down there. Special guests only. Best champagne and food." His lips tightened. "We'll get a list of them come daylight. It'll be bad."

"I know. Get an hour or two with your head down. We'll need all our wits when we have to haul the thing up. I've never lifted a big one. How do they do it?"

"What?"

"Raise the wreck," Monk replied. "We can't leave it there. Next thing you know, someone else'll run afoul of it and sink as well!"

"I'll take care of it, sir. We know builders with traction engines. It'll be slow, but we'll get 'er up." Orme looked pensive. "But it'll move everything inside 'er. Could wash a lot of the bodies out. And there must be a hundred an' fifty or more trapped below the decks. We'll have to bury them decent . . ."

Monk remembered another case he had had, years ago, before he had joined the River Police. The horror of that blind, underwater work still made his skin crawl, but he could not evade it.

"Maybe we should hire one of those diving suits and go down and look at it before we raise it."

Orme stared at him, his eyes wide with fear.

Monk smiled with a twist to his lips. "I've done it before. I'll go down. We've got to see what it's like, before everything moves."

"Yes, sir," Orme said hoarsely. "I suppose we have."

Monk woke up slowly, his head thumping. He came to consciousness as if rising from a great depth. For a moment he was confused. The light hurt his eyes. He was in his office in the police station. He sat up, aching all over, memory flooding back like a riptide, bringing with it all the fear and grief he had seen.

Sergeant Jackson passed Monk a cup of tea, hot and much too strong. He took a mouthful of it anyway, then bit into the thick heel of bread offered him. He looked around. The sun was bright through the windows. He realized with a jolt that it was well into the morning, nothing like as early as he had intended to be up.

"What time is it?" he demanded, rising to his feet stiffly, every joint aching. For a moment he swayed, his balance rocky. He was so tired his eyes felt gritted with sand.

"Time to go to the diving people, sir, that is if you've still got a mind to," Jackson replied. He was young, and he looked up to Monk.

Monk grunted, running his hands through his hair and over the stubble on his face. There was no time to think of his appearance now.

"Yes. Right," he agreed. Better not to think of it, not even to give himself time to think of it, or his nerve might fail him. The last thing on earth he wanted to do was climb into one of those heavy, unwieldy suits with the weighted feet, then have someone lower the helmet over his head with its glass-plated visor. They would screw him in so he breathed through a tube, a lifeline upon which his existence depended. One tangle in that, one knot, and he would suffocate—or if it was severed, he would drown. He must not think of it. He must control his mind lest he panic.

More than one hundred people had died. Quite apart from their families, they themselves deserved justice. He had to discover what had happened to them, who had caused it, and why.

He washed briefly, drank the rest of the tea, and finished the bread. It was fresh and really very pleasant. He could not remember when he had last eaten.

Then he walked out into the sun and across the open space to the steps that led from the dock edge down to the river. The steps were stone, running parallel to the wall, and many of them were now well below the swift-running tide, hidden until low water. Moored up against them was the boat that would take him down river to where they would anchor while he went over the side in the suit and walked along the riverbed to the wreck.

Of course he would not go into the river alone. No one dived without having someone else to watch, to help, to free you from snags if falling debris crossed your air line, or—just as bad—pinned you down.

He heard the shouts of men, the greetings. He answered automatically, forgetting what he replied even as he said the words.

He went through all the procedures as if in a dream. No one indulged in unnecessary conversation. The business they were about filled their minds. He listened to his instructions as the wind off the water stung his skin, and nodded as they told him step by step exactly what they were going to do and he in turn told them what he needed to see.

Amazingly, everything around them looked exactly the same as usual. Strings of barges, laden with goods, passed them, going upriver with the tide. Ferries plied back and forth from one bank to the other. There were plenty of small cargo or passenger boats, but none was out for pleasure this morning. He saw only one or two pieces of driftwood wreckage floating slowly upstream. There would be far more, farther down, spreading wider and wider from the point of the wreck.

They picked up speed away from the shore. The diving equipment was all laid out ready. They would drop anchor a short distance from where the boat had gone down, and then he would put on the heavy, clumsy-looking suit and helmet. And then there would be no avoiding the inevitable.

Monk stared at the water. It was murky brown, nothing like the dazzling blue sea he saw in the glimpses of memory that came to him now and again, a view sharp for an instant, then gone. Twelve years ago, just after the end of the Crimean War, he had had a serious carriage accident that had knocked him unconscious. When he had woken, his memory had been obliterated. He had not even recognized his own face in a looking glass.

Over time fragments had come back, like a picture painted on something fragile and shattered into a hundred pieces. Some of them had been painful, glimpses of a self he did not like. Others were good: lost moments from childhood, like the memory of the sea and of boats far in the north, on the coast of Northumberland.

He had learned to live with his loss of memory, and to rebuild himself. It would not have been possible had Hester not helped him. Her faith in him had been the spur to put the pieces together, to keep working at it even when the picture seemed ugly and full of darkness, as opaque as the water now swishing past the bow of the boat. He had come to believe that courage depended on knowing that there was somebody who believed in you.

No matter that the thought of going into that water, creeping his way through the gloom of the river mud and into the wreckage, frightened him; he must do it. Hester believed in him, in his ability to do the right thing, and he must never betray that faith.

They were there. He could see the men on the bank and make out the shape of the engines that would slowly haul what was left of the boat up to where it could be examined, and where it would no longer be a danger to the river traffic.

It was time to pay attention to the task, to listen, to climb into the suit, and let them bolt the glass over his face, then get into the water, sinking down while it closed over his head. Both his own life and that of his diving companion might rest on his remembering the instructions he was given exactly.

Obediently he climbed into the suit. He had rehearsed it mentally enough that he moved automatically, almost easily. Only when he felt the cold of the river and the weight of his boots pulling him down did it suddenly shock his senses in a way no nightmare could.

The darkness was almost immediate. Everything around him was brown, closed in, at once both swirling and shapeless; it was as if he were drifting in mud. The lamp in his helmet seemed absurdly feeble. Then his feet reached the bottom, sinking down as if he had landed on sludge, not stones. He struggled for a moment to keep his balance, arms out like a tightrope walker.

He moved his head so the light struck the murk around him. He felt a touch on his arm, and there was another grotesque figure beside him, lumbering and globe-headed like himself. It pointed forward. Awkwardly he obeyed.

It was only moments before he saw jagged ends of the wreck emerging in the gloom. It gaped like the jaws of some gigantic fish, and where the bow should have been there was nothing. At that instant he would have given almost anything to have backed away and gone up into the light.

He took a deep breath of the air coming to him through that fragile pipe, and stepped forward.

He had already visualized what he would see, but nothing prepared him for the reality. The hull had buckled. The floors lay at strange angles. In some places doors hung open. In others they were jammed fast shut. There were eddies of current where the tide was funneled unnaturally. More than once Monk was swept off balance, and realized with something close to panic how easy it would be to fall and become entangled in the debris and his own equipment.

Everywhere there were bodies, some lying on the decks, some piled on top of each other. Several were jammed in doorways as if they had rushed together to escape, and it had cost all of them their lives. A few here and there—mostly women with skirts floating around them—drifted with the current, bumping blindly into buckling walls. Their dead faces were ghostly pale in the beam of Monk's lamp.

Would he find anything here that could tell him what had happened? Any evidence that could implicate someone? The explosion had left the whole front end of the boat raw and wide to the river, flooding the decks and sweeping people off their feet and back into the prison of the lower rooms. The only ones with any chance of escape were those on the top deck. Those at the fancy party below, dressed in their best and smartest clothes, champagne glasses in their hands, were probably dead even before the boat plunged to the bottom. Was that chance, or intention?

The bodies would be taken out, identified where possible, and given decent burial. Several would be washed out by the very act of raising the boat. Some were already gone and would drift up on the banks in the days and weeks to come. And a few perhaps would never be found, washed out to sea, or snagged forever in the detritus of the deeper channels, eventually to be swallowed by the mud.

Monk moved forward very carefully, testing his footing, as far into the bow as he dared go. Once he slipped and was yanked back by his fellow diver. His heart was pounding and he forced himself to control his breathing before he choked. As he looked around, he could see what they had already suspected: the explosion had been caused by something placed in the bow deliberately. There were no boilers or other mechanical equipment anywhere near the heart of the destruction. But there was no evidence of what had caused the explosion either, at least in the area they were able to safely walk.

He signaled to his companion that it was time to go back up again. He had to force himself not to hurry as he made his way back toward the light, and finally up into the air and the day. When he reached the surface he was heaved back onto the deck of the boat and eager hands unfastened his face plate. He breathed in clean air in grateful gasps. When the helmet was unscrewed and lifted off, the width of the sky could have been heaven itself. For all the horror of what he had seen, he was smiling, gulping, almost wanting to laugh.

"Seen enough, sir?" his diving companion asked, struggling out of his own suit.

"Yes." Monk forced himself back to the moment. "Yes, thank you. We'll tell them to begin getting her up." He put the corpses out of his mind and concentrated on the fabric of the boat, the hole where the bow had been. The explosives must all have been there. Thinking about it coldly, it was the perfect place to put them. There was nothing dangerous or valuable there, so no reason for any of the crew to be on watch. No chance of an accidental ignition of the charge. It had been not only deliberate, but also clever and very carefully planned.

But why?

The exhilaration of surfacing passed and Monk found anger overtaking him again. He thanked the diving crew and asked them to put him ashore at the nearest steps. He made his way back to where Orme was standing with the overseer of the crew that was to raise the wreck. Orme looked exhausted, his face pale, the stubble of his beard adding to his crumpled air. But as always he stood straight, eyes narrowed against the light, pink-rimmed with weariness.

"Bow blown out, as we thought," Monk said quietly. "Pretty clean job. Couldn't see any other damage. People trapped below never had a chance."

Orme nodded but did not speak. He was a man who never forced words in where they had no meaning.

"It'll take a fair time to get her up," the overseer said grimly, giving Monk a slight gesture of acknowledgment. "Get the bodies off as we can. Bound to lose some of them as everything shifts inside. Send men after the rest. You just catch the bastards that did this."

"We will," Monk replied, knowing full well that it was a promise he might not be able to keep.

He watched a few moments longer, then nodded to Orme and turned away. He should not have said they would succeed, but how else did one answer to such an atrocity? "We'll try"? It would sound as if he thought it ordinary, just another case. It wasn't. Possibly a hundred and fifty completely innocent people had been drowned in the dark, filthy waters of the Thames. Some of them might never even be found for their relatives to bury. And for what? What end could it possibly serve?

But someone had to have planted the bomb. Perhaps they had even been paid to do so. And there were avenues along which to search for such a person. There were expert dealers in explosives, such as nitroglycerin. Amateurs did not handle it; it was far too volatile. There was always somebody who had seen something, heard something, who could be pressured to talk.

Monk walked across the open space toward the street. All around him were warehouses, cranes, men beginning the day's work of loading and unloading. It was May and the sun was already bright. Six weeks and it would be the longest day of the year.

One of the first things to look for was opportunity. Who had had the chance to place explosives in the bow of the ship? And nitroglycerin was the most common explosive, but in the last year or two there was also the new Swedish invention of dynamite. It was easy to carry, and needed an ignition device to set it off, so was far less prone to accidents. A few sticks of it would blow almost anything to kingdom come. So that was something to look into as well.

But why? That was the difficulty, and the key. The motive for whoever had committed such an act of barbarity, and the means by which they had done so.

He was so lost in his thoughts that he almost bumped into the man coming toward him. The man stopped abruptly to avoid the collision.

"Sorry," Monk said. "Wasn't looking where I was going." He stepped to the side but the man did not move. Instead, he held out his hand as if to introduce himself.

Monk was in no mood for conversation, but glancing at the man's face, he thought he seemed vaguely familiar, as if they might have met casually at some point. He had mild, almost sensitive features and a considerable gravity to him. Perhaps he had lost someone he cared for in the disaster. He deserved civility at least.

"Monk?" the man asked, but with the tone of voice as if he knew.

Monk forced himself to be responsive. He was exhausted, cold from the dive, and heartsick from what he had seen. He could not remember when he had last eaten anything except the heel of bread.

"Yes?" he said calmly, meeting the man's eyes and seeing pain in them. Yet, the look was not one of personal grief.

"John Lydiate," the man replied.

Monk was startled. He remembered him now. Sir John was commissioner of the London Metropolitan Police. Had he come here to find out the progress on the case so soon?

"Good morning, sir," Monk replied. "Sorry I didn't recognize you. I've just come up from the wreck."

Confusion on his face, Lydiate looked over toward the engines, which were now beginning to haul out the sunken hulk of the boat. "Do you mean you were diving?" he asked curiously.

"Need to see it before everything shifts as they get it out of the water," Monk explained. "Explosives were placed in the bow. Blew it right out. It went down in less than five minutes." He had meant to control himself, say it factually, but his voice shook as he saw it again in his mind's eye, the darkness as the ship plunged and the lights went out, then the screaming, the people he couldn't help.

Lydiate was pale. Perhaps he, too, had been up all night, even if not on the river. "You saw it?"

"I was on the water, about a hundred yards away," Monk replied.

"God in heaven!" Lydiate said quietly. It was a prayer, not a blasphemy. "I . . . I'm sorry."

Monk stared at him. It seemed an odd thing to say.

"It's an atrocity," Lydiate went on, now a very faint flush on his face. "Apparently there were quite a few very important people on board, foreigners. The government has . . ." He hesitated then started again. "They've said that because of the international implications we need to be seen to do everything we can. That's why I am here. They've put me in charge. You can stand down; go back to your normal responsibilities on the river."

Monk was stunned. He must have misheard what the man said. "It happened on the river!" he said sharply, too tired to be courteous. "The damn thing's in the river right now!" He waved his arms toward the half-submerged chains, which were dripping as they moved inch by inch, hauling the wreckage up.

"I know," Lydiate agreed. "Nevertheless, you are relieved of command. Home Office orders. I'm sorry."

Monk started to speak, and then realized he had nothing whatever to say. The decision was numbing, absurd, and also unarguable. If the government had made that decision for political reasons, no matter how idiotic, how unjust or self-serving, it was pointless to argue. And ultimately, it was certainly not Lydiate's fault that Monk was being relieved of command.

"I'll give you a written report of what I saw," Monk said, his voice rasping. "Whatever they find now you'll see for yourself. No doubt you'll speak to my men who interviewed people on the shore . . . and the survivors."

"I will. Thank you. You should go home and get some food, and some sleep," Lydiate said unhappily. His embarrassment was clearly acute and he did not seem able to add anything more.

Monk nodded and walked on up the incline and into the street. He barely saw the buildings around him or the people. His misery settled into a hard, white-hot rage inside him. This was his river, his responsibility. The people who had been killed had been in his charge. And now there was nothing he could do to keep his promise to find the truth, and exact whatever kind of justice there was to exact.

CHAPTER

2

Hester heard the explosion from their home in Paradise Place, which was about a quarter of a mile from the riverbank on the south side, opposite the Wapping Police Station. Like everyone else along the small street, she went outside immediately and stared across the rooftops of Greenwich and the darkening expanse of the river toward the Pool of London. The flames were brilliant orange, illuminating everything around them for a few terrible seconds, and then they were gone. All along the street there was only silence.

The woman next door stood paralyzed, a dish towel in her hands, her face contorted with horror. Farther down, where the street turned into Union Road, there were a couple of men, also motionless, shoulder to shoulder, staring toward the river. Then a youth came running up the cobbles shouting something.

Hester realized that Scuff was beside her and she had not even heard his feet on the stones. He was sixteen now, taller than she was, unrecognizable as the urchin she and Monk had befriended when he was, by his own estimation, roughly eleven. Then he had been narrow-shouldered, undersized, and frighteningly streetwise. Children did not survive in the London Docks alone if they were not. It was debatable whether they had adopted him, or he had adopted them. It was not discussed, but tacitly accepted, that his home with them had become permanent.

He touched her hand. "What 'appened?" he said huskily.

She did not hesitate to put her arm around him. "I don't know. A very big explosion and fire, and then it went out completely."

"Ship," he answered. "Must 'ave gone down like a stone. Monk won't . . . be . . ." His voice choked off with fear.

"No, of course he won't," Hester said firmly. "But he'll be going to it. I expect we won't see him again until tomorrow."

"Are you sure?"

"No, not absolutely." She had never lied to him. He was too much of a realist to have believed her if she had tried. Perhaps if she had known him since he was a baby there would have been a time when she would have offered only comfort, and let reality come later. But he had been a survivor when they met. His trust in them had grown slowly, and they must honor that trust with honesty, no matter how crushing the truth might be for him.

"I'll go . . ." he started.

"No you won't," she replied. "You'll stay here. I'll go down to the wharf and ask. I have the right to know, and, believe me, I won't take any soothing answers. I'll come back and tell you. Promise me you'll stay here?" She turned to face him. "I mean it, Scuff. I need to be able to trust you. And if it's bad, I'll need you to help me."

His eyes widened and he caught his breath, understanding filling his eyes. "Yes . . ." he nodded. "I'll stay 'ere, I promise. But . . . yer'll come back, won't yer?"

"Of course I will, as soon as I know anything. I promise that."

He sighed. "All right, then."

She returned a little before midnight.

Scuff was asleep in front of the remnants of the fire, but he woke as soon as she came into the room, fear stark in his face.

"He's all right," she said immediately. "It was a pleasure boat that sank. Almost everyone on it was lost." She came in and sat on the chair opposite him. In the dim light of the gaslamp he looked crumpled and terribly vulnerable, like any child woken from sleep.

"The River Police will be working all night, trying to save anyone they can," she went on. "I expect by daylight they'll still be finding out what happened. We'll just have to wait. Do you want a hot drink before you go to bed? I do. I know it's May, but it's still awfully cold out there."

He nodded. "'E's all right, then?"

"Yes. He'll be tired and cold, by the time he gets home, but safe—yes."

Scuff's face filled with relief. "Yeah. Can we 'ave some cocoa?"

"Good idea," Hester agreed. "Of course we can."

"I'm not going to school till 'e comes back . . ." Scuff said. He made it sound like a statement, but in his eyes there was a question, and he looked at her anxiously to try to judge her reaction.

She wanted to give in to him this time, and the little prickle of uncertainty within her made it easy. "This once," she agreed.

He smiled, but did not push his good fortune. "I'll make the cocoa?" he offered. "Stove's 'ot."

"Thank you." She accepted his offer, following him down the passage into the kitchen. She was momentarily overwhelmed by a wave of emotion. She loved this boy far more than she had imagined possible. He was an urchin from the dockside, and yet she understood his mind. She saw in his gestures and expressions a strange reflection of herself and now, as he matured, a greater measure of Monk also. Could the connection of love be as powerful as that of blood?

MONK CAME IN MIDMORNING. Hester had been watching for him through the window. He was still dressed in the borrowed clothes from the police station. He moved stiffly and his face was gray with exhaustion, and every few steps he hitched at his ill-fitting trousers as they slipped on his waist.

Hester met him in the passage, and after a glance into his eyes she silently put her arms around him. He stiffened for an instant as though he were too tender to bear her touch. Then he relaxed and his arms tightened around her until she had to bite her lip not to make a sound at the strength of his hold.

It was several moments before she looked up into his face, leaning back only inches. She could have asked him how he was, but words were insufficient for what she knew he must have seen. Instead she reached out and put her fingers gently to his cheek and gave a tiny smile.

"At the least a hundred and fifty dead." He gave the numbers that made the enormity of it unalterable. "Someone did it on purpose, put explosives in the bow and blew it out. I went down—"

She froze. "Down . . . ?"

"Diving suit," he explained. "I've done it before. They're most of them still there, trapped. They hadn't a chance, not ever."

Questions teemed in her mind, though none of them right to ask now. He could not know all the answers yet. The immediate things he needed were comfort, warmth, food, then as much sleep as possible.

"How long do you have before you need to go back?"

There was something in his face she could not read, a fury, a grief that surged into him until his body was rigid.

"William?" she said quickly. "What is it? Can't you stay?" She drew breath to argue that he must, but the look in his eyes stopped her.

"I can stay as long as I want to," he said gruffly, his voice catching in his throat. "They've taken the River Police off the case. Too many important people killed. They've given it to the commissioner—Lydiate."

All sorts of protests boiled up inside her. It was a ridiculous decision, and completely unfair. Whoever had made it was incompetent. But none of these objections would change anything. Years ago, when she had been a nurse to the army in the Crimea, she had fought hotly against injustice, vanity, and blind, towering stupidity. Occasionally, on the battlefield where death was a reality, she had won. But once back in England, making such arguments was like trying to write in the sand; the weight and complexities of the hierarchy of power erased her efforts like an incoming tide.

For seconds she did not answer, even though she knew Monk was waiting. Then at last she stepped back a little.

"How unfortunate for Lydiate," she said quietly, judging her words as she would the pressure of a bandage on a raw wound. "He'll be completely out of his depth because he doesn't know the river well enough to deal with this. But then I wonder if anyone can. It's going to be a terrible mess. Just at the moment we are all numb with shock, still trying to realize what has happened. But it won't be long before the anger comes. People will want to blame someone. Rage is so much easier than facing loss. They'll demand answers. The newspapers will be on it all the time. Why did it happen? Why didn't somebody prevent it? Why haven't the police caught whoever it is? No matter what Lydiate does, it won't be enough."

She smiled bleakly, and her voice became even softer. "That is, if he can do anything at all. Nothing will bring those people back. They'll want to blame somebody, hang somebody, even if it isn't the right person. Catching someone will make everyone feel as if they're not completely powerless. There'll be all kinds of crazy theories and rumors. It's stupid that they have taken the case from you. You're the one person who might have been able to solve it—but realistically, maybe no one can . . ."

He let out his breath in a sigh. His voice shook a little. "They should have let me try! The victims deserve that! I promised . . ." He blinked hard. "Hester, I spoke with the survivors, all huddled up, battered, freezing, and stunned with loss. One man was on the boat with his daughter. She had just recovered from a long illness. They were celebrating. One moment she was laughing, the next she was gone." His voice cracked. "I promised I'd find whoever did this . . ."

"I know," she whispered. "I've made promises I couldn't keep. I know how it hurts . . ."

"Do you?" he demanded, his voice tight with pain.

Memories of the battlefields surged back into her mind, drenched with the smell of blood. "I've promised soldiers I'd save them, and I couldn't always . . ."

He drew in a breath. "Oh, Hester! I'm sorry . . ." His arms tightened around her again and it was moments before he let her go. Only then did he notice Scuff standing in the doorway, pale-faced but with a thin, shy smile.

"You all right?" Scuff asked nervously. "You want a cup o' tea, or something?"

"Yes," Monk replied immediately. "Yes, please. And what are you doing here at this time of day? You should be at school. You ducking it again?"

"Couldn't go till I knew you was all right," Scuff replied.

"You—" Monk began.

"Couldn't leave Hester, could I?" Scuff glared at him. Then he swallowed hard and turned on his heel to go and make the tea.

Hester started to laugh a little jerkily, trying to stop it turning into tears.

As soon as he had drunk his tea, Scuff left Paradise Place, but he did not go to school. Actually he had not said that he would, not in so many words, although he knew both Hester and Monk had assumed he was headed there.

But this was not the time to go and learn things in books, however important they may be one day. Right now he must return to the river.

Some stupid man in a clean shirt and a woolen suit had taken away Monk's right to work this momentous case, when the damage was not just on the river but actually in it. Well, under it, now! Policing the river was Monk's job. That was who he was. They had no right to do this, no matter what Hester had said to comfort him about it being a bad case that maybe no one could solve. Monk could do all kinds of things other people couldn't. She just didn't want him hurt, which was all right, except life wasn't like that. All those people were dead and under the water. That was wicked, and had to be sorted out, and somebody needed to be punished, really punished, for it.

And it was Scuff's river too. He had been born on its banks and grown up within sight of it, to the sounds of it, feeling its damp all his life. Even in his sleep he could hear the lapping of its tide, and its foghorns booming in the distance. Almost all the treasures of his childhood had been saved from its depth, not to mention the pieces of coal, metal, china—even wood, now and then, that he had sold to feed himself. How could any ordinary land-bound London policeman know the river, or care about it as he and Monk did?

First he would go to where they were hauling the ship up, but quietly, not speaking to anyone who might know him. This must not get back to Monk, which meant that Scuff must steer clear of Mr. Orme as well. Although he would have been with Monk, so he had likely been up all night too, and sent home as Monk had been. Scuff figured he was safe for a while.

He walked briskly down to the ferry and used some of his savings to pay his fare to the other side. He climbed up the Wapping Stairs, keeping his face averted from the police station. He went as quickly as possible along the bank toward the dock where he knew from the ferryman that the pleasure boat was being dragged up. He tried to imagine what strength that would take, and what kind of engines it would need. And chains. They'd better be good! If one of them snapped it could take the heads of half a dozen men standing too close. He refused even to think of that!

He moved quickly, used to slipping by unnoticed. It was not so far, about a mile or so. There were loads of people standing around watching. What did they expect to see? A broken ship and a whole lot of dead bodies? They looked sort of huddled, even though it was a bright May morning. You would have thought it was winter! Maybe they were there because they'd lost someone they loved and they felt they had to come to see the boat pulled from the river, out of a kind of respect, like standing at the graveside at a funeral. Scuff did not like funerals. He did not want to see dead bodies here either. He'd seen people drowned before. It was horrible . . . the bodies all bloated out of shape, and squashy.

But if he was ever going to be a policeman like Monk, then he'd better get used to it. Even Hester could look at dead bodies! But then she could do a lot of things that most people couldn't.

He moved to stand beside a man and woman who were nicely dressed, but pale-faced and as close together as they could get. What would he say to them? Something that would not sound stupid, or childish, or cruel. Nobody was coming out of the wreck alive. Did they hope there was? They couldn't be that daft—could they?

There was a shout from the shore. Then as they watched, the funnel of the boat broke the surface. No one made a sound. It was so quiet he could hear the gushing of water out of the sides.

Without weighing his words, Scuff turned to the man.

"You shouldn't watch this, sir. If you lost someone, you don't need ter see it." Then he stopped abruptly. It was out of place. He had no right to speak. They had not asked him.

The man turned toward him in surprise, as if he had not realized Scuff was there. "You're right," he said quietly. "And maybe you shouldn't either. Did you lose someone, lad?"

"No. My pa's in the River Police. He worked all night trying to save people, an' now they've taken 'im off the case. Given it to the land police." Scuff's voice was bitter, but he could not help it.

The man's arm tightened around the woman beside him. "You're right. We can't do anything here. Come on, Jenny. Don't look. Remember him the way he was. Lad's right." He looked again at Scuff. "Your pa send you to report back to him?"

"No, sir! 'E thinks I'm at school! But I gotter do something. This in't right. It's our river. What kind of a cruise was it, sir? What kind o' people?"

The man began to move away from the place where he had been standing. His arm was still around the woman, but his glance included Scuff.

"Just a pleasure cruise," he replied. "The *Princess Mary*. Started up at Westminster Bridge and went as far as Gravesend, then back again. Expensive, at least for those attending the party. Very good food, lots of champagne and that sort of thing. Just . . . just people having fun." Suddenly his face tightened with fury. "What kind of a madman would want to hurt people like that? Why, for God's sake?"

"Albert . . ." The woman's hand tightened, dragging his arm down toward her. "The boy doesn't know. Nobody does. It's mad . . . mad things don't make sense."

Scuff wanted to say something that would make her feel better. What would Hester have said?

"They don't. But they can't stop us doing our best," he told her.

The man stared at him, but the woman suddenly smiled. It changed her face completely. "I'll try to remember that," she promised.

Scuff smiled back, then left them and started to work his way down the river toward the stretch he knew better. He must find some of the people he used to know before he went to live with Monk and Hester. They were the people who would never tell the police anything, either River Police or the ordinary sort. If the *Princess Mary* had started at Westminster Bridge, then whoever blew it up had got on before that— unless it was one of the people on the cruise. Most likely it was a porter or servant of some sort, what Monk called "invisible people." But Scuff knew beggars, peddlers, petty thieves, people on the fringes of life— they often walked unseen, but they saw everyone.

It took him most of the morning to find exactly the right ones. Far more had changed than he could have foreseen. People had grown up; some had gone away, perhaps to sea. Some had died. No one seemed to know him anymore, and the mudlarks—the boys who scavenged on the shore for bits and pieces they could sell, as he had once done—were all strangers to him. And they all looked so small! He had not really thought of it before, but when he remembered how many new pairs of trousers Hester had bought him, he realized he'd probably grown six inches in the last few years.

Suddenly he felt awkward. They should have grown too, and they hadn't. He saw one boy with no socks and odd boots, just as he had had. He had been going to speak to him and then changed his mind, feeling self-conscious—no, more than that, guilty. He could give this boy a few pence for a pie and a cup of tea, but what about all the others? Scuff now ate well, whenever he wanted to. Why not them? He had been no different from them, once.

He walked away along the bank. The wind in his face smelled of salt and fish and the fetid thickness of river mud. A string of barges went past, the lighterman balancing effortlessly.

Scuff did not know how he ought to feel. How could a few years make him into a different person?

Just beyond the New Crane Stairs by the West India Docks he found a boy he used to know. He was taller and heavier than before, but the wild pattern of his hair was just the same. He was standing in front of a pile of debris. There were glints of metal and brass in it, possibly something worth salvaging.

"'Allo, Mucker," Scuff said cheerfully. "'Ere, I'll 'elp yer." He took part of the weight Mucker was carrying, and his legs nearly buckled under it. Scuff was taller and heavier than he used to be, too, but he was not used to hard physical labor anymore.

Mucker looked startled. "'Oo the 'ell are you?"

"Scuff. Don't you remember me?"

"Scuff?" Mucker's blunt face twisted with disbelief. "Never! Scuff were a useless little article, a foot shorter'n you! Fly as an eel, but . . ." He stared at Scuff with narrowed eyes. "Wot 'appened to yer? Somebody stretch yer legs?"

"Yeah, summink like that," Scuff agreed, resting one foot on an old timber. "Want ter talk to yer. I'll get yer a decent pie an' a cup o' tea."

"Wi' wot?" Mucker asked suspiciously. Then he took a second look at Scuff's jacket and trousers and decided he was possibly on to a good thing. "Yeah, if yer want. But I ain't rattin' on nobody."

"Know anyone who were drowned in that boat what blew up?" Scuff asked casually.

Mucker's bushy eyebrows shot up. "Jeez! No. Do you? Yer gone up in the world, ain't yer? They was all toffs!"

"Crew as well?" Scuff asked drily.

"No, course not." Mucker stopped abruptly. "Why'd yer want to know? Wot's it ter you?"

Scuff was prepared for that one. He smiled. "Making my way," he replied. "Wouldn't rat on a friend, past or present. But I reckon as someone 'oo'd blow up two hundred people 'oo are just 'aving fun is no friend of anyone on our river. Would you?"

Mucker did not even hesitate. "No. It's bad for everyone. So wot d'yer think yer goin' ter do about it, then?"

"Boat picked up all these people at Westminster Bridge. Where'd it come from before that? Who got on wi' explosive stuff and set it in the bow?"

"'Ow d'you know it were in the bow?" Mucker asked instantly.

"'Cos I know someone 'oo was on the river an' saw it go up. Anyway, stands to reason. It went down bow first, not broke its back. They're pulling it up now." He waved his arm in the general direction of the wreck.

"Wot's it worth?" Mucker asked bluntly. "More'n a cup o' tea?"

"A blind eye now and then, when you need it," Scuff replied without hesitation. He had seen that one coming, too.

Mucker grinned. "I always thought you was a fly little sod," he said cheerfully. "Right—ye're on. Come back termorrer." He turned back to his work dismissively and resumed sorting through his find.

Scuff had never imagined he could learn enough in one day. School would have to be forfeited tomorrow and maybe the day after as well. He slapped Mucker on the shoulder in agreement. The promise was made. He might have to ask Hester for money for more pies, but he'd deal with that one only if he had to.

The next person he looked for was a bargee that he had known when he was a mudlark. Again, it took several moments before the man recognized him, and Scuff had to bite his tongue not to apologize for his good fortune. He gave the same reason for wanting to know about the wreck of the *Princess Mary:* that it was bad for the river.

"They'll be coming around asking everyone on the river what they know," he said reasonably. "If they think of it."

The bargee was busy splicing ropes. His gnarled fingers grasped the shiny hook and wove it in and out almost as if the task needed no thought. Scuff had seen old women knit the same way.

"River Police'll think of it," the bargee said with a downturn of his mouth. "Got their long bloody noses into everything. Still, according to old Sawyer down the way—an' 'e's ninety if 'e's a day—it used ter be a lot worse, before they came."

Scuff was startled. "When was that?"

The bargee grinned. "Afore your time, son. In the 1790s, or thereabouts. When the French were all cutting each other's 'eads off. Told yer, 'e's ninety or more. Says the river were the worst place in the world then. Pirates all over the place. Murder was as common then as thievin' is now. An' thievin' were as common as takin' a breath of air. So what is it yer want, then?"

"Could anyone 'ave got that stuff to blow them up an' put it in when they were on the river?" Scuff asked. "After dark, like? Or did it 'ave ter be when they was tied up somewhere? Like Westminster Bridge, or Gravesend?"

"Yer sayin' as maybe one of us did it?" The bargee's face was suddenly hard, his eyes angry.

"No I in't!" Scuff snapped back. "What d'yer take me for? I know that. And like as not, the River Police know. But they in't in it, are they! It's bin taken off them and given to the regular land police, 'oo don't know nothin'!"

The bargee glared at him, the splicing hook idle in his hand for a moment.

"An' 'ow do you know that, then?" he demanded. Scuff had his complete attention now.

"I know a lot o' things," Scuff replied darkly. "An' the sooner we get this sorted, the sooner we'll 'ave the reg'lar police off our river and get our own police back, what we know 'ow ter deal with."

"You cunning little sod!" the bargee said with feeling. He looked Scuff up and down again, this time taking more notice of his clothes, and particularly his boots.

Scuff wanted to tell him he had not earned them himself, but that would have destroyed what little respect this man had from him, so he smiled and said nothing.

He continued all day, searching out people he had known, either directly or by repute. He visited an "opulent receiver," a fencer of stolen goods who specialized in small and valuable pieces: jewelry, carvings in ivory, miniature portraits, and other easily hidden things worth a lot of money. Already several items had turned up, taken from the corpses that had washed onto the shore. Scuff thought robbing the dead was despicable. But he also knew hunger, cold, fear, and loneliness, and hated them; his experience made him slower to judge, and allowed him to hide his disgust. On the one hand it was like being a carrion animal; on the other, the dead had no more need of treasures, and to the living they could mean the difference between survival and death.

He must be home in time for dinner, but not because he could not go without eating. He could, and had. But if he were late Hester would want to know where he had been and he would have to come up with a very good explanation. He had no idea how she did it, but she was uncannily excellent at knowing when he was bending the truth.

Therefore he spent another few pence going back across the river in order to be able to walk up the hill to Paradise Place not so very long after he should have done were he coming home from school.

Had he accomplished anything? Possibly not. He had asked a lot of questions, trying to find out where the man with the explosives could have got into the boat, and learned that it would have been almost impossible anywhere in the first half of the voyage, partly because it would have been daylight, and to do anything unusual then would've been terribly risky.

But the explosives could have been loaded at Gravesend. How could he find out whether they had? Gravesend was miles away, down the estuary toward the sea.

His legs ached as he walked up the hill away from the ferry landing. He had become unused to being on his feet all day. He might be learning all kinds of interesting, useless things at school, but he was also getting soft.

He passed an old woman he knew and smiled at her. She pursed her lips and shook her head, but she wished him a good evening.

"Evenin,' ma'am," he answered politely. He was nearly home.

Who would do such a terrible thing as blow up a boat full of normal people, and in such a way that almost all of them drowned? Why? Did whoever had done it know that was what would happen? Of course! You put explosives in the bow of a ship, any fool knows it will sink. And any fool knows that all the people below deck will drown because there is no way on earth for them to get out in time.

He stopped still as if he had walked into a wall. That was it! It didn't matter where the bomber got into the boat! Anywhere would do. But it mattered more than anything else where he got off! He must have known when it would explode. It was a horrible way to die—he would have left the ship before that! But where? And how? Someone swimming in the river would surely draw attention. Apart from the fact that hardly anyone could swim, the water was filthy enough to poison you.

And swim to where? They would've been out in the middle in the current of the incoming tide. And the Thames tide was swift and strong.

There would have been other boats around: ferries, barges, large ships coming in to anchor in the Pool of London. They could see each other because they carried lights—they had to. Law of the sea. But a swimmer didn't! A swimmer could be struck, swamped in the wash, or, worst of all, caught in the paddles or the screws and hacked to pieces. Scuff shuddered at the thought of it and felt his legs go weak.

He put it out of his mind and hurried the last few steps home. He wanted lights, warmth, people, even if they scolded him for being late. It was very nice to be wanted.

"You're late," Hester said as soon as he was in the door. "Are you all right?"

Perhaps he should have been penitent—it would have been wiser—but he could not keep the huge smile from his face.

"Yes . . . I'm home." He saw the irritation in her eyes and was not absolutely certain what it was. "And I'm hungry," he added.

Monk came in a few moments later, and spoke only of the usual sort of business on the river. He did not even mention the *Princess Mary*, so Scuff thought he had better not mention it either. Hester did not refer to the fact that he had been late, and he was too grateful for that to risk anything but enjoying the good food and comfortable silence. He did not allow into his mind those who would be sleeping outside on the dock, as he once had.

CHAPTER

3

Monk tried to work as usual and put the atrocity of the pleasure boat loss at least to the back of his mind. Sometimes he succeeded for as much as half a day, but there was always something to remind him of it eventually. People were still talking about it. There was speculation in the newspapers and in fliers posted up on every wall and street corner, or passed from hand to hand. Even into June, wreckage was being washed up with each high tide: pieces of wood, broken furniture, waterlogged cushions, and the torn fabric of clothes. On the curved shore of the Isle of Dogs, three more bodies surfaced. A pall of grief hung over everything, in spite of the sunshine, and it was slowly hardening into anger.

Monk saw the Metropolitan Police on the banks, at the docks, even at times on the river itself, talking to lightermen and bargees. He did not envy them. At first they were resented, interlopers in an alien territory. Now they were being blamed because they seemed to have no idea who they were chasing, or even why the tragedy had happened.

Who would do such a thing? Possibilities teemed in Monk's mind. He could not think any ordinary river pirates or thieves could do anything so extreme. It would draw unwanted attention. But since the revolution that had swept Europe in 1848, some twenty years ago, London was full of refugees: people either fleeing the persecution that had followed the suppression of revolt, or simply looking for a different and better life. Occasionally old quarrels erupted into violence between groups; social change, overcrowding, strange languages and customs—all of it frightened people.

And yet standing on the quayside watching the river traffic passing, hearing the familiar shouts and clangs of men working their trades, Monk could not believe that any of the immigrants would commit such an atrocity. Apart from any morality involved, it would be pointless. All they wanted was a little space, and the chance to earn a living.

The speed with which Monk had been dismissed and Lydiate appointed smelled political, but to what end? Ships came and went from the Pool of London to every country on earth. Cargo included things as small as diamonds or as huge as timber.

Could the tragedy have to do with smuggling? The *Princess Mary* had been to Gravesend. Could it have met a coastal freighter there? The possibilities filled his mind. Smuggled goods deliberately sunk, to be plundered afterward? By whom? Pirates? Salvagers? Corrupt laborers, or even police?

Would Lydiate even think of that? Should Monk suggest it?

Or did Lydiate already know what or who was behind the explosion, but was keeping it quiet because it *was* political?

Whatever the reason, it had to be overwhelming for anyone to have committed such a horrific crime.

Years ago Monk had been in the regular Metropolitan Police himself. Whether he had resigned or been dismissed was an arguable point. Early in his career he had worked alongside a man named Runcorn, and they had trusted each other. Then Monk's darker nature had brought out the worst in Runcorn. Friendship had turned first to rivalry, later into something close to hatred.

The final straw came when Runcorn had been promoted, becoming Monk's superior. Runcorn was by nature obedient, loyal, unimaginative, and often pompous. All these things considered, it was surprising how long it had taken him to dismiss Monk. It had occurred at precisely the same moment when Monk had completely lost his temper and resigned.

For some time Monk had worked as a private agent of inquiry, but the living was dangerous and irregular. When he had been offered the position of commanding the Thames River Police, little as he liked either the responsibility or the discipline, he had accepted it. Commanding men had taught him much, humbled some of his arrogance and given him an unexpected sense of loyalty to his work and the people he worked with. He had even found, to his amazement, a kind of friendship with Runcorn, who had mellowed much since his unexpected marriage to a woman he had imagined hopelessly beyond his reach.

Now, at the end of the day on the river, Monk found he had finished his work a little earlier than expected. On impulse, he took a hansom to Runcorn's police station in Blackheath and asked to see him.

He had to wait about a quarter of an hour until Runcorn returned from some errand, but he did so with patience. He recognized Runcorn's rather heavy step ascending the stairs and found himself anticipating the meeting with pleasure, something he could not have imagined a few years ago.

Runcorn came into the room smiling and with his hand held out. He was a big man, tall and solid with a long face and thick gray curling hair.

Monk stood and gripped Runcorn's hand. The pressure expressed eloquently the strange mixture of memory and understanding that bound them.

Without asking Monk's preference, Runcorn called over his shoulder for two mugs of tea. Then he waved at the chair for Monk to resume his seat. He took off his jacket and sat down himself, crossing his legs comfortably, waiting for Monk to state his reason for having come.

"I expected to have to wait longer," Monk remarked. "Or have you got something else on at the moment?" He knew he would not have to tell Runcorn what case he was interested in.

Runcorn sighed. "Something else," he agreed. "Damn stupid knife fight in an alley. Lucky he isn't up for murder. Seems idiotic, doesn't it? Words! Man with the vocabulary of a pig insults you, and you risk spending the rest of your life in prison breaking rocks just to get back at him. And we've got a hundred corpses being hauled out of the river—and for what?"

"No idea yet, then?" Monk asked.

Runcorn sighed and answered the door as a constable arrived with the tea. He took it from him, thanked him, and then shut the door again. He passed one of the mugs over to Monk. "Take your pick. Theft, but there's nothing to steal that wouldn't have been taken a lot more effectively by half a dozen pickpockets, and sold on without anyone the wiser. Some sort of fraud?" He pursed his lips. "Can't see how. Extortion? 'Pay, or I'll sink your boat?' You'd have caught wind of anyone doing that sort of thing, on that level. Revenge seems to be the most likely scenario." Runcorn's face was sad, the anger in him unmistakable. "God knows for what."

"But it's puzzling," Monk said. "If it was out of revenge, why would the person behind the bombing not claim the act? Is revenge satisfying if you can't gloat?"

"Don't know," Runcorn replied. "Never hated anyone that much." Then a bright, sharp light came into his eyes and he half smiled. "Not lately, anyway . . ."

Monk laughed. It was the first time he had done so since the boat went down. It was a mark of the peace between them that Runcorn could refer to it. There was no longer the need to step around their former enmity with unease, like it was a patch of thin ice on a pond, likely to crack at any moment.

"Maybe it's something to do with all the talk of shipping changes," Runcorn went on. "Because of this new canal they're building between the Mediterranean and the Red Sea."

"That was de Lesseps's idea, not ours," Monk pointed out. "We're latecomers to that whole game. Why take revenge on us for it?"

Runcorn shrugged ruefully. "That's true, but I'm not sure whoever did this was thinking logically. We've got a lot of men working over there."

"But what could that have to do with the people on a pleasure boat on a day trip along the Thames? I could see it making sense if it were a freighter of some kind, perhaps," Monk said.

"I don't know," Runcorn said unhappily. "But there were all sorts of toffs on the guest list. Investors with money to burn. At least that's what Lord Ossett, the government adviser to the Home Office and the Foreign Office, told me. Not just British, but European, Middle Eastern, even American."

"Is that what it is about?" Monk began to see a much uglier and more complicated picture than he had initially imagined. He had assumed it was an isolated incident, but perhaps it wasn't. Perhaps he should be grateful that Lydiate had been given the burden of solving it—and preventing any further attacks. If what Runcorn was suggesting was true, this wasn't really a river crime. The fact that the first blow had taken place there might be incidental.

As if reading his thoughts, Runcorn spoke again. "Have you seen the papers? They're screaming so loudly they're getting in the way. All kinds of people are coming forward telling us things that don't matter, and the people that might know something relevant are so frightened they're hiding, lying, telling us whatever they think we want to hear. You've no idea how many one-eyed black dwarfs there are in the London docks . . ."

"What?" Monk was incredulous. Then he saw Runcorn's face and understood. "Monsters—anyone but us," he said, leaning back in his chair again. "Any real hope?"

Runcorn sighed. "A bit. We've spoken to a lot of people up and down the river. Could be getting closer to who actually planted the stuff—which incidentally we are certain was this new Swedish dynamite—but we still don't know why, or, more important, who is truly behind it."

For the first time Monk heard the real strain in Runcorn's voice. Monk knew what it was like to have those frightened demands for an answer ringing in your ears every day. You felt hounded. It was too easy to make mistakes, to tell your superiors anything just to make them go away. Every man would be doing his best, but there was just too little to grasp. It depended on luck, asking the right question at the right moment.

"Call if I can help," he said impulsively. "It doesn't have to be official."

Runcorn nodded. "I will, if I think of anything. I don't want to defy Ossett. He's a decent enough chap, but he's dead set on handling it his own way. I dare say a lot of people higher up are leaning on him."

Hester walked briskly along Portpool Lane to the huddle of interconnected houses that had once been a thriving brothel run by one Squeaky Robinson. A few years ago, at the successful conclusion of a case, Sir Oliver Rathbone had tricked Squeaky and his silent backers out of possession of the place. Several of them had ended up in prison, but Squeaky had remained in the place, not as owner or manager anymore, but as a peculiarly gifted bookkeeper.

The property itself had, with minor changes, been turned into a clinic for sick or injured prostitutes. Hester, with her military nursing experience in the Crimean War, ran the place. She managed to obtain professional help from one or two doctors willing to give their time without charge. Funds for simple maintenance were obtained by different volunteers: ladies of a charitable nature who were prepared to ask their friends, acquaintances, and even strangers for help.

Margaret Ballinger, later Oliver Rathbone's wife, and now his ex-wife, had been one of the best at raising funds. It was a sadness to Hester that she no longer worked with them. However, Hester's relationship with Margaret had suffered irreparable damage thanks to the tragedy that had struck Margaret's family, and the way in which Margaret had reacted to it.

Now, as Hester went in through the door to the room turned into a reception hall, she was greeted by Claudine Burroughs, a woman in her middle years, plain of countenance but remarkable of character. Her success here had given her a sense of freedom from her restrictive marriage, and the friendships she had won at some cost enriched her in all manner of ways. Her face lit up when she saw Hester.

"How are you?" she asked warmly. "We've missed you since that dreadful event on the river." She looked Hester up and down, assessing if she was really well enough, regardless of what she might say.

Hester smiled back. "Feeling totally useless," she replied. She felt comfortable being completely honest Claudine, and had for some time now. It was inevitable, given the work they faced together. They had shared triumphs and disasters both in the clinic and beyond. They helped people, sometimes cured them, but the very nature of their purpose meant that they came late into every battle against death, and often lost. Sometimes all they could give was warmth, peace, and a little dignity, making sure a woman didn't feel alone in the last days of her life.

Claudine frowned. "Come and have tea. The accounts are all done and we are in quite good shape. I didn't ask Mr. Robinson where our latest funds came from. I don't know if you care to know?" Her expression reflected her erratic opinion of and relationship with Squeaky. To begin with they had despised each other. He was a renegade in every respect, loathing the law and having little regard for women, particularly of the stiff, plain, middle-aged, and genteel variety—all of which Claudine so perfectly epitomized.

She saw him, in return, as devious, despicable, and personally repulsive. Experience had taught both of them their mistakes. Tolerance had very gradually turned into something almost resembling affection.

"Thank you," Hester said drily. "I have sufficient troubles not to go courting anymore. I have to say I miss Margaret's help in the funding."

"You mean Lady Rathbone . . ." Claudine said with a slight rasp to her voice. She was intensely loyal to those who had offered her friendship, but she regarded Margaret as one who had betrayed them all.

They went into Claudine's storeroom—now also her office—where Ruby was counting bandages, bottles of medicine, and packets of powder of one sort or another. She gave Hester a shy smile.

Claudine asked her if she would be kind enough to get them tea and she went off to do it, relieved she wouldn't have to focus on numbers in front of her superiors.

"She's improving," Claudine said the moment the door was closed. "She doesn't make many mistakes, although she hasn't really got the difference between three and five yet."

Hester smiled. It had been a long and wandering journey with Ruby, but the successes were joyous.

"How is Mr. Monk?" Claudine asked with a look of sudden gravity in her face. "I don't know whether to be furious that they have taken the investigation away from him, or relieved that he can't be blamed if they don't catch anyone. I think he is the only person who might have had a chance."

"That is precisely how I feel," Hester agreed. "But I am angry with myself for being angry that they took the case away from him. I'm sure the Home Office did what they thought was most beneficial to finding out the truth, and I ought to care only about the truth. A hundred and seventy-nine people died." She refused to visualize it in her mind; it was a hideous picture.

"One or two women we know were on it," Claudine said quietly.

Hester was startled. "Women we know? You mean contributors to the clinic?"

"No, I mean patients we've had," Claudine answered with a wry smile at Hester's misunderstanding. "It was a pleasure boat, with a big party on board. Apparently planned for some time. All sorts of people were there, several very wealthy, and liking their entertainment. And I heard talk that there were a good few army men expected, young and unattached." She did not elaborate on her meaning; it was obvious.

"I'm sorry, I didn't realize. That is terrible." Hester said quickly. She meant it. You cannot nurse someone and see them in extreme distress without feeling a degree of pity. Of course, the information should not have come as a surprise, considering their clientele. "How do you know?"

"From Kate Sawbridge," Claudine replied. "You know her? Big girl with a lot of fair hair. She said Jilly Ford told her about it, especially the soldiers, and she wished she'd been asked. Could have been fun, and good pay. Maybe something on the side. She said Jilly was showing off a bit." Suddenly her face was bleak. "Poor soul . . ."

Hester thought of Monk, remembering how he had looked when he came home after fishing the dead out of the river all night, and then diving to look at those left in the wreck before they raised it. It must have been like a battlefield under the water. She had seen enough of them on land. She thought that with time she would have forgotten, but she never did.

She forced her mind back to the present and practical things.

"Do you think Kate might know some details about the boat, if the party was talked about?" she asked. "There'll be other girls who wanted to go, and didn't. Or whose friends went. Let's see what the gossip is. There could be bits and pieces which, if we put them together, make something useful."

"Certainly," Claudine said quickly. "I dare say we'll get a lot of nonsense, wishful thinking, and gossip having to do with old scores, but we'll sort it out."

MONK WAS FRUSTRATED THAT he could do nothing to help the ongoing investigation. And he was still angry with the insult to the River Police. He found himself talking to his men more, encouraging them, even praising them at times. It was not his usual habit, and he knew he was saying to them what he felt the authorities should have: They had earned better regard than this.

Going upriver from Wapping toward Westminster, he found himself digging deep into the water and throwing all his weight behind the oar, forcing Orme to pull harder as well. His mind was full of questions about who had placed the dynamite, and why. The theft he was now investigating barely touched his thoughts.

Was Runcorn right and it was political? Personally he still thought smuggling was also a possibility. There was a lot of money in that, a fortune, if one really big shipment made it through all the barriers. The sinking of the boat might have been away to get the goods, whatever they were, past customs somehow; it might also convince the original owner that they were destroyed, lost forever!

Would Lydiate's men even think of such a thing? Or know who to ask, in order to find out?

Darker ideas invaded his mind. Was there corruption involved, and that was why the River Police were excluded? They knew the water officials, the excise men! They would be far less easily deceived by a web of lies. He drove the oar in deeper. The boat slewed slightly, because Orme had not been ready for such a surge forward.

Monk should apologize. More than that: He should measure his stroke more evenly.

It was a bright day, full of little shivering gusts that made the ripples scurry first one way then the other.

They rowed in silence, passing the usual river traffic of lighters, ferries, cargo-laden barges, and freighters low in the water. There were very few pleasure boats, although the weather was steadily improving.

He caught Orme's eye once or twice and knew his mind was filled with the same thoughts. He could see the suppressed anger in Orme's weathered face mirroring his own. This exclusion was an insult to the whole force. It didn't matter that the case was difficult, that maybe no one would solve it completely. This was their river, their beat.

They swung the boat shoreward and pulled in toward the bank just short of Westminster Bridge. This was where most of the pleasure boats left to go either up the river toward Kew Gardens, Lambeth Palace, and the little river islands; or downstream through the Pool of London, the Tower, the Isle of Dogs, and eventually Gravesend and the wide estuary to the sea.

They tied up and climbed out into the dock. It was good to stand after the long row.

Orme shook his head. His eyes were narrowed against the sun, and the cap he always wore was pulled down over his brow.

"Anyone could get on or off here," he said flatly, voicing what they were both thinking. "All you need is a peacoat on and a cap, and you'd be invisible. We don't even know who we're looking for. He could be anyone! Waterman, laborer, tourist, or even a gentleman. Or a soldier on leave."

"He must have been checked as he boarded," Monk replied. "He was either guest or crew."

"Crew," Orme said quietly. "Guests would have been known by name, and the survivors spoken to. That's a risk he wouldn't take."

"I wonder if they've thought to check that no guests got off again before she set sail," Monk thought aloud.

Orme gave a tight smile. "Don't think much of them, do you!"

"I wouldn't like to go through that guest list looking for whoever set the bomb off," Monk replied. "They'll have to do it, just in case they miss something. But apparently there's a lot of money, power, and privilege involved, people who don't expect to account to the police for anything."

Orme gave him a wide-eyed stare.

"All right," Monk agreed. "If they've any sense at all, Lydiate'll make damn sure they don't miss it! I wonder who was paid to turn a blind eye . . . and what they thought it was about."

Orme didn't answer, but turned slowly, gazing around the sheds and ticket offices, entrance booths and places for passengers to wait in an orderly fashion, without spilling over into the road above.

The wind had dropped here. The small sailboats barely moved, their hulls and slack sails reflected in the water. There were few sounds except the slurping of the tide and an occasional shout.

A string of barges came past slowly, lightermen balancing with an odd, almost awkward grace in the sterns. A ferry wove in and out, and then docked gently at the steps twenty yards downstream.

"Of course the dynamite itself could have come on board with the catering," Monk went on. "Orme, who are the invisible people?"

Orme looked startled. "What?"

"Who are the invisible people?" Monk repeated. "The ones who are always here, so much so that we end up not really seeing them; just like postmen, delivery boys, cabdrivers, maids coming out to shake carpets or fetch water, fill coal scuttles."

Orme stared at him. "Same sorts of people around here," he said slowly. "Men who fill and empty things, clean up, tidy after us, drive us on land or ferry us on the water. The landsmen investigating the bombing won't think to seek them out, I bet." There was frustration in his voice. "You're going to tell 'em that?" he said.

Monk hesitated, but not because he wasn't sure what the answer was. He was remembering the river at dusk, the lights of the pleasure boat, then the roar as the bow exploded and the screams that followed. And the darkness engulfing the water as the ship plunged down. He had to force out of his mind the people they had tried to help, and couldn't because their boat was too full already, too far away, too late.

Orme waited silently, as he so often did, like a ship for the tide.

"Yes, of course I will," Monk finally said. As he turned around and started walking back across the wooden quay up toward the street, he saw a police sergeant coming toward them.

The man stopped in front of them, glancing at Orme, then back at Monk.

"Sorry, sir," he said awkwardly. "I know as you're River Police, but this is still a restricted area, unless you got a reason you need to be here? There in't no one landed here this last couple of hours, I can swear to that."

Monk looked at him. The man was perhaps thirty, clean-shaven, eager, and at this moment embarrassed.

"Who *did* you see?" Monk asked him mildly.

The sergeant looked around. "No one, sir, as I said. Who were you looking for?"

"Who's that over there?" Monk gestured toward a ferry pulling away southward.

"No one, sir, just the regular ferry to the steps there."

"And over there?" Monk pointed again, a few yards across the water.

"Lighterman, sir. Going up with the tide. It's just turned. 'E'd 'ave had to wait or he'd 'ave been battling the current."

"Exactly," Monk agreed. "The river is full of invisible people like that. They come and go, and we don't see them, unless they do something out of character. Is your commander as observant as you are? Would he notice anyone different, a stranger, out of step with the tide? Or maybe not out of step, not different at all?"

The sergeant's face blanched in the late afternoon sun. He swallowed. "I don't know, sir. Do you think it could be a lighterman, or . . . someone like that who's behind this?"

"Well, if it wasn't someone you saw, then it was someone you didn't," Monk said reasonably. "Someone who was there, but that you expected to be there, so you didn't notice him."

The sergeant shook his head. "I don't think so, sir. From the looks of it, it's political. Least that's what they're reckoning. We've got a line on an Egyptian man. Worked for the caterers. Bit of a malcontent. Always complaining, and expressed some pretty ugly opinions when he wasn't being too careful. Quite a bit of evidence against him, I hear."

"Egyptian? On the Thames?" Monk affected to be polite rather than interested.

"World's getting smaller, sir," the sergeant replied. "They open up that canal and we'll be getting to the Indies in a matter of days rather than weeks. No more clipper ships, I reckon. And we'll miss them. Most beautiful thing I ever saw was one o' them under full sail. Couldn't take my eyes off it."

With a wave of sorrow Monk realized exactly what he meant.

Change was coming. And there was always a price to be paid for it.

He turned and looked at Orme in the waning light, and thought he saw the same understanding in his face, and perhaps also the same sense of inevitable loss. Change comes like a tide, and any seaman knows the tide waits for no one.

"Why would an Egyptian blow up an English pleasure boat on the Thames?" he asked the sergeant.

"No idea, sir," the man replied. "Not sure that I want to know. Lot of money involved in the canal project, though, an' Mr. Lydiate says it'll change all sorts of things for the Egyptians too. Lot of them died building it, that's for sure. Some say it was in the hundreds!"

Monk nodded. He saw very well the layers of money, influence, lies, and debts that could be connected to the canal project. There were infinite possibilities for secrets and distortion of facts. Perhaps Runcorn was right and none of them would unravel all that lay behind the sinking of the *Princess Mary*.

M ONK ARRIVED HOME SHORTLY after sunset, tired and disappointed. He had passed newspaper shops on the way and even one running patterer—a man who made a living reciting the news in a kind of singsong narrative rhyme, easy to memorize and carrying the essence of breaking events. They all agreed on two things: The tragedy had been an unparalleled evil, and the police were close to finding the man responsible.

"That true?" Scuff asked almost as soon as Monk was through the door. Now that he could read, he was devouring everything current and exciting, as if windows were flying open on all sides with amazing views he had never seen before. "They got someone?" He took Monk's coat from him and hung it up, all but stepping on his heels as he went into the kitchen where Hester was carving cold roast beef for supper.

She turned and smiled at him, and Monk felt some of his weariness slipping away, like a heavy garment discarded. He could smell hot mashed potatoes and onions frying in the pan, with fine-chopped cabbage stirred into them, a dish commonly known as "bubble and squeak."

"Looks as if they're close to arresting someone" he said. He had already made up his mind on the way home that he should tell them. Not to tell them would only make it harder to accept when it was the Metropolitan Police, and not the River Police, who brought some kind of resolution, even justice, to the tragedy.

Scuff tried to hide his sense of injustice, and failed. "That didn't take long," he said critically, his face clouded over. "Can't 'ave been that 'ard, so why'd they make such a fuss?"

Hester drew in her breath, then changed her mind and waited for Monk to answer.

"They haven't got him yet, but a sergeant near Westminster Bridge told me it'll be soon. He says it was an Egyptian man, reckons it has something to do with the Suez Canal . . ."

Hester looked startled, but it was Scuff who spoke.

"That's the stupidest thing I ever 'eard! How do they figure that?" he said hotly. "They're goin' to 'ang someone just so they can say they got 'im!" He was staring at Monk, and there was a tiny spark of panic in his eyes. Monk knew he must find an answer that was both honest and credible. It was hard enough lately to keep Scuff at school; believing in law and government— which were naturally alien to him— without seeing Monk do the same, would be impossible.

What could Monk say? Scuff did not need a lecture in geography and economics, the fortunes made and lost, the men who had died as the price of great undertakings. He needed to believe that the government who ruled his country was largely competent, and almost entirely honest. They figured Scuff to be around sixteen—they would never be sure exactly how old he was—and Monk knew it was age that carried with it a vulnerable mixture of naïveté and worldly wisdom, of hope in the face of the bitterest of experience. It was frightening that Scuff would likely accept whatever Monk or Hester would tell him. The responsibility of it was, for a moment, overwhelming.

Scuff was waiting for a reply. Monk had already taken too long.

"Sometimes we arrest the wrong people." He measured his words, watching Scuff's face. "There's often no solid proof, just bits of evidence. But they always have a trial and that's when the truth comes out . . ."

"They tried Sir Oliver," Scuff said immediately. "He weren't guilty! They still punished him. He can't do the law anymore. It would've bin too late for ever if they'd 'ave hanged him, wouldn't it!"

"He was guilty, Scuff," Monk said quietly.

"That man in court was wrong!" Scuff said angrily, challenging Monk, believing he was mistaken now, yet needing him to be right.

Monk was struck by how much of Scuff's precious, fragile new world depended upon his belief in Monk and Hester: that they were right, and that they loved him. Those two things would never change, even if food, shelter, and acceptance by others were all destroyed.

"I know he was wrong," Monk said as calmly as he could. Scuff should not hear anger or uncertainty in his voice. "And he paid for that. The one who killed those people was hanged for it. But Sir Oliver was wrong too."

"He had to do that!" Scuff protested.

"He thought so," Monk agreed. "And perhaps that was the truth. But what he did was against the law, and he knew he would have to pay for it."

"But he isn't doing law now." Scuff clung to his point. "That in't right. 'E was really, really good at it." There was desperation in his voice. "They shouldn't have put him out!"

"He's only out for a while," Monk assured him. "He's taking a holiday in Europe, going with his father, whom he loves very much." He made himself smile. "He'll come back. Then you can ask him if he thinks it was fair or not. I believe he'll say it was."

Scuff stared at him levelly for several seconds. Then he turned to Hester, his eyes demanding, waiting.

"Sometimes there isn't any good choice," she said gently, moving her shoulders a little in a gesture of acceptance. "You have to pick the one you think is least bad, and hope you're right. I think he was. But not everything comes with an easy answer, or without a price."

Scuff turned that over in his mind for a few more moments, and then he seemed satisfied. He looked at Monk again. "So what are they going to do about the boat and all those people what drowned?"

"Those people *who* drowned," Hester corrected him automatically. Scuff's grammar still tended to slip when he was upset.

"They're going to catch who did it, possibly this Egyptian man, and try him. And then if he's guilty they'll hang him," Monk replied.

"An' if he isn't?" Scuff persisted.

"Then they'll let him go, and start again," Monk said firmly.

Scuff looked a little doubtful. "They'll look stupid then, as they got it wrong. You think they'll own up to it? People'll be red-hot angry. They're bad enough now, 'cos it's taking weeks to catch him. If I was them, I'd be scared, and I wouldn't want to own up I got it wrong."

Monk drew in a quick breath, and then let it out again.

"Of course you would be scared," Hester said before he could find the words. "But I hope you'd be a lot more scared of how you would feel if you deliberately hanged the wrong person, and let the real one go free."

"'Course I would!" Scuff said angrily, his skin flushed.

Hester took a step closer and put her hand on his arm. It was not a caress, but it might as well have been, given the tenderness in it.

His face brightened immediately.

Hester kept on walking over to the stove without glancing back to see Monk's smile. She knew it would be there.

It was still over another week and well into June before the police arrested Habib Beshara, an Egyptian currently living in London. They charged him with the murder of one hundred and seventy-nine people by laying and detonating the explosive that blew up and sank the pleasure boat the *Princess Mary*.

There was jubilation throughout the city. Newspapers praised the police and looked forward to a speedy trial. Justice would be served. Order and faith in the rule of law returned. Many people even held parties.

Monk felt a wave of relief, and yet it was not absolute. No formality of a trial, no certainty or pain or fear of an execution could drive out of his mind the memories of the night of the drownings, or the corpses floating inside the hollow of the sunken ship.

CHAPTER

4

As the days passed leading up to the opening of the trial of Habib Beshara, Monk busied himself even more diligently on the river. He continued stretching his imagination and will to make his force excel, in order to keep up the reputation and morale of his men. The Thames River Police was the oldest force in the country, possibly in the world. It was even older than the "Peelers," and it deserved every word of praise it had gained over the years. The government's choice to take the *Princess Mary* case from them might have been politically expedient, but it was still an insult that was deeply felt.

There was plenty to do. There had been a major robbery from one of the waterside warehouses along the Blackwall Reach, and several minor thefts from docksides, lighters, and other vulnerable places. There was always smuggling, often of brandy, especially farther down by Bugsby's Marshes, beyond Greenwich, where small boats came and went under cover of darkness.

There were drunken fights, most of which inflicted little injury and were easily settled, but there were bad ones as well. A knife could make it lethal. One moment a fight could be wild, but with only a punch here and there landing; the next someone was bleeding to death and it was murder.

Added to that, every few days a piece of wreckage from the *Princess Mary* washed up, bits of wood carved and elegant, made for pleasure, not utility.

Monk stood in the sun beside the water now, hearing it slurp on the steps below him as the tide rose slowly, each ripple a little higher. He held a carved leg and part of a strut in his hand. It had been turned on a router, making it smooth, showing off the grain. It had once been part of something useful.

There was no reason to stand here holding it. It was not evidence of anything. Everyone already knew what had happened. He just felt that if he threw it back into the water he was abandoning it, clogging up the river with more detritus. It was too small to salvage, good only to burn in someone's fire. And yet it had been beautifully made. Somebody had taken time and care with it.

He put it down on the dockside. Someone would find and make use it. He did not want to burn it on his own fire. Right at this moment, as the trial was starting, he was glad the government had given the case to someone else. It would be Lydiate, and not he, who would have to give evidence and relive the whole thing, witness by witness. Lydiate had not seen the disaster and Monk had, but the salvage crew would be the ones testifying. No one had sent for Monk, probably because they would then have to explain why the case had been taken from him—a fact that would undoubtedly be exploited by Beshara's defense.

He turned and walked with his back to the sun, feeling its midsummer heat on his shoulders.

If Rathbone were here, and still able to practice, would he have taken the case for the defense? Or would he have wanted to prosecute? It was all irrelevant; they were none of them involved. Maybe that was not entirely bad. Rathbone had been promising his father for years that they would spend some time traveling together. One case or another had always intruded. He might have gone on delaying until it was too late. Then his grief would be with him always.

And, in an oblique way, Monk was feeling a new sense of loyalty to his own men. They had served in the River Police long before he came to it. They were as good as any police in the world, better than most, and they deserved recognition of that, not this cavalier bypassing as if they were less than the regular police. Few of them had said anything, but he saw it in their eyes and heard it in the silences. There was an edge of bitterness to the usual jokes. Everyone worked even harder, most of all Monk himself, as if to prove something.

He increased his pace across to the warehouse entrance, his attention fully returned to this present robbery.

Hester did not find it easy to gain a seat in the gallery for the trial of Habib Beshara. After several failed attempts through the normal routes, she called on Rufus Brancaster, who had so ably defended Rathbone when he needed it. In pleading for volunteers or money to support the clinic in Portpool Lane, she was no longer abashed to state a case; but when asking a favor for herself she found it much harder. However, as it happened, Brancaster was both able and very willing to assist. He asked after Rathbone's well-being with respect and some degree of feeling.

"He'll hate missing this," she said honestly. "That's really why I'm here, so I can write and tell him what I see. But on the other hand, for years he has been wanting to travel with his father, and always changed his mind at the last moment, or had it changed for him. Do you know Mr. Henry Rathbone?"

"No," Brancaster admitted. "But I have seen in Sir Oliver's face how fond of him he is. And frankly, I think this case has become so political that it's going to be something of a mess."

She smiled agreement, but refrained from adding her opinion. She had said nothing to Monk about her sense of betrayal at the case having been taken from the River Police but only because she knew that would make it even harder for him to deal with. And perhaps also she was a little wiser in political matters than he, having tried so hard when she had returned from the Crimean War to alter some of the worst habits in nursing. She had had high ideals then, like her mentor, Florence Nightingale. Both of them had largely failed, learning lessons as to the power and immovability of the Establishment, especially where its vested interests were concerned. It still raised her anger to explosive levels, if she allowed it to, but she had long discovered that loss of temper more often damaged oneself than anyone else.

She thanked Brancaster warmly, and on the first day of the trial arrived in plenty of time to claim her seat.

The very first shock of the morning came with the arrival of the judge, before the case was even introduced. Hester was watching without particular interest when they were asked to rise and the judge entered, robed in scarlet and wearing the customary full-bottomed wig. As he took his seat in the high, carved chair and faced the court, she felt a stab of recognition so sharp as to be almost physical. It was Ingram York, the senior judge who had first favored Rathbone, then sought to destroy him.

He still had the same sheen of complacency on his broad face, but the lines of quick temper were deeper around his mouth than she remembered. To some he might look pleasantly avuncular, but to Hester he was a dangerous man, his loyalties ready to turn in an instant.

Thank heaven Rathbone was not here—or worse, involved in the case!

Who was? She turned to the defense table and saw a lean man. She realized he was of average height, although he looked taller at first glance, perhaps because of the elegance with which he rose to his feet, and gave a slight bow. It was impossible to tell the color of his hair beneath his obligatory barrister's wig, but his skin and brows suggested it would be fair. His expression was unreadable. But then he was in an impossible situation. To satisfy the law, he must attempt to defend the indefensible. The court clerk addressed him as Mr. Juniver.

The prosecution was led by Sir Oswald Camborne. He was a thickset man, powerful, heavy-shouldered. His bushy eyebrows and the shadow around his broad jawline suggested dark hair, beginning to gray. At the moment he looked satisfied, and he had good cause.

Finally Hester made herself look up at the dock where the accused man sat, well guarded on either side by uniformed wardens. He was dark-skinned and his thick hair was black, gray at the temples. He appeared to be in his late forties, which she had not expected. Somehow she had imagined a younger, more fanatical-looking man. She could see no passion in his face, no fire at all. He looked more ill than frightened. It was hard to imagine that he had exacted such a terrible revenge on the people of a country he possibly hated. It seemed not to have brought him satisfaction. But then perhaps revenge never did.

At last the jury were sworn in and the proceedings began in earnest. Both prosecution and defense gave powerful and lengthy statements of their respective cases before Camborne called his first witness, a ferryman who had been on the river the night of the atrocity.

Hester found herself stiff, her hands clenched. This was where Monk should have testified. Would Juniver ask why he was not here? But then did any of this actually matter at all, or make any difference to the outcome? Or was it a charade to satisfy the law, so Beshara could be hanged and the public feel that justice had been accomplished?

The ferryman's name was Albert Hodge. He stood uncomfortably in the high witness box above the floor of the court. He was an ordinary-seeming man, tired-looking and clearly a little frightened. His face was weathered from spending day and night in the open air, in all seasons. He wore what was probably his best coat. Even so, it strained a little across the breadth of his shoulders, which had been made powerful by a lifetime's drag of the oars through the water, battling the current and the tides.

Camborne walked out into the middle of the floor, like an actor to center stage.

"Mr. Hodge," he began smoothly, even sympathetically, "I'm sorry to ask you to relive what was probably one of the worst nights of your life, but you speak for all the brave men on the river that night who witnessed what happened, and worked until daylight and beyond, trying to rescue the drowning and bring back the bodies of the dead."

Hester shivered. The emotion was already so highly charged in the room that she could feel it like a coming storm, heavy and churning with unspent electricity. In a few sentences Camborne had set the tone. Juniver must know that. If he tried to defuse it he would be guilty of seeming to diminish the tragedy, and that would be a fatal mistake.

Hodge began almost awkwardly, repeating himself and apologizing for it. He need not have; his simple language and obvious distress were far more affecting than any ease of vocabulary would have been.

In the gallery no one moved. There was just the occasional exhalation of breath and creak of a wooden seat.

As Hester listened to him speak, she heard Monk's voice in her mind, saw him at the oars, straining his back to get to the drowning in time, peering through the darkness to see the white of a desperate face, the drift of a woman's gown beneath the filthy water. She felt the helplessness Hodge tried to express, forgetting the present and the lawyers in their wigs and gowns, even oblivious of Ingram York presiding above them.

Hodge had worked all night, first receiving the desperate living, then hauling the tragic dead into his boat. Finally there were no more dead, only the shattered pieces of the boat.

When at last Juniver rose, he was facing hostility so strong it was palpable. It was unforgivable that anyone should try to excuse this or disregard the grief, and he had to know that.

Hester swallowed nervously, wondering what on earth he could say. Did he feel as lost, as overwhelmed as she did? From his face she could not tell. Even the way he stood revealed nothing.

"We thank you for your time and your honesty, Mr. Hodge," Juniver began gravely. "The experience is beyond anything we know, but you have made it as real for us as anybody could." He cleared his throat. "You have said there were others who struggled to save anyone they could reach at the time, and long into the night after that, to find the bodies and bring them ashore. Did that include the police, do you know?"

"Oh, yes, sir," Hodge agreed quickly. "River Police was there all night. Saw 'em meself. Mr. Monk—'e's the boss o' them—'e were there right from the start, an' even went down in one o' them suits inter the wreck the next day, God 'elp 'im!"

Juniver's thin face registered surprise. "Really? You're sure of that?"

Hodge could not keep a flicker of anger from his face. "'Course I am. Anyone wot works the river knows 'im."

"Can you think of any reason why he has not been called to give evidence here: an experienced river policeman who actually saw it all?" Juniver asked innocently.

York leaned forward as if to interrupt, but Hodge spoke before he did.

"No, sir, I can't," Hodge replied.

"Perhaps my learned friend has some reason that has not occurred to us?" Juniver looked across at Camborne. It was a small point, and in the heat of the moment it might mean nothing, but it was a valid one. Should there be an appeal, it would be remembered.

Hester looked at York and saw a flash of irritation cross his face, cutting the lines more deeply around his mouth.

Camborne affected indifference and did not respond. Instead he called his next witness, a bargee named Baker. He gave a similar account of the horror and pity he had felt at pulling bodies out of the water.

"Did you see the ship itself go down?" Camborne asked, his brows raised, his eyes wide.

There was not a movement in the room.

"'Appened in moments, sir," Baker told Camborne. "One minute it was all lights and music an' laughter I could 'ear from where I was, mebbe fifty yards away. I were close. Then that terrible roar, an' flames shot out of 'er bow, lit up the night." He blinked. "'Urt the eyes ter look at it. An' before yer could come to yer senses and realize wot yer'd seen, she up-tailed an' plunged inter the water, an' everything went dark—black dark like the night swallowed 'er up." There were gasps around the room, and the sound of one person weeping with inconsolable grief.

"Thank you, Mr. Baker," Camborne murmured quietly. "Your witness," he offered Juniver.

Juniver had enough sense not to invite further disaster upon himself; he politely declined to ask any questions.

Baker left the stand. The court adjourned for luncheon.

The afternoon began with one of the doctors who had treated some of the survivors, and later examined the bodies of at least thirty of the dead. He was a quietly spoken, solid man with gentle eyes and thick, white side-whiskers. Gravely, his voice tight and cracking with emotion, he described what he had seen. He showed no hysteria, no anger, just grief.

Hester recognized Camborne's skill. Anyone not moved by the account—the terrible state of the bodies, the range of victims from the youngest of the women to the white-haired men, all enjoying a summer evening on the river, when out of nowhere the party had been torn apart, drowned in the dark and filthy water, some washed to sea, never to be recovered—must be devoid of all human feeling; yet there was nothing for Juniver to inquire after, nothing to question or doubt.

It was early in the afternoon, but the entire courtroom was already exhausted from the emotion of it. It was both merciful to adjourn, and a wise tactic on Camborne's part. No one who had sat through the evidence would sleep unhaunted by nightmares, or leave unaware of the precious fragility of such happiness as they had. All would ache for the small comfort that would be offered by knowledge that justice had been meted against the man who had caused such grief.

The second day began with the testimony of the man in charge of raising the wreck of the *Princess Mary* and hauling it ashore. His name was Worthington. He was in his forties, lean and strong, his hair thinning a little, his face weathered dark by the elements. He looked uncomfortable in his suit. Several times he half lifted his head, as if to ease the high-collared white shirt around his neck, then changed his mind.

He told the story of hauling up the wreck with as little emotion as possible. He could have been speaking of raising any wreck: the practical difficulties, the skills and the equipment needed.

Hester sat in almost the same seat as she had the previous day, and listened as Camborne led the witness through the process of raising a shattered and sunken ship. The tension in the room eased a little as he allowed the people present to concentrate on the technical details. When this part was over he would ask about the bodies. She had watched him long enough to know that he would time it perfectly: asking enough to horrify the jurors, to draw every ounce of pity from them, but not so much that the listeners were exhausted and their emotions numbed. He would leave scope for the imagination to work.

She looked across at the faces of the jurors: twelve ordinary men. Except, of course, that they were not ordinary. They must by law all own property, which ruled out far more people than it included. They must be worthy citizens, themselves above reproach. That ruled out a few more. All women were excluded automatically. Was this truly a jury of peers? Hardly. Did it matter? Probably not at all in this case. For once there was no social division over the crime, no sympathy at all for the accused, no difference in the rage or the pain between rich and poor, man or woman, churchgoer or atheist.

They might register their feelings in slightly varying ways, but the result would be the same. Hester might be one of very few in the courtroom who realized that Camborne had not connected any of the events with the silent man who sat in the dock.

For the rest of the morning Worthington gave expert evidence on exactly what had caused the *Princess Mary* to sink so disastrously quickly that only a few of those on deck at the time had managed to escape.

In the afternoon he told in specific detail how the explosion was caused by a heavy charge of dynamite, where it had been placed and how it ignited.

As to who had done it, that was entirely another matter, and Camborne said that would be explained when the trial resumed the following Monday.

York adjourned them for the weekend.

Hester did not discuss the trial with Monk over the Saturday and Sunday, and he did not ask her. She had told both him and Scuff that she had attended, but had heard nothing they hadn't already deduced. They were not satisfied, but they did not press her, and she guided the conversation to other subjects: family things, and what Scuff was learning at school—a subject he avoided answering with some skill. She made a mental note to inquire further later on.

The conversation shifted to what they would like to do when they had a weekend free and could travel. Brighton was not far. Or Hastings? Scuff wished to see Leeds Castle, which, despite its name, was in Kent, not in Yorkshire. Perhaps they could go to Canterbury Cathedral and the high altar before which Archbishop Thomas à Becket had been murdered by the king's men, seven hundred years ago. They discussed that at some length, and in detail, and the *Princess Mary* was temporarily forgotten.

On Monday morning the whole tragedy returned with renewed force as Hester took her seat in the courtroom again. She had written once to Oliver Rathbone, sending the letter to Rome to await his arrival. She had done so largely because she wished to record her impressions while they were still fresh in her mind rather than remember them in the light of whatever should happen subsequently.

Listening to the conversations around her as the public waited for the proceedings to begin, she heard no arguments as to guilt or innocence, only anger that the whole series of events had occurred. In one or two instances there was a degree of irritation that Juniver should defend Beshara at all.

Hester had a considerable sympathy for Juniver. She did not imagine he was speaking for Beshara for any reason except that without a legal defense, there could be no conviction, and therefore no sentence. She had to exercise more control than usual over her tongue to keep from pointing this out to the people behind her. But experience had taught her that such arguments failed. You cannot tell people to take into account what they do not wish to know.

She sat silently, feeling extraordinarily alone. Was she the only person here who was even considering the possibility that Beshara was not guilty at all? There was no doubt as to the crime or its horror, but the prosecution had not yet produced any connection with the man supposedly guilty of the act!

The first witness to be called was Sir John Lydiate, the man who had replaced Monk at the head of the investigation.

To begin with Hester had been angry with him, until sense prevailed and she realized that he also had no choice in the matter. Now, looking at him in the witness stand, isolated from the rest of the court by the high box at the top of its own winding steps, and the fact that it was several yards from anyone else, stared at by all, she felt sorry for him.

Camborne was respectful of Lydiate's rank and spoke with great courtesy, but he was very much in control of the entire exchange. He stretched it from the opening of the court on Monday morning, right through until the adjournment for luncheon on Tuesday. It was masterful. Every fact of the explosion was raised, every detail was dealt with regarding the entire investigation and every piece of evidence Lydiate's men had found, every witness they questioned and every conclusion drawn.

Lydiate looked tired and distressed, but he was meticulous in his answers and the jury watched his face almost unblinkingly.

Hester felt the weight of it settle on her like a smothering blanket. Lydiate had followed the rules precisely. He did not exaggerate or assume anything. He erred on the side of caution. There was nothing for Juniver to attack. He tried, and was overruled. He stopped before he lost more of his remaining credibility.

On Tuesday afternoon the eyewitnesses began. Camborne played it for drama, leaving the few survivors until last. Hester understood that, but there was an essence of deliberate exploitation of their grief in it that she found ugly. Added to that, it was now unnecessary.

First were the dockside workers who had seen Beshara, or someone like him, watching pleasure boats, even traveling on the *Princess Mary* himself at an earlier date. Was it definitely him? Yes, they remembered him because he was not one of them. Occasionally he used words they did not understand.

A dockworker named Kent had seen him. Again—was he certain it was Beshara? Yes? Yes, absolutely.

Juniver objected and York ruled against him. The crowd in the gallery murmured their approval.

Juniver rose to question the man.

"You remember him, Mr. Kent?" he said politely.

"Yes, I do," Kent said firmly.

"Why?" Juniver asked.

Kent looked puzzled. "You asked me."

"I beg your pardon. I mean, why is he so memorable to you?" Juniver explained. "He looks very ordinary to me. Except that he's not English, of course. But there are hundreds of men on the docks who are not English."

Camborne moved restlessly in his seat, but he did not overtly interrupt.

Kent shook his head. "I know he's not English."

"He is one of several hundred men on the docks who are not English," Juniver tried again. "Why is it that you are sure you remember seeing this man in particular, and not any of a score of others?"

"I never said that," Kent answered with an edge of irritation. "I seen lots of 'em. But I seen him." He looked up at the dock and nodded. "Came ashore from the *Princess Mary*, he did."

"How do you know—" Juniver began again.

Camborne rose to his feet. "My lord, Mr. Juniver has already asked that question, and been answered. He is badgering the witness."

"Mr. Juniver," York said curtly, "you are doing yourself no favor by harassing honest men reliving painful experiences. I do not wish to have to tell you this again."

"My lord," Juniver protested, "if I cannot question a witness's recollection or point out inconsistencies in his account, I am left nothing but silence—and the accused is left unrepresented in this court."

York clenched his fist on top of his bench and leaned a little across it.

"Mr. Juniver, do I take it that you do not accept my ruling in this matter? If that is the case, then you will be correct, and the accused will not be represented in this court, until we find a replacement for you! Is that your position, sir?"

Juniver could do nothing but retreat.

"No, my lord," he said quietly.

Others all gave variations of the same evidence. They had seen Beshara near the *Princess Mary* shortly before she set out on her last, tragic voyage. A deckhand had seen him hanging around on the quayside. A waiter had served him with a drink on deck and then seen him leave the boat.

A young woman survivor, ashen-faced and clearly afraid, said she had seen him on the deck talking to someone shortly before they left Westminster Bridge. Yes, she nodded vehemently. She was certain.

As soon as Juniver questioned her she burst into tears. Ingram looked at him inquiringly, eyebrows raised. It was obviously against his interest to pursue her further, and he abandoned it. Whatever she said, he would have utterly lost the sympathy of the jury. It was a battle he could never have won, even had Camborne been less skillful and York less impatient.

When, by Wednesday, all the prosecution evidence was in, it

seemed as if the case had to be over. For Juniver to say anything was pointless, except to fulfill the requirement of the law. He had been stalled in all the attempts he had made during the prosecutor's case. On the few occasions York had ruled for him the victories had been small: procedural rather than emotional.

Hester felt her heart sink as Juniver rose to his feet. She had a deep sympathy for him, and pity for Beshara. Camborne had still suggested no motive for the atrocity, except a general hatred of the British! He had given no reason for it: no personal injury or loss, no cause at all. Did he think it unnecessary? Or could it be that the cause might involve some kind of information that he had reason to conceal? Political? Financial? Personal to someone too important to offend? Was that what this was all about?

Was that in fact why the case had been taken from Monk and given to Lydiate? Was it even why York had been chosen to preside?

Juniver did everything a lawyer for the defense could do. He presented witnesses who stated that they had seen Beshara in places and at times that contradicted the previous evidence given.

Camborne rose to cross-examine.

"Mr. Collins, you say you were unloading your wagon just outside the Pig and Whistle when you saw the accused, and you are certain that it was lunchtime on the day of the tragedy?" he asked politely.

"Yes, sir," Collins replied.

"You carry kegs of ale?"

"Yes, sir."

"To supply the Pig and Whistle, among other taverns?"

"Yes, sir."

"Good ale?"

"Yes, sir, the best." Collins straightened up a little.

Camborne smiled.

Juniver half rose, then caught York's eye and changed his mind.

"Lunchtime," Camborne observed. "An interesting way of recalling the hour. Did you have lunch there, Mr. Collins?"

Collins hesitated only a second. "Yes, sir."

"What did you have?"

"Ploughman's, sir. Cheese and pickle."

"You're quite sure?"

Juniver rose. "My lord, this is all completely irrelevant."

"You are precipitate, Mr. Juniver," York replied. "It may prove to be of importance. Proceed, Sir Oswald."

"Thank you, my lord. Mr. Collins, why are you so sure that you had a ploughman's sandwich on that day? Was there something remarkable about it?"

"No, sir. It's what I always 'ave. They do a very good pickle at the Pig and Whistle," Collins said with approval.

"Always? And always at the Pig and Whistle?" Camborne asked.

"Yes, sir."

"And there was nothing different about this day?"

Collins stared at him. Suddenly he realized the trap he had fallen into. "I know I saw Beshara on the street there that very day!" he insisted.

Camborne's eyebrows shot up. "You know him? You are acquainted?"

"No! But I saw him!"

Camborne smiled. "But how can you be certain it was the day of the explosion, if there was nothing else to set it apart? Thank you, Mr. Collins. That is all."

Juniver stood up to try to save his witness, but he realized that he could only make it worse. Collins might repeat all he had said, but his confidence was gone. He would be replying in anger, to save his dignity. Juniver sat down again.

The others largely followed suit, and what was left was likely to be disregarded by the jury.

Juniver did not call Beshara to the stand. It was a wise decision. His manner was not particularly pleasing, his English only moderately good. All he could do was deny his guilt, and of course testifying would open him up to being cross-examined by Camborne. Like many people accused of terrible crimes he accepted his lawyer's advice to remain silent.

The jury barely needed to retire to bring back a verdict of guilty. The court sat late in order for York to place the black cap upon his head and pass sentence of death upon Habib Beshara for the murders of one hundred and seventy-nine men and women. He would be taken to jail, and in three weeks' time would be hanged by the neck until he was dead.

CHAPTER

5

Monk ate dinner in the comfort of the kitchen, with Hester and Scuff. There was a checked cloth on the table, and the yellow china jug full of flowers on the dresser at the side was so big it hid half of the plates kept there. The back door was open to let in the warmth of the summer evening and the faint smell of earth and cut grass.

"Why's it matter so much?" Scuff asked.

They had been speaking of the new canal at Suez.

"Because it will take about five thousand miles off the journey from Britain to the Far East," Hester replied, eager to sharpen his interest in anything connected with schoolwork. She was certain that he had been skipping attendance recently, but nagging him would not help.

He still looked slightly puzzled.

She started to explain how hard Britain had fought for mastery of the seas over the previous hundred years. Her narrative was full of terrific naval battles, especially in the period of the Napoleonic Wars, battles such as Copenhagen, the Nile, and finally Trafalgar, and at last she had his full attention.

They were interrupted by a knock on the front door. Monk looked up in surprise, fearing that it would be one of his men calling on him about some case too urgent to leave until the next day.

Scuff had finished his dinner. He had not yet lost the habit of eating as fast as he could in case his food were taken, as it had been sometimes in his years living in the docks. He stood up.

"I'll get it . . ." he said willingly, going toward the door before Monk could check him.

He returned a moment later, closely followed by Runcorn.

"Sorry," Runcorn said, more to Hester than to Monk. He stood awkwardly, his height seeming to crowd the room. His eyes went to Monk's unfinished meal. "I thought you'd want to know, maybe hear all there is, rather than whatever the papers say, which'll be plenty."

Hester stood up, smiling. "Would you like tea, and maybe a piece of cake?"

Runcorn shook his head, and then changed his mind instantly. "If it's not a trouble?"

"None at all," Hester answered him, ignoring her own plate. "Why don't you go and sit in the parlor? You'll be more comfortable. Scuff, you can help me . . ." It was an order. He obeyed with only one backward glance, his brow puckered with worry.

Runcorn accepted the suggestion, and followed as Monk stood up and led the way. In the parlor they sat down opposite each other. Monk waited.

Runcorn shook his head. "You'll hear tomorrow morning. It'll be all over the place, and I'm reckoning it'll be ugly. It seems this Egyptian fellow, Beshara, comes from a pretty important family back at home. To be precise, in the port of Suez, which I gather is small, scruffy, and very busy. But his family is in a way of business, and has quite a lot of money."

Monk was skeptical. "Who says so? And if he comes from an important family, why was he working in the London docks? Why did none of this important family come and speak for him during his trial?"

Runcorn looked tired. He pushed his fingers through his thick, grizzled hair. "He always claimed he wasn't working at the dockside." He looked very directly at Monk, a shadow in his eyes. "Actually, the Egyptian embassy said as much, but nobody believed them—or, more accurately, everyone thought they were mistaken."

Monk felt the chill of unease touch him. Why had Runcorn come with this now? Was it anything more than what they must have expected, even if a little late? "Several people identified him," he pointed out. "It didn't rest on one."

Runcorn looked down at the table. "I know . . ."

Memories flickered through Monk's mind, other cases they had worked on together, long ago, people who had been certain of what they had seen—and wrong. Something else stirred in his mind, but eluded him before he could identify it. Something that night on the river.

"Have you doubts?" he asked gently. If Runcorn had, he would understand. In a couple of days Beshara could be hanged and it would be too late to correct errors then, however obvious in hindsight. Mistakes would be sealed in death, unalterable. Nightmares of error would creep into the dreams of every man, no matter how honest his investigation had been. Monk had woken with the same fear himself, cold sweat on his body at the finality of it. Did jurors feel it too? Or did the company of eleven other "good men and true" relieve the responsibility?

Runcorn was staring at him again. Whatever he said, the truth of it was in his eyes, but also a bitter humor, surely horribly misplaced.

"What is it?" Monk asked.

"They're not going to hang him," Runcorn replied. "At least not yet. He's ill, so the doctors say. Can't hang a sick man. Got to cure him first. Except I'm not sure there is a cure for that. Instead of hanging him quickly, they'll let him die slowly."

Now Monk understood what he had seen in Runcorn's eyes.

Hester came in with the tea on a tray, and several slices of cake.

Both men thanked her for it, unintentionally speaking at the same time, as she reached the door. She smiled briefly, and went out, leaving them alone.

Silently, Monk poured both cups of tea and took a slice of the cake.

Runcorn helped himself to one also. "Actually I do have doubts," he answered the first question. "At least . . . I think I do." He bit into the cake and smiled with satisfaction. He finished the mouthful before he went on. "Eyewitnesses see what they expect to see, and when they've said something to the police, unless they're scared out of it, they tend to stay with whatever it was. And when they've said it a dozen times, they're sure anyway."

"I know," Monk agreed. "And by the time they've sworn to it in court, they're boxed in and can't change. Do you think they're all wrong?"

Runcorn bit his lip. "How much does anyone really remember faces? Especially of people you don't know? I believe they probably saw someone who was an Egyptian, or similar looking, but how could they know with absolute certainty it was him . . ."

"What do you know about Beshara, his background?"

"He's a very questionable dealer in artifacts, beyond doubt some of them stolen. Uncertain temper and . . . different . . . ideas about what qualifies as customs and excise duty," Runcorn replied. "Not all cultures see bribery as a crime. To some it's a way of life, a necessary expense of doing business."

"So a man on the edge of the law . . ."

"Over the edge," Runcorn corrected him.

"That's still a long way from killing the best part of two hundred people," Monk pointed out.

Runcorn sighed and ate another piece of cake. "I know," he said with his mouth full. "But that isn't going to change people's reaction when the news breaks tomorrow that he won't be hanged. I just want you to be prepared for that."

Monk's own feelings were momentarily lost in pity for Runcorn himself. Monk understood the man's confusion and sense of futility; even though Monk had been taken off the case almost as soon as he began, he felt the same emotions.

Had they all allowed intense, almost unbearable shock and emotion to blind their vision? After all, Beshara had never admitted his guilt.

But then, why would he? Most guilty criminals never did.

"Did you ever really learn why he blew up the ship?" Monk asked abruptly.

"No," Runcorn replied. "The belief is that it was just anger because foreigners were making all the money out of chopping up Egyptian land and digging a canal."

"Did you think so?"

"Actually I assumed he was paid by someone," Runcorn confessed. "It fits the past patterns we could find; he has done questionable things for money several times. And he had no incentive to say who paid him. I supposed that was for his family's sake, not his own. Maybe they were even hostages to someone . . ." He let the idea hang in the air, an ugly, complicated thought, which changed the balance of everything. "He's sick anyway," he added.

Monk nodded.

The memory he had half glimpsed was still gnawing at the back of his mind, just beyond his reach.

"Yes," Hester answered Monk's question when she and Monk were alone in the sitting room an hour later, after Runcorn had gone and Scuff was in bed. "It's a nasty disease, and there isn't a lot we can do to help people. Just—care . . ." She stopped, aware of what she was saying, and where Beshara would be, growing more and more ill, and eventually dying. She lifted her chin a little. "Perhaps it would show more mercy if they did hang him," she conceded, her face pale. "But I know that isn't the way they do it. I am sorry for him, but I feel more pity is for the families who lost the people they loved in the river that night. I can only imagine how I would feel if you were dead." She stared at him defensively, daring him to argue with her.

"I'm alive and well," he answered gently. Then he looked at her more closely, seeing the stiffness in her shoulders, the way she carried her head. "I wasn't in any danger," he added.

"I know! I . . ." She stopped, her voice choked in gathering tears. "Oh damn!" she swore, completely uncharacteristically.

He put his arms around her and held her tightly. He knew acutely the tide of fear and gratitude that had overwhelmed her. Life was so precious, loss so rending, that there were moments when the passion of it slipped beyond control. He wanted to find something to say, but what he felt was too enormous for words at all. In the end all he said was, "I love you," and then felt her arms tighten around him in answer.

THE NEXT MORNING MONK was returning from an early check on a missing cargo of hides. Since it was now midsummer, it had long been daylight. He walked down from the Licensed Victuallers' Dock to the Dog and Duck Stairs, keeping his eye out for a ferry to take him back upriver, and to the north bank again. He reached the top of the steps with still nothing in sight.

He had been there only a couple of minutes when he saw Hooper coming along from the other direction.

"Morning, sir," Hooper said cheerfully.

"Morning," Monk replied. "Going over the river?"

"Yes, sir." Hooper shaded his eyes and scanned the water for sign of a ferry. Then, seeing one, he raised his arm. "What do you make of the news, sir?" he asked.

Monk had no doubt that he was referring to Beshara's stay of execution.

"Surprised," he answered. "I thought they would have kept quiet about the illness and just got on with it."

Hooper's face was grim. "It's not over yet, sir. They should've left it with us. Got 'emselves in a right mess now."

Monk looked at him, studying his face in the bright morning light. He saw resigned anger in it. Hooper was a man he had learned to respect since he had joined the River Police.

"An inevitable mess?" he asked. "Or would we have done better?"

Hooper smiled—a surprisingly gentle expression. "Maybe not, but our mistakes would 'ave been different. We know the water, and the watermen. We'd 'ave known who'd be out in the river, an' who wouldn't, who's scared of wot, and who owes."

"Do you think they're wrong?" Monk asked.

"They went about it wrong," Hooper replied. "They asked the questions as would get them the answers they wanted. Not lies so much as truths shaved to fit. We'd 'ave known that."

"Is that all that is bothering you?" Monk asked.

"No," Hooper answered firmly. "You work the streets, you work the river. You know the people. You know when something don't smell right, even if you don't know why. This don't smell right." He looked straight at Monk, prepared to defend himself.

"Do you think it was Beshara?" Monk asked.

"Could be, could be not. Too much hurry. He fits well enough, least if you don't look too close, too long. Everyone wanted it over with."

"You think they made mistakes?" Monk pressed.

Hooper nodded. "Maybe they got the right man. I'm not saying they didn't. Just they didn't get 'im the right way. That's the trouble with real bad crimes—people look at it an' don't see straight."

"There's going to be a lot of feeling about not hanging Beshara after all," Monk said thoughtfully. "I've heard some of it already, and it's early yet."

Hooper smiled. "There'll be a lot more." He shook his head. "We in't more than halfway through this yet."

The ferry bumped gently at the bottom of the steps and Monk straightened up and started to go down to it, Hooper on his heels. He did not answer, but he knew Hooper was right.

When Monk went into the police station at Wapping there was a sudden silence. Half a dozen men stared at him, waiting for his reaction. He had expected that.

"Good morning," he said cheerfully. "Any word on the brandy smuggling in Bugsby's Marshes? Mr. Orme?"

"Yes, sir," Orme answered gravely. "All dealt with, sir. Quiet day, by the look of it. Except that everyone's hopping mad about that Egyptian. Bit of smashing up of property owned by foreigners, that kind of thing. And of course everybody's jumpy about it happening again. Pleasure boats losing custom. Should've 'anged him when we had the chance. Like before arresting him!"

"We didn't arrest him," Monk pointed out bleakly. "The regular police did."

Orme pulled a face of disgust. "Yes, sir. That's what they're complaining about. Walpole, that old tosher down the King's Arms Stairs, says he was never asked anything, an' he doesn't miss a trick. They took the word o' Nifty Pete instead, skinny little toad, an' he wouldn't tell you straight what day it was." His face was dark with disgust. "He'd tell you it was the prime minister who did it, for a ham sandwich an' a cup o' tea. If that was what you wanted to hear."

"Do you think it wasn't Beshara?"

Orme shook his head. "No idea, sir. I've got to go and see about that boat that Huggins says was stolen." He said it politely, but his anger made his voice cold, and as he walked away his body was stiff; there was no ease to his gait.

Hester had given Monk a list of the witnesses who had been called, and he studied it that evening for the first time. Perhaps it was foolish of him, since the case was closed. There was no evidence to be added.

But for his own peace of mind, he went through it, along with the lists and statements of all the witnesses the police had questioned. He compared their evidence with what he knew of them, and thought about whom he would have asked for the same judgments and observations.

It carried him over into the following day, when the anger at Beshara's escape from the rope had grown more intense. The newspapers were full of it. He saw posters on walls demanding justice, even slurs daubed in paint, ugly and uneven and filled with rage.

It was nothing to do with him, or with anyone in the Thames River Police, and yet he felt a sense of responsibility, as if he had failed.

As the day wore on, it nagged at the back of his mind. Lydiate was a good man—in all probability an honest one—but investigation needed more than that. It needed knowledge of the area, of the people, and it needed luck. It usually required more time than this also—and that, Lydiate had been denied.

Monk had occasion to be on the dockside where one of the witnesses, a man named Field, had been working at the time he claimed to have seen Beshara. He mentioned it to Landry, a squat, heavily built man whose back was bent from years of lifting heavy sacks and barrels.

"Did you see Beshara?" Monk asked with interest, wondering why Lydiate had chosen to question Field instead. He was far less respected and given to invention.

Landry shook his head, squinting sideways at Monk. "You try carryin' a few o' them sacks, an' see if yer've got time ter see yer own mother walking past yer, never mind some foreign feller wi' a box o' fancy food up ter 'is face."

Monk pictured it in his mind. "So Field was lying?" he said bluntly.

"'E were sayin' wot they wanted 'im ter say," Landry snapped back. "If yer ask the question the right way, yer get the right answer, don't yer? 'Yer din't see this man, did yer?' 'No sir, I didn't.' 'D'yer think you might 'ave seen this one?' 'Yeah. I might 'ave.'" His voice was heavy with sarcasm. "Field weren't lyin', 'e were bein' 'elpful. We all want ter catch the bastard wot sank the *Princess Mary* an' all them people! I wouldn't 'ang the swine. I'd drown 'im, slow! Down a bit—up a bit. Know wot I mean?"

"Yes," Monk agreed with feeling. "I saw it happen."

"I know yer did! So why'd they take the case from yer? That's wot I'd like ter know."

"Politics, I dare say," Monk replied, then realized he would be most unwise to continue the conversation. "Thanks, Landry."

Landry shook his head and went back to work.

Monk continued on his current robbery investigation. He was trying to trace the passage of the goods both before they were stolen, and then afterward, and that involved speaking to several stevedores, bargees, and ferrymen—some of who had given evidence at the trial. He could not help asking them a few questions about what they had seen.

He soon realized that each time they had told their stories to others the words had been exactly the same. They were remembering not what had happened, but what they had said about it.

"Did you see the Egyptian?" he said casually to a lighterman called Bartlett, who hadn't been questioned extensively or called to the witness stand. "You were there, weren't you?"

Bartlett looked at him narrowly.

"I'm not looking for evidence," Monk said. "It's all over. Doesn't matter now."

"It's not bleedin' well all over," Bartlett snarled back at him, swaying slightly as he kept his balance on the stern of his barge. "Damn Egyptian's still alive! An' goin' ter stay that way, looks like."

"You saw him?" Monk said quickly.

"Saw him? How the hell do I know? I watch wot I'm doin', not a couple o' dozen Egyptians, lascars, Levantines, Africans, or 'oo ever comes an' goes. This is London, mate. The 'ole world's got its business 'ere, one time or another. You think I've got time ter sit 'ere an' watch 'em?"

Monk thanked him and walked away, turning his words over and over. A man passed by him carrying a load. Monk looked at him, but knew he would not have remembered his face a moment later, or differentiated him from the next man ten seconds after that.

Was any of the evidence that had been given worth a conviction? A man's life?

There was a frustrating lack of factual evidence here, of details that could be examined as many times as needed and were the same to everyone who looked at them later. Not memories. Not things affected by emotion, by loss and the need to settle on some truth and move on.

And he still hadn't been able to recall that fleeting memory from the night of the explosion, which bothered him. Every time he thought he had it, it was replaced by the horror of the ship exploding and then the bodies thrashing around in the water. He had woken in the night with his muscles clenched, his throat aching almost intolerably with the strain of shouting, and trying to be heard above the noise of the rushing water and the oars, the cries of the drowning. And then he was awake, and the silence was worse. The only thing that made it bearable was being able to reach out and touch Hester beside him, move closer to her, feel her breathing and the warmth of her body.

How often had she been awake already, disturbed by him but pretending not to be? Sometimes she had moved and her hand had found his. He had held on to her until he went to sleep again. There was nothing to say. No words were needed.

AT THE END OF the week, Orme came in pale-faced, his usual brisk color faded. He looked tired, even though it was not yet eight in the morning.

"Found another body, way down Greenwich Reach," he said quietly. "Just a girl, less than seventeen, by the looks of 'er. Just started 'er life." He stopped abruptly and shoved the side office door open hard so it banged into the wall to the side of it.

Hooper was standing at the entrance, the sounds of the river drifting behind him, and the warm, dusty salt air off the dock.

"Feelings are running high," he said, coming in and closing off the sounds. "Thought we had 'em all, an' now she turns up. Must've been snagged on some wreckage, or she'd have turned up days ago. Papers'll make it worse."

"There's bound to be more bodies for a while," Monk replied as levelly as he could, but his voice grated as if his throat were tight. "Even if they're as far off as Gravesend. I suppose it's just harder when it's someone so young."

"I didn't mean that." Hooper walked slowly across the floor. He had a very slight swagger, as a man might have who had grown up at sea. "Comes the same day as they've officially commuted Beshara's sentence to life in prison."

Monk jerked his head up, staring at Hooper to see if he was serious, although he was not a man known for an irresponsible sense of humor. He saw nothing in his face but a brooding anger.

Around the room other men shifted position, muttering half-swallowed words of fury or disgust. There were several blasphemies that Monk did not often hear from them. He felt they had a right to feel doubly betrayed, first with the loss of the case, now with the commuting of the sentence.

"What are you going to do, sir?" one of them asked, looking at Monk.

Monk realized that they were all looking at him, even Hooper. He had no idea what answer he could give that made any sense. The case was finished. He had never had the power to do anything, from the moment they had taken the case from him. But to say so was to make himself helpless, a figure of submission, a follower.

But did he want to lead what amounted to a mutiny, in effect if not in law? He felt the rage swell inside himself, fueled by his own knowledge of what it was like to be cornered and weaponless.

It was Hooper who saved him from an immediate answer.

"They'd 'ave been better to leave the case with us," he remarked, leaning against one of the desks. "We'd 'ave solved it so the whole world would 'ave known he was guilty, an' no one who valued their own skin would 'ave gone back on the sentence. Or maybe we could 'ave managed to let 'im drown as we were bringing 'im in. Dangerous places, rivers . . ." He let the suggestion linger in the still air of the room.

Before the commuting of the sentence Monk might have argued. But who could have foreseen that? Like everyone else, he had believed that the death sentence was final.

The men were waiting for his reaction. He knew their trust in him depended on his response, not only for the next few days, but in the weeks and years to come. All sorts of ideas raced through his mind. He knew of no one on whom to model himself! He was alone, and the seconds were ticking by. If he did not answer he would be effectively abdicating his leadership, and he would never get it back again.

He took the plunge.

"I know a politician called Quither is saying that it's mercy to do with his illness and Lord Ossett is saying more discreetly that there are diplomatic reasons also, to do with Suez and the canal. And I expect the Egyptian embassy has had something to say."

They stared at him, no one speaking or moving.

"I think they made a mess of the case," Monk went on. "I've been up and down the docks in the last week. Spoken to a few people, listened to a lot. We all have. We know the Metropolitan Police didn't do it as we would have done. They took people's word we'd have known better than to trust. I think they've got cold feet now that they might have the wrong man—or at best that they haven't proved it's the right one. Once he's hanged, they can't go back on it."

One of the men vented his opinion in unrepeatable language. Several others growled agreement.

Hooper straightened up and watched, his eyes moving from them to Monk, and back again.

"If anybody's going to put it right, it's us," Monk went on recklessly. "But carefully. It may take a long time, because we've no authority. A court's found Beshara guilty, and it could be right. If we find real proof of that, the kind that we know is right, then we'll make it public, and see what happens."

He looked around them slowly, catching each man's eyes. "But one stupid mistake, one word out of turn, and we'll be finished; our whole case will be shot full of holes like a sinking ship. Got that? If we don't want to wind up on the bottom in the Thames mud, like the *Princess Mary*, then we've got to be careful, clever, and lucky."

He gave a bitter smile. "My wife's a nurse; she was with Miss Nightingale in the Crimea. She says Beshara will die of his illness, and it'll be slower and crueler than a rope and a quick drop. Now let's turn our attention to the missing brandy from Mills & Sons."

Hooper stood up. One by one the other men picked up what they had been doing and resumed work.

Monk waited a moment. His hand was still clenched, and he knew he was not yet ready to hold a pen and write anything legible. He had put his career on the line, his credibility as a leader of men, and all that it meant to him. More than he wanted it to, more than in the past when he had been a loner, not caring what anyone else thought or believed. He had not respected his seniors, nor really cared whether his juniors respected him. In fact they had feared him, and—before the accident that had erased his memory—that had been sufficient.

How much he had changed! It was not sufficient now, not to him, and not to the man he wanted to be.

THE FOLLOWING MORNING WAS Saturday and Monk was free to take a whole weekend off. It was a mixed blessing. At any other time he would have been totally happy, looking forward to a day with Hester and Scuff. However, the morning papers were full of the reprieve for Beshara, and wild speculation as to the reason for it. Various political motives were mentioned and also a few far uglier financial ones. The words "bribery" and "corruption" were used.

Monk saw Scuff staring at it and knew Scuff now could read the article without difficulty.

"Why'd they change their minds?" Scuff asked, looking across the breakfast table at Monk. The question was simple and he wanted a simple answer. "He blew up the boat, didn't he?" His eyes lowered again to look at the portrait of the girl in white that had been printed. She had been the daughter of an important man, one with enough wealth and influence to have had her photographed. It was a real person who stared back at him from the page, not an artist's impression. She was individual, with a life and a name, a mole high on her left cheek, and a shy, slightly crooked smile, as if she understood a joke and would have shared it with you.

This moment it was Scuff whom Monk had to answer to. There was no question in his mind that he must not lie, but how much truth should he tell him? How much was helpful, how much a burden it was unfair to place on him?

If he looked at Hester, he would seem to be asking her to lead. That was not what he wanted to do.

"They're saying that it is because he's ill," he replied, judging his words carefully, even though his voice was rough-edged with emotion, and Scuff would hear that, too. "We don't execute people when they're ill."

Scuff blinked. "Why not? If they're going to be dead anyway, what difference does it make?"

"I don't know," Monk admitted. "I don't think that's the real reason, anyway. Apparently his family is important in Egypt, near where they're making the canal."

"Why does that make it all right?" Scuff asked.

"It doesn't," Monk said. "It makes it expedient." He looked at Scuff's confusion. "It is the convenient thing for them to do for their own purposes," he explained.

Scuff's contempt was plain in his expression.

Instantly Monk regretted his choice of words. If he showed no respect at all for the men who governed the country, how could he expect Scuff to respect authority either? He had made a mistake.

"I'm sorry," he said grimly. "I'm so upset about all the dead people it makes me angry. I think they should have done better with Beshara's trial, but I don't know why they decided to let him live. Maybe they know something about it that we don't."

Scuff bit his lip. "Like what? Didn't he do it, then?"

Monk hesitated. "I wasn't on the case. I really don't know. It is possible he didn't . . ."

Hester spoke for the first time. She looked far calmer than Monk felt.

"If you think about it," she said quietly, "it doesn't seem likely he did it all by himself. In fact, I don't think it's even possible. But he refused to mention anybody else. If they hang him, he'll never tell them who else was with him."

"I see!" Scuff said quickly. "An' if he's alone an' sick, they could get him to tell them."

Hester looked uncertain.

Monk bit back the ghost of a smile.

"Possibly," Hester conceded. "At least that's what they might think."

"So then we can hang all of them," Scuff concluded.

"Well, at least we could catch all of them," she amended. "We really don't want them going free, if we can prevent it."

Scuff looked satisfied. "You going to help?" he asked Monk.

It was time for certainty. "Yes."

"They let yer?" Scuff said with doubt.

This time Monk smiled properly. "I wasn't intending to ask."

Scuff grinned back and went on with his breakfast.

When he left the table to get ready for the day, Monk looked at Hester.

"You don't look as angry as I feel. How do you manage it? Do you really have some kind of pity for them? I mean the politicians who wriggle and twist as the wind turns?"

"You know me better than that," she replied, putting the used plates on top of each other. "I've seen too many battlefields to feel the same raw shock that you do, that's all. It doesn't hurt any less, just differently. I've learned to keep my powder dry..."

"Gunpowder?" he said with a twist of his mouth. "Do we have any?"

"I don't know. Nobody's given a real reason yet for Beshara, or anyone else, to have blown up the *Princess Mary*, have they?"

"No. It doesn't make a lot of sense. Unless there's something about Beshara or his family that we don't know about."

"Could we have cheated them out of something, or vice versa?" she asked very quietly. "Land, for example?"

He had thought of that and hoped it was not so. Of course, there were vast shipping companies whose fortunes were built on Britain's dominance of the seas. With a canal from the Mediterranean to the Red Sea that power would largely disappear.

"Paid by someone to do it? Or someone paid to make it look like he did it?" he said, hating the words.

"It could be... William, please..." She did not finish.

"I know," he said very quietly. "Don't tell Scuff."

"He has enough trouble with authority," she agreed. "All his natural instincts are to deny it. Don't add to that. He needs to stay in school. If he rebels now he'll lose all he's gained so far. He'll close so many doors that won't open for him again."

"I know," he said gently. "I'll be careful."

"Is Beshara guilty?" she asked.

"I don't know. I'm not happy with the evidence. The whole investigation was too quick, too pressured. I'm not blaming Lydiate for that, but his men don't know the river the way we do. I've found some oddities, but I don't know if they make any real difference."

"Enough for a retrial?"

"No. Just for a lot of doubt and ugliness."

She looked even more worried. "People are talking about riots to force them to hang him. They don't know what they're talking about, but they're so angry that doesn't matter anymore."

"I know. Please . . . you be careful . . ." He did not know how to say what he wanted. He felt a nameless fear, a darkness just beyond grasping.

It was Runcorn who told him the following day that Habib Beshara had been attacked in prison and was now in a critical condition.

Monk was stunned. "Attacked?" he repeated, as if saying the word again would explain it. He stared at Runcorn standing in the Greenwich dockside in the sun, the busy river bright behind him, endlessly moving. "Who? Were they moving him, or something? Why?"

Runcorn looked unhappy and just as confused. "No. He was safe in prison. At least he was supposed to be safe. Fortridge-Smith isn't saying a damn thing!"

"Prison governor?" Monk assumed. "Who did it? Someone lashing out because they decided not to hang him? Someone who lost a relative in the *Princess Mary*?" It was a natural assumption.

"Nobody's saying anything," Runcorn stared across the choppy water. "It's a bloody mess! Could be revenge, outrage, or sheer temper. Or it could be an old score to settle over something else. Beshara's been here on and off for several years. He's probably made a few enemies even before the *Princess Mary*."

"Or it could be to make sure he keeps silent about whoever else was involved in the sinking," Monk said quietly.

Runcorn turned to face him, his eyes narrowed against the light off the water. "Yes, it could," he agreed. "I've heard that the Chinese have a saying, something like: 'Before you go looking for revenge, you had better dig two graves.'"

"Very wise people," Monk agreed. "Except this time I don't think we are looking at just two."

CHAPTER

6

"I wasnae there!" McFee complained bitterly, glaring at Monk. "That's down river o' me, you daft . . ." He bit his tongue. Whatever his thoughts on the mental inadequacies of the River Police, it was not wise to antagonize them. "The tide was going out . . . sir."

Monk ignored Orme's flash of irritation, and affected interest. They were standing on the steps at Charlton Wharf, just short of Woolwich Reach. They had caught the whip-thin Scotsman with a couple of kegs of single malt whisky, and no papers to explain them. They looked extraordinarily like part of a shipment that was missing from a warehouse a mile and a half farther up the river.

Orme waited.

"I know what you're thinkin'," McFee began again. "They barrels was like this, but I got this one from Old Wilkin at Bugsby's Marshes, right legal. An' I can prove it! Ask Jimmy Kent. He was with me."

"When was that?" Monk said quickly. Jimmy Kent had only recently gone into the Coldbath Fields Prison for a short stretch.

"Ha! You think I cannae count, eh?" McFee said triumphantly. "I know exactly what day that was, 'cos the *Princess Mary* got sunk that night—see!"

"And Jimmy Kent was with you when you bought those?" Monk asked.

"That's right!" McFee nodded vigorously. "Up at Blackfriars." His lips thinned in a crooked smile. "And you know where to find that poor sod!"

"I do indeed," Monk nodded. "But he wasn't at Blackfriars on the evening before the *Princess Mary* sunk. You picked the wrong man—or the wrong night, McFee. He swore in court that he was at the Surrey Docks. He was one of the witnesses who saw Habib Beshara coming ashore before the *Princess Mary* went down."

McFee paled but he did not retreat.

"Then he's a liar! I was there! You ask . . ." He looked from Monk to Orme, and back again, then swore solidly for a full minute without repeating himself.

Orme arrested him, curling his lip with distaste.

An hour later Monk and Orme were back at Wapping taking a hot cup of tea and a cold beef sandwich each. The room was over-warm and the air stuffy. Someone had left the door open to remedy it, and the slight breeze was ruffling papers on the nearest desk.

Orme was deep in thought, ignoring the sound of river traffic, the drift of accordion music, the odd shout of a bargee, the constant hiss and slurp of water.

"He's a nasty little swine," he said suddenly, turning to look at Monk. "But what if he was telling the truth?"

"McFee?" Monk said incredulously.

Orme swallowed a mouthful of tea. "Yes . . ."

Monk thought for a moment. "Then Jimmy Kent was lying." He recalled what he could of Kent. Not much of it was to his credit.

Orme sat still, his blunt face set in stubborn concentration.

"Why would Jimmy lie?" Monk pursued the train of thought.

"If he wasn't where he said, then he was somewhere else." Orme held his finger up to stop Monk arguing. "Somewhere worse—stands to reason."

"With McFee at Blackfriars?" Monk shook his head. "Fiddling a barrel or two of whisky? We couldn't have proved it. Jimmy's sharper than that."

"Yes. So what was he doing?" Orme raised his eyebrows and stared at Monk.

"Fiddling the whole shipment," Monk concluded.

"Right!" Orme agreed. He watched Monk closely.

Hooper was leaning against the wall, his ankles crossed, listening.

Monk gave it words. "Which means he lied when he testified. If he saw Beshara at all, it wasn't when he said it was!"

"And if it was somewhere else, but still Beshara," Orme pointed out, "then Beshara wasn't where anyone said he was!"

"Yes," Monk said slowly. "Yes. I wonder how many said what they thought we wanted them to say—"

"Not us!" Orme interrupted, a shadow across his face. "Lydiate's men . . ."

"Police," Monk explained. "The authorities, the State. We all wanted it tidied up as soon as possible. Deal with it and forget it. Punish someone, then move on. It's natural. The government would have pushed us, too, had we been on the case."

Orme said nothing. It pained him, but he was a fair man. He could not argue.

"I wonder how many of them could tell one man from another in a hurry, just a glimpse of a face. Could you, Orme?" Monk pursued it. "If they were people you didn't know," he added.

"No," Orme conceded. "But I wouldn't swear to it . . ." He stopped. Monk smiled.

"Maybe I would," Orme said very quietly. "Maybe I'd get surer of it the more times I said it, and the more I thought of all of them that had gone down. An' maybe I'd think the police grateful to me, and off my back forever asking me what I know."

"And maybe," Monk added, "if I had a lot of business I'd sooner that the police weren't poking into too much, I'd look to be in their favor for a while."

"You going to Lydiate?" Orme asked. No one would like the investigation being opened up again, after people had begun to forget it and move on with life. Beshara was a man with a reputation for dealing and bribing. He was not an innocent, simply in the wrong place at the wrong time. Even if he wasn't guilty of sinking the *Princess Mary*, he was guilty of other things for which he had not paid.

"I have to," Monk replied. "To Lydiate, anyway. It'll come out, sooner or later."

Orme nodded and gave a downward twisted smile. There was no need for him to add anything. Their thoughts were the same.

MONK DID NOT WANT to tell Lydiate in his office. He would allow the man time to accept it alone, or reject it, and possibly dispute it. He invited him to one of the small pubs along the river where there were seats overlooking the water. Everyone else there would be too busy watching the boats or listening to the occasional song to bother overhearing two men talking over a pint of ale and a pie.

Lydiate arrived after Monk. He was casually dressed, attempting to blend in, but he still looked like a gentleman. His careful grooming, and the grace with which he walked, would always give him away.

He came over carrying a tankard of ale and sat down next to Monk on the bench. It was only when he was closer, in the lower, more direct evening light off the water, that Monk noticed how tired he was. The fine lines on his face seemed to drag down, and there was little color in his skin. The experience of the *Princess Mary* case had weighed heavily on him. He had had to be closer to the reality of it, the massive loss, than his position usually required of him. This was going to be bitter.

"Put away a petty thief yesterday," Monk began. There was no kindness in stringing it out, beginning with pleasantries. "But while I was doing so, he inadvertently gave me some information about another man involved in the robbery. That was odd, because the other man had a perfect alibi. I checked it very carefully."

Lydiate was studying his face, waiting.

Monk looked at him. "He was with one of the witnesses who saw Habib Beshara at the time he was supposed to be putting the dynamite on board the *Princess Mary*."

"But . . ." Lydiate began, and then sighed. "I suppose there's no doubt?"

"Not that I can see. It raises the whole question of how many others were saying what they thought we wanted them to."

"He fitted perfectly," Lydiate said, more to himself than to Monk. "He was an unpleasant man, and for sale. He'd committed many other small acts for money, which he knew were going to end in brawls, or worse. But admittedly, this was far more serious. He had a record of dislike of the British, small acts of vandalism." He took a sip of his ale, then put it down, as if it tasted sour to him. "This was far more serious than anything else we've know him to do, but it wasn't out of character." He looked at Monk. "Everyone was so keen to help. We weeded out a hundred or more who only wanted the limelight, or thought they knew something and were nowhere near. Lord Ossett's people called every day."

He did not need to add more than that. Monk could imagine the pressure. He had experienced it himself, in other cases, albeit to a lesser degree. He was familiar with the constant calls, the demands for results.

He looked at Lydiate and saw the weariness in him. Had those who demanded answers any idea what they were asking? Or the danger of error when there was such hunger for quick solutions? It was juggling the possibility, even the probability, of lies. First one, then another to explain the first, then more and more to prove the ones you had already built on.

"It's political," Lydiate said suddenly, anger and pain in his voice.

"This damned canal is going to change so much! Everybody with money invested in shipping, import and export, travel, is trying to foresee what differences it'll make, and guard themselves against loss. For decades, ever since Trafalgar, we've been lords of all the major seaways in the world." He shrugged very slightly, his expression rueful. "Now suddenly there are shortcuts! The Mediterranean is the center of the world again and we're on the edge. We can be bypassed, and fortunes are going to be made and lost!"

"Not all the seaways," Monk corrected him. "It won't affect the Atlantic, and that will get more and more important as America grows. But it will still mean a whole lot of change in investment, if the canal is a success."

"There was talk about a new land route to the east, through Turkey," Lydiate added, shaking his head. "Or trains from Alexandria to Suez, and then reloading everything again to go by sea. Even if this canal is a success, it will take ships slowly, and only up to a certain size. It's inevitable. Haven't they read about Canute?" He smiled with a bitter amusement.

Monk struggled to remember. "Holding back the tide? I saw a drawing of him, sitting on his throne with the sea up to his knees! Unbelievably stupid!"

"No!" Lydiate said sharply, as if this were the trigger to the anger he had been so long holding in. "He was trying to show his people that, great as he was, he could *not* hold back the tide. That was the whole point of the exercise. Even kings cannot stop the inevitable."

Monk was considerably sobered. He felt a sudden warmth for this beleaguered man sitting on the bench beside him in the last of the sunlight. Lydiate was fighting against men's political ambitions, and probably a king's ransom in invested money. He was dealing with men who demanded miracles, and did not seem to understand the tide in any sense—of the sea, or of history.

"I don't know whether Beshara was guilty," Monk said. "But I do know that the verdict was unsafe. And there's a very strong chance that sooner or later something is going arise that will prove it. Do some of our political masters know that, and that's why they won't hang him?"

Lydiate looked at him curiously, the fine lines of his face etched deeply in the waning sunlight, his eyes very clear. "I hadn't thought of that. Perhaps because I didn't want to. Perhaps. The other possibility is just as ugly, come to think of it. I assumed Beshara's family had got to them. He's a wayward son, something of a disappointment, but he has brothers and cousins who own a good deal of land around the canal, which means now that they have a lot of money."

Monk raised his eyebrows. "And do they want him released?"

"That's a very good question," Lydiate answered, pulling his mouth into a bitter line.

"Can you prove anything?" Monk asked, turning a little in his seat. The sun was sliding below a cloud bank, spreading color over the water, but in ten minutes or so it would fade, and the wind would turn colder. There were fewer people on the bank already.

"I don't have the right even to look," Lydiate replied.

"Motive?" Monk pointed out. "No one gave a motive for Beshara blowing up the *Princess Mary*, beyond a general hatred of Britain, and that's as thin as tissue paper. Millions of people the world over must have a pretty mixed view of the British Empire, just as millions admire it or depend on it. It doesn't make them blow up a pleasure boat with a couple of hundred ordinary people on board."

"I know," Lydiate agreed. "Nobody seemed to care very much about finding a more substantial reason."

Monk said what he was afraid Lydiate was also thinking. "Or else they know damn well what it was, and didn't want it to come out?"

"I didn't see that at the time," Lydiate confessed, staring across the water again. "I thought it was just the weight of public outrage and loss. Damn it, Monk, you saw the bodies! You, of all people, know how bloody awful it was! It was like a battlefield! Only it wasn't soldiers dead, it was ordinary people, most of them women and children. What kind of a . . . monster does that?"

"Greedy . . . frightened . . . filled with hate for his own lost," Monk replied. "Think about how many Egyptian lives have been sacrificed, digging this canal."

Lydiate sighed. "Thousands—but the bloody thing's French, not English!"

"You're right," Monk conceded. "It doesn't make any sense. But mass murder doesn't, however you look at it."

They sat in silence for a few minutes. The sun disappeared, taking the glow with it, and suddenly it was dark and the air chill.

"I'm sorry," Monk said. "It might make some kind of sense if we had all the facts. It was very carefully planned. It wasn't a sudden impulse of a lunatic, and we both know that."

"It's about all we do know, for certain," Lydiate said miserably. "How can so many men, and the constituencies they serve, be so wrong? There is so much we assumed, and could be totally mistaken about." He looked helpless. "What government deals or policies are involved? What's really in the balance, naturally, or intentionally? What private deals are in place, and with whom? Or is it all something else entirely, and we aren't even on the right track?"

Monk gave a bitter little smile. "With luck we can give it back to the Home Office and let the minister worry about that."

Lydiate flinched. "And give it right back to me again!"

"I'm sorry," Monk said sincerely.

"I know. You had no choice," Lydiate answered graciously, rising to his feet as if his muscles ached. "I'll tell him tomorrow morning."

THE FOLLOWING AFTERNOON MONK was in Wapping; he had tidied up the last reports on the smuggling case and had just left the police station when Hooper strode after him.

"Sir!"

Monk turned round as Hooper caught up with him. He saw from the look in Hooper's face that the news was not good. He waited in silence to hear it.

"Lord Ossett wants to see you, sir," Hooper said expressionlessly, his brown eyes meeting Monk's and waiting.

Monk was surprised. Ossett was very senior indeed, a man of great power, highly respected in government circles. A member of the House of Lords rather than the House of Commons, he was an adviser to both the Home and Foreign Offices and occasionally to the prime minister himself on important matters of international trade and finance.

"Are you sure?" he asked.

"Yes, sir," Hooper replied steadily, his face unreadable.

"When?" Monk asked, his stomach knotting tight.

"Now . . . sir." Hooper took a deep breath. "Maybe we're getting back on the case, sir. Do you want me to tell Mr. Orme, and start sorting the duties out?"

Monk felt a sense of dread, but he didn't let it show on his face. "Yes . . . please," he agreed. I think you'd better. Don't change anything yet, but get ready."

Hooper's smile was twisted, and without replying he turned and walked with his easy, loping gait toward the station.

Monk caught the first passing hansom toward Lord Ossett's office in Whitehall. On the ride through the docklands he was all but unaware of the high, barn-like warehouses, wagons laden with all kinds of goods, the towering cranes and the creak of loads, shouts of stevedores, and the rattle of wheels on the stones. His mind was on the case of Habib Beshara and the sinking of the *Princess Mary*.

Was he going to be given back the investigation, now that it was thoroughly contaminated? Could he refuse? What would it mean for his career if he did? No—that was not the issue. He was irritated with himself for having thought of it at all. What mattered was the reputation of the River Police, and whether they had any chance of finding the truth, for Beshara, and for those who were dead or bereaved.

Was it important to find those beyond, the incompetent, and the corrupt? Or was that expecting miracles, which might also take down a great many people who were only peripherally involved? In eagerness to find the guilty, he could destroy the bystanders as well, those who were misguided, afraid, confused, guilty only of not understanding.

He had found no answers to any of his questions when he alighted. He paid the driver and walked across the pavement and in through the imposing doorway of Lord Ossett's office.

He was received immediately. He had the distinct impression from Ossett's lean and rather somber secretary that Monk was not so much paying a visit as obeying a summons.

Ossett was waiting in his office. He was a striking man, slender, a little over average height, and with a bearing that made it obvious that he had served many years in the army. He stood like a soldier, back straight, shoulders square, but quite clearly with the ease of an officer well used to command. Monk respected that whatever rank he had borne, Ossett did not now use it. He had no urge to impress.

"Ah," he said with evident satisfaction. "I'm obliged you have come." He did not even obliquely refer to the fact that Monk had had no choice. "I'm afraid we have a very ugly situation." He waved his arm toward one of the well-upholstered leather armchairs near the classic fireplace, which was at present unlit and masked by a tapestry screen.

As Monk sat down, he noticed that above the marble mantel hung a four-foot-high portrait of what appeared to be Ossett himself as a young man. His face was quite plainly recognizable. His hair was thicker and several shades fairer, but the way it grew from his brow was exactly the same. He was handsome, his chin held high, a half-smile on his mouth. His military scarlet was immaculate.

Ossett sat in the chair opposite Monk, leaning forward a little so as to indicate the urgency of the matter. There was no time for the indulgence of relaxation.

"Lydiate tells me that you have discovered a serious flaw in some of the evidence against Beshara," he said gravely. "Evidence that wouldn't stand up to exposure, should you pursue your inquiries. Is that true?"

"Yes, sir, I'm afraid it is," Monk replied.

"Lydiate gave me some of the details, but I would like to hear it from you. Please be specific. If it really does cast doubt on the verdict, then it is so serious it would be hard to overstate the damage it could do."

Monk recounted exactly what he had learned, and how.

Ossett listened to him silently, but with clearly growing concern.

"So if this is accurate, then Beshara *may* be involved," Ossett said finally. "But we cannot confirm that he is the person who placed the dynamite on the *Princess Mary*."

"No, sir," Monk agreed.

"And have we any idea who did?"

"Not yet," Monk answered. "I assume the investigation will have to be reopened."

Ossett bit his lip. Monk noticed that his hands were tight, knuckles pale as he sat. He was deeply disturbed by the situation. All the comfort and familiarity of the office with its leather chairs, glowing Turkey carpet, shelves of well-used books on the history of the Empire, the exploration of the world and the arts and sciences of the mind, could have been another man's possessions for any sense of comfort they offered him.

"I regret this," Ossett said quietly. "But we cannot turn a blind eye to the new evidence. It would not be morally unacceptable to ignore it, even if we could. But it is a moot point. It will emerge somehow, sooner or later, and that will damage Britain's reputation beyond anyone's ability to repair. Some mistakes can be salvaged. This would be one that cannot."

Monk did not reply. He knew that Ossett was speaking as much to himself as to Monk.

"This will be highly political," he said at last.

Again Monk did not speak. He felt a deep sympathy for the man. He was caught in the horror of a dilemma that might be partially of his own making. He had acceded to the decision to take the case from the River Police and give it to the regular metropolitan force, although perhaps he had had little choice in that too.

"Yes, sir," Monk said, not that his agreement mattered. He spoke to break the silence, and possibly even to indicate that he understood the burden, and the decision.

Ossett looked up at him. "You have a considerable loyalty to your men, I hear. Which is as it should be. A leader has no right to expect loyalty if he does not first give it." His eyes were for a moment far away, as if he were thinking of other times, and other people. "The reputation of the Thames River Police, by implication, has been insulted. I know their history, and they are owed better."

Monk looked at him questioningly, a sinking in the pit of his stomach warning him of something ugly to come.

"I regret taking this from Lydiate, but it has been too compromised for him to retain it." His voice was tight, almost gravelly with his own dislike of what he felt forced to do. "But he is no longer in a position to handle the further investigation. I am handing it back to the River Police. It should never have been taken from you. It was a political decision, in light of the many foreign merchants and dignitaries who were lost on the *Princess Mary*. It is now painfully clear that it was a mistake."

Monk had anticipated this news from the moment Hooper had told him Lord Ossett wished to see him. The whole issue was poisoned beyond any possibility of finding evidence uncontaminated by time, interference, emotion, or confusion. And—worse than that—when they failed, as they certainly would, the blame would rest with them, not the Metropolitan Police who had actually mishandled it. People would remember only that it was the River Police who had ended it in disaster, confusion, and injustice.

Ossett took a deep breath. "And now with this attack on Beshara in prison," he went on, his face bleak with misery, "our reputation suffers even more. It was very severe. He is a sick man, and now he may not live. It will appear as if we deliberately allowed it to happen." He lowered his eyes, no longer able to meet Monk's gaze. "I wish I could be absolutely certain that that is not so."

CHAPTER

7

Hester knew the moment Monk came in through the door that there had been a major change. There was something more than tiredness in his face: a mixture of surprise, anger, and resolution. If he did not tell her what had happened, then she would press him. But first she would pretend that she had not noticed and allow him time to choose his words and tell her when he had caught his breath, and had a cup of tea.

Actually he left it until after they had eaten, and they were sitting by the door to the back garden, open to let in the summer breeze. He was sorely trying her patience. Even Scuff was aware that something was amiss. He looked at her, then at Monk, started to speak, and changed his mind. He excused himself and went upstairs.

"What's the matter with him?" Monk asked as they heard Scuff's feet on the stairs.

"He's wondering what it is you're not saying," Hester replied. "He won't ask you . . . but I will. What is it?"

He gave a bleak smile. "You know me too well."

It was on the tip of her tongue to tell him to stop being so evasive. It was not a time for word games. But from the look in his eyes it was too serious even for that.

"Wouldn't you ask me?" she said more gently. "If I were so troubled about something?"

"That's different," he started, then realized his mistake. "I was finding the right words. I'm still not sure that I have them."

"Try anyway," she said, controlling with effort the fear mounting inside her.

He had not told her about McFee's evidence. He did so now. She had been at Beshara's trial. She did not need to have any part of its importance explained to her. The evidence against him had been cumulative. It was like a house of cards. To remove any part of it would make it collapse on itself.

"Who have you reported it to?" she asked quietly, trying to assess the weight of the problem, and the potential damage.

"Lydiate. He deserved to know. He told Lord Ossett, who sent for me." He gave a little grunt. "And Ossett has given the case back to me."

"You're taking it?" She made it a question, although she knew the answer. The only alternative was one Monk would never have accepted.

"I have to," he said flatly, but he was searching her eyes, not for answer so much as understanding as to why he had to.

"Where do you begin?" She said "you" deliberately, not because she did not intend to help, but because she would do it her own way, and not necessarily discuss it with him until such time as she had learned something of use.

"Back to the beginning," he answered. "Ever since that night there's been something at the edge of my memory. I didn't know whether it was important or just part of the general horror and sense of helplessness. But it came back to me when I was on the ferry. That evening Orme and I were rowing toward Wapping, but from the south. We were facing backward, as always, so we were looking directly at the ship, and she was faster than we were, and gaining on us. I was watching her, and I saw a man on the deck, and he jumped off into the water, just seconds before the explosion. Afterward I put it all together, as if he'd been part of the explosion, but he wasn't. He leaped several seconds before."

"Escaping . . ." she said slowly, realizing what it meant. "He set the fuse. Man? Just one?"

"Unless anyone went over the other side, away from us, yes, one."

"Beshara did it alone?" she said doubtfully.

"I'm not sure now that he had anything to do with it at all," Monk replied. "But whoever laid the explosives or detonated them in the first place, there are a hell of a lot more people involved now."

She knew he was watching her, waiting to see if she understood all the things he had not yet said about the investigation and the trial, the commuting of the death sentence to life in prison, then the attack on Beshara in prison, which had so nearly been fatal.

She wished there were some way he could avoid accepting the case. The coldness inside her was fear, and there was no way at all she could think of to protect him.

She even played with the idea of asking him to find whatever solution they wanted, short of blaming an innocent man: to say it was an Egyptian who had escaped, gone back to the Middle East, a conspiracy of some sort, not involving anyone still in England; to say it quickly, before they knew beyond doubt that it was not true.

Then she was ashamed of herself. She might understand any woman who asked a man she loved to do such a thing, but it could only be because she thought his morality would allow it. Monk's would not. She had known that since their first dark days together after the murder of Joscelyn Grey.

And what could she ever tell Scuff, if he knew she'd done that? Don't do anything dangerous! If it gets really tough, to hell with the right. Just run away!

Outside the light was fading. The starlings were circling back and settling in the trees.

"What is it?" Monk said quietly.

"Nothing," she answered. "Just thinking. You'll . . . be extremely careful, won't you? Perhaps . . ." She was fumbling for words, ideas. "Perhaps it would be a good idea if whatever you do, you do it so many people know? I mean people other than Orme and your own men."

"Hester, I don't know who else is complicit in this," he said patiently. "It stretches a long way! I might be telling the very people I'm trying to catch!"

She clenched her fists in her lap, where he could not see them. "I know that, William! That is precisely what I mean. If they know that there are plenty of other people who know all that you do, there would be no point in hurting you! In fact, it would only make matters worse for them." She sat motionless, holding her breath for his reaction.

He laughed, but it had a harsh note to it, not of anger but fear. The fact that she knew it too made it impossible for him to deny without putting a barrier between them that neither of them could live with. However much he might wish to protect her, they had experienced too much together for him to pretend now.

"That's probably good advice," he conceded. "I'll keep Orme in the picture, and probably Hooper. I'm beginning to appreciate what a good man he is. Maybe I'll speak to Runcorn too."

"Promise me you will!" she urged. "Especially Runcorn! He's a . . . a safety escape."

"I know. Fancy that, after all these years of hating each other."

There was a lot she could have said about that, but this was not the time.

"William . . ."

He was waiting, watching her.

"You don't know how high up this goes," she began tentatively. As an army nurse she had more experience than he with the hierarchy of authority, men who felt that a threat to their authority was a threat to their lives, and to question orders was treason. They might break, if the pressure were overwhelming, but could not bend.

"No, I don't," he agreed, smiling at her because he understood what she was trying to say, and why there were no words. "And you're right . . . a degree of openness is the only safety. It really is a bag of snakes, isn't it!"

Scuff stood in the kitchen doorway, taller now than Hester, an achievement he was immensely pleased about.

"Another cup of tea?" she asked without turning around.

He sat down at the kitchen table, dropping his bag of school books on the floor. "Not yet," he replied. "Wot's 'appened?"

She must include him as if he were an adult. In wisdom of the street, he was so more than she. If she in any way excluded him she would not be able to make up for it later.

"One of the people who gave testimony in court about seeing Beshara in a certain place was lying," she told him. "Or at best he was badly mistaken. That means that now all the evidence needs to be questioned to see what else could be wrong. They call it an 'unsafe' verdict." She wanted to see if he understood.

"'E din't do it, then?" he summed it up.

"We don't know. But it means it hasn't been proved that he did. So they are asking that the River Police take the case back and start all over again."

Scuff's eyes widened. "Can they do that? Take it from us, mess it all up, then say, ''Ere y'are, 'ave it back!'"

"Yes, it looks as if they can," she admitted.

"I'd tell them ter—" He remembered who he was speaking to and blushed.

She tried to hide her smile, failing conspicuously. "I'd be tempted to as well," she agreed. "But that would be like saying that you didn't think you could do it. And somebody has to. All those people are still dead. It's not just a matter of finding the guilty ones; it's clearing the innocent ones as well."

He looked at her for a long, steady moment, and then he nodded. "Yeah. So 'ow are we goin' ter start, then?"

She felt a sudden sting of tears in her eyes and blinked an extra time. "First we think very carefully, and make plans—which we keep to ourselves."

"O' course," he agreed. "We will tell 'im when we know anything, though, won't we?"

"Yes, the moment we are sure it makes sense," she agreed. "The important thing is that we tell each other, just to keep safe. You must promise me?"

He hesitated.

"Scuff! If you don't tell me where you are going to be, I will be so worried about you I won't be able to think straight myself. If I didn't tell you, wouldn't you worry?"

"'Course I would! You—" Then he saw he was cornered. "Yeah . . . that's fair . . . I s'pose."

She smiled and held out her hand.

Soberly he took it and they shook on the deal.

She could remember most of the evidence in the trial, and checking on that was a good way to start. She wrote everything down, trusting that Scuff would be able to read her writing. She had long practiced making it clearer than character and nature had intended. A mistake in medical notes could be fatal.

"'Oo are they?" he asked, taking the paper from her and scowling at it.

"All the people who say they saw something, or somebody," she replied. "As clearly as I recall."

He searched her face. "You think they're lying?"

"Not necessarily. But they might have been saying what they thought people wanted to hear. Have you ever seen something happen, and then asked three different people what it was?"

"Yeah," he nodded, understanding bright in his face. "They all remember it different. You reckon that's what 'appened 'ere?"

"Maybe. But they've said it so many times now that they're remembering what they said, not what they saw. We need to know what evidence is there that's not about faces and memories. Or at least is not from people who've already testified; they will feel that they can't afford to go back on what they said now, because they'll look stupid, and everyone will know. And, of course, they could be charged with perjury—lying in court when you've sworn to tell the truth."

"You mean we need to speak to the people what isn't noticed, like?"

"People who aren't noticed," she corrected automatically.

"Them too," he grinned. "I can find out. An' before you tell me, I'll be careful. I know people who the police don't. Even the River Police."

She didn't have the heart to tell him it should have been "whom."

"Thank you. And be careful! Whoever really did it could still be out there." Now she had misgivings about including Scuff in the hunt. Hurt feelings were much easier to deal with than if Scuff should be physically harmed. "People who will blow up a boat with two hundred men and women on it won't think twice about drowning one inquisitive boy!" she said sharply.

He winced. "I know," he answered almost under his breath. "Or one woman either. Is that going to stop you?"

"It's going to make me very careful indeed," she replied.

He looked at her absolutely levelly. "Good. I'll tell Monk that, if he asks me."

She would dearly like to have clipped his ears for impertinence, but that would keep for another time. "I'm going to the clinic," she told him. "To see what help I can get from Squeaky Robinson, and anyone else."

Hester arrived at the clinic to find it very pleasantly free of urgencies. Perhaps the summer weather had helped. There were the usual slight injuries, bruises, dislocations, a cut or stab, but none of them life-threatening. Nor were there any of the chronic diseases of colder seasons: no pneumonia, bronchitis, or pleurisy.

"Morning," Squeaky said cheerfully as she came into his office, which was lined with bookshelves and locked cupboards. There were engravings on the wall that Squeaky said were worthless, and she knew were very good indeed. As usual he had the ledgers open and spread out across the table, and the top off the inkwell. It made him look busy, should Claudine come in and ask him to do anything that he did not want to—something Claudine knew perfectly well. "We need money," he added.

"I know," Hester replied, ignoring the subject. She knew from Claudine that the situation was far from desperate.

"You haven't been here for days," Squeaky complained. "How do you know?"

"We always need money," she answered with a smile, pulling out the chair opposite the desk and sitting down. "Is this a sudden crisis, or just the usual state of affairs?"

He looked at her carefully, assessing her mood. "Usual," he said with uncharacteristic candor. "What's wrong?"

She could seldom fool Squeaky. Actually she very rarely tried. Quite simply and in as few words as possible, she told him about Monk being given back the case of the *Princess Mary*, and why he could not refuse it.

Squeaky grunted. "So we've got to sort it, then?" he concluded. "Could have told them in the beginning it wouldn't work, putting them regular police on it. Stupid sods . . ."

"They're not stupid," Hester said reasonably. "They just don't know the river . . ."

"Not the police, the government!" Squeaky said indignantly. "They're covering up something, just bad at it, like everything else. Now everybody's going to know. It's a wonder they can even get their clothes on straight, that lot! Couldn't cover their backsides with a bed sheet!"

Hester swallowed her laughter at the vision in her mind. "We still have to sort the mess," she pointed out.

"Why? To save them what made it? Or to get vengeance on whatever evil bastard drowned all these people?" he asked reasonably.

"I prefer the word 'justice' to 'vengeance,'" she answered.

He pulled a face, but made no comment.

"But it's fair, either way," she continued reasonably. "If I'd lost somebody I'd want a better answer than this. And it makes us look terribly incompetent. What faith can anyone have in justice if this is all it can do? This doesn't comfort the innocent or scare the guilty into thinking twice."

Squeaky shook his head. "Sometimes I wonder about you. You bin to war, you seen hundreds of men hurt and dying, you seen what boneheaded idiots the military are. You seen hospitals where they don't change nothing, and don't learn nothing, you seen the police and the government and the streets, not to mention this place!" He swung his arm around, indicating the warren of a building around them. "And you still believe in fairies! I sometimes wonder if you're all there!" He tapped his head.

Perhaps she should have been hurt, but she wasn't. "It's called survival, Squeaky. Now, we must begin with the people we know. Who do we have in here at the moment that could help?"

He looked dubious. "Don't know as they want to . . ." he pointed out.

"They want to," she assured him. "It's the price of medicine next time they're cold, sick, hurt, or scared."

His face lit up. "I think I just seen a fairy! Little one, up in the air—with wings!"

"Good. I'm going to see Claudine." Hiding her smile, Hester stood up and went out of the room.

She found her in the pantry with its shelves of powders, leaves, bottles of lotion or spirits, creams, and bandages. She was assessing what supplies they had, and how much more of anything they needed, or could afford. After the briefest greeting—they knew each other too well to need more—Hester began to assist. When they had reached a satisfactory conclusion, she told Claudine roughly what she had already explained to Squeaky. They discussed it further in the kitchen over a cup of tea. Claudine was angry.

"I said they had no right to take the investigation from Mr. Monk in the first place," she said bitterly as she added the boiling water from the kettle into the already warmed teapot. It was an old and very battered pewter one that somebody had thrown out, but it made an excellent cup of tea, and the crooked spout still did not drip. The crockery also was mismatched, but not chipped. What did it matter if a bluebell cup sat on a wild-rose saucer? Or poppy or daisy on anything else?

"And now that they've made a complete mess of it, hand it back," she added indignantly. "It's like being given cold porridge that somebody else has already half eaten."

"What a disgusting thought!" Hester turned her mouth down. "But regrettably accurate."

"What are we going to do?" Claudine also automatically included herself in the problem. "There were quite a few prostitutes at that party, we know, from the survivors and the bodies. We'll get help. And I dare say some will speak to us who wouldn't to the police."

"I'm counting on it. I've already told Squeaky that cooperation in this is the price of help in the future: sick, injured, or just hungry." Hester bit her lip, looking very steadily at Claudine. "I've never put a price on it before. I don't like doing it."

Claudine did not hesitate. She had been watching Hester's face as she listened, and she knew trouble when she saw it. Her own long, unhappy marriage had taught her a lot about bargains and prices. Since working at the Portpool Lane clinic, a new world of possibilities had opened up to her, most particularly the realization of her ability to make friends, to be clever, helpful, and liked by the oddest of people. Years ago she would have helped prostitutes with suggestions for their salvation, and considered it her Christian duty. Most of her acquaintances would still do that, or less.

Now she knew prostitutes as individual people. Some she liked, some she didn't. She helped them in practical ways regardless. They were to be treated in whatever way was possible for their illness or injuries: fed, and occasionally given better clothes, warmer ones. No comment was made on their occupation. That generous silence had not come easily to her, at first.

Now Claudine amazed Hester.

"I think it's a good idea," she said firmly. "Sometimes you can do too much for people. No self-respect in always taking. Price can be part of value. It's time we showed them that. They'll be the wiser for it."

Hester thought about it for a moment or two, and realized with surprise how deeply she agreed. And she was relieved because up to then she had felt guilty about it. Nursing help was never conditional, no judgment involved, except as to the best treatment. But food, shelter, clothes, dignity . . . that was different. Above all other things, worth could not be given.

"Good," she agreed.

The information about the party on the *Princess Mary* was teased out slowly, and with much impatience on Squeaky's part. He counted every spoonful of food given in reward as if it were a potato off his own plate.

He quarreled with Claudine over the portions, and was amazed to come out of it second best. He had had no idea she had such spirit. It was disconcerting, and yet he was also oddly pleased, as if a protégée of his had developed a sudden talent.

One of the most unfortunate was a particularly recalcitrant young woman named Amy.

"Describe the people you saw at this party," Claudine asked her. "How did they speak? How were they dressed? It's your business to size up what money people have and whether they'll spend it or not."

"More'n I got, that's for sure!" Amy responded. "Yer should 'ave seen some o' their dresses."

"Not good enough!" Squeaky snapped.

"I dunno," she said tartly, glaring back at him. "Wot's it ter you, anyway? They're all dead now, in't they? Yer can't buy an' sell 'em anyway."

"No, nor they can't eat a nice hot dinner," Squeaky retaliated. "Like you can't neither."

"You said . . ." she started.

Squeaky rose in his seat. He was taller than one might have expected, seeing him slouched in the chair.

She glanced at him, her face pallid with fear.

Claudine stood up also. "There is no point in hitting her, Mr. Robinson," she said coldly.

Squeaky was amazed and angered. He had had no intention of hitting the stupid girl. How could Claudine have thought that of him? It was unjust . . . and hurtful.

Claudine turned to Amy and regarded her coldly. "If you have nothing else to tell us then you had better leave. You should set about earning your dinner, you'll get none here. You can go out through the kitchen into the back alley. I'll take you."

Amy rose to her feet sullenly and edged around the table, keeping as far from Squeaky as possible. She followed Claudine into the passage and—after many twists and turns—through the kitchen door. She knew she was there by the rich, delicate aroma of frying potatoes and onions that wafted toward her. The crackle and spit of a frying pan suggested someone was making sausages as well. She stopped abruptly.

"What is it?" Claudine asked. "The back door out is at the other side."

Amy turned round to face her. "I might know summink about 'oo were on that boat—names, like."

Claudine put her hands on the girl's shoulders and turned her back toward the door. "Then come back when you're sure you do."

"D'yer 'ave that every day?" Amy sniffed and gestured toward the kitchen stove.

"No," Claudine answered unequivocally. "On you go!"

"I 'membered summink!" Amy protested.

"Did you? What was it, then?"

Amy drew in a deep breath, studied Claudine's face for a moment, and decided she had better give value for money, now, specifically, for fried sausages, onions, and mash.

"That party were planned least a couple o' weeks before it 'appened," she answered with the firmness of truth rather than the flair of invention. "All the guest list wrote up, an' everything. Least, special guests, people wot should be got special girls for, an' like that. If yer gonna do it right, yer gotter know wot kind o' girls different folks go fer."

"I see," Claudine replied, as if she did see. "And who would know that information?"

"Big Bessie, o' course! 'Oo'd yer think? That's worth an extra sausage, in't it?"

Claudine considered for a split second. "Yes, I think it is. So Big Bessie would know anyone that was important early. Asked by whom?"

"Eh?"

"By whom were they invited? Who was paying for it?"

"Geez! Ow the 'ell do I know? I got me sausage? Or are yer a liar, an' all?"

"You have your sausage. You don't yet have your pudding."

"Yeah? An' wot's pudding?"

"Jam tart and custard."

That did not require any considering at all. "Wot else d'yer wanna know?"

Big Bessie could be found easily enough. Squeaky would certainly be able to do that, and probably know the appropriate pressure to bear on her to gain the desired information. That it was so carefully planned at all was interesting in itself—well worth a fried sausage.

"I would like to know Big Bessie's clients, but I don't imagine you have access to that. Perhaps at least whoever she usually uses to provide the food and drink for such occasions, and music? Or anything else that would be customary."

"Be wot?"

"Anyone else involved." Claudine looked narrowly at the girl and saw fear, hunger, and an underlying, constant rage. Her life held little pleasure, and much uncertainty and pain. "If you can bring me anything like that, for certain, or if it's a guess, then say so—no lies—then it's worth a meal. We eat every day, about this time."

Amy weighed her up. "Wot about that 'ol git? Wot if you in't 'ere?"

"Then tell Mr. Robinson. I shall let him know of our bargain. But don't lie. He will be very unpleasant if he's lied to."

"Yer mean worse than 'e is now?" Amy asked incredulously.

"Yes, I do. Very much worse. But if I've given you my word then he will honor it."

Amy took a deep breath. "Yeah . . . all right. Now I want me sausage an' mash. An' onions!"

"You will have it. Go and sit at the table."

"You did what?" Squeaky demanded of Claudine. "That dozy piece o' string? You—"

Claudine raised her eyebrows and stared at him coolly. "I beg your pardon, Mr. Robinson?"

Squeaky muttered under his breath, but conceded the victory. It *was* a very interesting piece of information, well worth a couple of sausages.

CHAPTER

8

Monk went back to the beginning, starting with sitting on the river in one of the police boats, oars at rest, facing Orme, who was at the tiller keeping the boat headed into the stream. They ignored the steady flow of traffic passing them: pleasure boats, ferries, heavy-laden barges. They were barely conscious of the sound of the hurdy-gurdy music on the shore.

"What do you remember?" Monk asked grimly. He did not want to have to go over this again, but there was no other sensible way to begin. He did not prompt Orme. He wanted to see if he too had noticed the man going over the side of the *Princess Mary* the moment before the explosion.

Orme was quiet, his face somber. Yesterday he had been full of anecdotes about the new granddaughter. Today it seemed bad taste, even bad luck, to speak of her at the same time as of those who had died so suddenly and violently.

"Seemed like any other summer evening," Orme began. "Lots of traffic, just the usual stuff. Remember someone crossing off toward mid-stream. String o' barges near the far bank, and another about thirty yards behind them."

"How many ferries?" Monk interrupted.

Orme thought a moment, visualizing it. "Three that I remember. One coming crosswise, about twenty yards behind us, level with the *Princess Mary;* another nearer the bank, as if they were waiting for her to get out of the way, and the rest to pass, before going in to the stairs. Another one out there," he gestured. "Level with us. Don't remember any more close. Don't know what was behind, upriver of us."

"Do you remember the explosion?"

Orme's eyes widened. "Like I'd forget!"

"What did you see?"

Orme started to speak, then stopped. He stared at Monk.

Monk waited.

"You saw it, didn't you?" Orme said softly. "Something going over the side, in the air one moment, then going down first, before the explosion. What was it? Was it a man?"

"I thought so," Monk answered. "Which would have to be whoever set it off. There's no other reason anyone would leap overboard into the Thames. Did you see a boat in the water anywhere near him?"

"The closest ferry could have made it." Orme clenched his jaw. "Or, of course, maybe it wasn't a ferry."

"Then the moment after it would be picking people out of the water, rescuing survivors," Monk pointed out. "Perfect disguise. What's a couple more wet and shocked people?"

"The swine!" Orme said bitterly. "No wonder we never found him. Invisible man. Survivors, like anyone else. Where the devil do we even look?"

"With the ferryman," Monk replied. "God! That's cold! Blow them into the sky one moment, then the next, stretch out your hands to pull them out of the water, as if you were one of them."

"D'you suppose he was a real ferryman?" Orme asked, revulsion making his voice shake.

"We'll have to go back and question all the survivors we can find," Monk answered grimly. "And the ferrymen we know were there. Go over and over it! Someone will have seen something, or remembered something they didn't then."

"You reckon?" Orme's eyes widened.

"I saw someone," Monk pointed out. "So did you. And another thing I'd really like to know, who did the police speak to? Did they speak to you? They didn't ask me what I saw."

Orme considered it for several seconds, his hand gripping the tiller, keeping the boat facing into the current.

"Odd, that," he agreed, chewing his lip. "We were there. You'd think they'd try to jog some memory, wouldn't you? What do you make of this Lydiate fellow?"

"Decent man in an impossible situation," Monk replied honestly. "But none of us has dealt with a tragedy on this scale, not when it's a deliberate crime, and the victims are all random and completely blameless. At least as far as we know, it was the ship itself that was the target, or possibly the owners of it. The poor damn people in the water were incidental. They could have been anybody."

"Do you think the owners had anything to do with it?" Orme said dubiously.

"No. That's another thing; we've had no motive except general hatred of the way England behaved in the digging of the canal. That's good for whipping up emotion and making everyone believe that in giving evidence they're being patriotic, fighting the country's enemies, but it doesn't make any real sense. Have you ever come across a crime like that before?"

"No." Orme's mouth pulled down at the corners.

"Let's go back to Wapping and start again," Monk answered, moving back to his seat at the oars. "You and Hooper talk to the ferrymen and bargees. I'll take the survivors."

Orme drew in his breath to argue that Monk had given himself by far the grimmest job, then looked at Monk's face, and fell silent.

IT WAS INDEED HARD. It took Monk two days to find the men left alive from the disaster and trace them to where they were now living. There was one woman who had survived also, but he wasn't sure if he should cause her further distress. Then, thinking of Hester, he decided that she might be more insulted by being excluded than grateful for the consideration. And it was always possible that she would recall some detail no one else did.

There were seventeen of them well enough to be interviewed, still in the London area, and willing to speak to him. Most remembered little, repeating only what they had already said. Monk sat patiently listening to the pain in their voices, saw the blocked-out horror return, and felt as if he were being pointlessly cruel. The things that were uppermost in their minds were the sense of coldness and suffocation, and the helplessness as they watched their wives, friends, or families sinking in the dark river, fighting for life, and losing.

He feared he was being brutal and he loathed himself for it.

The ninth person he spoke to was a brickmaker's laborer with powerful arms and a chest like an ox. He still looked faintly bewildered as he recalled the night.

"I can't 'ardly remember where I was, or what 'appened," the man said, as if admitting to some deep failure in himself. "One minute I were standing on the steps going up to the deck, next I were in the water an' I couldn't see nor 'ear nothing, 'cept cold an' choking. It were moments before I even 'eard other folks cryin' out." His face was pinched with misery and there was a haunting guilt in his eyes.

Monk did not want to press him, but there was no other way to discover if there was anything more to learn. Silence, fear, shame, and pain were all the allies of whoever had done this.

"Who was with you on the boat, Mr. Hall?"

Hall's face tightened. "My ma and pa. It was a special trip for them. Wedding anniversary." He breathed in deeply, his massive chest expanding and contracting, but he could not control the tears that slid down his cheeks, embarrassing him for the show of weakness in front of a stranger.

Monk felt bruised himself for his failure to have prevented this, or at the very least to have caught the right man for it. Would an explanation help? An apology? The man deserved it.

"I'm sorry," Monk said quietly. He wished he could comfort the man by blaming someone else. "It looks now as if Habib Beshara was not the right man. We wanted to catch someone so desperately we weren't careful enough."

Hall shook his head slowly, not taking his eyes off Monk's. "You mean that man in prison isn't guilty?"

"Possibly not. Certainly not alone. If it weren't necessary, I wouldn't ask you again."

Hall was quiet for several moments, as if thinking this over. Then he nodded for Monk to continue.

"Who picked you up out of the water?" Monk asked.

"Ferryman. 'E might 'ave said 'is name, but what did it matter?"

"Are you sure it was a ferry?"

"Yeah. Why?"

"It might matter. Were you the first person in the boat, apart from the ferryman himself?"

"No. There were one other man in it. 'E were 'elpin' all 'e could."

"Do you remember him?"

"No . . ."

"But a man?"

"Yeah." His face crumpled. "Weren't many women as were got out. I . . . I couldn't find me ma . . ." He stopped, his voice choking. "I swam around looking for 'er, calling out . . . but she were gone . . ."

Monk could imagine it, the increasing panic as hope faded, the desperate search among the survivors, going from place to place, asking. Had he ever found her body? He must bring the man back to the present. It seemed uncaring, but it was probably better than the memory he was reliving.

"And the man, what was he wearing? Party clothes? Black suit, fitted jacket, white shirt?" he asked.

Hall frowned, searching his memory, finding the image. "No jacket, least, not like . . . it was like them jackets waiters wear, waistcoats, to move easy in, just . . ."

Monk felt a sharp jolt of excitement, recognition of a moment of truth. Could this have been the man he had seen leap off the *Princess Mary* just before the explosion?

"Anything else you remember about him?" He clung to the tiny thread, afraid to pull too hard and have it disintegrate. "Voice, actions? Did the ferryman seem to know him? A name?"

"I . . . I can't remember." Hall shook his head, like a dog coming out of water. "I can't remember what anyone said."

"Anything at all that you can think of?" Monk pressed.

"No! No, 'e said something, but I can't remember. I was so desperate, none of it made sense. I'm sorry . . ."

Monk reached out and grasped Hall's hand. He had been there, seen it all.

"What did the police ask you?" he said quietly.

"Police? Nothing really, just if I'd seen anything before the explosion. Where I was, that kind o' thing. I weren't any 'elp to them."

"They didn't ask anything about after the explosion?"

"No. Nothing. They knew I'd been rescued, and that I'd lost my ma. Nothing else."

Monk withdrew his hand slowly.

"I think you might have been a great help to me, Mr. Hall," he said with growing conviction. "I appreciate it, and I grieve for your loss."

Hall nodded, too full of emotion to risk words again, which anyway would have been inadequate to the weight of meaning.

Monk asked others but no one else had more to add to what he already knew, just confirmation. What stood out, over and over, were the omissions, the questions Lydiate's men had not asked, and the people they had not spoken to. They had inquired about events leading up to the explosion, and hardly anyone had had more than a few passing observations to offer: anonymous people who played music, waited on them with drinks or at table. Most of the evidence that was of value came from the deckhands. It could have implicated Habib Beshara, or almost anyone else with a darker than average skin.

Crossing the river again at dusk, on the way home, Monk was haunted by his disjointed memories of the screams, the bewilderment, and the look of abiding pain in the faces of survivors. When it came down to reality, what mattered except the lives of those you loved? All that was precious was made up of passions and of love, of belief in a purpose beyond the habits of living from day to day.

The meaning of it all could be taken in a few moments. What would his life be without Hester, and now also without Scuff?

Even memory could be torn from you. He could not remember his accident, all those years ago, or who he had been before that. All he could recollect was waking up in the hospital with no idea even who he was, let alone the life he had built. He had lost both the good and the bad, the dreams and the nightmares. No one knew what lurked in that long silence before he woke up.

He vividly remembered everything since then, the things he wanted to and the things he would prefer not to: mistakes, discoveries about his own nature, including the reasons why some people feared or hated him. Better than that were the good things, and like a strong thread through all of it was Hester, in all her roles. They had fought like cats in a bag at one time, each trying so hard not to be vulnerable, not to care. Always she had been loyal, believing in his worth even when he did not.

Thinking, even for an instant, how he would feel if she had been lost in that dark water was horrifying; it gave him a deep empathy for the grief the survivors and the victims' families lived with, day and night. It was not like someone dying from a long illness, when you know to prepare yourself and have the time to do it. This was sudden and brutal, total, like an amputation of part of you.

He came to the further shore, paid the ferryman, and alighted. He walked up the hill in long, swift strides, far faster than usual—eager to be home.

M<small>ONK CONTINUED WITH THE</small> search, going through all the reports from Lydiate's men, comparing each with the others. He found no reference to the man he had seen dive overboard. Did that mean they had not found him? Or that they had, and he was of no importance? Or that they just weren't aware of his existence?

He read them all again, to be sure of his impressions. There was a pattern of interference from various officials working for a politician, Mr. Quither, who appeared to report directly to Lord Ossett himself. They had steered the police away from the whole subject of shipping. The suggestions had apparently been discreet, but quite firm. A man of Lydiate's political sensitivity would not have misunderstood. Why had they done that? To protect specific interests—friends, supporters, men who would reward them amply? Or because it was genuinely irrelevant to the sinking? But that raised the question as to how they could know such a thing, unless the government also knew far more about the sinking than they had told the police, or the court.

Comparing police notes with instructions from Lydiate, it was increasingly clear that certain pieces of evidence to do with eyewitness accounts had been buried within irrelevant testimony. Because they were actually irrelevant? Or because such accounts would be inconvenient to officials such as customs and excise men, port authorities, one or two members of the Home Office? One testimony was labeled as interfering with a current investigation into smuggling, a case Monk knew nothing about. He suspected it was fictitious.

Similarly, with very careful reading of what was left of the guest list, the numbers of survivors and dead did not tally with the list. The guest list had been difficult to get hold of, and then suddenly it had reappeared from being mislaid. Had it been altered, names erased, because some people who should not have been there were listed originally? But why would someone have to hide being on a pleasure boat? Perhaps if they had lied about their whereabouts, or were keeping company with the wrong people?

Some people had not been questioned at all, let alone investigated. Or had they been discreetly not mentioned because their presence was found to be irrelevant?

Or maybe this was merely the degree of error one might expect in a highly emotional case pushed to the limit for quick results, castigated by the press, interfered with by politicians.

The atrocity had been monumental. The shock waves had spread throughout the country, and no doubt to neighboring countries, particularly France. Perhaps it was inevitable that a government minister like Lord Ossett should have kept his finger on the pulse of the investigation. He had to have feared the possibility of something like it happening again.

Nevertheless, cumulatively all these directions and enquiries had failed to encompass all the evidence and come up with an accurate picture. There seemed to have been considerable misinterpretation, due to ignorance of the river and its people. And there had been a foreseeable prejudice against the regular police by those who resented them usurping what they viewed as a Thames River Police job. They were only small lies, withholding of information, but together they added up to larger error.

Above all, what was striking was the general weakness of the accounts by eyewitnesses. They were swayed so easily by horror, fear, loss, pressure, or simply the wish to please those who were questioning them. Not to mention some clearly desired attention, hoped for reward, or saw the tragedy as an opportunity to take a little revenge here and there.

When he had completed his review and compared his conclusions with those of Orme and Hooper—who largely agreed with him—Monk went to see Lydiate at his home.

It was a very pleasant house in Mayfair, a highly fashionable area. It was set in a Georgian terrace with elegant façades and rows of white columns in a gentle arc between the pavement and the steps up to the front doors. Monk found number 72, and pulled the shining brass lever for the bell.

A few moments later a butler answered and welcomed him in. Monk followed the servant across the marble floor and to the door of a comfortable, book-lined study.

Lydiate rose from the desk, told the butler to leave the decanter of whisky and glasses. The man inclined his head and withdrew, closing the door behind him.

"Please sit down." Lydiate indicated the other beautifully upholstered captain's chair with its polished woodwork and leather seat. He looked tired, as he had the last time Monk had seen him, and no more at ease, in spite of being in his own home.

He offered Monk whisky, which Monk declined. Lydiate's tension was palpable; he wasn't hostile, but rather more like a patient waiting for bad news from his doctor.

Was the quick blow more or less merciful than careful explanations? This would not be easy for either of them.

"We've been over all the reports," Monk began. "Thank you for giving me access to them. I don't believe that any of my men have seen anything in them that your men didn't."

None of the tension in Lydiate relaxed. In fact, if anything, it increased. There was a tiny muscle twitching in his temple.

It was time for honesty.

"It was the omissions that were interesting, the people you chose not to speak to, or were instructed not to."

"Such as whom?" Lydiate was not defensive so much as confused.

"Some of the survivors . . ."

Lydiate bit his lip. "That was a cruelty I was advised against, and I admit I was happy to obey. The few we did speak to could tell us absolutely nothing useful. It was brutal to ask them to relive such a nightmare." There was pain in his face, and a soft note of disappointment in his voice.

"Investigation is often painful," Monk said in reply. "Most of it is also useless, but sometimes memory returns and something comes up."

"Such as what?" Lydiate sounded dubious.

"When I was going over it again, thinking about it one evening as I crossed the river from Wapping back home, I remembered a moment before the explosion. I saw a figure leaping off the *Princess Mary* into the water. He was there against the light only for an instant, then the whole bow went up in flames and I forgot about him."

Lydiate leaned forward a little. "A figure. A man jumping before the explosion?"

"Yes."

"Why would anyone leap off before? Are you certain you are not transposing the events in your memory?"

"Yes, because I saw him against the evening sky, not against flames. If he was responsible for the explosion, then he was escaping—"

"Into the water? Hardly!" Lydiate interrupted.

"There was a small boat in the water, near the ship," Monk explained. "Later, I was interviewing a survivor, one of the first off. He was picked up by a ferry, near the ship, and there was another passenger in it already, soaking wet, but dressed as a waiter or servant, not a guest."

Lydiate sat back with a long sigh. "Not Beshara," he said softly. "He was caught having been at the dockside, and not dressed as you describe. He only went into the ship at Westminster when they boarded. He got off again somewhere around Limehouse, judging by the longest possible time for a fuse."

"Eyewitness's testimony," Monk pointed out. "Which we now know might not be entirely accurate. Did you find anything that could be considered a decent motive since we last spoke?" Monk pressed.

"No," Lydiate shrugged as if it were an old wound aching again.

Monk would like to have let him off the hook, but he could not afford to. "I saw a lot of direction from government ministers," he said. "Do they normally interfere with police investigation this much?"

"It was a spectacular case," Lydiate pointed out, a touch of defensiveness in his tone. "It was imperative we clear it as swiftly as possible, for several reasons. Justice demanded it. Public safety was at issue. And for reasons of international diplomacy we needed to be seen to have solved the whole thing and dealt with the perpetrators."

"Because there were important people on board?" Monk said. "Some of them foreign?"

"Precisely."

"And constant interference was considered the best course of action?" He allowed his disbelief to ring sharply in his voice.

"They were distressed," Lydiate protested. "Everyone was."

"All the more reason to keep a cool head. I presume you told him as much?"

"Lord Ossett?" Lydiate's eyebrows rose sharply.

"You're in command of the police." Monk made no allowances.

"I don't think you quite grasp the situation—" Lydiate began.

"Then help me!" Monk cut across him. "Whoever sank the *Princess Mary* and drowned nearly two hundred people is still out there and, for all we know, ready and willing to do it again! Unless you know something about who it was that you are not telling me?"

Lydiate went white.

Monk moved forward instinctively, to catch him were he to faint.

Lydiate righted himself with an effort. He did not apologize, but the shame of it was in his face.

"I had little choice in the course of my investigation. These were powerful suggestions—"

"Pressure!" Monk said for him.

"Yes, I suppose so." He looked down. "I thought it was just a judgment call, an encouragement to guide me, make me aware of the desperate importance of dealing with the tragedy quickly and firmly."

"Did you need pressure to do that?" Monk could not afford to let him off the hook.

"I would have done it differently, left to myself," Lydiate said quietly.

"What pressure did they bring to bear?" Monk replied. "Your job? Your home? Your fitness for leadership?"

Lydiate gave him a look of disgust. "Do you think I would have changed my direction of enquiry for any of those reasons? Would you?"

Monk found the answer died on his tongue. He should not have asked.

"My sister," Lydiate replied slowly, forcing the painful words out softly. "She is married to a man who is peculiarly vulnerable: not just to disgrace but to a grief he could not bear, because it would be compounded with guilt. His daughter by his first wife has committed an indiscretion that, if revealed, would cause her ruin. It was not a crime! A... a desperate error of judgment." He swallowed. "If I allowed that to happen my loss would be compounded by guilt also. I understand that very well. I was not compassionate to my sister when she needed me in the past; too busy with my career. Too full of judgment. I will not make that mistake again." He faced Monk now, quietly defiant; ready to take whatever blame was given.

Monk felt a monumental anger, not against Lydiate but against the person who had known this and deliberately given the case to a man that he could manipulate in this way. Now it was all very clear why the matter had been taken from the River Police.

What would he have done himself, if the threat had been to Hester? Please God, he would never have to find out! However, this did not alter the fact that he still had to pursue every aspect of the sinking of the *Princess Mary*, including the motive for it, wherever it led. The passion and confusion, the fiasco of Beshara's arrest, trial, sentence, and now the attempt on his life, had made it imperative. Did whoever was behind this need him silenced, and was willing to reach out, even into prison, in order to make certain of it?

"Why was Beshara reprieved?" Monk asked Lydiate.

"I don't know," Lydiate admitted miserably. "I was told it was to do with his illness, which seems absurd, since it is apparently incurable. I assumed it was some kind of concession to the Egyptian embassy."

"Or that the government wanted to know who else was involved," Monk pointed out. "And wanted to know who paid him!"

"I believed that the motive was hate, revenge for something that happened in Egypt," Lydiate answered.

Looking at him, Monk knew that Lydiate really believed what he was saying. And why shouldn't he? Monk had originally thought such a motive made sense as well, but he also hadn't accepted it without question. That explained why the case was given to Lydiate—he was a man who was clearly vulnerable to such subtle and corrosive persuasion.

"And what do you believe now?" he asked as gently as he could.

"I have no idea," Lydiate confessed. "I would go back to the beginning, without presupposition."

Monk said nothing. He was working blindly, and with the whole case already contaminated.

When Lydiate offered him whisky again, he accepted.

CHAPTER

9

Scuff did not have any clear plan in mind when he bypassed the road toward school and turned in the direction of the river instead. He knew only that now the regular police had messed up the case of the *Princess Mary,* and got the wrong person almost killed, and still stuck in prison, and had given the whole thing back to Monk. He was left with having to sort out the problem—if he could!

It was warm already. The sun glittered bright and hard on the water, making him squint a little.

Of course there was no way Monk could keep the police's mistakes concealed. He had to go back to the very beginning and untangle all the knots. How was he supposed to do that? It wasn't just a matter of witnesses telling lies; it was people saying something over and over until they believed it, and then getting all angry and scared when someone suggested it wasn't true.

Now it was too late, and nobody remembered what they'd really seen or done anyway, even if they wanted to tell the truth. People would make fun of them, laugh at them, and most likely never let them forget it. Who wanted that? Scuff had experienced it and it was horrible. Much easier to insist you were right, regardless of anything anyone else said. Just stick it out! Who could prove you wrong weeks afterward?

Better than being labeled a fool who didn't know what was right in front of your own eyes!

He reached the steps. The tide was high and slapping over the concrete, making it slippery. He climbed onto the ferry carefully and paid for his passage across the river. He needed to be on the north bank, because the *Princess Mary* had gone down nearer to it, and, as far as he knew, most of the stops had been on that side. Then he walked steadily along the dockside downstream toward the Isle of Dogs.

He found one little urchin who was inquisitive, and probably hungry.

"Find anything good?" Scuff asked him casually.

The urchin sized him up, and did not know quite what to make of him. "Wot yer lookin' fer, mister?"

"Mister!" Scuff felt instantly taller, and at the same time alienated. "Mister?" What did the boy think he was? Some kind of stranger here?

Use it. The child was being practical, surviving. Without thinking about it Scuff put his hand in his pocket and felt to see how much money he had. It was mostly pennies, but he also had a threepenny bit and two or three sixpences. Sixpence was too much to give anyone! But for a really good piece of information he might share a cup of tea and even a sticky bun.

He must be inventive, quickly.

"You got anything off the *Princess Mary*?"

The urchin looked at him as if he had crawled out of the mud. His small, dirt-stained face was a picture of disgust.

"Not for you, I in't. Why? Wot's it worth?"

Scuff changed tack instantly. "If you'd lost anyone on it you wouldn't need to ask that," he said tartly. "I'd get anything I could for me uncle Bert, but it would just hurt the more if it weren't Aunt Lou's at all, an' he knew it."

"Yer aunt Lou got drownded?" The urchin's expression was unreadable. It could well have been his version of embarrassment.

Scuff did not hesitate. "Yeah. Why? You know people who fished stuff out o' the river what might 'ave come from them?"

"I could see," the urchin said more carefully.

"Like what?"

The boy gave a shrug. "Combs, pins, bits o' cloth, but they in't much. What's it worth?"

"Help me find a few things, ask a few questions, an' it's worth a cup o' tea and a sandwich," Scuff answered, watching the child's face. "Were you here?" he went on. "Did you see it blow up?"

The urchin considered, looked Scuff up and down, and made his decision. "No, but I can take you to someone 'oo were! But it'll cost yer an 'ot meat pie." He was pushing his luck, and they both knew it.

Scuff weighed his choices. His decision must be quick, or he would look weak. On the riverbank the weak did not survive.

"We'll have a pie for lunch," he gave his verdict. "You'll get half of it. If what you find is any good, you can have a whole one, and pudding an' custard for dessert."

"Done," the urchin said instantly.

"What's your name?" Scuff asked him.

"Warren, but they call me Worm."

"All right, Worm. Start being useful. And don't think you can play me for a fool. When I was your size, I was on the river just like you are, so I know all about mudlarking."

Worm looked at him with total disbelief.

Scuff glanced down at Worm's feet. "You got better boots than I had," Scuff observed. "You can't be as daft as you're acting."

Worm shrugged. "I'm all right. C'mon then."

THEY SPENT MOST OF the day searching for information about the imaginary Aunt Lou, and mementos that did not exist. But along the way Scuff began to learn the things he had wanted to know about what had changed recently: who was afraid of whom, who was richer, who owed money, who had found things and sold them, because they had information about where they'd fetch up that other people didn't. He had names now, specific debts paid off, people who had gone to ground, even if not yet the reason why.

Scuff treated Worm to a jolly good pie for supper, and the pudding with custard.

Early the next morning they began again. Worm was now fully expecting to be well fed, and Scuff had been forced to borrow money from Hester. He had managed to avoid telling her what he needed it for, but he didn't think that would last long.

By the middle of the day Scuff had stopped trying to base it all on Aunt Lou's lost bracelet or pendant, and Worm knew perfectly well that they were trying to get information about the disaster itself.

"Yer reckon as it weren't the feller as they've got in prison, then?" he said, skipping a couple of steps to keep up with Scuff's longer strides.

"Yeah, I reckon not," Scuff agreed, actually rather relieved it wasn't the accused, even if he didn't know how to explain it further. A good explanation eluded him; his mind was so burning with the truth.

Worm was quiet for several minutes as they climbed up a long row of steps and across the uneven planks of a wharf. Scuff did not look down at the tide through the missing slats, but he could hear it suck and squelch beneath them.

"Why'd you care?" Worm said at length as they went back up onto the stone dock again and passed a horse and cart standing patiently waiting to be loaded. Scuff wondered if horses were as bored as they looked. "'E were a bad one anyway. Even I know that."

"I don't care about 'is being a bad one," Scuff said with deep conviction. "You shouldn't 'ang someone for something as they didn't do.

'Ow'd you take it if they done you for something you didn't do?" The moment he had said it he wondered if perhaps it was a bad question.

"I'd be cross as hell," Worm admitted. "Unless it were about right for summink I 'ad done? Mebbe!"

"An' what if it wasn't?"

"That in't fair." This time there was no doubt in Worm's voice.

"And who gets to decide?" Scuff went on.

Worm thought about it for some time. "I guess it in't right," he conceded at length.

"And what else?" Scuff added. "What about the feller what did do it? He needs putting away."

"'Anging?" Worm said thoughtfully. "Ye're daft, you are. They'll never get 'im now."

Scuff could think of no suitable reply to that, not one that would impress this dirty, hungry, opinionated little urchin.

"I think I'm gonner be daft too," Worm said at last, matching his step to Scuff's. "Where are we goin' ter next?"

"To find out how Wally Scammell got to pay off all his debts just after the *Princess Mary* went down.

"Ye're not going ter Jacob's Island?" Worm said anxiously, looking up at the sky, whose light was already fading.

Scuff was not happy about it either, but that was where Wally was.

"Wot about yer dinner?" Worm asked. "Won't yer ma be cross if yer late?"

That was another very sobering thought—not that Hester would be angry with him, but that she would be afraid for him. He did not miss meals. Sometimes she cooked something he especially liked. He thought of the look on her face when she watched him eat. She would tell him he was eating too quickly—it was bad manners—but he could see how pleased she was to be looking after him.

Knowing that Hester cared for him raised a powerful—and very complicated—feeling in him. It was the best thing in his life to be loved, and yet it was also a fence around his freedom. There were things he could not do, and responsibilities.

Worm would understand that.

"Yeah," he said slowly. "It wouldn't be good if she made my supper an' it didn't get ate. And she'd worry."

The light went out of Worm's face. "Then yer'd better go, eh?"

"I think I'd better send you to go tell 'er I've got a job to do, an' I'll be late," Scuff replied. "I got enough money to get a pie. I'll be fine. But . . ." He hesitated. Was this the right thing to do? Well, whether it was or not, he was going to do it. "You'd better ask her to give you summink to eat, as well. 'Cos I promised, an' I'm not going to be able to keep it, like I said. I live at number four, in Paradise Place. Over the river. You know it?"

Worm shook his head.

"Useless little article! Go ask!" Scuff said. "Get the ferry over the river from Wapping to Greenwich Pier, then go up the hill and ask! You can remember Paradise, can't you?"

Worm nodded, his eyes wide.

"Yer looking for Mrs. Monk. Can you remember that?"

"Like 'im wot's in the River Police? Yer tryin' ter get me locked up?"

"I'm trying to get Hester not to worry 'erself I'm drownded, an' throw away my dinner!" Scuff snapped at him. He fished in his pocket and came out with a threepenny bit. "Give that to the ferryman and get yourself off, then!"

Worm took the coin, bit it automatically to make sure it wasn't a wooden one, then turned tail and ran.

Scuff swallowed hard, wondering if he'd lost his wits. Then as Worm disappeared, he went resolutely toward Jacob's Island, his hands clenched and his stomach sinking.

HESTER HEARD THE TAP on the door as she was staring out of the kitchen window at the gathering darkness. She was unable to concentrate because she was too anxious wondering where Scuff had got to.

She flung the door open and saw on the step a small, very thin, and very dirty child with a cap too large for him and trousers held up by string.

"This number four?" he asked, clearly frightened.

"Yes, it is. Can I help you?"

He took a deep breath. "Scuff sent me ter tell yer not ter throw away 'is dinner—'e's got money for a pie, an' 'e'll be late." It was out all in one breath.

"Thank you," Hester said with a wave of relief. "You look cold."

He pulled a face, and shrugged as if it were nothing.

"Tell me what else Scuff said," she asked. "Perhaps you had better do it inside, if you don't mind?"

"I don' mind," he agreed, stepping inside and following her down to the warm kitchen. He tried not to stare around, but he couldn't help it. He had never seen a place like it before. It was warm and smelled of wonderful food. There were lots of pots and pans, shiny ones, and clean china. There was a jug with flowers in on a table.

"So Scuff is going to have a pie?" she asked as if to clarify it.

He nodded, his eyes wide.

"So he won't be waiting for supper?" she went on.

He shook his head.

"It would be a shame to waste it. Would you eat it?" she asked, as if she doubted his answer.

He swallowed hard. "I don't mind if I do . . ."

"Good. Then you'd better wash your hands and sit down." She turned on the tap and ran water for him, and it was straight out of the tap into a bowl. She gave him a towel to dry his hands. Washing left a little mark around his skinny wrists, but it was good enough.

She served him fried potatoes and two fried eggs. Then she realized he probably did not know how to use a knife and fork, so she cut it up for him and gave him a spoon as well.

She did the same for herself and ate quite slowly, knowing he was watching and copying her very, very carefully.

"My name is Hester," she said when they were both finished. "What's yours?"

"Worm . . ."

"Good. Would you like a piece of cake, Worm? And perhaps a cup of tea?"

He nodded, temporarily beyond speech.

"Then we'll have that. And you can tell me exactly what you and Scuff have been doing."

He froze.

"Oh, that's quite all right," she assured him. "He has been asking people questions, hasn't he?"

Worm nodded.

"Very good. So have I. I shall tell you what I have done, and you will tell me what he has done."

Worm nodded again and settled a little farther into his seat on the kitchen chair.

CHAPTER

10

Monk arrived home late to find Hester sitting in the kitchen talking to a very small urchin whose hands were immaculately clean, while the rest of him was remarkably filthy.

Hester smiled up at him. "This is Worm," she said, as if that in itself were an explanation. "He has come to tell us that Scuff is busy following clues on Jacob's Island, and will be home too late to eat his dinner. He suggested that Worm eat it for him." She kept her face perfectly straight, but Monk could see that it was an effort for her. She was so amused she could have laughed, so sorry for the child that she could have fed him permanently, but above all she was terrified for Scuff's safety. With a sudden tightening of the chest, he understood perfectly.

"Hello, Worm," he replied, looking at the child and fearing he would find him here from now on. "Did Scuff say what he was going to Jacob's Island for?"

Worm shook his head. "'E were goin' ter look for someone." He took a deep breath. "But we found out about some real funny stuff goin' on, like they knowed where the boat were goin' ter go down, an' it 'ad ter be there. But there weren't nothing much stole. I dunno wot 'e's after, but it'll mean summink." He looked at Monk with wide, bright blue eyes.

"Thank you," Monk said, swallowing his fear for Scuff as much as he could.

"'S nothin'." Worm stood up very slowly, glancing at the window and the darkness outside. "Can you lend me tuppence for the ferry? I only got a penny and I gotta get back ter the other side." He looked hopeful, then frightened at the realization of his own temerity.

"It's a bit late," Monk answered. "And there are a couple more things I'd like to know about what you found out. Perhaps you'd better sleep here by the fire. I'm sure we can find you a blanket, and a cushion for your head."

Hester gave him a beautiful smile. Monk refused to look back and meet her eyes. He suddenly felt absurdly vulnerable.

Worm looked startled, then he smiled as well—not that he imagined this generosity was going to come cheap. He would have a lot of questions to answer, but maybe another cup of tea before bedtime. If he got all the answers right, he might even get another piece of cake!

In the morning, Monk gave Scuff a stiff warning about staying out so late, but also thanked him for the consideration of sending Worm with the message. It turned out Scuff had found Wally, but that it had been a dead end—it was mere coincidence that he had come into some money right after the sinking of the ship.

As he went to the front door, Monk saw Hester standing alone.

"What are you going to do with Worm?" he asked, without any preamble.

"Find out if he has a mother," she answered. "He might belong to someone."

"Rubbish!" Monk said smartly. "He has nowhere to go . . ." He took a deep breath. "And we're not housing half the orphans on the river! Scuff was fine . . . but—"

"I know!" she said quickly. "I thought we could make use of him in the clinic. We need a permanent messenger."

"Hester!"

"What?" She opened her eyes wide and seemed to look right inside him.

"What a good idea," he said meekly.

MONK CROSSED THE RIVER and took a hansom cab to Lincoln's Inn, where most of the top lawyers had their offices. He intended to see Alan Juniver, but was informed by his clerk that Mr. Juniver was in court at the Old Bailey and would not be available today. Monk had no intention of accepting such an answer, but the luncheon adjournment would be his first opportunity to force the issue. First he would see Sir Oswald Camborne, who had led the prosecution in the trial of Habib Beshara, before he went to see Beshara himself. He needed all the information he could obtain.

It took a degree of pressure, and then a thirty-five-minute wait, but finally Monk was shown into Camborne's somber and imposing office. The bookshelves towered up the walls, giving the impression that too heavy a tread on the floor might bring them crashing down. The gas brackets were ornate and someone kept them meticulously polished.

Camborne rose from behind a large desk piled with papers. It was Monk's instinct to catch a few and re-pile them less precariously, but he resisted with an effort. It would seem officious.

"I don't know what you think I can help you with," Camborne said immediately. "I have very little time, and there really is nothing to add. It was regrettable that the case was not more secure, but that doesn't mean that Beshara wasn't involved, even if not exactly as it seemed at first."

Monk sat down, making himself as comfortable as he could in the chair facing the desk. He had the alarming feeling that one of the springs was about to break.

"There is nothing to prove beyond reasonable doubt that Beshara was involved at all," he pointed out.

"Of course he was involved!" Camborne snapped. "You don't know the history of the man as I do. In fact I dare say you've never even spoken to him, eh? No, I thought as much." There was a flush in his face. He leaned forward. "You are meddling in things you know very little about, Mr. Monk. Stick to solving your petty little river thefts and stabbings and the things you understand."

Camborne's arrogance was astonishing. Monk reminded himself that it was a measure of the man's insecurity in his situation. He kept his temper with great difficulty.

"And you understand the sabotage and sinking of ships, Sir Oswald?" he said very levelly.

Camborne paled. "No, of course not!" he retorted. "I don't know what you mean by that remark! But I understand politics and international finance. You have no idea the weight of the affairs you're meddling in. Possibly Beshara's part in this atrocity was different from the precise act he was charged with. Does it matter who actually lit the fuse? The intent was there. A conspirator is both legally and morally guilty."

"What conspiracy?" Monk asked, raising his eyebrows.

"For God's sake, man!" Camborne said with exasperation. "The conspiracy to blow up the *Princess Mary* and drown all aboard her. Don't play the fool with me!"

"Was there a conspiracy?" Monk affected innocence. "I was taken off the case almost immediately, and have only just been put back in charge. Clearly there is evidence I have not been given. A conspiracy requires a number of people to be involved. At the very least, more than one."

Camborne forced the words between his teeth. "Of course it's a conspiracy! You don't imagine he did all that without help, do you? He acquired the dynamite, got it on board the ship, and set it up in the bow. Then somehow he got off before it exploded, killing nearly two hundred people."

"Somehow?" Monk repeated the word carefully.

"You don't have to demonstrate how a thing was done to prove that it was," Camborne pointed out.

"Not exactly right," Monk corrected him. "If you can prove that something couldn't have been done, then you can infer that it was not."

Camborne blinked. "The ship was blown up. I believe you saw it yourself. Scores of men and women were drowned. There is no possible argument that that happened, and that it was deliberate mass murder." He enunciated the words carefully. "Beshara was closely involved. We don't know how he escaped before the explosion, but he was on the ship beforehand, and he survived. Presumably he managed to get off when they were close enough to the shore around the Isle of Dogs. It seems the clearest explanation. We may never know exactly, and it doesn't matter. It would be very satisfactory if we could find and prove who helped him. That may be what is in the minds of the authorities who commuted his sentence." He smiled bleakly, with little more than a baring of the teeth. "When he gets ill enough, and frightened enough, he may decide that silence is not his best choice."

"By which time I imagine his coconspirators will be a thousand miles away," Monk responded drily. "Unless, of course, he has nothing to do with the sinking, but just happens to be Egyptian."

"For a man who has spent so many years in the police, you are astoundingly naïve," Camborne said coldly. "I had heard that you had a reputation for being reasonably astute, even ruthless. I can't imagine how you got it." Again he leaned forward over the piles of paper on the desk. "Leave it alone, man! Stick to the crimes you understand and the criminals you can catch. If you interfere you may do far more damage than you can begin to understand."

Monk considered confronting him and asking if that was a threat.

However, he thought he saw a flicker of fear as well as anger in Camborne's eyes, and that was a far greater warning than anything the man could have said.

There was a heavy silence in the room. Footsteps passed in the corridor outside.

Slowly Monk rose to his feet. Camborne did not; he merely craned his neck and stared upward.

"Do you really believe Beshara is guilty?" Monk asked.

"Yes, I do." There was no hesitation in Camborne, only a flat, evasive anger.

"Alone? Or with others?"

"With others," Camborne replied. "But he escaped the explosion. Perhaps they were not so lucky. Or again, perhaps he did not mean them to be? Had you thought of that?"

"There's a lot to think about," Monk said with a tight smile. He now thought of Camborne not as an ally at all, but as a possible conspirator himself—by his silence, if nothing more. "Thank you for your time," he added, and went to the door as Camborne declined to reply.

Monk found Juniver almost as soon as the court had adjourned. He fell in step behind him on the pavement as he left the Old Bailey.

Juniver looked unhappy. "Miserable business," he commiserated. "But I don't know how I can help." He drew in breath as if to add something, then changed his mind and continued walking briskly to the intersection. They crossed Ludgate Hill and went into one of the small alleys toward a quiet little pub.

Monk kept pace with him all the way to the door. Inside, when Juniver ordered food, Monk ordered some as well.

"All right," Juniver said wearily, pushing his way through the throng with Monk on his heels. "What is it you think I can tell you? I represented Beshara as far as the law allows. There was nothing more that I could have done for him. I certainly did not know any of the evidence you've since brought to light to cast doubt on the eyewitness identifications."

"Interesting choice of words," Monk observed.

"What, 'cast doubt on'?" Juniver said skeptically. "That's what it is, isn't it? Doubt? Would you prefer me to add 'reasonable'?"

Monk smiled. "The words I was thinking of were that you 'represented Beshara, as far as the law allows.' I think the usual phrase is 'to the best of my ability.' Was it to the best of your ability? Or did you avoid that phrase because it would not have been strictly true?"

Juniver winced.

"The man was guilty, Monk—if not of actually placing the explosives on the *Princess Mary,* then of obtaining them, or hiring those who did, and probably of helping them escape as well. He was up to his eyes in intrigue of one sort or another. He hated Britain, and everything we've done, from raiding Egyptian antiquities to dominating the sea lanes around Africa, and anything else you can think of that's profitable. We're arrogant and show off the fact that many of us think we rule the earth by some kind of divine right."

Monk regarded Juniver with greatly increased interest. He had previously seen him as a good lawyer, and possibly ambitious, but curbed by both discipline and honor from exceeding what he perceived to be justice. Now it seemed as if he had an emotional involvement in politics and the ambivalent values of patriotism. Monk wondered what bigotry and greed lay behind the claim of love for a narrow group, be it family or country. What was it acceptable to buy at the expense of others? Loyalty to one's own country above everything? "My family before all others"? How far was that from "me first"? "You can have only what I don't want, or can't hold"? "Might is right"? "Duty is only whatever I say it is"?

The other hurried diners chattered around them, oblivious of their isolated intensity.

Juniver looked at Monk with curiosity also. He had clearly expected an immediate answer: probably one of anger, even an accusation of disloyalty.

"You disliked the man," Monk said thoughtfully. "Yet you could see very clearly why he might hate Britain from the various examples of arrogance we have exercised in pretty well all corners of the globe. You defended him because it was your job, but only as far as the law required, because you found the offense with which he was charged to be abominable."

"Fair," Juniver replied wryly. "But incomplete. I also honestly believed the man to be guilty."

"Morally if not legally," Monk pointed out.

"A distinction without a difference," Juniver replied. "The law is rather often an inexact art." He smiled bleakly and ate a slice of his cold pork pie.

Monk ate also. There was more to Juniver's actions than he had admitted. There was a discomfort in the man as if some internal conflict had been reawakened.

"Camborne said there were fortunes to be made and lost," he said. Monk was aware as he did so that perhaps he was taking too much of a risk in revealing this. He had no idea of Juniver's deeper loyalties. Perhaps he should have investigated the lawyers concerned as well as the facts of the case regarding Habib Beshara. Was Beshara not a prime mover at all, but possibly just a pawn?

Suddenly the cold game pie in its rich pastry lost its flavor. He could have been eating cold porridge. Camborne's advice not to probe too deeply would be cowardly to follow, but perhaps wise.

Juniver put down his knife and fork and leaned forward a little. "Camborne would say that," he replied very quietly. "He has to. He's a decent enough man, or he used to be, if a bit pedestrian. His wife is very handsome, but more importantly, heiress to a great deal of money."

"In shipping?" Monk asked.

But Juniver did not add any more. He was unhappy to have said even as much. It sat like a mask of embarrassment on his face, and Monk liked him for that. It was not envy when he spoke of Camborne, but pity for a certain kind of captivity.

"So both Camborne and Beshara are pawns in the game?" he said, picking up his own fork again.

"Willing pawns," Juniver replied. "Both could have chosen otherwise, even if at a certain cost."

"In order to pay a high price for freedom you have to be aware that you are not free," Monk pointed out. "Sometimes that knowledge comes too late."

"For trapped animals, yes," Juniver agreed with a touch of bitterness. "But if you'd met Beshara before the trial, you would believe as I do, that he was perfectly willing. And you would have disliked him as much as I did, and been quite aware of it, and the reasons. I believe he knew what was going to happen to the *Princess Mary*, and was perfectly willing that it should."

"That is a sin," Monk agreed. "But it is not a crime. I dare say many of those with shares in the Suez Canal were quite aware of how many people were going to die needlessly in the digging of it, and yet they do not protest."

Juniver drew in his breath, and let it out again. He too appeared to have lost an appetite for his meal. "There's nothing useful I can tell you, Monk. I couldn't prove anyone else guilty because there was no one else involved that I could point to. I didn't have the evidence you dug up to prove Beshara was in the wrong place. All I could do was try to raise reasonable doubt. That was pretty well doomed from the start, because of the horror of the crime. Most of our eyewitnesses couldn't tell one middle-aged Egyptian from another. But far more importantly than that, they didn't want to."

He took a sip of his ale and set the tankard down again, shaking his head as if he could loosen the grip of memory.

"They were horrified, grief-stricken, and quite honestly afraid of being blamed for disloyalty, cowardice, even sympathy, with the enemy, if they didn't stick to the testimony they'd given in the first place—in the heat of the moment. The more I pushed them, the more threatened they felt, and the more they clung to what they'd said. No one wants to be accused by his neighbors of being an apologist for the man who sank the *Princess Mary!*"

Monk made no reply. Juniver was right. By the time of the trial they had all entrenched themselves so deeply they could not move. They would be destroyed before they could recant willingly. Honest men, frightened, grieved, confused by hatred they could not possibly understand.

Monk finished his ale and set the tankard down.

"Thank you. I wish I didn't have to prove them wrong, but someone else is guilty of this crime, far more than Habib Beshara."

THE FOLLOWING DAY MONK was sent for again by Lord Ossett. He took the long hansom ride without pleasure, in spite of the sunlit streets, and the sight of the open carriages containing ladies in gaily colored dresses, drawn by horses whose harness brasses gleamed and winked in the sun.

He went up the steps and into the government buildings' shade with no sense of relief from either heat or noise. He did not have anything to report that was worth Ossett's time, or his own. All he knew was a mass of details, many of which conflicted with each other. He had little choice but to tell Ossett as much.

Ossett looked tired. The lines around his eyes and mouth were more deeply etched and there was pallor to his skin. He nodded slowly. "I am very much afraid that the whole issue is now so clouded with irrelevant evidence that there is little chance of learning the truth, far less proving it," he said unhappily. "I had hoped that you might turn up something unexpected, but I admit that that is unlikely. I think I have too often been overoptimistic."

"In all that I've found," Monk replied, "there is nothing that would stand up in court to implicate anyone. The only certainty is that Beshara's conviction is unsafe. There is no doubt of that."

Ossett considered for several moments before replying, as if he might still find some thought to grasp on to.

"Then if we can find nothing at all," he said finally, "even to prove him a conspirator, we shall be obliged to let him go." He regarded Monk intensely. His eyes were shadowed, and the small muscles in his jaw tight. The depth of emotion in him was palpable.

"I haven't given up," Monk said quickly, then wished he had not. He felt obliged to add the only piece of evidence he had not yet mentioned. "I recall seeing a man jump off the *Princess Mary* moments before the explosion . . ."

"Before?" Ossett said quickly. "Are you absolutely certain he went before?"

"Yes. There was a ferry within yards of where he went in. They pulled him out straightaway."

"Good man," Ossett said absentmindedly, not as if he did not believe it, but as if it were now irrelevant. And perhaps it was. "What do you plan to do to find this man . . . assuming he survived? He may have been injured, or died from swallowing river water."

That was the question Monk had been dreading. He had no answer that satisfied him, but silence would not do. Ossett needed and deserved more than that.

"I know. We are looking for him, but as you say, he may not have survived. We are comparing all the witness statements and finding the differences to see if they matter," he answered. "We are also speaking to a few people who saw a great deal but were not questioned the first time. It was an inconsistency in connection with another case that proved a key eyewitness was not where he said he was when he supposedly spotted Beshara. And his guilt depended almost entirely on the testimony of eyewitnesses. If they were mistaken then the rest was irrelevant."

"Yes . . . yes, I am aware of that," Ossett said very quietly. The acknowledgment was clearly painful to him. Monk wondered how much he knew that he was not free to say. Who else was involved, perhaps innocently? Who else did he wish to protect, or maybe had no choice? What edifice might collapse, crushing the people who relied on it, were stones from the foundation to be removed?

"It is an impossible situation," Ossett went on. "What else is there, but what your own eyes tell you? But clearly even the most honest people, when terrified and bereaved, can make mistakes, or become uncertain afterward." He folded his hands across his stomach. "Be careful, Monk. The newspapers are making a very large issue of this. And—as I dare say you will have noticed—they are angry that we have not yet found all those to blame, but very few have much sympathy with Beshara. He's a nasty piece of work, whether he is guilty of this particular crime, or not."

Monk understood exactly what Ossett was saying and agreed with him. It was Ossett's reasons that troubled him. Was he offering advice for Monk's own sake, as if perhaps Monk might not have thought of such things? Was it an attempt at commiseration for the difficulties Monk now faced? Or was it as Monk feared: a very skillfully phrased warning not to question too far into a matter which, for all its violence and grief, was still better left undisturbed?

Under his mask of office, Ossett was as tense as a dog on guard, the emotion barely held within him. Was his fear general, amorphous, or hideously specific? Further violence? Even worse, miscarriage of justice? Diplomatic crises to do with blame for the atrocity? With whom? The French? Did it really have anything to do with the Suez Canal, or was that a distraction from the reality?

"Monk!" Ossett's voice cut sharply across his distraction.

"Yes, sir," Monk said quickly. "I appreciate that the eyewitnesses were men recounting in some distress what they recollected, and in many cases wishing desperately to be of any assistance at all. This case might be larger than any other, but it is not different except in scale. Either we want to have as much of the truth as we can find, and act only in accordance with it; or we are willing to blame anyone, and probably hang them, regardless if they are guilty or not. And, of course, consequently allow the real guilty parties to escape. If the latter is the case, then I need it in writing, or I may very well find myself charged with being an accessory."

Suddenly Ossett lost the control he had been guarding since Monk had come in. The veneer over his pain was as thin as a coat of varnish.

"Don't be a damn fool, man!" His voice creaked with emotion. "If you can't act in the best interests of your country without some idiotic and totally impossible written permission, which would excuse anything you choose to do, even murder and treason, then you are not fit for a reasonable position of any kind, let alone the one you hold—at Her Majesty's pleasure, I might add! In fact you are not even fit to be called a loyal subject."

It looked like rage in his face, close to hysteria, but Monk knew now that it was fear. What could a man of Lord Ossett's power and influence be so deeply afraid of?

"I am loyal to Her Majesty," Monk said quietly. "My only higher loyalty is to the honor of justice and the law. At least I believe it is. I have never before been in a position where I perceived them not to be the same."

The color bled from Ossett's face. For several seconds he said nothing, and then he spoke slowly, choosing each word.

"You misunderstand me. Perhaps I was not clear." He swallowed. "There are aspects of this case that you are unaware of, and will remain so, for reasons that should not need explaining to you." He pushed a lock of hair back off his brow. "It is distressing, profoundly so, and I apologize for my loss of temper. This whole matter is abnormal to me. The crime was horrific, and therefore acutely sensitive in public opinion. I made an error in giving it to the Metropolitan Police. I appreciate that now, and you have my apologies. You are now handed back a case that is far more difficult to solve than it would have been in the beginning. The waters have been muddied, perhaps hopelessly. It is a matter not only for detection but for delicacy and discretion."

Ossett hesitated, still finding his thoughts slowly, as if treading on ice already cracking beneath his feet.

"It may be necessary to admit defeat, but it will leave a highly dissatisfied public, no longer believing in the power or the skill of their police force. That is a result I profoundly desire to avoid. Lies are difficult, dangerous, and usually immoral. But the truth is not always the answer either. There may be a fire in a theater, but to shout it out is still dangerous, even fatal. I'm sure you take my point without the necessity of elaboration."

Monk was startled by the wave of pity he felt for the man. "Yes, sir. I understand, and I will make certain that my men do also. It is not yet impossible that we will find whoever is guilty, and it may include Habib Beshara as an accessory."

Ossett smiled bleakly, the anger had melted away.

"That would be the best answer imaginable," he said with a faint smile. "If I can be of assistance in any way at all, ask me. Regardless, keep me informed. That is an order." He kept his eyes, tense and dark with misgiving, on Monk's to assure himself that Monk had understood.

"Yes, sir." Monk rose to his feet and excused himself.

Outside in the sun he walked slowly, his mind still turning over what he had heard, and even more the intense depth of emotion that he had seen in Ossett.

He claimed that appointing Lydiate and the regular police instead of the Thames River Police was a misjudgment, clumsy but understandable. Under normal circumstances, Monk would not have questioned that explanation. But after talking to Lydiate, Monk had felt that the man been put in charge because he was impressionable, and perhaps more easily manipulated. What was the truth?

Why was Beshara's motive, or anyone's, so difficult to find? Why had Lydiate and his men not pushed harder to find it, clarify it, and prove it so the jury understood? Was it a motive that, if revealed, would be acutely embarrassing to the government? Or to some major supporter of the government? A financial giant? Heaven knew there were enough of them in the shipping world. Some of the finest and richest port cities in Britain had been built on the wealth of those who shipped slaves across the Atlantic.

What else? The Opium Wars were as ugly as anything committed by any nation, but they were old history now.

Did it have anything at all to do with Egypt and the canal through Suez, or was that a convenient diversion? That was where there might be a possible current diplomatic clash that would matter—with the French. Or was it Egypt, and the Turkish Empire to whom Egypt was subject?

He crossed the street to the shady side of the pavement, still deep in thought.

CHAPTER 11

Monk had Orme and Hooper continue to pursue the witnesses along the river, and look for any who had not testified in court.

Monk himself considered Habib Beshara and the mounting number of times his attempts to speak with the man personally had been denied for one reason or another. He was ill and too weak to talk, or there was restlessness in the prison and it was not convenient, not safe, or the governor, Fortridge-Smith, was occupied with other matters and unavailable. Each reason alone was understandable. Collectively they amounted to obstruction. He read through all the reports on Beshara twice, shuffling papers in his office in the Wapping Police Station, looking in the backs of drawers, among the records of other cases to see if pages had been mislaid. There seemed to be so much that was missing: details of Beshara's life, friends, enemies, debts, and weaknesses, anything that could be followed through to learn more of him.

It was all facts, no flavor of the man. There was no history to him, nothing at all about who he was before he appeared in the London docks, already speaking English and with a considerable art in making money across the line of the law.

He had said his family was prominent in one of the small villages very close to the Suez Canal, which had profited them greatly, but he had said little as to in what way.

Camborne had not raised the subject at all at the trial, and Juniver had not challenged him, nor given any account of his own, and Beshara had very wisely not insisted on taking the stand himself. But if the truth was damning, why had Camborne not disclosed it?

The obvious answer to that was that it involved other people whom Camborne did not wish to call, either because of their own dubious reputations, or because they would implicate others of great influence, and possibly high office. And as it had transpired, none of it was necessary for a conviction.

Regarding the present case, several people had testified to seeing Beshara in the neighborhood of the *Princess Mary*'s sinking. Unfortunately their descriptions did not agree. One said he wore a high-collared shirt and a jacket similar to those worn by waiters on the ship. Another made him appear much more like a river man. A third and fourth were too emotional to have more than impressions, but these grew firmer with each retelling.

It all added up to no more than impressions, beliefs: nothing that should have carried a verdict in a court of law, but emotions were too high and York had overruled Juniver's few objections.

Then there was also the question as to who had attacked him in prison, and came so close to actually killing him that he was still kept segregated in the prison infirmary. Had Lydiate looked into that? No report had been made public, and there was nothing regarding it in the notes that had been given to Monk. Monk decided he must press that with Lydiate, to find out whether it was an oversight or a deliberate omission.

Wʜᴇɴ Mᴏɴᴋ ғᴀᴄᴇᴅ Lʏᴅɪᴀᴛᴇ in his tidy, comfortable office, which was at least three times the size of Monk's own, it was an awkward interview. Monk disliked having to force the issue, so he did it directly and without misleading pleasantries.

"I was told it was simply a prison fight," Lydiate said grimly. "I accepted that. I thought it was possible someone had taken their own revenge, and frankly I didn't blame them." He bit his lip, but there was defiance in his eyes. "Or it may have been some prison quarrel. He is not a pleasant man."

"Did you speak to him?" Monk could not let it go so easily. It was one of the few threads he had to follow that might lead somewhere.

"No. I asked to, but was refused," Lydiate replied as if the answer were both expected and adequate.

"You accepted that?" Monk could not keep the incredulity from his voice.

"No," Lydiate replied with a touch of coldness. "I took the matter higher; the best I could achieve was to see Fortridge-Smith, which was unsatisfactory, but it was better than nothing."

"What did Fortridge-Smith say?" Monk asked.

"That Beshara was an unpleasant man, guilty of this particular crime and many others, and fully deserved to be hanged, which he gave me credit for proving," Lydiate replied with a flush of embarrassment. "The government had seen fit to commute his sentence, for reasons he did not understand and had not been told, but if the man was killed in prison then it was no more than his due." Clearly Lydiate did not admire Fortridge-Smith.

Monk changed tack slightly. "I see from your notes that you and your men tried to get any information you could from Beshara when you arrested him, and he said nothing at all about any coconspirators?"

"Yes. You can try talking to him if you want to," Lydiate acknowledged. "But I think it's a waste of time. Looking at it with hindsight, it is even possible that he may not actually know anything."

"I've been trying. I think I will try again." Monk stood up. "Thank you."

Monk duly asked for official permission to speak to Habib Beshara again, in order to question him about certain times and places he had been near the river on the night of the explosion, and what he might have seen or heard. He did not expect to learn anything useful, at least not intentionally from Beshara, but sometimes a creative lie revealed other truths.

Beyond that, he was very interested indeed as to what Beshara would say about the attack on him. Was it a prison quarrel, as Fortridge-Smith had claimed, or was it revenge by someone who believed him responsible for the atrocity? Or—far more interestingly—was it to keep him silent about whatever he knew: either a warning, or a failed attempt to kill him?

Permission was again refused. Monk asked for an explanation and was denied one. It made him more determined than ever.

Hooper was less known to the authorities than Orme. Monk had Hooper find out the news and backgrounds of those currently in the same prison block as Beshara. When Hooper returned with a list of names Monk chose one that the Thames River Police could justifiably wish to question. It had to be regarding a crime currently under investigation.

Giles Witherspoon had been found guilty of receiving stolen goods of considerable value. Orme had already tried to elicit information from him as to who had stolen them in the first place, and gained nothing. He had not really expected to. Giles was an opulent receiver, and a man did not succeed in that calling if he betrayed his clients, either buyers or sellers.

Monk went to the prison armed with the permission he needed.

Fortridge-Smith was a tall, lean man with sandy hair and a closely clipped mustache. His military bearing made him seem to be in uniform, even though he was not. He stood very straight, almost to attention, when he spoke to Monk as he arrived at the prison and reported to the governor's office.

Fortridge-Smith read the letter of permission closely, then handed it back. "Seems to be in order," he said with a slight nod.

"Yes, sir," Monk agreed, sensing the hostility immediately and making more effort than he wished to conceal his own.

"You'll get nothing from him," Fortridge-Smith continued, looking Monk up and down to assess him. "You can't threaten him with anything like the kind of punishment the thieves could!"

"I know that," Monk said quietly. "But sometimes people say more than they mean to."

Fortridge-Smith shrugged. "If you say so." He looked at Monk with sudden suspicion. "Commander Monk, Thames River Police? Didn't you apply to see Habib Beshara?"

Monk tensed. "Yes. I was refused. Is he too ill?"

"No!" Fortridge-Smith colored slightly. "I mean—we cannot comment on his health. The situation is very delicate."

"So it would seem," Monk observed drily. "Fortunately for me, it is Giles Witherspoon I have come to see."

"Indeed," Fortridge-Smith said stiffly. "I shall conduct you to the interview room."

Monk had no grounds to argue and followed the governor's rigid back along the stone-floored passageway, their footsteps echoing. However, he wondered if he might create the opportunity to deviate from the prescribed path and make an attempt to see Beshara, even if he were not able to speak with him. How ill was he really? Monk had never seen him. In the newspaper sketches of the trial he had looked sallow, a little too fleshy, black hair graying at the sides. What did he look like now? How badly had he been beaten? Was that why Monk had been refused access to him—because his injuries were more serious than they were saying?

If that were true, it was a serious dereliction of duty, of course. Or was it something they had deliberately allowed, for any number of reasons—at the worst, that they had been requested to do it?

He increased his pace and caught up with Fortridge-Smith.

"What happened to the man who beat Beshara?" he said abruptly.

Fortridge-Smith stumbled and regained his step awkwardly. "That is an internal prison matter, Mr. Monk. Not the concern of the River Police." He kept his face forward and increased his pace along the corridor.

"In other words, you don't know," Monk concluded, continuing to match his stride.

Fortridge-Smith spun around, glaring at him. "That is an irresponsible conclusion, sir! You will repeat that at your peril. Do you understand me?"

"I think so," Monk faced him with a very slight smile. "Beshara was questioned with some violence, and he refused to betray his associates, with the result that he was beaten very badly indeed, and still refused to speak." He watched Fortridge-Smith's eyes and the high color in his skin. "He will probably die here," he went on. "A political martyr to the cause of whatever it is he believes in. Presumably that does not include Westerners cutting canals through his country and laying claim to the profits it earns. Or something like that."

Fortridge-Smith was shaking with fury, his cheeks mottled. "Who the devil put you up to this? The idea is monstrous! No one has tortured the wretched man. He was beaten by other prisoners, because he is a devious, oily wretch who is guilty of being involved in the mass murder of almost two hundred innocent men and women. He should have been hanged for it! It is only by dint of some trumped-up diplomatic necessity that he was not." He stood in front of Monk, stiff as a ramrod, shoulders square, hands clenched so his knuckles shone. His jaw was so tight he kept repeatedly raising and lowering his chin as if his collar restricted his breath.

"So either you do not know who beat him, or you do not care," Monk concluded.

"I do not care," Fortridge-Smith said briskly, snapping out the words. "But if you repeat to any man outside this prison that the damn man was beaten in anything other than a prison brawl, you will pay a very heavy price for your foolishness. Not to mention your betrayal of your own, which sin is beyond pardon. Do you understand me? I make no threat. I shall do nothing whatever. It is simply a warning, not because I care about you, but because I care very much about the damage you can do."

Monk felt a chill as if the sky had suddenly darkened. This stiff, frightened man, with his bristling mustache, understood something he himself was only groping toward. He might seem absurd, but the danger he spoke of was perfectly real.

"I want to know the truth, sir," Monk replied, his voice holding something resembling respect. "I do not necessarily intend to repeat it, and certainly not publicly, but the bereaved deserve better than lies."

"Beshara may not have acted alone, but he had a part of it," Fortridge-Smith insisted. "If he dies here, he deserves it." He jerked his chin up again. "Now go and interview your wretched thief, or fence, or whatever he is!"

"Opulent receiver, sir. Thank you." Had Monk been a military man, he might have saluted, but then he would feel just as ridiculous as Fortridge-Smith.

THE SKY WAS DARK when Monk left the prison and made his way to the ferry, even though it was July.

The ferryman was gray-haired and lean-faced. His powerful arms were built up by years at the oar. They spoke to each other casually, agreeable tones that meant nothing except that they had both worked a long day and were pleased to see the end of it.

The shadows stretched across the water and there was a hard edge to the wind. The warmth had gone and the ripples on the incoming tide were deeper, one or two with white edges.

There were other craft out, ferries from one bank to the other, strings of barges making the last trip on the incoming tide, a trifle late. No pleasure boats anymore, as it was too late in the day.

There was no sound but the rhythmic creak of the oars in the rowlocks and the hiss and splash of the water. Monk found himself lulled by it, his attention wandering. Giles Witherspoon had given him more information than he expected. Perhaps that was what he ought to be pursuing, instead of trying to pick up the pieces of Lydiate's investigation. Whoever was responsible, apart from Beshara, had probably long since left the Thames, even left England. Monk's continuing investigation of the case was not going to bring justice or peace, only more fear, more doubt and blame, more anger.

Out of nowhere another boat appeared and struck them hard. The weight of the bow and the impetus behind it drove the boat right through the ferry's hull. Within seconds Monk was floundering in the water. It was ice-cold and filthy, soaking his clothes until they imprisoned him like ropes, stopping him from trying to swim. The waves were high and rough, closing over his face again and again.

He fought, lashing out for a moment blindly, panicking. He shot upward, feeling that he was torn apart by the current dragging at his legs. Something was grasping him from below while he fought for the air. He gulped, the water washed over his head, the sound of the water deafening him. Where was the ferryman? Was he unconscious somewhere in these churning, suffocating waves?

He tried to swim, to stay afloat, anything so he could breathe. One moment he gulped air, the next a length of wood struck him in the side so hard he almost lost consciousness with the pain. He could think of nothing else. The surface receded from him and he was dragged under the river, going down, blinded, deafened, his lungs bursting. Now he knew what it was like to drown, to be sucked into the belly of the tide and swallowed, knowing what was happening and helpless to stop it.

He must compose himself. Up! He must go up toward the light, the air—life! He kicked out with all his strength, thrashing his arms and legs. It seemed like forever before he broke the surface again, gasping hard. The water sloshed over his face, waves too high, buffeting him, washing him one way then the other.

He heard cries, a human voice, sharp and desperate. He could see a large shadow almost overhead, as if an enormous craft, six, seven feet high, were bearing down on him. He had not the strength to claw his way out of its path—the waves and the current were too strong. He was going to be hit, knocked senseless, his head smashed. He had seconds! He could not move in the current. It was sweeping him into the ship's path!

Down. Down was the only way to get out of its reach. He took as huge a gulp of air as he could and let the drag take him under the water again, his mind screaming out to defy it, not to go down.

What was happening? Did no one even know they had been hit, cut in half? Or had somebody meant to kill him? And the poor helpless ferryman. Where was he? The man didn't deserve this!

Lungs bursting, he fought his way to the surface again. He sucked in the air, starving for it, and swiveled around in the darkness to look for the ferryman. He shouted, "Hey! Where are you? Hey!"

He heard a cry. He strained to hear it again, but there was only the water.

Then it came, growing fainter.

He struck out toward it. It was years since he had swum, but fury and the impulse for survival took him across the current toward the cry.

He had almost struck the ferryman before he knew he had reached him. There was a brief flailing of arms in the air, a lot of splashing. A few times Monk went under again. The ferryman was dead weight, seemingly unconscious. Please God he was not dead!

Monk held the man's face above the waves, and shouted as loudly as he could, simply, "Help! Help!"

It seemed like ages. He was growing weaker. His legs were so cold he could hardly feel them. The water came over him, suffocating, as if hungry to devour him. Each time it was longer before he came to the surface again.

Then he lost the ferryman. The current swept the man out of his grasp; his hands were too numb to keep hold. He was sinking. Despair overwhelmed him. They would both die, like all those from the *Princess Mary* that he had failed to save—and for whom there would be no justice.

Then something heaved him up by his arms, something very strong. Was he caught in a net? A rope? He was losing consciousness.

WHEN HE OPENED HIS eyes he could feel a touch on his face, something wet. He gasped, then vomited up river water. But he was breathing?

He tried to sit up, and collapsed as he was pushed down again.

"You stay there, sir," a man's voice said out of the darkness. "We'll be ashore soon. You was just about a goner. You take it easy. I'll get you a stiff brandy. Take the taste o' the river out o' yer mouth."

"Ferryman?" Monk struggled to make his voice audible. It mattered. It would be all wrong if he were alive and that poor man were dead. He couldn't remember why, but he was certain of it. "What happened?"

"Looks like someone rammed yer," the voice replied. "Ferryman'll be all right. Take a little time, mind. Broke 'is arm bad, poor devil. Ought to be drownded 'isself, whoever was in that boat, but we gotter catch the bastard first. Yer got a few bones good an' broke too, I reckon. You'll 'ave the mother an' father o' bruises on yer by termorrer."

"Thank you," Monk said weakly. His head ached, his chest ached, and he felt sick. He felt he must have swallowed half the filthy river. Still, he was alive, and so was the ferryman. He closed his eyes and gave in to the pain and the cold, gratefully.

WHEN THEY REACHED THE shore on the south side Hester and Scuff were waiting. She was white-faced, hollow-eyed, trying to hold her panic in. Scuff was standing beside her, suddenly looking very grown up. Then as soon as Monk clambered out of the boat—with help, but alive and comparatively unhurt—Scuff had to struggle not to show his tears of relief.

Hester went to Monk immediately, not caring who watched her take him in her arms, touching him gently, as if he might break. Scuff hung back, self-conscious, uncertain if at this particular moment he really belonged.

Monk looked at him over Hester's shoulder and smiled, holding out his hand.

Scuff hesitated, and then came forward, still not sure. Only as Monk's hand closed over his did he grasp it back, then abandoned all pretense and threw his arms around him, barely aware of Monk's gasp and the gritted teeth as he returned the embrace, pain ignored.

A few of the local men insisted on helping him home in their wagon, which was waiting just nearby. With Hester and Scuff on either side of Monk, he limped over to it, thanking the men with startling gratitude. The climb from the dockside to Paradise Place would have been nightmarish.

It was a rattling, bumping ride home. Little was said. Monk was shaking with cold, pain filling him. When they stopped outside his house, Scuff helped him out of the wagon again onto the ground, and then inside and into the kitchen. He was stronger than Monk had expected.

Hester questioned him as to where he was injured and checked everything he said, then helped him slip off his sodden clothes. She washed off the river mud and as much as she could out of his hair. She regarded his bruises with a practiced eye, hiding her own distress.

"Your ribs need some binding up." She said it as calmly as she could, but her voice trembled. She was acutely aware that Scuff was beside her, fetching hot water and bandages, and holding things for her, tense with deep, awful fear that his world was coming apart in front of him and he could do nothing to save it.

"It'll be all right," Monk insisted. His teeth were chattering with shock and cold, so his words emerged mumbled.

"Of course it will," Hester agreed. "As long as you do as you're told."

"Hester . . ."

"Be quiet," she said softly, blinking as the tears slid down her cheeks. "Unless there's something medical I need to know, just sit still. Scuff, will you make us all some hot, very strong tea, please? And put sugar in it. I know you don't like it, neither do I, but it's medicine. I'll add the brandy."

Monk sank into a deep sleep almost as soon as he got into his own bed. He ached all over, but Hester had given him various powders, which he had accepted gratefully, to help ease the pain. He hurt too much to stand on his pride.

But his sleep was not untroubled. He woke up gasping for air, still feeling the icy water holding him prisoner, hungry, sucking him down. No matter how he struggled, he could not break free. His whole body was filled with pain, throbbing in his chest, his belly, his limbs, even his head. He was imprisoned by the binding Hester had put on his chest. The blankets suffocated him, tying his arms to prevent him escaping.

Then the next moment it seemed as if he was in the water again. The fetid stink of the river mud choked him, clogged his throat and stopped him swallowing. He was drowning. Everything was dark. He could see nothing, touch nothing. This was what death was like. No lights, no comfort, just ice-cold, clinging, consuming darkness.

This was what it must have been like for those people on the *Princess Mary*. One moment they were laughing, drinking, dancing in the lights; the next they were alone in the dark, stifled, being sucked down and choked to death. Every one of them, one hundred and seventy-nine! And for the others dragged down also: the men in the small boats close to the explosion, as she went down. All of them! He was at one with them.

He beat his way free and sat up in his own bed. It was pitch-dark, but he could hear Hester breathing beside him, feel the warmth of her body. This was his life, and everything that mattered and made it sweet beyond words.

He reached out slowly, waiting for the bite of pain. It came, and he ignored it. He touched her gently, and relaxed back into the pillow again, holding her.

Then a preposterous thought came to him. All those deaths were acute, agonizing, totally individual, and final. Was it conceivable that someone had sunk an entire ship in order to kill one specific person?

CHAPTER

12

At first Hester slept out of exhaustion, but by about three in the morning she was awake again, listening to Monk turn restlessly, although he was clearly too sore to move much. Now and then she knew he was dreaming. Several times he cried out, and she reached across to touch him. But this seemed to make it worse, and she didn't want to waken him.

Eventually there was one nightmare that seemed so bad that she shook him awake. She could hold him only awkwardly, because of his injuries, but she kept him in her arms until he slept again.

In the morning he was still tired and in considerable pain. She gave him the small breakfast he wanted, redressed the few wounds on his arms where the skin was broken, then gave him a little laudanum for pain. After that there was nothing else she could do for him except to instruct Scuff carefully how to care for Monk, since she had an errand to run. Scuff was to make sure that Monk rested all day and that he did not even think of going out.

"Now repeat that back to me," she said gravely, when they were alone in the kitchen.

Keeping his eyes on hers, Scuff obeyed. "Lots o' tea, but no more brandy in it," he said. "No more laudanum."

"I've put it away safely anyhow," she answered.

"I'd not 'ave given it 'im!" he protested.

"I know, but he knows where it is."

"Yer don't trust 'im?" Scuff's face was crumpled, his eyes sad.

"We're not always ourselves when we're sick, hurt, and had a very bad fright," she explained. "We need those who love us to take care of us as well. That's a big part of what loving is. Not just the good times, or the battles side by side, but the bad times too, and the battles we have to fight alone."

"Where're you going?" he asked anxiously.

"I'm going to look for Crow. I think he might be able to help us with this boat problem. He knows the river even better than the police do."

"You can't do that!" he protested, all kinds of dangers whirling in his mind. She was a woman. Anything could happen to her. And she was quite pretty, in a sort of way . . . maybe? Women were supposed to stay home where it was safe. They had to work hard, and having babies was dangerous—which was something he could not even think about. But they weren't supposed to go out and get into trouble, and fights, and bad places.

"You stay 'ome and look after Monk, an' I'll go an' find Crow!" His voice was sharp and high, full of fear. "He might need you!" he added for good measure. "You're the nurse. You'd know what to do. Anyhow, what if 'e won't listen to me? What if 'e won't do what I tell 'im?"

She smiled and gave Scuff a light kiss on the cheek, which took him utterly by surprise, and felt nice, very nice.

"He will," she promised rashly. "He's too sore to argue right now.

Just make tea and toast for him. Get him anything else from the pantry that he wants, except more brandy. And I'll be back when I've found Crow."

"But you shouldn't—" he protested.

"Don't worry," she said, moving toward the door. "No need to be bored. Get one of your schoolbooks to read!"

"But—" he began, just as she closed the door behind her.

It was a calm, sunny day. Yesterday's sharp wind had fallen completely and the air was heavy, the smell of the river pungent. She was accustomed to it, but it was still unpleasant: a mixture of fresh salt and sour mud—mostly the latter, on a day like this.

In spite of the heat, she found herself shivering as she sat in the ferry going across to the north bank. The tide was low, showing the mud banks on either side. The water itself was gleaming and flat, tinged brown, almost as if one could walk across it. It was impossible to imagine yesterday's rough, white-capped waves pitching a boat, tossing it.

Had the other boat really rammed Monk's ferry by accident? Were their riding lights invisible? Could anyone ram another boat and not be aware of what they had done, or going at such a speed that they could not stop and turn to look for them, even in the near dark?

Her knuckles were white where she clenched her hands on the wooden edge of her seat. Was she afraid of the water too? Or was she just imagining Monk drowning, struggling, and believing that someone had deliberately tried to kill him?

She could feel her heart beating, and her hands were clammy. She was panicking. She must stop. Regain some control. She was no use to anyone like this. She was a nurse. She had dealt with terror, mutilation, and death on the battlefield. What was wrong with her?

She knew the answer to that with a jolt of surprise, and complete understanding. Life was far sweeter, immeasurably more precious to her now, because she had everything that mattered to her—love, purpose.

They were close to the far side already. She took out her money. As they drew in to the steps she paid the ferryman, thanked him, and climbed out. It was odd to think that he did not even know who she was or that someone had almost drowned her husband the night before. The river was so intimate, and yet at times so anonymous. That brown water could close over your head and you were gone as if you had never been. You became nothing, except a memory in the minds of those who had loved you.

She walked up the steps and along the cobbled road to the high street, catching an omnibus eastward to the Isle of Dogs, the bulge formed by the large curve in the river between Limehouse and Blackwall. She alighted at the nearest stop to where Crow had set up his new premises. She knew the address, but had not visited it before.

She counted the numbers along the street, and tried to recall the exact description he had given her. She followed Wharf Road, running parallel to the shore, if such an irregular line could be described as parallel.

She knew the landmark she was looking for, but she was passing it for the third time before she recognized it and went up the narrow stairs to what eventually became a large loft with huge skylight windows. It was full of beds and suddenly it was as if she were back in the hospital in Scutari among the soldiers. Until that instant the Crimean War had become a memory so distant it could have been a story told her by someone else. Now it was real again: the smells of lye, carbolic, and blood so sharp she inhaled rapidly and started coughing.

Then she saw Crow coming toward her, tall, and lanky as ever. His shirt was stained with chemicals and in places with blood, his black hair untrimmed and flapping over his forehead.

"Hester!" He had never bothered with formalities. "Come to see my new establishment?" He grinned with pleasure, both to see her, and with pride in his wider, cleaner, airier rooms. Then he regarded her more closely and frowned. "What is it? What's happened?"

She had always been too candid—"undiplomatic," her family had said. That was why in the past she had left the raising of funds for the

Portpool Lane clinic to others. She found it almost impossible to be roundabout with words. The more important the subject, the more direct she was.

"The *Princess Mary*," she told Crow. "Beshara is probably not the one who laid the explosives and set them off. Now that Monk has raised this doubt, they have given him back the case."

Crow nodded as understanding opened up to him. "Tea?" he offered. It was a good way to start any serious discussion.

She nodded and followed him out of the big room, so like one of Miss Nightingale's new wards in the Crimea, and into a small room with a woodstove and two chairs. It was clearly Crow's office.

She sat down while he put the kettle on the hot surface, then sat opposite her. Briefly she summarized the whole story, from Monk's part in the rescue on the night of the sinking, right up to the present time, with Monk at home in bed, dazed and injured.

Crow pursed his lips. "You need me to help, until he gets better?" he asked, his voice gentle but full of doubt. "I'd be glad to. God knows, we need to find whoever did this, and string the bastard up by his . . . feet. But I'm not much good at detecting. I'll ask everyone I know, see what debts I can collect, but if anyone—"

"No . . . thank you," she interrupted him. "Orme and Hooper will do that. I'm afraid I need much more from you."

He looked puzzled. "What could be more important than finding who really did it? I don't understand."

The kettle came to the boil. He made the tea in an old tin teapot.

"Finding out who tried to kill Beshara in prison," she answered as he waited a moment before pouring a cup for her and one for himself. "If we knew that," she went on, "it might lead to the person who is behind all the lies and the pressure. Possibly also tell us why."

"It might," Crow agreed. "In fact it probably would. But I have no idea, and I don't know anybody who would."

"Don't you think Beshara himself knows?" she asked with as much innocence as she could affect.

He still did not understand. She knew him well enough to pick up even the faintest glint of humor in his bright, dark eyes. He had never been able to hide it, in fact he had seldom seen any need to try.

"He's ill," she added.

"I know . . ." Suddenly his eyes widened and his jaw dropped a little. "No!" he said, sitting upright. "No, Hester . . ."

"Nearly two hundred people were drowned in that disaster," she pointed out.

"One hundred and seventy-nine," he corrected her. "Don't exaggerate."

"And sixteen more in other small boats, people who tried to rescue them. A rowing boat was pulled into the vortex, with five people in it."

"All right, nearly two hundred." His voice wavered a little. "I still can't do that! I might never get out!"

"We're on the right track," she went on. "Monk was nearly killed last night. The ferry he was in was rammed. If the ferryman dies, I suppose you could count another one. And, by the way, two of the rescued people died of pneumonia afterward."

"And I'd make it one more!" he said. It was a last attempt to avoid being drawn in, but his eyes reflected his defeat already.

"They wouldn't dare kill you!" she assured him, but her voice wavered. "You're a doctor."

"I'm a quack," he said, wincing at the word. "If you're going to flatter me, do it better than that."

She smiled at him. "You're a friend, one of us."

Several emotions chased each other across his face. Twice he drew in breath to argue, but the words eluded him. Perhaps he did not really want to.

She said nothing, waiting.

"How do I get in?" he said at last.

"I haven't worked that out, but I will! I'll come back and tell you. I really am . . . very grateful." She finished the rest of her tea in a gulp, and then rose to leave, before he could gather his wits and change his mind.

She hurried along Wharf Road to the omnibus stop, and took the first one that was going all the way into the city. Now that Crow had more or less agreed to help, she had a favor to collect. After she had returned from the Crimea, and before marrying Monk, she had kept herself by working as a private nurse to patients who needed constant care. She had not failed in her medical duties, but she had not always pleased her charges. She was far too blunt for that, too honest as to the nature of illness. But she had made a few deep and lasting friendships, and it was to two of these people that she now went.

First she called on Colonel Brentwood, retired from the army, but still alive largely because of her quick action at the time he lost his left hand in Crimea. Next she visited Sir Matthew Rivers, a junior minister in the government whose son she had nursed during a severe fever.

She did not make any pretense as to her reasons, and in truth, there was no necessity. With the help of Colonel Brentwood and Sir Matthew, Hester was able to get Crow an immediate position as doctor to the prison where Habib Beshara was being held in the infirmary.

She had to contort the truth, but she was still quite candid to both her previous patrons as to what she wished to achieve, and why. They had both been men of adventure in their youth, and very much admired Hester's spirit now.

She left, confident that the following day she would be able to hand to Crow the papers that he would need. The disease that affected Habib Beshara might not be curable, but his injuries were another matter. She herself was possibly more used to dealing with such things than the doctor who regularly visited the prison. She would tell Crow all she could, and hope for the best. He had studied medicine with a single-minded devotion, but he lacked the paper qualifications, for reasons she knew, but he preferred not to discuss. She trusted both his intelligence and his instinct. His dedication had never been in doubt.

It was still light out when she finally arrived at the Portpool Lane clinic, though she was far later than she had wished.

She went straight to Squeaky's office where she knew he would be, whether he was actually working on anything or not. It was his domain, his kingdom.

He looked up at her with indignation the moment she was in the room and had closed the door.

"What do you mean by sending me that dreadful little urchin?" he demanded, his eyes flashing. "What in hell's name am I supposed to do with him? Are we an orphanage now, as well as a refuge for every tart in London who has a disease?"

"Are you referring to Worm?" Hester said innocently.

He collapsed melodramatically into his seat—slightly crookedly, having misjudged the distance. "God in heaven! Is there more than one?"

She was too tired to laugh at him, although she wanted to. "Not so far as I know. Why? Do you want two? I'm sure I could find . . ."

He raised his eyebrows and glared at her. "No I do not!" he snarled.

"Good. I think one is better." She sat down opposite him.

"Better than what? None is better. What on earth am I supposed to do with him?" He hitched himself upright again. "Tell me that, then?"

"Use him, of course," she said reasonably. "He's an obliging child. He can clear up, run errands, and do whatever you want. All that matters is that you give him breakfast and supper, and a place to sleep. A blanket on the kitchen floor, if all the beds are full."

"If all the beds are full?" he said incredulously. "What's the matter with you? Is one urchin child not enough for you?"

"Yes. That's precisely why I brought him here. I dare say Claudine can find a job for him, if you can't."

"I can!" he said instantly, still glaring at her. "You—you can leave him with me. If you've got the wits you were born with, you won't give him to that woman. She'll—she'll spoil him till he's no use to man or beast."

"That's what I thought," Hester said complacently, looking at his outrage with a smile. "Now I need your help getting some documents for Crow to be temporarily employed as a prison doctor. I've taken the liberty of telling certain people that he is properly qualified, but unfortunately I cannot provide any documentary support for that."

"You what?" he squawked. "Not that prison isn't where he probably belongs," he added smugly.

"If you can't do it, just say so." She gave a shrug. "Don't make a song and dance out of it."

"'Course I can do it! Give it here." He reached over and snatched the piece of paper she was holding in her hand. "Do you want to wait here for it, or you got something useful to do while I work, eh?"

She rose to her feet. "I'll go and see Claudine. Thank you, Squeaky. I appreciate your discretion." She did not mention that she also wanted to make sure that Worm was all right, and had had breakfast that morning.

Squeaky grunted his assent.

She need not have worried. Worm was well fed and occupied sufficiently to justify lunch and even dinner as well. He gave her an enormous grin, and then ran off to his duties, full of importance.

Hester arrived home in Paradise Place after ten o'clock that night. She found Monk sitting in the parlor with a cup of tea, but looking tired and extremely uncomfortable. Scuff, sitting opposite him and watching anxiously, shot to his feet the moment he heard Hester's footsteps.

He took a look at her face and must have seen the exhaustion in the droop of her shoulders, but relief at seeing her at all overwhelmed everything else.

"You all right? I'll get yer a cup o' tea. Can I . . ." He gulped at his own temerity. "Can I get yer something to eat? There's still pie an' . . ." He could not think what else.

She sat down, leaning back into the chair, ease washing through her. "Yes, please, that would be very good. Pie and a cup of tea would be perfect."

Scuff glanced at Monk. "'E's all right . . . I think," he assured her.

"Thank you," she nodded. She waited for him to go so she could look more closely at Monk, and see whether he was feverish or just sore and frustrated with being a prisoner of his own debility.

Scuff disappeared and Monk stared at her, speaking in a low, urgent voice. "I need to get back into the case." He leaned forward a little and winced. "The more I think about it, the more certain I am that that boat rammed us on purpose. Ferries go across at that point all the time. Anyone on the river would know that and keep a watch. He wasn't even in the usual lane for the tide. It was only dusk, and we had riding lights. I'm close to something."

"We'll see how you are tomorrow—" she began.

"You don't understand!" he cut across her. "I must have—"

"Yes, I do," she assured him with as much calm as she could, but she heard the fear in her own voice. "Someone rammed you on purpose, which means they want you out of the way. Maybe they even think you're stupid enough to come after them when you're wounded and at less than half your usual strength. Fortunately they're wrong. You aren't."

Giving her a twisted smile, he moved slightly, winced, and decided it was a bad idea. "Hester, it won't work! Where have you been all day, anyway?"

"Getting Crow into the prison to see Beshara," she replied.

He stiffened. "What? You went to the prison? Hester, I told you . . ." He stopped, crippled by his own helplessness.

She saw the pain, the emotional momentarily deeper than the physical, in his face.

"No, I didn't," she said levelly. "Just sit back and let me look at how that wound is coming on."

"It hurts. It'll get better," he retorted. "Did you tell Scuff where you were going?"

"No, I didn't. If I'd told anyone, it would have been you. Now sit still!"

"Do you realize what could have happened to you?" he demanded.

"Of course," she assured him with a touch of sarcasm. "I could have been rammed in a ferry, and nearly drowned. But fortunately I wasn't. Now will you please sit still?" That last came out sounding like an order.

"Hester—"

"And be quiet! I need to concentrate on binding your ribs again. And I want to be finished by the time Scuff gets back with my tea."

He started to speak again, but he was too tired and too sore to argue.

She smiled at him gently, hiding her own anxiety. "It'll get better," she promised.

His eyes searched hers for a long moment, and then he relaxed and smiled back.

Two days later she received a letter from Crow, asking her to meet him at his new surgery the following morning.

Monk was considerably better by then, although still in some pain. He was expecting Orme to come to see him, as he had the day before. Hester made sure she told him her own plans while he was busy deliberating what he would ask the men at Wapping to do in furtherance of the case.

It was another hot, still morning and the river was full of traffic. It took her longer than she expected to reach the surgery off Wharf Road, and Crow was waiting for her impatiently. He looked eager, his face alive with anticipation of her reaction, and his own increasing interest in the case. He did not even offer her tea but plunged straight into his report.

"Poor devil is genuinely ill," he said, sitting opposite her in his private room, leaning forward in his chair. "It's what's called myasthenia gravis. Gets the muscles all through the body. Comes and goes. One day he'll be pretty good, the next thoroughly weak and ill and looks like hell. That's why they think he's putting it on half the time."

"I've seen it before," Hester replied. "Not often. How far on is he?"

"Long way, I'd judge. But he's good for a few years yet, if no one kills him," he said wryly. "And that's not something I'd bet on."

"Did you get a chance to speak to him?"

"Briefly. Surly bastard. But I think he's scared. Knows he's not likely to get out, and even if he does, he'll be lucky to last long. Someone's out to get him."

"Does he know who?"

"I think he does, but he certainly isn't saying so. They've got him sorted, as far as telling anyone is concerned."

"Is anybody else trying to find out who attacked him?"

"That's the funny thing; it doesn't seem as if anyone is." He screwed up his face. "The governor doesn't seem to care. In fact I'd say he would definitely prefer not to know. Which makes me wonder if actually he does, and values his ignorance all the more for that reason. Sometimes it isn't what you know that matters so much as what other people think you know. Keeps his nose down, does Mr. Fortridge-Smith, and his eyes closed."

"Cowardice?" she asked grimly. "Or well-rewarded self-interest?"

"From the little I saw of him, I'd guess both," Crow said with disgust. "But Beshara's scared for his life, that's pretty clear. You know he wasn't the main person who sunk the *Princess Mary*, but I'll bet he knows who was. And they know he knows . . . which is a death sentence a damn sight more certain than the official hangman's noose. Poor sod just doesn't know when, or by whom."

"There's no pity in your voice," she observed.

"There wouldn't be much in yours either, if you'd met him," Crow said with a grimace. "He may not have been the one who put the dynamite in the *Princess Mary*, or lit the fuse, but he knew what was going to happen, and he chose to let it. If he's scared to hell of someone silencing him on the chance he might testify to it, I, for one, have little grief for him."

"Is it someone in the prison already, there with him?" It was a question to which he might have no answer, but she had to ask.

"I think so, although they may be getting their orders from outside."

"Why do you think so?"

"Because he's locked away in the infirmary, but he's still scared."

"Was he frightened of you?"

He thought for a moment. "No," he said with slight surprise.

"Then he knows who it is," she deduced. "Or at least he knows something about them. How interesting." She smiled. "Thank you very much."

It was only four days since the ramming of the ferry, but Monk was increasingly restless. His ribs still ached, but the wounds on his arms were practically healed. As long as he moved carefully, the pain was far more bearable than even the day before. It was time he went back to Wapping and started doing more himself than listening to reports from Orme and Hooper, and giving directions. They were closing in, but it seemed desperately slow.

He received Hester's news from Crow with considerable interest. He drew in breath to tell her never to dare take such a risk again, but saw the foreboding in her eyes, and realized it would hurt her, without making any difference to what she would do. It would drive a wedge of distrust between them, not of lies but of lack of confidence. That was too high a price.

"Thank you," he said quietly. "It all points the way to the same answer. Beshara was not guilty, but he knows who was, or has a pretty good idea. And whoever it is will quite willingly kill him to keep his silence."

"And ramming the ferry?" she pressed. "It wasn't an accident, was it?"

"No . . ."

"Be careful . . ." Her voice was hoarse, the words forced between her lips. This was real fear now, not for her own safety, but for the loss that she could not bear.

He stood up awkwardly, and, ignoring the stab of pain in his chest, took her in his arms. Neither of them noticed Scuff come into the room with the tea, then turn around and go out again, to wait for a better moment.

CHAPTER

13

Four days later, aching and still wearing the strapping around his ribs that Hester had put on for him, Monk returned to work. After checking in at the Wapping station and speaking with Orme, and then with Hooper, to assess the latest information and relate it to all that they had so far gathered, he went to see Rogers, the ferryman who had so nearly been drowned. He felt guilty because he was now convinced the sinking of the ferry had been deliberate, and the poor man had suffered only because Monk had been his passenger.

Hooper had found the man's address and visited him a couple of times, at Monk's request, largely to see if he was safe, and recovering. His house was easy to find and, as Monk walked along the narrow road fronting on the water, he saw Rogers sitting in the tiny garden, his eyes closed in the sun. As Monk drew closer, he noticed the broken arm bound up in a splint and the dark bruises on the cheek and jaw of his pale face. It was apparently still too tender for him to shave and dark stubble dotted his chin.

The ferryman opened his eyes as he heard Monk's footsteps crunching on the gravel.

"Good morning, Mr. Rogers," Monk said, stopping in front of him. "How's the arm?"

"Hurts like hell," Rogers replied, looking up at him with a bleak smile. "But it'll mend. Not the first bone I broke. Thing is, I feel so damn useless! Wife has to cut up my food for me, like a baby."

"I'm sorry." Monk sat on the bench opposite him.

"Not your fault," Rogers said, shaking his head very slightly. Clearly the movement still caused him pain. He regarded Monk's girth, increased by the strapping. "Not much better off, eh?"

"Some," Monk agreed ruefully. "Got both my arms, with difficulty. And I don't need to row, although I'd like to. I'm in command of the River Police at Wapping . . ."

Rogers nodded. "I know. Think I been on the river and didn't know that?"

"Probably not. The point is I think that we were rammed on purpose, to get me." He watched Rogers's face and saw no surprise in it at all. "You knew . . ." he said quietly.

Rogers pursed his lips. "Pretty sure. I seen nobody on the river that damn clumsy before. Get new people who are awkward sometimes, ain't used to shiftin' weight an' 'ow the boat rocks. But them lot was pretty good at 'andling 'er. Turned fast once they'd rammed us."

"You saw that?" Monk said curiously.

"Yeah. I remember, 'cos I ain't never seen that boat before, as I can recall. Saw the stern of 'er. And a picture on it that I'd 'ave known if it were reg'lar."

Something stirred faintly in Monk's mind: a recollection of the stern of a boat with something unique painted on it. The whole image was blurry, streaked with the red light of flames in the air. It was the boat he had seen moving away just after the explosion on the *Princess Mary*, in the four minutes between the eruption of the fire and her final plunge beneath the water.

"What was it like—the picture on the boat?" he asked, his voice cracking as he stared at the ferryman's eyes. "Describe it!"

Rogers sat motionless. Not even his fingers moved in his lap. "You seen it before?" he said huskily.

"Maybe. What was it like? Describe it as much as you can."

Rogers concentrated.

"Like an 'orse's 'ead, with bumps on it, not real. And its body weren't really there, just neck going inter a sort o' lump, with a long tail curled in a circle. Something were written inside the circle, numbers I think. Not sure about that. Just saw it for a moment, like."

"What color was this horse without a body?"

"Pale. Maybe white. An' . . . an' there was something else . . . can't bring back what it was . . ."

There had been a rope around the animal depicted on the side of the boat Monk had seen the night of the explosion, but he kept silent. He didn't want to prompt Rogers into remembering it . . .

"It was a rope, I think!" Rogers said suddenly. "Yeah, there was a rope around it! You seen it?"

"Yes! I saw it the night of the sinking, just for a moment in the glare, between the time it exploded and the time she went down. In those minutes the boat was picking up survivors."

Rogers's eyes narrowed. "That were quick! Are you sure?"

They sat a couple of feet apart in the summer sun, two men who knew the river. Monk: its crime, its darkness, still learning; Rogers, all his life: its ways, its moods, its people.

There was silence between them. The distant sounds of the river, the shouts, the slurp of water only forty feet away. The crack and clang of machinery could have been in another world.

"That were them, weren't it?" Rogers said at last. "That boat with the 'orse on it. They picked somebody up out o' the river before the explosion, didn't they? An' then they tried ter kill you—an' me—'cos you knew summink about them."

There was no point insulting Rogers by pretending he was wrong. "Yes," Monk agreed. "I think so. If I draw a rough picture of what I remember, will you tell me if it looks like what you saw?"

Rogers smiled. "Yer'd better. I can't draw nothin', one arm's busted."

"Your left arm," Monk observed.

"Yeah. I'm left-'anded."

Monk took out his notebook and pencil and made a pretty good sketch of the image he had seen for those few moments after the explosion. He turned it round for Rogers to look at.

Rogers's face paled. "Yeah, that's it, pretty exact. You get yer men ter find that boat, yer got 'oo sank the *Princess Mary*—an' all them poor souls on board."

WHEN HE RETURNED TO Wapping Monk told Orme and Hooper about his visit to Rogers, and showed them the sketch he had made. It was Hooper who identified it.

"It's a seahorse," he said with interest. "It's real. Have 'em in the waters of the Caribbean."

"You been there?" Orme asked skeptically. He liked Hooper, even respected him, but he did not pretend to understand his nature. He distrusted men who told tall stories about faraway places and seemed to have no family or roots that they spoke of. Never mind Hooper's odd sense of humor.

Hooper gave him a sudden, wide smile. "Long time ago. When I was at sea." He passed the sketch back to Monk. "We'll find that boat, unless they scrapped her. Even if they did, someone'll know who had it. We're a whole lot closer."

Orme looked at Monk, his blue eyes narrow, careful. "You still look rough, Mr. Monk. They damn near killed you, not to mention Rogers. Innocent man, an' it's all the same to them. But they took a risk, right out there on the open water, and still almost daylight." He shook his head. "You never said where you were that day, or the day before. Who'd yer get so close to that they did that?"

Monk hesitated. It had been going around in his mind and he was not yet sure if he wished to tell anyone else. It was ugly, and he was uncertain. And at the back of his mind he was aware how close he had come to being killed. It was dangerous knowledge. He did not want Orme to see how rattled he was, how suddenly the knowledge of death had made life almost unbearably sweet. For years he had avoided such awareness. It was crippling, robbing him of the nerve he needed to do his job.

Orme was still looking at him, almost unblinkingly.

"Someone you respect, sir?" Hooper put it into words. "You don't want it to be true?"

Monk was startled. He also owed Hooper better than this. "Not at all! I don't want it to be true because it would go so deep and maybe so far to the top that we'd bring down a lot of people, if we could prove it." That also was totally true. The rest—the doubts, the knowledge of pain and fallibility—a man fit to lead kept to himself.

"And if we couldn't?" Orme asked.

"Maybe they'd bring us down," Monk replied quietly.

Hooper tensed. He was a big man, rangy, usually quiet, but now his anger was palpable in the air. "Can't let that happen," he replied. "We can't let ourselves be beat, or there's no more decency left. No one's safe."

"You're right," Monk agreed. "We have to win. Find that—what did you call it—'seahorse'? Quietly. Find who owns it, who uses it, and be very careful. Remember, they've already killed close to two hundred people. They won't think twice about killing you, if they think they need to."

Orme drew in his breath to make light of the idea, then changed his mind. Since the birth of his granddaughter, life had become sweeter to him also, and more precious. Nothing was to be taken quite so lightly.

"Yes, sir," he agreed, and Monk heard the gravity in his voice.

Monk had retrieved the passenger list from the *Princess Mary* again, and was happy to sit down to study it. He was annoyed with himself for feeling so tired, and he was increasingly aware of how persistently his ribs hurt. He was unpleasantly conscious of every breath.

Certainly he worked hard. He had many late nights and early mornings. He was often tired, and far more often than most people, he was cold and wet. Working on the river was arduous and sometimes dangerous. But he was in the best health he had been in his life. He could row all day and be no more than agreeably tired at the end of it. He could always afford to eat, and his house was warm and extremely comfortable. He did not worry about being able to keep it.

Above all, the deep, wounding loneliness that had dogged his half-remembered past, the dark places within himself that he dared not look at, were no longer there. He had done nothing to earn or deserve such wealth. The fear of losing it, of being somehow unworthy, was more frightening than anything his past imagination could have created. No one could deserve such riches, but one could at the very least treasure them.

He had to avoid the thought but it was there in his mind—pervasive, undeniable—that he must take the risks his duty demanded. It was the price of all he valued. Second best was never, ever good enough.

He read the passenger list over carefully, then again, even more carefully. He already knew who most of these people were: ordinary men and women who had saved up to take a river cruise perhaps to celebrate some special occasion—a birthday or anniversary, an engagement, anticipation of a happy future. Could he exclude all the families from suspicion? Most of them came from parts of London close to the riverbank. Their families would be known to neighbors, their lives easily investigated. They were shopkeepers, clerks, petty government officials in town halls, merchants who had done well, good tradesmen.

Hester had told him that there were also street women paid to attend. They must have been for the bachelor groups, and perhaps wealthier men who had not taken wives or fiancées with them. Which among them could have any imaginable connection to the explosion?

Comparing those with the lists of the dead was the place to start. The victims had all been identified and buried. In some cases their affairs had been settled and their circumstances known. He could probably rule out a hundred people that way.

It took him the rest of the day to be certain of his conclusions, and it was well into the following morning before he could look at the remaining fifty-six people and begin to see which among them might have been the intended victim—if that theory were indeed reasonable and not a product of his desperate imagination.

He was looking for wealth—connections of any sort with Egypt or the Middle East in general: investment in shipping, either to own or to use the great cargo vessels that sailed around the Cape of Good Hope to India, China, or the great trading ports such as Singapore and Hong Kong.

Interests in passenger liners must be included, and possibly connections with South Africa and the ports along its coast, which would no longer be used by ships taking the vastly different and faster route through the Mediterranean and the new canal. It was tedious and time-consuming, but he could not afford to miss any detail.

He was so tired his eyes felt gritty, and he was on his fifth or sixth mug of tea, feeling the whole exercise was pointless, when Hooper came in. His face was lined, his shirt grimy and jacket hanging loose, but there was a spring in his step.

Monk looked up at him, the papers sliding out of his hands. Suddenly his mouth was dry. He took a breath, and then did not ask.

"Got him," Hooper said, his face lighting with a rare smile. "Feller called Gamal Sabri. Egyptian. Been over here for several years, but still got strong connections to the places along the new canal route."

"For hire?" Monk asked, sitting upright again. "Or for himself?"

"For hire." Hooper sat down in the seat opposite Monk's desk, sprawling a little as if he were too tired to sit up straight. "Nasty little bastard. Got a few other marks against his name, but nothing we could prove before."

"Can we prove this?" Monk felt his muscles tighten. He could not bear the thought that they might actually know who had sunk the *Princess Mary* and not be able to convict him of it. It was only an idea on the edge of his imagination, yet already he was thinking of ways to get around a lack of proof and still get a legal verdict against Sabri that would withstand any appeal. He despised himself for it. It was frightening that he could entertain the thought so easily. "Are you sure?" he asked Hooper.

Hooper nodded. "Yes, sir. Found the boat. Called the *Seahorse*. Got the painting on the back just like your drawing, but more than that: the bow's been smashed in and repaired within the last few days. Good job done, but the paint's still different, and you can see it. It's for show. Took a good look inside, and it's been hit pretty hard. Can't tell at a glance, but you can if you look."

"How is this Sabri connected to the boat?" Monk was almost afraid to ask. They were all too keen to succeed, he most of all.

"He owns it," Hooper said. "Lots of witnesses that he was out on the night of the *Princess Mary* sinking, well before anyone was called to the rescue. He was on the water when it happened. And we did check to make sure no one reported the boat stolen."

"And on the night it rammed us?" Monk asked, beginning to feel the weight lift from his mind, and a warmth inside him as if he had had a shot of brandy.

"Sabri was out again," Hooper replied. "And again, no report of the boat being missing or anyone borrowing it. Got statements from people who saw him go out in it, about an hour before you were hit."

Monk found he was smiling too. "Why? Any idea why Sabri would sink the *Princess Mary*?"

"Because somebody paid him to," Hooper said sourly. "He's settled up a good few of his debts since then. Quietly. No flashing nothing around. But a few collectors that were after him aren't anymore."

Monk allowed himself to relax. "And where is he, this Gamal Sabri? Don't tell me we don't know . . ."

"Yes, we do. Left a man watching it, but it's like a rabbit warren down there. Best to take him at night." Hooper glanced up at the clock on the mantel. It said half past seven. "Tonight, sir. Before he gets wind of it tomorrow. We should take half a dozen men. He won't be alone and he has to know that the rope's waiting for him."

Monk rose to his feet. "Pick your men. Well done, Hooper. Any idea when Orme'll be back? He went upriver. I dare say he won't have found anything . . ."

"You can tell him when he comes." Hooper stood as well. "I'd best be starting. Dusk is a good time . . ."

"We'll take Mercer and—"

Hooper stopped still. "No, sir. I need your permission to go get him, but you're not coming . . ."

"Who the hell do you—" Monk began.

"You're injured, sir, and you'll get in the way. Somebody'll be too busy looking out for you to do his own job. I may not be able to stop you, but I'll try." He stood squarely in front of Monk, unmoving as a wall, his eyes hard.

Monk faced him.

"They're my men too," Hooper said quietly. "I owe them to look out for them. Not run them into danger they don't need. We'll get him to the police jail. Break his legs if we have to. He won't get away." He did not add, "Unless you move too slowly and give him a hostage to take," but it was in his face.

Monk could give in either with grace, or without it. Or he could make a really bad command decision and lose the confidence of his men, and insist on coming. It might even be a fatal mistake for the case.

"Right," he said quietly. "I'll wait here. I want to know when you've got him."

"You should still be at home, sick," Hooper told him. "Go back there now. I know where Paradise Place is. I'll come and tell you."

"Stop treating me like a child!" Monk snapped at him.

Hooper grinned. Even his eyes were bright. The retort was in his face, but he did not make it. "I'll see you later," he said, and went to the door.

Monk tidied up his papers, left a note for Orme, then took his jacket off the hook and went out.

A***n hour later he*** was sitting in the parlor in his own house. He was so tired he longed to sleep, but he felt compelled to stay up until Hooper should come.

"How did Lydiate go so wrong?" Hester asked. She looked up at him from the sofa, where she was sitting sideways with her feet curled up half underneath her.

"I didn't remember the painting of the seahorse on the boat I saw," he replied regretfully. "And of course it hadn't rammed us then."

"That's not what I meant," she replied, shaking her head. "It can't be so easy to get the wrong man, and come so close to hanging him, just from the lack of one clue. Are we ever sure we have the right person, if it's this simple to be wrong? And how many innocent others have we punished for crimes they didn't commit, if that's the case?"

"I know," he admitted. "We quite often get confessions, once the evidence is in. But not always."

"But was Beshara guilty at all?" she asked. "I know he's apparently an unpleasant man, but that's irrelevant—or it should be."

He smiled at her sleepily. "Sometimes you're more innocent than Scuff."

"There was a pretty big cover-up, wasn't there?" Her face was grave.

"Probably," he agreed, moving a little in the seat to ease the ache of his ribs.

She stood up and very gently moved the cushion behind him to make him more comfortable. Then she went back to the sofa and curled up on it herself.

It was after midnight—closer to one in the morning—when there was an insistent knock on the front door. It was a moment before Hester realized what it was. By then Scuff had pattered downstairs in his nightshirt and was standing in the hall, troubled but wide awake.

"It's all right," she assured him. "It's probably Hooper come to say they arrested the right man."

Scuff did not move.

"It's all right," she said again, more gently. She saw the fear in his face and felt a stab of guilt for it. They should have protected him from disturbance this late in the evening.

The knock came again, more heavily.

There was no time to say anything now. She unfastened the bolt and opened the door.

Hooper was standing on the step. His face was pale even in the yellow light from the hall, and there was blood on his shirt under his old pea jacket.

Hester stepped back immediately, her fear now even stronger than Scuff's. "Come in. Come to the kitchen. Scuff, get hot water and towels." She held out her hand to Hooper as if to steady him, although he was probably about twice her weight. "Come with me."

"I'm all right," he insisted, but he came in through the door staggering a little.

She led him along the passage to the kitchen and he followed without speaking again.

"Sit down," she told him, pointing to the hard-backed chair closest to the table and away from the stove. The last thing she wanted was him passing out and falling against the hot surface.

Scuff was busy somewhere behind her. He passed her towels without being asked.

She eased Hooper's jacket off gently and saw where most of the blood was.

"Is that it?" she asked. "Are you hurt anywhere else?"

"I'm all right," he said again, but quietly and with less certainty in his voice.

"Don't argue," she said firmly. She took the scissors out of the cutlery drawer and began to slice away his shirt to expose the wound in his shoulder.

"That's a good shirt!" he protested.

She did not bother to reply, but took the basin of hot water from Scuff and began to clean the excess blood away and expose the jagged tear in the flesh. She heard Scuff gasp, and then quickly recover. She did not turn to look at him.

"It's not bleeding too badly," she told Hooper. "But it would be a good idea to put a stitch or two in it. You could very easily pull it open again accidentally."

Hooper's eyes widened.

"It just takes a needle and some strong, clean thread. I'll sterilize it, I promise you." She continued, "Scuff, would you please fetch me the brandy, and my sewing basket from the parlor? If you can do it without wakening Monk, that would be good."

"Yes," Scuff said, swallowing hard. Two or three minutes later he was back again, holding out both the basket and the brandy.

"I don't like brandy," Hooper said between his teeth.

"It isn't for you," Hester smiled at him. "It's for the needle and the thread. Now please sit still. It will feel unpleasant maybe, a bit of pulling, but it won't hurt nearly as much as the stab did."

Hooper clenched his teeth, but apart from a slight grunt he neither moved nor made a noise.

Quickly and deftly, Hester washed the wound with the spirit. Then with Scuff's assistance she threaded the needle with linen and stitched up the wound, drawing the sides together carefully. Finally, she knotted the finished work and cut off the ends.

"There," she said, looking at Hooper's ashen face. "In a few days, a week or so, I'll take them out. In the meantime you should go and see a doctor named Crow. I'll give you his address. Tell him who you are, and that I sent you. He'll be happy to help. Are you still sure you don't like brandy?"

"I might manage to swallow it down," he said, clearing his throat. "Thank you, ma'am." He looked at Scuff. "And you too."

Scuff smiled but had no idea what to say.

"You'd better stay here for tonight," Hester went on.

"Yer can have my bed," Scuff said quickly. "I'll sleep on the couch."

"Thank you," Hester said to Scuff. "That's an excellent idea. Now we should all go to bed. It's halfway to morning already. Mr. Hooper, Scuff will show you upstairs. I will come to see you through the night, just to make sure you aren't feverish. Don't pay any attention to me. I'm a nurse, and used to wounded men."

Hooper nodded very slowly, and then, with Scuff at his side, ready to help, he went up to bed.

OVER THE NEXT FEW days the newspapers were full of the arrest of Gamal Sabri, and the questions it raised as to the original trial and conviction of Habib Beshara.

How much of that error had been incompetence, and on whose part? Lydiate, who had been in command? Or the Metropolitan Police in general? The entire idea of a police force was relatively new; doubts were raised again as to whether it was a good one, or did society require something different? Those who could remember the original "peelers" were still alive, having objected then to their power, and the consequent invasion of privacy to the respectable citizen.

Monk swore under his breath, and then continued reading. He was at his desk in Wapping, still sore, and more easily tired than he would wish, but well enough to be back working a full day. Hooper he could order to stay at home until he was better recovered, although he was doing well. This he heard from Hester, who insisted on visiting him regularly, since he had no family and she did not trust him to care sufficiently for himself. She had actually asked Monk if he thought Hooper would stay for a few nights at the clinic, but Monk had been unequivocally certain Hooper would refuse.

The newspapers all went on to speculate that if the police were not incompetent, were they then corrupt? Or did the corruption possibly lie in the judicial system? If they were both competent and totally honest, then how had an innocent man been convicted and sentenced to death? In fact how was it that his guilt had never been seriously questioned? Might such a thing happen to any man? Or woman, for that matter? How safe was anyone at all?

Others asked still further: Did a verdict in the courts, or even a police charge in the first place, depend upon money, privilege of birth, influence, the color of your skin, or a tragic combination of all these things?

Such questions were asked not only in the newspapers, and on the streets, but in the House of Commons. The words "corruption" and "collusion" were spoken.

As the week progressed the questions became deeper, more probing, and spread into other spheres. International and diplomatic issues were raised. Lord Ossett was mentioned as not having dealt with the matter in an open and competent way. What political favors were being offered, or called in? Inevitably the Suez Canal was mentioned also, and all the old arguments for it and against.

Letters to *The Times* became more and more open in their challenges to authority, and demands that deeper inquiries be made. They named several prominent ship owners with questions that were close to libelous. Lawsuits were threatened.

Everyone was uneasy, even on the streets and docksides along the river. Several policemen were hurt in brawls that began in taverns and spilled out into the streets and alleys. Leaflets demanding justice were nailed up on doors. Crude pictures of a hanged man were painted on walls, with the words "It could be you next" scrawled beside it.

Two weeks after the arrest of Gamal Sabri, his trial was announced. The haste was a matter of keeping some kind of control on public opinion, both at home and abroad.

Rufus Brancaster, the young lawyer who had so brilliantly defended Rathbone at his trial, was chosen to prosecute Sabri.

The following evening he knocked tentatively at the front door of Monk's house in Paradise Place.

Monk had just arrived home, tired and disheveled but beginning to regain his strength. He was pleased to have Hooper back, even if restricted to duty at the Wapping station for a further week or two.

Hester brought Brancaster straight into the kitchen where Monk was eating a late supper. She offered the barrister something to eat, and he accepted tea and a thick slice of cake.

"I suppose you know I've been asked to prosecute Sabri?" he asked, looking from Monk to Hester and then back again.

"No." Monk's face lit with interest, and he momentarily ignored his food. "When does the trial begin?"

"Three weeks. Doesn't give me much time. But I think they're terrified public unrest will boil over if they don't settle this soon. It's been a long, wretched summer since the sinking, and people are beginning to think it won't ever be properly resolved. It's one hell of a mess!"

"The handling of it was," Monk agreed, now taking his last mouthful.

"It's a mess itself," Brancaster said, pulling his mouth into a tight line. "Pryor has already been engaged to defend Sabri, and he won't defer to anyone, whomever or whatever he brings down. He's already made his mark, and his money." The muscles in his face tightened. "I know him. He'd rather win this and go down in history, even if it means he never practices again. He won't be swayed by loyalty, offers of a seat in the House of Lords, or threat of never working again if he gets Sabri off."

"Sabri is guilty," Monk pointed out. "The evidence is physical this time, no eyewitness identifications to be mistaken. The *Seahorse* is unmistakable. And before you ask, there are no other boats on the river with that particular device on them, not to mention the fact that the damages from the ramming of the ferry are still present. They're structural; they can't be painted over as the outside was, or replaced with new wood—that would make it even more obvious. I can give you half a dozen witnesses, apart from myself. I'm sure Pryor will try, but you have the facts."

"Precedent," Brancaster said unhappily. "He'll make a big play of the fact that we already convicted Beshara for it. He'll attack the police, the prison system that let Beshara be beaten, the whole shambles of the investigation. I wouldn't be surprised if he brings in the issue of Suez, or the debate as to whether it'll ruin British shipping and the mastery of the sea lanes we've given a century's blood to secure."

He accepted a mug of tea and the cake from Hester with a smile of thanks.

"And don't think he wouldn't do it!" he went on with his mouth full. "He would. And draw in all the weight and influence he can to protect those like Ossett, who stand to be ridiculed if the courts convict Sabri, thereby vindicating Beshara."

"I'll give you all the evidence I can," Monk promised. "And I'll testify."

"I need more than that," Brancaster said grimly. "I want Rathbone's advice. I know he can't appear until his disbarment is over, but I need his counsel, his ideas. I can't find him!"

"He's in Paris," Hester told him. "I'm sure he'll come home for this, if you want him to."

"Yes, please," Brancaster said with intense relief. "I know that technically it should be a simple case, but it's only partially a matter of law. Mostly it's emotions, beliefs, rage, and grief, and fear of chaos. And we need to win, not just for the victims of the *Princess Mary*—for all of us."

CHAPTER

14

OLIVER RATHBONE SAT IN the ferry across the Thames with the westerly sun hot on his face, in spite of the fact that it was early evening and the heat of the day gone. After nearly three years traveling around with his father, he was home again, in his new apartment, and on his way to see Hester and Monk, and, of course, Scuff.

He had promised his father for years that they would take a trip together, and yet he had always had some reason to put it off. Then with the Taft case he had been disbarred and legal matters no longer kept him in England.

With that event many of his values had changed. His wife, Margaret, had left him. There was no possibility of a reconciliation, nor did he now want one. He had seized the chance to go abroad, and travel with Henry Rathbone wherever they wished. It had been marvelous. They had walked miles in old cities steeped in history, in rich countryside; they had eaten good food, laughed at jokes and stories, and talked of every subject imaginable. It had enriched him immeasurably. They had come to know each other as friends in a way that made him feel as if their entire past life had led toward this. Friendship, generous and unforced, without duty or obligation—that was surely the foundation of all the love that mattered.

Now it was time to return to the present, to London, and to pick up what threads were left of his life. It was a strange, bittersweet feeling. All the old familiarity was here. He had known this city and its river all his life. Yet the time in Egypt, and then in Italy and France, had changed the way he saw almost everything.

Had he grown up, became wiser? Or simply different?

He looked around at the other craft on the water. The tiny waves were no more than ripples. Barely a breeze moved as they cut their way across for Wapping Stairs toward Greenwich. The air smelled of salt and mud. Usually he did not even notice it except perhaps with slight distaste. Today it filled him as if it had been strange and new. He had been to so many other places that he was drenched with all their various tastes and sounds, the smells of different foods, different lives. In his imagination he could feel the desert sand itch his skin, or recall the silence of the Egyptian night, alone with that great, ancient river and the ghosts of pharaohs lost in the dimness of time.

His hands were knotted in his lap, his shoulders tight. He was home again, facing challenges, a life different from all he was accustomed to, which was sometimes awkward. He could either handle it well, or handle it badly. Every day when he got up from his bed in the new flat he had rented, away from the beautiful, lonely house he had shared with Margaret, once so full of hope, the choice was his.

The ferry bumped gently against the Greenwich dock. He paid the fare and got out onto the steps. He thanked the ferryman and began to make his way up the hill toward Paradise Place. He realized he was walking rapidly, expectantly, pleased at the thought of seeing Monk and Hester again. He refused to acknowledge that it was still mainly Hester he was looking forward to seeing.

They welcomed him with surprise and a warmth that wrapped

around him like the odor of all the things he liked: clean sheets, fresh bread from the oven, mown grass, sunset wind off the Downs.

They asked after Henry Rathbone, and about their travels.

"Excellent," he replied. "A week in the recounting, even to begin. But first tell me about the *Princess Mary*, and Beshara, and the trial of Gamal Sabri. What evidence was there before? How was it so mistaken? What is there now?"

Monk smiled.

Rathbone noticed how tired he looked, and that he sat a little awkwardly. "What is it?" he asked, anxiety biting him with a sudden chill.

Monk told briefly him about the *Seahorse* ramming the ferry and how close he had come to drowning. He did not use emotional words, or describe his fear. Perhaps his tale was the more powerful for it.

"And now?" Rathbone asked with concern.

"All healed up. Just a little stiff."

Rathbone looked at Hester to confirm it, or not.

"Near enough to the truth," she conceded. "And Hooper was wounded also, when they arrested Sabri."

Rathbone relaxed a little. He had not expected to be so alarmed for Monk's welfare. He did not normally give consideration to the physical dangers of his calling, only the always-looming possibility of failure.

"And you said in your letter that Rufus Brancaster is going to prosecute. I can already see dozens of questions, difficulties, tactics the defense is likely to use."

That was a bleak half truth, but he needed to approach the real subject crowding his mind a step at a time.

All the papers were clamoring for justice, but the more deep-thinking ones were asking who was behind the incompetence of convicting the wrong man. Where were the vested interests that had weighed the balances so crookedly? Whose money, whose political power had done this?

It was the shadow of incompetence and almost certainly corruption within the law that weighed most heavily on Rathbone, the failure that had so easily condemned Beshara, an innocent man, at least as far as this crime went. So what if he was apparently unpleasant and a foreigner? None of these things should be relevant to a fair trial and a true verdict.

How deeply had the error and corruption eaten into the soul of the law? With his own recent acts, for which he was now disbarred, was he another part of the same disease, excusing himself for his personal morality's sake?

Monk was regarding him with a slightly twisted smile, but it was an acknowledgment of both his presence and his help.

"Let's start with what evidence we have that is physical, and not capable of more than one interpretation." Rathbone glanced at Hester and saw the corners of her mouth twitch in amusement at his inclusion of himself in the case.

He colored very slightly but did not make it worse by trying to explain. She did not need to know how important it was to him, how much a part of being "at home" again. He would not try to explain to anyone, even his father, his hunger to know that he was intellectually and morally honest in his service of justice. That was too poisoned a wound to touch.

"What does this evidence prove?" he continued. "What does it only indicate, and what more is needed? Is there anything that specifically implicates Beshara, or can we ignore him now? What about the eyewitnesses? Are any of them reliable? Any we need to explain, or discredit, to prove Sabri guilty?"

Monk named a few, but added that there was no way to predict in advance who might change their story under pressure, or what the changes might be.

"That's the whole issue, isn't it!" Rathbone leaned back in his chair. "What's really behind this?" He looked from one to the other of them. "Does anybody know what Beshara's motive was supposed to have been? Hester didn't mention anything more than emotion and supposition in her letters. Do you know anything, Monk?"

Monk shook his head slightly. "Talk of revenge, but we don't know for what, if it was on his own behalf, or that of his family, his community, or if it was merely someone who paid him. We found no evidence of money passing hands—but if it were well done, there wouldn't be. It needn't have been paid to him; anyone could have received it on his behalf. Maybe it's sitting in a bank in Egypt."

"There's the devil of a lot to find out," Rathbone said with a touch of both exhilaration and awe. He remembered their past battles, the long nights when he was so tired he could barely see straight, the nagging ache in the back of the head, the prickle of desperation as the answers eluded him. But no triumph comes without work and the corresponding possibility of loss.

The difference now was that the last case he had sat through at trial was his own. He was not the one who fought, he was the one whose life would pay the price for win or lose. He was never going to have been hanged, but he could have spent years in that wretched prison with the noise, the stench, the utter lack of privacy. It had seemed to him as if that penetrated even his mind and his soul, and he would slowly have changed into the man they thought he was.

"Oliver!"

He heard Hester's voice, sharp, demanding his attention. Had she sensed what he was thinking? Even seen something of it in his face? Surely the hot Mediterranean sun had burned away the prison pallor? Or would there always be the sick shadow of it in his eyes?

He trusted Hester. She was his friend, not because of who he was, but who she was. His ex-wife no longer mattered. She would hate him and think the worst of him, regardless of facts. Hers was a hate born of disillusion, out of something that had once been love, and perhaps an unreal hope. Thinking about Hester and Margaret automatically made him think of Beata York. But she was also different, from both Hester and Margaret. He had met and become fast friends with her in a rash moment; possibly more than that, in dreams.

He must discipline his mind not to think of her. He had been getting better at it, until now. But this case—the struggle, the insatiable desire to fight for the truth—was as much part of his life and his nature as was breathing. He could not stand up in court and speak, but he could put the words into Brancaster's mouth, and he was grateful for that opportunity.

"Oliver!" Hester said more sharply.

"I am trying to think through to the key questions we must answer. The eyewitnesses are not the issue. I think we may safely conclude that they were emotionally distressed, pressured by the police and by circumstances and the desire to please. It is also obvious that Lydiate's men were given no time to investigate properly, as public feeling was running so high about a crime so appalling. But what are the officers of the court concealing, and for whom?"

"For whom?" Hester asked, puzzled.

"Who has the power to order such a thing?" he explained. "What would be revealed by a complete exposure? Who would it damage?" He looked from Hester to Monk, and back again.

Hester shivered.

"Is this thing they are concealing related to the sinking of the *Princess Mary*? Or is the connection only incidental?"

"It has to be," she replied.

"No, actually it doesn't," Rathbone argued. "Not more than by chance, or the coincidence of one man who is implicated in both the sinking and something else involving money or power, position, even reputation. I am only exploring possibilities."

Monk nodded slowly but said nothing.

"Lydiate's motives are easy enough to understand," Rathbone continued. "His professional reputation, and that of his men, is on the line for a quick and unquestioned solution that damages no one of importance."

Hester winced.

Rathbone smiled ruefully, but he made no excuses.

"Is Oswald Camborne guilty of overzealousness to the point of ignoring the truth, cutting corners of legal process? He's an arrogant man with extraordinary ambition, but he is usually very careful indeed not to cross the line of acceptability. And Juniver? He's honest enough, but did he allow himself to be pressured, and if so, by whom?"

"Camborne?" Monk asked.

Rathbone shook his head. "No. Juniver's good for a fight. If anyone affected him, it would be someone with a more honorable argument; threat and promises would not work on him. And another thing, have you evidence as to whether this new man, Gamal Sabri, sank the ship on his own account, and if so, for God's sake why? Or was he paid by someone else? Or has he hostages to fortune of some sort?"

"No family," Monk replied. "We found no personal connections in England, or in Egypt. We could find no motive except for money."

"You've questioned him?" Rathbone glanced at Monk's still heavily bandaged chest.

"Once," Monk replied. "Briefly, before they took him away and his lawyer refused to allow him to speak. He need not have bothered. Sabri wasn't saying anything."

"Your opinion?" Rathbone asked.

"Paid by someone," Monk said without hesitation. "You don't get a lawyer of the quality of Pryor without both influence and money."

"Fame," Rathbone said simply.

"Defending the man who sank the *Princess Mary*?" Monk's voice rose with disbelief.

Rathbone smiled bitterly. "Or defending the justice system and showing that they got the right man in the first place. You could gain a lot of friends that way, and comfort a vast number of Londoners who want to feel safe."

Monk closed his eyes and leaned back a little in his chair, as if suddenly too weary to sit upright.

Rathbone could not afford to let it go yet.

"Any idea who tried to kill Beshara? And for that matter, do you know if Beshara has any connection to Sabri?"

Monk looked tired. There were blue shadows around his eyes. "No. Everything leads to a dead end."

Rathbone asked the final question. "And is there anything to indicate whether it has even the most oblique connection to the canal on Suez?"

"Nothing but speculation." Monk pushed himself upright again. "One man you didn't mention, and that's the judge in the first case. His rulings were . . . eccentric."

"York," Rathbone repeated the name to himself. He had known that. Had he deliberately forgotten it? "Do you think that is relevant to this trial now?"

Monk looked straight at him, unblinking. "It could be. I imagine he wasn't put in it by chance. A different judge might have handled it in other ways."

"How?" Rathbone tried to steady himself. York's hatred of him should have nothing to do with this. The fact that he could not get York's wife, Beata, out of his mind, his memories, his dreams, should have nothing to do with it either.

"Rulings, mainly," Monk replied. "But also the issue remains that in his summing-up Juniver raised the question of motive again, and York came pretty close to telling the jury that the facts were sufficient. If they believed Beshara guilty, the precise nature of his motives did not matter. It killed the only real point Juniver had."

"And Sabri's motive?" Rathbone asked. "Aren't we in the same position now?"

Monk acknowledged it ruefully. "All we can do is point out that he comes from the region of Suez."

"What a vast, complex, and hideous case." Rathbone looked at Monk. "Are you still involved, even though you have arrested Sabri? Can I call on you for some of the information Brancaster will need, if he is to win?"

"He has to win," Monk answered. "The price of losing is one we can't afford. It would be the biggest scandal in the justice system this century. We can't measure what is at stake."

"Then I need to know all I can about the people who were exercising the pressure, even Lydiate. And, of course, the people in the first trial. How did this all go so terribly wrong?"

After Rathbone had gone, Monk and Hester sat up long into the night talking. No matter how heavy the problem or how tangled, there were ways in which these were Monk's happiest times. There was a deep pleasure, a peace of the soul, in sharing even the most desperate battles with a woman he loved with whom he shared not just passion, but an abiding friendship.

They were in the parlor where the chairs were comfortable. The door was closed, so the murmur of their voices would not waken Scuff.

"Are you satisfied it was this man, Sabri, who ignited the dynamite and then jumped off the deck before the explosion?" Hester asked gravely. "He was taking a terrible risk, wasn't he? Most of the people who get into the Thames don't get out. Even if they don't drown, the filth in the water poisons them."

"He must have been paid a very great deal," Monk reasoned.

She frowned. "Do you think that's all it was: simple greed? He didn't do it alone, did he?"

"No. But other than possibly Beshara, we have no idea who else could be involved."

She gave a deep sigh and her face pinched with a sad understanding. "Then we don't have much chance, do we?"

"Actually, what I really want," Monk went on, "is to find the people behind this, who may not know anything about the actual explosion, but compromised our system of justice by lying, suborning lies, overlooking things, all the accumulated concealment that made it so easy for an innocent man to be condemned to death."

He saw her draw in breath. "I know he wasn't innocent altogether," he said quickly. "But that isn't the point. He would have been hanged just the same if he'd been charming and not involved at all. We got the wrong man! If it could happen to Beshara, then it could happen to anyone! You. Me." He bit his lip. "Scuff . . ."

She was pale now, shaken. "All right. I see. Yes. It's far bigger than just getting Sabri instead of Beshara. What do you need to do?" She did not say "we," but he knew she meant it.

"Find out how all these mistakes happened," he replied. "But more than that, find out who was behind it. Who, at best, allowed it to happen."

"And at worst?" she asked.

"Who applied the pressure," he replied. "Who took the case from us and gave it to Lydiate. Find out who is behind Ossett, pressuring him! And how, with what?" He told her what Lydiate had said about his appointment, and the implication that his sister would suffer were he to conduct himself without the required discretion.

She said nothing, but her face reflected her disgust, and the pity he would have expected of her.

"I need to know who was behind that," he went on. "It was Ossett who spoke to Lydiate, but where did the suggestion come from before that? What has Ossett to gain or lose? So far I see no connection. He has no money in shipping, or in the Middle East; I did check on that. He comes from an excellent family with a history of serving the country in many places, all the way back to Waterloo."

"Could it be someone else pressuring him?" she asked. "Family? An old debt or obligation?"

"It could. But what about all the others? Why did they twist, misinform? There's no one answer I can find that explains them all."

"Perhaps there isn't one," she said, thinking slowly as she found the words. "Maybe they each had different reasons? Sometimes we make mistakes, and then are afraid to admit them, and just dig ourselves further in. Sometimes we fear other people's opinions."

"So, based on pride and error, we hang an innocent man," Monk said grimly, appalled at his own words. "And now we have either to unravel the whole thing, or compound it and make it worse. I can give the ordinary witnesses to Orme and Hooper, but I have to look at people like Ossett myself."

"And the lawyers," Hester added. "They may have started out simply taking the briefs they were given, and doing what they thought best, with possibly a little ambition or self-interest thrown in. But what about now, when it's questioned and all the little details are thrown in? What about the things they overlooked, or chose to ignore, the small instances of selfishness that add up to a major error, when they're all piled on top of each other?"

"I know. I'll start with Lydiate. I'll go and see him tomorrow. If I can get him to help, it will be a place to start. But it's the River Police's case now, and he can wash his hands of it if he wants to."

"No, he can't," she said quickly. "Not if he wants to keep the respect he needs in order to do his job. Unless he's a complete coward, he'll help. I'm far more afraid you'll get little from the lawyers. But Oliver will help Brancaster. He's longing for a good, tough fight." There was laughter on her mouth and sadness in her eyes. "He'll have a hard one here, all the struggle he wants . . ."

"I know," Monk agreed. "I'll do whatever I can. I've got some idea of how much it matters."

She smiled at him, and stifled a yawn.

LYDIATE RECEIVED MONK THE following morning as if he had been expecting him; in fact he was more than prepared. He looked tired, rather like a man with an aching tooth who finally faces the dentist.

"Yes," he agreed when Monk put the situation to him. "Of course. The truth, whatever it is, will have to come out in court. There'll never be an end to it if it doesn't. I don't know how deep it goes." That was an admission, and he said it with shame. But along with that pain Monk saw a rising anger in him. He had been manipulated, and he was beginning to realize just how deeply.

"It's going to be difficult," he said, facing Monk across his very handsome desk, which was much more ornate than Monk's, but almost as untidy. "Many of the people concerned are very powerful and they are going to resent any of their actions being questioned."

"Of course," Monk nodded. "And the more dubious they are, the more crucial to the investigation, and the more they will resent it. I'm sorry. I wish it wasn't necessary, but it is. It goes to the core of justice for anyone."

"I understand that!" There was a momentary sharpness to Lydiate's voice. "To allow a guilty man to escape is to connive at his crimes, but to cause an innocent man to be hanged is an offence against humanity . . . for all I know, against God. It can't be overlooked."

"No one could have put it more succinctly," Monk said with a degree of respect. "But they will come up with excuses. Public pressure. Public good. Diplomatic necessity. Things too important and secret to be revealed—where in reality it is fear, greed, loyalty, or sheer stupidity. One mistake to cover another."

Lydiate looked at him levelly. "You might be well advised to allow some people to hide behind excuses. And don't look at me like that. If you are to succeed, you need to learn a little diplomacy. Or, if you prefer, the art of being devious."

Monk shut his eyes for a moment, then opened them and smiled. "I appreciate your advice," he said honestly, and wondered what on earth had happened to him that he was suddenly so tactful. Then he knew that it was not only an acknowledgment of the truth, but that he also liked Lydiate. He knew that in his place he, too, might have bent to pressure, if the price of it were the safety of those he loved. It was possible. He, too, had hostages to fortune.

CHAPTER

15

Rathbone stood in the center of the sitting-room floor in his new apartment. It was elegant: exactly his own taste; no one else was catered for. Yet it felt unfamiliar and almost unused. There were all the books and artifacts he had collected in more than a quarter of a century of independent life, and yet it was not home. Would time make it so, eventually? Perhaps after he had entertained guests here, returned after a full day doing something that mattered. Or might he always feel rootless now? Was failure so relentless, so deep?

That was what was missing: purpose. Before going away with his father, he had been looking for something to do rather than trying to make the day long enough for all that mattered most, and still feeling he carried things over and had to hurry the next day.

Purpose. Perhaps it was the next best thing to happiness. Empty time was a dark hole in which monsters lived and too easily came to the surface.

But this apartment was a new start. He had no profession, which was inescapable. It was a fair price to pay for what he had done, but that did not take away the void inside him.

It was also free of any reminder of Margaret, and that was a relief. His marriage was the thing in which he had signally failed, but his freedom was good. Only now did he realize that in acknowledging the end of his marriage, he had also escaped from the need to lie to himself about its possibilities. It had been hard work to deceive himself, and in the end the battle was always lost. Admitting defeat hurt, even when he knew he was wrong.

He should be used to that now. No longer could or should he always win. His endeavors should be in the service of truth, with perhaps a degree of mitigation.

He smiled to himself, walked over to the window, and drew the curtains. He was happy to gaze at the trees in full leaf, and the clipped grass of the square. They were not quite the same as the garden of his previous home, but he had no time to stroll around it anyway, and no inclination whatever to work in it.

Even though he could not speak in court until his punishment was served and he had reapplied to be accepted again, he could attend court, as could anyone else, and he could certainly assist Rufus Brancaster in this vital prosecution.

Assist! Brancaster would once have been honored to be his pupil, to be permitted to occupy the second chair next to him! Oh, "how are the mighty fallen!" Humble pie had a bitter taste, but much necessary medicine did. You could swallow it with a good grace, or a poor one, but taking it was the only way back to where he wished to be.

He sat down at the walnut desk and wrote a brief, gracious letter to Rufus Brancaster asking him when it would be convenient for them to meet and discuss this most interesting case. If Brancaster wished, he was welcome to come to Rathbone's apartment for dinner, and speak at leisure, neither unobserved nor commented on by others.

He sealed it, placed a stamp on it, and rang the bell for his manservant to take it to the postbox. He realized as he did so that there was a knot of anxiety inside him, almost an excitement. He cared that Brancaster had asked for his help. He was touched with fear that he would not justify the expectations. Did he still have the imagination, the confidence to win the seemingly impossible?

WHEN BRANCASTER ARRIVED FOR dinner, carrying a briefcase full of papers, he looked nervous. This case was one of the most important of the decade, if not of the half century. His own reputation was only a small part of what would be made, or ruined by the result.

Did Rathbone envy him? Yes. Yes, he did. To use the skills nature had given you was necessary, as a horse must run, or a bird must fly.

It was the measure of himself how he helped: to do the very best he could do, and none of it for personal reward, even in admiration. Far more was at stake than any man's vanity.

"Come in," he invited, standing back. Dover, his only manservant now, was in the kitchen. Serving a good meal was his pride as well as his duty.

Brancaster followed Rathbone into the sitting room and accepted a fine, very dry sherry, which Rathbone poured from the silver-mouthed decanter on the sideboard.

Brancaster smiled. "Should I ask you about your trip around Europe?" he said, his voice only barely showing the tension he felt. "Or shall we turn to business straightaway?"

"My trip around Europe was marvelous," Rathbone replied smoothly. He understood what Brancaster was feeling. In fact, since his own trial, and his experience of prison, he was aware of a great many things he had failed to grasp before. It was almost as if a film had been lifted from his eyes. Everything was both uglier and more precious. Life itself was shorter. Every hour should be cherished.

The sun through the window shone on their sherry glasses, and it was as if they had been carved out of topaz.

He smiled. "But having dispensed with that, we can turn to the most pressing areas of business."

Brancaster relaxed. "I've received a lot of background on people from both Lydiate and Monk. There seem to be a score of little inconsistencies, but they are errors anyone might make. Nothing even remotely indicates deliberate complicity in a crime of this magnitude."

"Are you satisfied beyond any reasonable doubt that Gamal Sabri is the man who detonated the dynamite on the *Princess Mary*, and then leaped overboard to escape the explosion?" Rathbone asked.

Brancaster did not hesitate. "Absolutely. And I rest on provable facts, not eyewitness accounts. And that boat is unquestionably the one that rammed the ferry. They pulled the ferry up and examined it. Apart from the accounts of both Monk and the ferryman, the structural damage is there for anyone to see. We have experts who can swear to the pattern of damage. For that matter, we could bring the thing itself into court. But that won't—"

"I know," Rathbone agreed. "Emotions are too high for sense to override them. Trying to force belief won't work. You need to lead them gently until they are ready to accept the truth. In fact, until they want to. It will be a long and very careful task, and there'll be many people who will try to sabotage it. One of the dangers is that you could draw it out so long that the jury loses the thread, and—worse than that—loses the rage and grief. There comes a point of exhaustion beyond which all one wants is to end the matter, and escape."

He wondered how far he dared tell Brancaster the far deeper issue that troubled him. Was it wiser to address the conviction of Sabri first, and leave the corruption until that was established in law? Or did they necessarily proceed together, locked in step toward one conclusion?

Was it his responsibility to make that decision? Or was he succumbing to arrogance?

Brancaster sighed. "The rage is against us for having got it wrong in the first place," he said gravely. "We offered them an answer—a murderer to hang—then we took it away by saying he was ill and we wanted to cure him first, when what we probably meant was that we needed him alive to get more information from him. Now we're saying he's the wrong man and they need to start all over again with somebody else. You can't blame them for directing their fury at the one source that is certain: us! Whoever else is at fault as well, we have no escape. The grief is stirred up all over again."

"Do you want to pass it to someone else?" Rathbone asked, afraid that, if he were honest, Brancaster might admit that he did. He was young, in his late thirties. He had an excellent practice and was respected by the legal community in general. He had enough imagination to succeed where others might have failed. This was a risk he did not need to take. Rathbone's own experience should be enough to warn him off crusading!

Perhaps some of the disappointment Rathbone felt was shadowed in his eyes.

Brancaster shifted slightly and raised his chin. "No, thank you. I don't know of anyone else who could do it better. Do you?" He smiled suddenly, showing strong teeth. "Because I'll have you to help me—won't I?"

Rathbone felt the color burn up his face momentarily. The praise should not have meant so much. He was too vulnerable. "Indeed . . ." he said drily. "And Monk."

Brancaster was instantly sober again. "They've given me a lot of evidence, this time largely bolstered by facts, and—where it's observation—we've got several people who all saw the same thing. But it was unarguable that Beshara is a very nasty piece of work, and likely that he knows Sabri and could have had knowledge of what Sabri was doing. Unfortunately, we have no specific motive for Sabri."

"I know," Rathbone agreed. "But before we get that far, we have to explain why Lydiate's men slipped up so totally. Why the men in charge behind him gave the orders they did. Why did the legal system convict and damn nearly hang the wrong man? Nobody wants to believe that could happen. It's a very frightening thought. It's like taking a step and realizing the ground in front of you has disappeared and you're hanging over a chasm. Beshara could be everyman. In a way, he is!"

Brancaster looked down at the floor. "I know that. That's the main thing I haven't worked out how to use—the fear."

Dover came in and coughed discreetly, then announced that dinner was served. They went through to the small dining room with its window overlooking the square and the trees.

"You can guarantee that Pryor will use it," Rathbone answered the remark as they began the first course. "He will make it seem as if the safety of the whole system depends upon upholding the original verdict. The details might be wrong, but the conviction wasn't. The jurors will want to believe him. Don't ever forget that. They won't care who's right or wrong, whose reputation falls, but they'll want desperately to be safe. They'll want it for themselves and for those they love. And Pryor will know that as well as you do. He'll play on their fears that justice and law will collapse if you prove they were wrong the first time. He'll frighten them out of thinking clearly at all. And once you've lost them your chance is pretty slight of getting them back."

Brancaster nodded grimly. "I know."

"Who is presiding?" Rathbone asked, feeling his muscles knotting as he approached the subject he dreaded.

"Antrobus," Brancaster replied. "That's something in our favor, I think. From what I've heard, he isn't afraid of anything, which should make for a fair trial. And he's reputed to have a hell of a temper if he's crossed."

Rathbone smiled. "That's right. Don't even try to put anything across him." He hesitated. "I understand Ingram York presided over the first one . . ." He left the sentence unfinished. Suddenly he was embarrassed, not sure how much Brancaster knew or guessed about his past with York.

Brancaster's expression did not change at all. "I've read and reread those transcriptions," he said thoughtfully. "I think in a different, less highly charged case there would even have been error sufficient to appeal. But then considering the degree of the atrocity, and public feeling at the time, anyone else might have ruled similarly. They all appeared to believe Beshara was guilty."

"It also seemed as if they didn't look very far beyond him," Rathbone pointed out. "Did anybody at all assume that he could have done it alone?"

"That's the whole other issue," Brancaster replied. "They were happy to settle for someone to blame and not dig any deeper."

Rathbone thought for a moment.

The manservant cleared the dishes and brought the main course.

"Sabri is being defended by Pryor," Rathbone resumed as soon as the door was closed. "Who is paying him?"

For an instant Brancaster looked startled, his eyes widened. "I don't know," he admitted. "It's possible Pryor is doing it for nothing, or at least for nothing that we can see. But it would be most interesting to know."

"Favor for favor?" Rathbone wondered. "It should be looked into. Discreetly, of course. Now let's get down to tactics, because that's where it will all lie. The evidence is for us, but the emotions are against."

Brancaster smiled and obeyed. He did not comment on Rathbone using the word "us," although he undoubtedly heard it. He began to lay out the ground plan of his prosecution.

Rathbone listened and commented here or there.

They had dessert, then coffee and brandy, and sat far into the night, debating facts and tactics.

It was Brancaster who finally put words to the question Rathbone had been skirting around.

"What if Pryor can prove that Sabri has no connection with Suez or anything to do with it? Or worse, that he has some interest in its success? Why on earth would he kill two hundred British people he doesn't even know?"

"For money," Rathbone replied, although that was merely opening the door to the answer they both feared. "But I have heard no proof that anyone paid him. If they did, it will have been in some way we can't trace, probably all done in Egypt."

"Why?" Brancaster said simply. "And probably far worse than that, who? Even if nobody else wants to know, Pryor is going to ask, because he'll know damned well that if we don't say who, it's because we don't know."

"Worse than that," Rathbone added. "Who colluded to frame Beshara, and why? Lydiate? Camborne? Even York? Who put pressure on Ossett to direct it as he did, or to get Monk back on it after the case against Beshara collapsed?"

Brancaster did not even attempt to answer.

OVER THE NEXT WEEK, Rathbone learned everything he could about the main players in the trial of Habib Beshara, and those like Lydiate and Lord Ossett who had been instrumental in handling the whole tragedy. He contacted Alan Juniver for much of the background. It was a difficult meeting, as it always was for Rathbone when encountering anyone he had known prior to his fall from grace. Before it he had been one of the most senior lawyers, and later, briefly, a judge. His downfall was spectacular, because it had been from such a height.

Had his long trip to Europe been an escape, a running away that had only made his return harder? Possibly. But whatever the cost now, he would not regret it. The time with his father had been beyond price.

Juniver was embarrassed to see him, but he concealed it moderately well. He had once admired Rathbone immensely, and told him so. Now he was uncertain, and that, too, was in his face.

"You're looking well," he said with sincerity. Rathbone's skin had been burned brown by the Mediterranean sun. He was leaner and he knew it. He had had to ask his tailor to alter some of his suits by a couple of inches to fit his shape, having lost the softness he had gained from too many good lunches and hours sitting at a desk studying depositions and briefs.

"Thank you." Rathbone accepted the compliment. "Good travel broadens the mind and narrows the waist."

Juniver smiled. "I hear you were in Egypt. Was it all that the romantics say? Newspapers, travel books, novelists, and poets seem to be full of it."

"More than all," Rathbone said sincerely. The memories of it were sharp in his mind: not just the grandeur to the eye but the tastes and smells, the sting and heat of the sun, the murmur of the Nile fingering its way through the reeds. It was not hard to think of the basket with the infant Moses caught up in those reeds, or, centuries later, the gilded barge with the young Cleopatra returning to her capital after lying with Caesar.

"And Italy," he added. "No visit there is long enough. Must be one of the most beautiful coastlines in the world. But there is much to return to here."

Juniver bit his lip. Now he was wrong-footed. He did not know what Rathbone was going to say next, so he did not know what reply to prepare.

"I need your help," Rathbone said, concealing his faint amusement. For all his potential, Juniver was not as quick, as intuitive at questioning, as he would need to be.

Juniver saw it in his eyes and caught the lesson.

"Of course," he said quickly. "You want to know about the Beshara case. I assume there is no doubt this time that Sabri is guilty?"

"None at all," Rathbone answered. "But that is only part of the issue, as I imagine you must know. I've read the transcript of Beshara's trial. There was never any possibility that you could have got him off, unless you had had the evidence that Monk later discovered. Even then I am not certain. The emotional tide might have prevailed, even so." He looked steadily at Juniver, seeing the uncertainty in his eyes, and finally the acknowledgment that he himself had believed Beshara guilty. That had inevitably colored his voice, his face, the way he stood. The jury had read that too.

"Tell me all you can," Rathbone asked, and knew Juniver would.

RATHBONE WOKE IN THE morning a trifle later than usual. It was funny how in just a few months, years of mental discipline had loosened their hold.

Dover was standing beside the bed with a steaming cup of tea, and the newspaper in his other hand. Rathbone relaxed again, feeling the smooth surface of the sheets with his feet, smelling the cotton. It would be a long time, maybe years, before the luxury of that wore off, after his time in prison during trial, when he could see no end to his incarceration.

"Good morning, sir," Dover said punctiliously. His expression gave no indication that he was aware of anything unusual having occurred. It was extraordinarily comforting. "I'm afraid the news is not very pleasant this morning." He put the cup of tea on the bedside table beside Rathbone, and then the newspaper, still folded, on the top of the bedcover.

Rathbone sat up. "What is it?" he asked, suddenly cold in spite of the fact that the room was warm.

"Mr. Beshara, the Egyptian who was accused of—"

"I know who Beshara is," Rathbone interrupted. "What about him?"

"I'm sorry to say, sir, he has been murdered, in the prison where he was being held . . . and treated for his illness."

Rathbone was stunned. "Are you sure?" It was a stupid question, and yet he could hardly grasp the facts. It was like some parody of the past, hideous, ironic, not even remotely funny. "Murdered?" he repeated the word. "By whom?"

"No one knows, sir."

"No, of course they don't! Damn it! Damn it! How could they let that happen?"

"Dead men don't speak, sir," Dover replied.

SEVERAL DAYS LATER, RATHBONE had dinner at the house on Primrose Hill where his father still lived. It was a late August evening and the shortening of the days was noticeable. Sunset came earlier, and there was a golden haze in the air as Oliver and Henry walked down the lawn toward the hedge and the orchard beyond. The boughs were heavy with fruit, and here and there birds were already pecking at the riper ones.

"Don't worry about them," Henry said casually. "There'll be plenty for us. I grew them mostly for the birds anyway. Although I hope they don't take all the plums."

They went through the gate and into the longer grass. Oliver drew in his breath deeply, smelling the richness of it: the ripe seed heads of the longer wild grass, the damp earth where the ditches ran. It would not be long before the hips and the haws turned scarlet. There were a few trumpets of late honeysuckle in bloom. It was far enough into the evening for their scent to be heavy and sweet in the air.

Above them the breeze was stirring the elm leaves in a soft whisper, and the starlings were beginning to gather. In an hour or so, there would be small bats flittering in their odd, jerky way between the branches and the eaves of the house.

Traveling had been wonderful, full of adventure, walking in the ancient places where men had built monuments to their lives and beliefs for thousands of years. But nothing exceeded the deep and abiding pleasure of a late-summer evening at home.

Returning to London also meant facing emotions that Oliver had been able to bury while filling his mind daily with new and absorbing experiences, then sharing them afterward with Henry and discussing all manner of ideas and philosophies long into the night. But one cannot escape forever; even such freedom has its caverns that cry out to be filled.

Now the awareness that intruded on him, no matter how he tried to escape it, was of how much Beata York was in his mind. Even as he stood here in the familiar orchard, steeping himself in its scents and letting the silence wash over him, he thought what joy it would bring him to share it with her. Everything, sweet or painful, would be better shared, and he could think of no one else with whom that would be so.

He had finally accepted in his mind that Henry would not be here forever. Whether it was years from now, or sooner, the day would come. He could not yet grasp the loneliness it would bring, but he had gained the courage to face it.

With Beata it could be accepted as one of the great milestones of life, not an irreparable loss. He did not even know what he believed of death, or of eternity. Perhaps very few people really knew, until the test of bereavement came.

He had thought of it when visiting the tombs of Egypt, the burial mounds of people who died a thousand years before Christ was born, or even longer. They had unquestionably believed in immortality. But life had held more mystery then. It was easier to believe in the unknowable.

He had thought of it also standing in the streets of Rome, the same city to which St. Peter had come after the death of Christ, and from which pope after pope had ruled the Catholic Church, which at that time was synonymous with the Christian world.

Perhaps he should have gone to Jerusalem?

Except that it should not make a ha'p'orth of difference where a man stood. What closer place was there to heaven than an English garden at sunset as the wind shimmered the leaves of the elms above them and flocks of starlings were crowded black pin dots against the gold of the sky?

Henry's gentle voice broke into his thoughts. "This trial you're advising Rufus Brancaster about, have you thought of the consequences?"

Oliver returned his mind to the immediate present with a jolt. "Beshara will be vindicated, although it's too late to be of much use to him," he answered. "Sabri will be sentenced to death."

"That will be the beginning," Henry agreed. "And in some senses, the least of it. This appalling miscarriage did not happen by accident, or because of one or two chance pieces of evidence. There was error, misjudgment, and corruption all the way through. If you succeed—and I know that you must if it is humanly possible, and whatever the cost—

then you will also expose that. Once you have begun, you will not be able to stop it. Have you considered the full impact?"

That was precisely what Oliver had been avoiding, keeping his mind too occupied to tread there.

"We don't know who is behind it," he said reasonably as they began to walk back toward the house.

Henry sighed. "Yes you do. You've read the transcripts by now. Don't tell me you haven't. You are not incompetent."

Oliver did not answer.

"Part of your argument regarding the first trial, and a flaw you will certainly expose, is that no one proved a motive for Beshara to risk his own life to kill so many British that he did not even know."

"The only answer is the general one, that he hated us and was paid to do it," Oliver replied.

"Precisely," Henry agreed. "And have you considered who may have paid Sabri? I hope you don't imagine that Pryor will not ask?"

"No . . . of course he will," Oliver agreed.

Henry shook his head. "And do you know?"

"Not yet. There are several possibilities. Ossett has nothing to gain by it. I looked into his background, his financial investments, even his social connections. There is nothing to suggest he's anything but the decent, slightly stuffy, ex-military man he appears to be. The same is true of everyone else connected with changing the case from Monk to Lydiate. And Lydiate himself is a victim of it. He was put in over his head, granted. He felt coerced because of his brother-in-law's vulnerability, but it didn't affect how he behaved. And there's Camborne, but I can't find any reason for him to prosecute so passionately, except his ambition."

"Do I have to spell it out for you?" Henry asked as they reached the French windows and went inside. The air was cooling as the light faded, and he was happy to close and lock them for the night.

Oliver waited.

"Ingram York presided over the first trial," Henry went on, sitting down in his favorite chair and waving Oliver to take the opposite one, where he habitually sat. "You will be forced to expose his conduct of it, with every ruling he made. Are you prepared for what you may find? Do you want to prove him at best incompetent, losing his mental grasp, or at worst, actually corrupt?"

Oliver faced it at last. Henry had left him no escape. Such an exposure would inevitably hurt Beata, even if at the same time it began to free her from York. He did not know if that was a price he was willing to pay.

Would it even free her? Was it not more in her character that loyalty would bind her to her husband even more tightly?

Henry was watching him, not saying the obvious, but the knowledge of it was in his eyes, and the pain he would share if Oliver were hurt.

Either way, it should make no difference to the decision as to what was the right thing to do. He could not recuse himself! What would he say? I am in love with Sir Ingram York's wife?

Of course not. He would embarrass her beyond bearing, not to mention what he would do to himself—and to the case. It was not a time for personal considerations. And he was not officially representing anyone. He had no standing. All he could do was advise Rufus Brancaster—and serve the law.

Inevitably it raised memories of Margaret, and the failure of their marriage. Her loyalty to her father had risen above her loyalty to the law, or truth, or even moral justice. When it was only in theory, she had said that whatever the cost, one's first loyalty had to be to what was right.

Such easy words—before something cuts to the heart and the bone. Before it is your father, your husband or wife who is to be imprisoned, or executed! Arthur Ballinger had been sentenced to be hanged for a crime Oliver knew he had committed. In their last, terrible meeting he had not even denied it. But only Oliver had heard that.

Margaret still believed that her father had been innocent, and that Oliver had put his own career before loyalty to family in allowing Arthur to be convicted and not mounting an appeal. When Oliver's career had crashed in ruins, because of his decision as to what was right in the Taft case, she had rejoiced, and seized the opportunity to ask him for a divorce.

He had faced a prison sentence and could not morally deny her her freedom. Not, honestly, that he had wanted to. Freedom was lonely, but sweet for all that.

Could he stand by his loyalty to the truth, no matter the price, if it were asked of him? Did he really believe that without honor, nothing else survives?

If it were Henry charged . . . but Henry wouldn't be guilty!

Then again, Margaret had been unable to believe that her father was guilty, whatever the evidence.

What would Beata believe of her husband?

Henry was waiting, a sad, gentle smile on his face.

"I've paid that price once," Oliver replied. "I think, if I have to, I'll pay it again. I'm not sure."

Henry nodded. "I thought so. But you cannot know what you will find. Someone is guilty."

"I know . . ."

CHAPTER

16

MONK WAS IMPATIENT WITH how long his wounds took to heal, but it was actually as fast as anyone could expect. Broken bones mend at their own rate, and neither Hester's care nor his own annoyance could hasten it. Once or twice she reminded him that his constant irritation was actually more likely to make him feel worse.

Hooper was less volatile or, as Hester observed, to Monk's surprise, he was more stoic. Her remark had the desired effect of making Monk bite back his anger. He gave Orme authority to act in his place, to choose which cases were given priority, and direct his men accordingly.

Monk accepted his physical inactivity and turned his mind wholly toward investigating what other dark and complicated motives might emerge when the trial of Gamal Sabri proved that Beshara was innocent, and his trial had been flawed by serious error, and almost certainly a degree of corruption.

Monk liked Lydiate and understood why he had yielded to the pressure applied to him regarding the case, even if he was forced to agree also that it jeopardized his impartiality. But once you yield to pressure, even with the smallest, most harmless-seeming deviation from the path, have you then made the next step inevitable? When do you refuse: the third step, the fourth? Or is there no longer a way left to escape?

He began with the most unpleasant of the tasks, which was to check all the facts Lydiate had told him of his sister's marriage, and consequent vulnerability to pressure. The initial inquiries were simple enough; being discreet was another matter. Once he was beyond what was common knowledge, he went to see Runcorn. He chose to meet him in Greenwich Park, rather than at the police station. They walked side by side along the wide gravel paths between the lawns and flowerbeds, under the great magnolia trees, which had long finished their blooming. To the casual eye they were simply two men who had time to spare in the middle of the summer day.

Runcorn looked unhappy. "You think Lydiate's corrupt?" he said very quietly, although there was no one else within earshot. "Or you're trying to prove he's not . . . just a bit slipshod in this?"

"Both," Monk said with an attempt at lightness that failed.

Runcorn moved on several paces before he spoke again. "What does a good man do if he's blackmailed, not for himself but for someone he loves, and who has a right to expect his protection? Do you sacrifice your family to what you see as justice, even if they don't?" He shook his head. "I know it's his sister's stepdaughter, but that is irrelevant to the question. What if it were his wife?" This time he looked at Monk. "What if it were your wife? Or mine? I couldn't tell Melisande, 'No, I won't protect you. My job comes first.'" He stopped on the path, challenging, waiting for Monk's reply.

Monk stopped also. "And she would tell you to pass the case to someone else," he said. "And accept the consequences. She's wise enough and brave enough to know that the other choice leads to an even worse ending."

"That is only half the answer." Runcorn refused to move. "Would I ask that of her, knowing what she would do? Maybe the only honest thing is simply to make the decision yourself. Isn't that what true protection is? You make the choice?"

Monk pushed his hands into his pockets, fists slowly clenched. "Perhaps you have to make the wrong choice once or twice to know how much darker it is in the end."

Runcorn kept up with him. "And you want me to find out if Lydiate took the wrong choice?"

Trust Runcorn to be blunt. "I need to know. I need to know for sure how far he bent the facts. I've been over and over the reports, but that isn't enough," Monk answered.

Runcorn pulled his mouth into a thin line. "Are you trying to protect him or to expose him?"

"How the hell do I know, until I find out what he did?" Monk demanded. There was far more he wanted to say. He wanted Runcorn to understand the pity he felt for Lydiate, that he did not know himself what he would have done, only that to yield was never the answer. He might have protected him, if he could, but it was no longer an option. Brancaster would tear Lydiate's case apart anyway. He had no choice.

"I can't do anything if I'm caught on the blind side," Monk added. "Lydiate's family is as vulnerable as he told me, and nothing has happened to them."

"Who threatened him?" Runcorn asked.

"Ossett was the one who told him," Monk said unhappily. "But I had the strong feeling that someone else was pressuring Ossett. It's almost like something you can feel in the air." He searched for words that would not sound melodramatic, and failed. "A desperation," he finished. "You can find the real records without being as obvious as I'd have to be. If Brancaster is any good, he'll find them. We need to do it before he does."

Runcorn gritted his teeth but he did not disagree.

By the time the trial of Gamal Sabri was a couple of days away, Monk had provided Rathbone, and thus Brancaster, with all the information he could find on Lord Ossett, Sir John Lydiate, and all the lawyers who had conducted the trial of Habib Beshara. There were errors of judgment, vulnerabilities, oversights, occasional contradictions, but nothing that individually amounted to more than anyone might make in a hasty and deeply emotional investigation. And there was no apparent connection to the murder in prison of Beshara, which Monk had also been looking for.

He did, with some difficulty, discover that Gamal Sabri's legal counsel had been hired by a wealthy Egyptian named Farouk Halwani, currently living in Cairo, and unavailable for comment.

Monk had tried to speak to Fortridge-Smith, but had been evaded, and then outright refused, by his secretary. He had no great hope that he would be able to learn how Beshara had died, still less who might have been responsible. There were so many possibilities he had little expectation of it being useful in the trial of Sabri. Still, it angered him to be refused access.

Accordingly, he went to see Lord Ossett, and was received in his large and very handsome office, with the haunting portrait of himself as a young man.

Monk came straight to the point.

"I'm sorry to disturb you with this, sir, but time is short, and I have done everything I can to persuade Fortridge-Smith to see me, but he refuses. I believe it is imperative that I have all the information possible regarding Habib Beshara before Sabri's trial begins. We cannot afford to be caught off balance." He watched Ossett's face and saw the shadows in it: apprehension, perhaps more. He was increasingly certain that Ossett was distressed to the point of endangering his health. He was struggling within his own mind for an escape from some overwhelming burden. He looked all but exhausted by it.

"I appreciate that the situation is difficult," Ossett began, his voice rasping a little. "But surely a prison tragedy like the death of Beshara, even if it was intentional and malicious, has no real bearing on convicting Sabri?"

His mouth pinched in an expression of pain rather than revulsion. "Or are you suggesting that the timing of Beshara's death is not coincidental?" He did not move in his chair, as if he lacked the energy. "Surely you were not hoping that he could be made to testify? The man was a wreck, and very seriously ill. In fact, he may well have died within weeks, if not days, regardless. Fortridge-Smith informed me that to label his death as murder was irresponsible. Some journalist seeking to make headlines for himself." His expression was quite clearly one of disgust.

Monk was obliged to retreat at least a step or two. "Possibly the journalist was guessing," he conceded. "And in that case, he is totally irresponsible, and before the trial of Sabri we should give the newspapers the truth." He kept his face as expressionless as he could. "Who investigated the death?"

Ossett stared at him. "I beg your pardon?"

Monk did not look away. He saw the shadows in Ossett's eyes, a sudden flicker of anxiety, something that eluded him.

Monk drew in his breath to prompt a reply, and sensed a pain in Ossett, one that Monk didn't understand. Then it was gone again, masked.

"I don't know," Ossett answered. "It must surely be a very narrow circle of possibilities. I admit, I have been too concentrated on the difficulties of this wretched trial of Gamal Sabri to consider Beshara's death." He looked back at Monk now, his eyes steady. "Between us all we seem to have brought the justice system to the brink of disrepute. I don't know if you have thought of the damage we might do if there is no satisfying explanation as to what happened that brought us to condemn the wrong man in such a terrible case. It is the grace of God, and no more, that we did not hang him! No sensible man is now going to feel that his own life is safe should he be charged with a crime. Therefore we must both explain it, and show that it cannot happen again."

"I know that, sir," Monk said quietly. "And it is just as important that we do not now blame someone who is innocent for that mistake."

Ossett moved. "Dear God! Don't even think of such a thing. I don't want poor Lydiate sacrificed. He's a decent man . . ."

"I know," Monk agreed. "But not a politician and not a policeman."

Ossett paled. "That's harsh . . ."

Monk knew it was harsh, and he loathed saying it, most particularly because it was true. "He is a good administrator, sir, and, above all, an honest man, deserving of the respect his men have for him. They would rightly see it as unjust if you were to remove him from his post over this."

Ossett looked at him curiously, as if trying to weigh him up, to see the answer to something that had troubled him.

Monk resisted the temptation to overexplain himself, and remained silent.

"Will you win the case?" Ossett changed his line of approach. "Brancaster is good, but he lacks experience. Rathbone would have been better. Making such a fool of himself over the Taft case did a great disservice to the British legal system." He shook his head very slightly. His shoulders were painfully tight. "It's full of pitfalls, Monk. Full of them! It's still possible, if he gets into a tight corner, that Brancaster could rip some of York's decisions apart." He sighed. "But it could possibly come to the same thing whoever had presided. Emotions were hot. The whole country was demanding that we condemn someone. And who can blame them? It was an atrocity. The ordinary man in the street wants to believe that we—the police, the government—have some kind of control over what's happening!"

"And that it won't happen again," Monk added.

Ossett looked at him sharply. "For God's sake, don't ever whisper such a thing! Don't think it!"

"We have to think it," Monk replied. "That's the only chance we have of seeing that it doesn't."

Ossett's face was haggard. Monk glanced at Ossett's younger self in the portrait on the wall, but noticed that Ossett avoided looking at it. Did it remind him of a happier time when decisions were simpler? Or had he failed to become the man that young soldier had dreamed of?

"Are you thinking of the sinking of the *Princess Mary*, or the abominable mess of the investigation and the trial convicting the wrong man?" Ossett asked.

"Both," Monk replied. "And also the possibility of making it even worse by now failing to convict the right one."

"Are you sure he is the right man, Monk?"

"Yes, sir. But I need to find out before the trial as much as I can about how Beshara died, and who was responsible. That is something Brancaster at least will ask, and he will only be the first. Every thinking man in England will be asking it before the trial is finished." It sounded a little like a threat, and he had meant it to.

Ossett's voice was gravelly when he answered, as if he were finding it difficult to control.

"I will see that Fortridge-Smith answers your questions—today," he promised. "If he has nothing to hide he won't mind, and if he has, then you are going to learn what it is!"

"Yes, sir."

OSSETT WAS AS GOOD as his word. Fortridge-Smith received Monk at a little after four o'clock that afternoon, albeit with an ill grace. They were in his office, a bleak room with shelves on one wall. Books sat in regimented rows, awaiting his interest. A red Turkey rug relieved the dark painted stone floor and muffled the sound of footsteps.

"I don't know what good you think you can do in raking up the issue again," he said angrily. "The man was guilty, and he was dying of his wretched disease anyway! He got into a quarrel with someone and they may well have hastened his death, but that's all. Men quarrel in prison, Monk! It's not a nice place. It's not meant to be. There are fights and men get hurt. It's not good for your health. People die younger in here than they would outside. Nobody starves or freezes, and that's about the best you can say for it."

Monk drew in his breath to argue, but Fortridge-Smith continued.

"And as for Beshara, I know that, thanks to you, it appears he didn't actually put the dynamite on board the *Princess Mary*, but he was involved in the atrocity, and that makes him a guilty man. He deserved to be here."

Monk controlled his anger with difficulty. He could feel it welling up inside him and he wanted to argue, to point out the difference between personal judgment and the law. The whole principle of private vengeance was against everything the law was supposed to embody. But his common sense told him Fortridge-Smith was not listening, either intellectually or emotionally. Monk's anger would only make it worse.

"For the upcoming trial of Sabri, who is also guilty," Monk said lightly, and so very levelly that he was clearly governing himself not to speak his mind, which Fortridge-Smith had to know, "I need to speak to the people in charge of the prison infirmary at the time of Beshara's death. I may be called to testify."

"To what, for heaven's sake?" Fortridge-Smith said sharply. "The way Beshara died, long after the explosion, has nothing to do with Sabri's guilt!"

"Don't be naïve," Monk snapped back. "Since when did a defense lawyer's questions have to have immediate relevance to the crime?"

"Then don't answer them!" Fortridge-Smith retorted.

Monk's eyebrows shot up. "And leave them to realize not only that I don't know, but that I don't care enough to have found out? That would hand the defense the perfect opening to suggest that Beshara was guilty after all. Or alternatively, that he knew something so important that he had to be silenced. And we, the authorities, connived at it." He watched Fortridge-Smith's eyes as the skin tightened across his cheeks. "Or worse, that we actually did it ourselves," he went on. "To save our embarrassment at the complete mess we made of the first trial, and everything since." He could not keep his contempt hidden. "And that would not please our lords and masters."

The blood surged up Fortridge-Smith's face, but he was cornered. He had to reply to that last challenge, and he knew it.

"Then go and speak to whomever you like," he said bitterly. "I'll have one of the guards accompany you. And don't get rash and lose him, Mr. Monk. As you have observed for yourself, this is a violent place. The prisoners here are not good people. I might very well be able to find out who killed you, and even prove it, but it would be little use to you . . . or your family."

Monk felt a moment's sharp, tight fear. It knotted his stomach and ran through his veins with heat, and then cold.

"I'm obliged," he said with less panache than he would have liked. "Lord Ossett will be too."

"Indeed," Fortridge-Smith said, almost without expression.

A senior guard was sent for. As soon as he appeared he conducted Monk to the prison infirmary, where Monk interviewed the nurses—all men, naturally—and the part-time doctor who had been hired since Crow, having found out as much as he could, had left. Monk gave no indication of having heard of Crow, much less known him.

As soon as he entered the high-ceilinged room, the smells of lye and carbolic, mixed with that of human waste, seized Monk's stomach and twisted it so hard he found it difficult not to retch. There were ten beds ranged along two walls facing each other. Eight of them were occupied by men in various stages of pain or resignation. Many were bandaged; two clearly had broken bones; others were feverish, flushed, sweating, and moving uneasily on the hard mattresses.

There were two nurses on duty, presently occupied in cleaning or tidying, rolling bandages, emptying slops.

After Monk had acknowledged them, introduced himself, and explained why he was here, he asked them who had been on duty immediately before Habib Beshara had been found dead.

The answer was that it was Elphick, the larger of the two, and another man called Stockton. Monk told them that he needed to speak with them, one at a time, in a closed room where they were guaranteed not to be overheard. The guard whom Fortridge-Smith had ordered to be with him for his safety would wait outside.

Elphick was a tall, wiry man with a nervous habit of drumming his fingers on the top of the table between them. It was irritating. Monk had to discipline himself not to order the man to stop, as it would be a bad start to what was almost certainly the only chance he would have to speak with him alone.

He began with something to which he knew the answer.

"What was wrong with Beshara?"

Elphick pulled a face of disgust. "Slow thing. Called something gravis . . ."

"Myasthenia gravis?" Monk suggested.

"Yeah, that's right. Least that's what they said." He looked up at Monk with sudden directness. "Don't kill yer, though. Sometimes 'e were like normal, others 'e could 'ardly lift 'isself off 'is backside. 'E weren't putting it on, for all that. Why should 'e? Don't make no difference to us."

"Was he having a bad spell when he died?" Monk asked.

"Yeah, pretty much."

"So it wouldn't have taken much to overpower him?"

Elphick shrugged. "We gotter know 'ow ter do that anyway."

"Why wait until now to kill him?" Monk asked without warning.

Elphick looked surprised. "Geez! I dunno! Nasty sod, but no worse than usual."

Monk persisted for another ten minutes and learned nothing he considered useful.

Stockton was different. He described in some detail how he found Beshara dead, and said he had no idea how it had happened. There had been two other prisoners in the infirmary at the time. One had been asleep all night, and both claimed not to have seen or heard anything. Both of them had been released since then and disappeared back into the underworld from which they came. Might even have gone to sea, for all he knew.

"Did you look into it at the time?" Monk asked, keeping his tone light, as if it were something quite casual.

"Yeah, o' course we did," Stockton said indignantly. "Reckon 'e must 'ave choked, or something. 'E were a nasty swine anyway, and we all knew as 'e'd bin part o' the sinking o' that ship, whether 'e actually done it personal like or not. No one were sorry 'e'd gone." He met Monk's eyes without evasion.

"So one of the prisoners in the infirmary killed him?" Monk asked.

"If 'e were killed, then it must 'ave bin," Stockton said reasonably. He stayed looking straight into Monk's eyes a second too long.

"And of course they've gone," Monk said. "Disappeared."

"'S'right," Stockton nodded. "Pity, mebbe. But there's no 'elp for it now. Save yer the price of a rope."

"You were the one who found him? When you came back on duty?"

"'S'right."

"Was he cold?"

"Yeah."

"Were there marks of a fight on the body?"

Stockton breathed out slowly. "No, 'e looked like 'e could 'a gone in 'is sleep."

"No struggle. So he wasn't expecting it?"

Stockton hesitated. "I were a bit shook up . . . finding 'im dead, like."

Monk measured his words. "Do you think one of the other prisoners might have been paid to kill him? It seems certain from what you say that it was someone he knew. Both the other prisoners, perhaps? Odd that one woke and the other didn't, don't you think?"

"Maybe 'e'd 'ad a bit o' medicine?" Stockton moved very slightly on his seat.

"Very possible," Monk agreed. "Or maybe both of them had?"

Stockton's shoulders tensed, as if under the table his fists had clenched.

"Dunno," he said.

"Perhaps I had better check the infirmary records of sedatives," Monk suggested. "And at the same time, get the Metropolitan Police to look at your spending habits around about that time. Did you come into a little extra money that week?"

"I didn't kill him!" Stockton said sharply. A whisper of panic in his voice: thin, but Monk heard it.

"But you know who did." That was a statement. "You have a big decision to make, Mr. Stockton. Which side are you on? The same as you have been up until now: the prison guards, the law? Or did you change sides to be with the prisoners, the men like Habib Beshara, who colluded in the murder of nearly two hundred people?"

"I weren't never on 'is side!" Stockton cried out, rising slightly from his chair, his face white with fury. "And I never killed 'im neither. But I in't sayin' I'm sorry the bastard is dead. Nor should you be, if you 'ad any 'uman blood in yer."

"Indeed?" Monk raised his eyebrows. "But if it wasn't the other prisoners, it has to have been you. You've just said there was no one else here." He pushed his chair back as if to stand up.

"Wait!" Stockton said sharply.

Monk relaxed. "What for?"

"I let someone in ter visit 'im. I didn't know 'e were goin' ter do anything like that. 'E said 'e were a friend, come ter say goodbye."

Monk filled his expression with disbelief. "I've got you; I haven't got this imaginary person of yours. The trial begins on Tuesday."

"So you'd 'ang me ter cover yerself, even though yer knew I didn't do it?" Stockton could hardly grasp such dishonor. "That's p'lice for yer! Lyin,' murderin' filth!"

Monk shook his head. "I'm not hanging you rather than him, you are! You give me him, and all you'll get is a rap on the knuckles for taking a bribe . . . providing you give us enough evidence to convict him, of course."

Stockton looked at him with pure hate, made deeper by the fact there was nothing he could do about it.

"Stand up, Mr. Stockton," Monk ordered.

Stockton did, awkwardly, as though his joints hurt him.

Monk moved around slowly, aware of Stockton's balance, the tension in his body, and his own vulnerable ribs, which were still aching from the ferry ramming. He locked the manacles around one wrist before attempting to do the other. For an instant Stockton went rigid, as if he would have fought, and Monk twisted his arm up toward the shoulder in what he knew could end in a dislocation. He could not afford to use less strength. If Stockton managed to overpower Monk, he would likely kill him. There was no other way out. He might have already killed once. The unseen visitor to Beshara could be an invention. There was no proof. Stockton himself must know that.

What would the guard waiting outside do? Keeping Stockton in front of him, Monk rapped on the inside of the door.

It opened, and he pushed Stockton out, keeping his own hands low and tight around Stockton's left wrist, pressing hard enough on the pulse to stop it if he tightened his grip a quarter of an inch.

"Take me to the governor's office," he ordered the other guard.

The man stared at him, then at Stockton's contorted face.

Monk saw the indecision in him. Monk's heart was hammering against his aching ribs. He was too weak to fight. One good elbow in the chest and he would be finished, possibly even dead with a punctured lung. He swallowed hard, and yanked Stockton's arm higher. The man let out a squeal of pain.

"Geez! Do it, for Gawd's sake. Don't let this son of a bitch . . ." The rest was lost in another howl.

The guard obeyed, leading the way. It was a short distance, only twenty-five feet or so, but Monk realized with a ripple of horror that perhaps Fortridge-Smith would not side with the law, as he had assumed. He might turn his back and allow Monk to be disposed of. He could claim complete ignorance of it all. He could say that Monk had gone out another way, without calling in to pay his respects as he left. Who would argue?

For the second time in a space of weeks, he was going to have to fight for his life! Why the hell hadn't he brought Orme with him, or even Hooper, who was as close to healed as he was himself?

With a burn of shame, he knew the answer. Because he had intended to get a confession from someone regarding Beshara's death, and he preferred that neither Hooper nor Orme saw him do it. The anger inside him at the atrocity, first of murdering the passengers on the *Princess Mary*, then the corruption of justice in the trial, was tempting the man he used to be before the accident and before the amnesia that had forced him to begin again: a ruthless man, respected and feared, not liked. It was not who he wanted to be. Hester would not lie easily beside him. There would be no more laughter, no comfortable silences. Scuff would not trust him.

And yet they expected him to solve Beshara's death and see not only Sabri convicted, but those who had lied in court, taken money or praise to convict an innocent man.

They were at Fortridge-Smith's office, and he had no plan.

Then suddenly it was there in his mind's eye: the photograph on Fortridge-Smith's desk, a family group. Probably it was his wife and sons, but it did not matter. He could recall the light on the glass.

He told Stockton to knock on the door. The moment it was answered he pushed Stockton's head inside, and then hit him on the side of the skull so hard he tripped and fell, rolling on his injured shoulder. He stayed motionless on the floor.

Monk followed him in, slipping his own jacket off his left arm so his right sleeve hung over his hand. He seized the photograph off the desk and smashed it on the hard, wooden corner, shattering the glass. He picked up the longest, sharpest shard, using his coat sleeve to protect his palm, then he lunged behind the still gaping Fortridge-Smith.

"Sorry," he said as calmly as he could, his breath making the words jerky. "But I need to get out of here, and send someone back for Stockton. Either he murdered Habib Beshara, or he took money to let in the man who did. And I have no idea whether you were part of this or not. I can't afford to take the chance."

"God Almighty, man! Are you insane?" Fortridge-Smith's voice rose to falsetto with outrage. "I'll have you arrested for this!"

"We both have to get out of here alive first," Monk replied, forcing the words between his teeth.

"Then put down that damn piece of glass, before you slip and kill me with it!" Fortridge-Smith shouted.

"Don't waste time," Monk told him bitterly. "We might not have it to spare. The prisoners have no love for either of us. It won't matter to me who they blame for my death. I don't know if it does to you—for your death, I mean."

Fortridge-Smith gulped. "You'll not get out of here alive!"

"In that case, neither will you," Monk pointed out, giving the shard of glass a little nudge, enough to go through Fortridge-Smith's jacket and nick the flesh.

"All right! But I'll see you pay for this!" Fortridge-Smith walked carefully over to the door. He opened it and peered out.

"Take the key from the lock," Monk ordered. "And lock it from the outside. We'll send someone to let Stockton out."

Fortridge-Smith did as he was told. Then slowly they walked along the corridor to the entrance, nodding as they passed the guards on duty. One footstep after another, they went through into the outside air.

Fortridge-Smith hesitated.

"You realize that if the prisoners break my office door down, they could kill Stockton to stop him telling you who killed Beshara?" he said. "Then what will this insane action have cost you?"

"Probably my job," Monk replied. "And yours."

Fortridge-Smith tried to swing round, and earned another hard prick in the flesh. He swore in language that Monk was surprised he knew. It was ugly, and yet it made the man more human.

"Perhaps it would be wise to move a little more sharply," Monk told him. "Until we get some reinforcements." Now he, too, was shaking beyond control. The very streets around him, the open air, the regular police constable, who had accompanied him to the gate earlier and was now walking purposefully toward them, were all more sane and beautiful than gardens full of flowers.

The constable stopped. He looked from one to the other of them. "Everything all right, gentlemen?" He blinked, hesitated. "Commander Monk?"

"Yes." Monk's voice was scratchy. "There's been an unpleasantness at the prison. Governor Fortridge-Smith is coming with me to report the matter, and see a doctor. He had a slight injury. Not serious, but best to get it seen to."

"Yes, sir! And are you all right, sir?" the constable said with concern.

Monk touched his ribs tenderly where he was still bruised from the ferry attack. He smiled with absurd gratitude. "Yes, I'm perfectly fine, thank you."

IN THE SHORT TIME until the trial of Gamal Sabri began, Monk questioned Stockton over and over, and gained from him very little of value. He described the man who paid him to allow a visit to Beshara, but his account was so general it could have applied to thousands of people.

"Between twenty-five an' thirty, I reckon," Stockton said. "But the light were bad. Could 'ave bin morning. Stubble on 'is chin. That makes yer look different. 'Bout my weight, I'd say."

Monk estimated Stockton to be a couple of inches short of six feet. Stockton added, "Kind o' greasy 'air, cut short."

"Color?" Monk said without hope.

"Brown. Medium brown. Blue eyes, I think."

"In fact an average Englishman," Monk concluded. "I suppose he was English? He wasn't Welsh, or Scots was he? Or perhaps Irish?"

"Can't say." Stockton shook his head. "Looked like hell, but he spoke like a gentleman. 'Course that could 'ave bin put on. Mimic, like."

"But you took his money and let him in to see Beshara, and murder him. Oddly gullible, for a prison guard," Monk said sarcastically.

"That's a fault," Stockton said with mock contrition. "Not a crime. P'raps I should get a different employment?"

"You'll be employed breaking rocks for a good few years," Monk said tartly. "Unless they think you killed Beshara yourself."

"Then I'll get a medal!" Stockton said with a sneer.

"Then I'll see you hang!" Monk snapped. He stood up and went to the door. He turned before he opened it. "If this man who killed Beshara really exists, are you supposing he did it in revenge for the sinking of the *Princess Mary*?"

"'Course," Stockton replied. "Wot else?"

"How about to make sure of his silence?" Monk suggested.

The color bled out of Stockton's face.

"Watch your back," Monk said softly, and went out of the door, closing it behind him.

CHAPTER 17

Rathbone sat behind Brancaster at the Old Bailey, as the Central Criminal Court in London was known. Last time he had been here, he himself had been in the dock. Brancaster had defended him, with courage, eloquence, and, now and then, flares of brilliance.

In the past Rathbone had appeared here as a barrister, sometimes prosecuting and at others defending. Now he was merely an observer, an assistant to Brancaster without the right to address the court at all. It was a strange feeling, as if he were not quite real to those who were part of the proceedings.

The jury had been chosen and sworn in. The court had begun proceedings with Lord Justice Antrobus presiding. He was a lean man, ascetic, with a quick mind and a dry sense of humor. He was perceived as a man who relied on his intellect more than his heart. Rathbone, though, had seen the rarely shown side of him that was capable of compassion, and deep anger at those times when the law was unable to punish cruelty. He had warned Brancaster of Antrobus's nature, but he wondered now if he had done so with sufficient vehemence.

Brancaster was on his feet addressing the judge and jury. He must be acutely aware of the crowded gallery, the journalists, and the vast mass of men and women beyond the building, who would know only what the newspaper headlines told them.

Rathbone watched with his body clenched, his hands rigid in his lap. Would Brancaster judge well how to press his case? Would he horrify people too much, or just enough? Or might he allow them to become complacent that justice had already been done, and they should not question it now?

"The crime of sinking the *Princess Mary*, and drowning nearly two hundred human beings, is a terrible one," Brancaster was saying. He spoke quietly, but his voice carried in the silent room. Everyone was looking at him.

"We have lived with this knowledge for several months now," he continued. "We had been led to believe that the man responsible for it was in prison, ill, and possibly dying, in some degree of pain."

He waited for the effect of his remark and looked at the faces of the jurors. "Twelve good men, like yourselves, had been presented with evidence and reached that conclusion." He took a long breath. "I am now here to tell you that they were given only part of the evidence: Some evidence was misguided, some incomplete, some was false, possibly deliberately so. I will ask you to reach a different conclusion."

At the defense table, Pryor dropped a piece of paper and bent to retrieve it. His movement broke the spell.

Brancaster smiled. "Gentlemen, it seems I have startled my learned friend for the defense to the point where he let his work fall onto the floor." He looked at Pryor. "I hope you did not get ink on your clothes?"

Everyone, even those in the gallery, turned to look at Pryor again. There was a slight titter of amusement.

Pryor flushed. "Not at all," he said sharply.

Brancaster resumed his remarks to the jury.

"I shall ask you to reach a different conclusion," he repeated. "Not necessarily that Habib Beshara was a nice man, or innocent of all wrongdoing, but that he was not guilty of the crime with which he was charged. Indeed, that he could not have been. Whether he was implicated at all in this tragedy is another matter, and not one for us to decide today."

He became suddenly very grave. "There is also another very serious question that you will inevitably face, and that is, what happened that we were so disastrously wrong in our earlier judgment? How many people lied? Was it simply a series of errors? Or was there corruption?"

Pryor was fuming. He was close to the point where his outrage would erupt into words, inappropriate as that would be.

Brancaster went on, "This is not a legal question for you to address, but these thoughts will come into your mind. It is impossible to avoid them. Is our legal system so totally flawed that this could happen? Do you fear that you yourself, or someone you love, could be falsely accused and convicted of a crime, and no one but you will know their innocence until it is too late?"

"My lord!" Pryor could bear it no longer.

"Mr. Brancaster," Antrobus said quietly, "I think you are a trifle ahead of yourself. Mr. Pryor may well be going to suggest such things, but you do him an injustice to assume so in advance."

"Yes, my lord," Brancaster agreed. It was not difficult to concede; he had already made his point. He resumed his address to the jury.

"We shall show you how this crime was committed using evidence you can see: physical objects rather than people's recollections from what must have been one of the worst nights of their lives. We will not ask terrified and bereaved people to remember what they saw or heard. We know that they must have been suffering appallingly."

He inclined his head a little. "No one man did this. It was a conspiracy of, at the very least, two men. Habib Beshara may have been one of them, but he was not the man who took the dynamite on board the *Princess Mary*, or the one who ignited it. Whatever he is guilty of, he is now facing God's judgment for it. Gamal Sabri is the one who set off the dynamite that blew the bow off the *Princess Mary* and sank it, and all who were on board, to the bottom of the Thames."

Brancaster returned to his place.

Pryor rose to his feet, still pink-faced with anger. He paced back and forth as he spoke, recapitulating the leading testimony of the first trial, painting a picture of the devastated survivors and their grief. He mentioned only the points on which the witnesses had agreed.

Rathbone, listening intently to every word, realized that what he was actually doing was reminding them of the horror of the event, moving them gently, step by step, to see themselves, their families, and friends as the victims of the nightmare it had been. It was not reason he was appealing to, it was their terror and grief, and he did it well.

By the time Brancaster stood up again, Rathbone could feel the fear in the courtroom like thunder in the air.

Brancaster called his first witness. No matter how much it played into Pryor's hands, he was forced to establish the facts of the case, and that included details about the explosion and the sinking itself. He kept it as technical as possible. Rathbone had warned him that if he did that, he might seem cold, even unsympathetic to the victims, as if this were all an exercise in law, not the stories of the awful deaths of nearly two hundred people.

Now he folded a blank piece of paper, and passed it forward.

Pryor saw him. He rose to his feet.

"My lord! I see that we have in court a very distinguished visitor, Sir Oliver Rathbone, who has just passed a note to my learned friend. I regret having to remind the court of the tragic and rather grubby facts, but Sir Oliver is no longer permitted to practice law. I believe Mr. Brancaster defended him at his own trial here, and cannot therefore be ignorant of that fact."

There was an instant, total silence.

As one man, the jury turned to stare at Rathbone, who felt as if he were a butterfly pinned to a board.

It was Brancaster who spoke, even before Antrobus could intervene.

"My lord, Mr. Pryor is within his rights, of course, but I believe he has exceeded even his own boundaries of good taste. The piece of paper he refers to is blank." He held it up, turning it over so they could all see both sides of it. Brancaster offered it to the usher. "If you wish to examine it, my lord?"

"No, thank you," Antrobus declined. "But perhaps you would tell us the purpose of such a note?"

Brancaster smiled self-deprecatingly. "I imagine, my lord, it is to tell me that my remarks have no substance, which I regret is true. Sir Oliver has from time to time warned me about giving the court more technical detail than it requires, and failing to give them the emotional side of things, which my learned friend Mr. Pryor is so skilled in doing."

"Indeed," Antrobus said with a slight upward curve of his lips. "It is good advice, Mr. Brancaster."

"Thank you, my lord. If I may continue?"

"Please do."

Brancaster resumed, this time being sure to speak of the fear that saturated the night of the sinking and to talk about people's wonderful eagerness to help catch the perpetrator—which perhaps led some of them to be less than accurate, and understandably so. He was detailed but sympathetic. It was a fine performance.

Nevertheless, Pryor was on his feet after the luncheon adjournment. In covering the evidence yet again, he managed to refer to the note that Rathbone had slipped to Brancaster—not for what was in it, but for the necessity of passing it at all.

"It seems my learned friend has become a pupil of Sir Oliver, or should I say a puppet? Sir Oliver is accepting his banishment from the courts with an ill grace."

Rathbone felt a chill as if he had been robbed of some necessary garment. There was a cruelty in Pryor he had not foreseen. Was it a taste of how bitter this battle would become?

Antrobus thought for a moment or two, and the look on his face could have been irritation or distaste.

Most of the jurors seemed to be staring at Rathbone as if they expected him to defend himself, not understanding what was going on and seeing him painted as some kind of villain.

Brancaster was obviously taken by surprise.

It was Antrobus who spoke. "Mr. Pryor, as you are well aware, grace of manner or judgment is not a requirement in court. Were it necessary, you would not find yourself here either. Sir Oliver may attend the court, and listen, as may anyone else who does not interrupt the proceedings."

"Thank you, my lord," Brancaster said. He hesitated a moment, then took a deep breath, and called his next witness.

This time Pryor did not interrupt him.

Brancaster had a slightly different list of witnesses from those at Beshara's trial, as he had indicated in his opening address. He did not call Monk regarding his witness of the actual explosion and the long night of work afterward; he chose Orme instead, as Rathbone had suggested. Orme was a quiet man, born and bred on the river. He spoke with a soft voice and with the local accent. His anger and his distress found no words, bringing barely a change in the dignity with which he answered Brancaster's questions. Rathbone had known that, to the jurors, who were unfamiliar with the working life of the river, this would be more authentic than if the testimony had been expressed in Monk's more educated accent, or with his confidence and his rank behind it.

It was the following morning before he drew from Orme an account of how the case was taken from them and given to the Metropolitan Police, under Lydiate.

"Do you remember that, Mr. Orme?"

"'Course I do." Orme said it quietly, but there was a darkness in his voice, a strain anyone could hear.

"Do you know why that was?" Brancaster asked.

Pryor rose to his feet. "Objection, my lord. Mr. Orme, for all his worthiness, is not privy to the command decisions of the senior police officers in charge of—"

"I apologize, my lord," Brancaster said with spurious contrition. "Mr. Orme, may I put that a different way? Were you informed of the reason for this decision?"

"No, sir," Orme replied. "Didn't see a reason for it, myself."

"And then the case was given back to you?" Brancaster asked. "After Habib Beshara had been tried, found guilty, sentenced, and then reprieved, that is?"

Orme's face was a study of disgust. "'Cos by that time it were a first-class mess no one wanted to tangle with," he said heavily.

There was a murmur of sympathy around the gallery and several jurors clearly felt the same.

Brancaster proceeded to draw from Orme an account of the evidence he and Monk had gained from witnesses that clearly exonerated Beshara from having placed the dynamite on the *Princess Mary*, or having been on board the boat himself.

Pryor appeared to consider questioning Orme, and then decided against it.

Throughout the rest of that day, and the next, Brancaster questioned more witnesses, always careful to stick to material facts. Where an eyewitness observation was unavoidable, he had at least two separate people speak.

Pryor attempted to discredit them, but after the third time he appreciated that he was losing more than he gained. The jury might not remember the detail, but they would not forget that he had lost the point.

By the fourth day a picture had been created of a carefully planned crime involving at least two people, more probably three. It was supported by interlaced facts, details that did not depend upon anyone remembering a face or a walk, exact words or the clothes a person was wearing. Orme had described the boat he and Monk had seen on the night of the sinking. The ferryman, still with a splint on his broken forearm, described exactly the same boat, and his glimpse of the seahorse emblem. Pryor tried to shake his testimony, but he could not.

Hooper was called. He told briefly and powerfully how he had seen the boat on the Isle of Dogs, and found Sabri and arrested him. Witnesses were produced who could connect Sabri to the boat, not on one occasion but a score. Pryor failed to discredit Hooper at all.

Brancaster was careful not to suggest Beshara was a good man, or innocent of any involvement in the sinking, only that he had not been placed on or near the *Princess Mary* himself, and Sabri had.

The court was adjourned for the weekend.

"Not a completely unassailable case," Rathbone said as he and Brancaster walked out of the Old Bailey and down the shallow steps to the noise and bustle of the street.

"I know," Brancaster admitted, turning to go down toward Ludgate Hill. He fitted his step automatically to Rathbone's. "It could be enough for any other case, but not this. They'll still take reasonable doubt—it's easier. Nobody wants to think the justice system is so fragile we could have hanged the wrong man for this. We were all so sure."

"It's not only a matter of not hanging the wrong one," Rathbone argued. "It's about hanging the right one. Did you see Camborne in court today?"

Brancaster drew in a sharp breath. "No, I didn't. Of course he'll fight pretty hard not to have Beshara vindicated." They reached the corner and turned into Ludgate Hill, the sun at their backs. The traffic was heavy in the late afternoon. It was Friday. There was a weariness in the air.

Rathbone debated with himself whether to raise the subject that was clamoring in his mind. Was it a weakness to mention it now, or cowardly not to? It would have to come, if not today, then on Monday.

"And York," he added. "He won't want to be effectively reversed."

Brancaster shot a sideways glance at him.

Rathbone wondered how much he had guessed, or deduced, about his feelings for York's wife. Was he as transparent as he felt?

They walked fifty feet without speaking.

"They've all got reasons," Brancaster said at last. "Pride, fear, money, advancement, something."

"Protecting somebody," Rathbone added.

Brancaster kept step with him.

"So Sabri put the dynamite in the *Princess Mary*, and he detonated it and then leaped over in time to escape the explosion. Do you think he did it to protect somebody?"

"It's possible. And we still don't know who picked him up," Rathbone added. "That wasn't left to chance."

"That's the whole issue, isn't it?" Brancaster sighed. "Who else was part of it at the time, and—even worse—who else covered it up afterward?"

"I know," Rathbone said quietly. They were now on a side street and there was no clatter of traffic to drown their voices.

"The other thing that is troublesome," Brancaster went on, "is that we still have no motive. Sheer hatred of Britain can be powerful, but why this particular reaction, and why now? If the jury is going to believe me, then I need to show a reason they can understand."

"Not only that," Rathbone warned him. "You need to have something that speaks to ordinary human passion, not something financial or to do with trade routes and shipping, if that's what it turns out to be. And I would advise you very seriously not to get into a political train of thought that may end by painting Britain in general as being greedy, exploitative, and destructive of other people's lives and homes, in order to increase our own profits. It may well be true, but your jury will not wish to accept it." He glanced sideways at Brancaster as they crossed the road. "You can force them to accept it, if the weight of your evidence is heavy enough, but it will be against their hearts, and they'll make you pay for it. No one wants their dreams broken. Patriotism is a very powerful force. God only knows how many people, what families down the ages, have given their lives for their country. Don't try telling them now that they did it for an unworthy cause."

Brancaster stopped, his face bleak, mouth pulled tight. He stared at Rathbone. "Why the hell did Sabri do it? Am I going to end up with nothing better than a plea of insanity? Play to their belief in a foreigner having a different and baser morality than ours? That's not only untrue, it's . . ." He struggled for a word. "Degrading myself. I'm not sure I'm prepared to do that, even for a conviction."

Rathbone looked back at him. "And what about our justice system that latched on to Habib Beshara because he's an unpleasant character, and was prepared to twist and distort, overlook or misrepresent the facts, a detail here, a detail there, to convict him? Hang him and get the whole thing out of the way? Are you prepared to take off the garments clothing our system's less public parts, and expose that for what it is?"

"How the devil else can I put this right?" Brancaster asked with a note of desperation in his voice.

"I don't know," Rathbone said frankly.

THE TRIAL RESUMED ON Monday morning. Brancaster knew that if he did not discredit the conviction of Beshara he had no chance of having Sabri found guilty in his place. He and Rathbone had debated the wisdom of a preemptive strike. Would it seem unnecessarily spiteful? Might it even betray a sense of vulnerability in their own arguments to defend them before they were attacked?

Rathbone looked across at the table where Pryor sat waiting, listening, his pencil ready to take notes. There was a keen doggedness in his face. His heavy jaw was clenched so the muscles showed very slightly in the slant of the light from the windows.

Brancaster called a young policeman by the name of Rivers, who gave an account of his search for witnesses, when the case had been given to Lydiate's men. He seemed both serious and candid. He was very polite.

Brancaster treated him gently.

Rathbone sat fidgeting, aware that it was a mass of detail, and inevitably boring. He saw the attention of the jury begin to wander.

Pryor yawned and hunched his shoulders, then relaxed them.

It was more than time that Brancaster elicited something of value. Much longer and it would fall on deaf ears, regardless of its relevance.

"Can you describe this particular witness, Sergeant Rivers?" Brancaster asked pleasantly.

Pryor had had enough. "My lord, how can it possibly matter what the witness looked like? I began to fear that Mr. Brancaster is stretching this out to impossible lengths in the hope of boring us to death!"

Antrobus looked inquiringly at Brancaster.

"Not at all, my lord," Brancaster said respectfully. "Were Mr. Pryor to die, we should have to begin all over again, and I, for one, have no wish to do that."

There was a titter of amusement around the gallery.

"Nor I," Antrobus agreed. "I doubt I should survive that myself. Perhaps you will be good enough to reach your point, on the assumption that you have one?"

"Yes, my lord," Brancaster said obediently. "You were going to describe the witness for us, Sergeant Rivers."

Rivers looked puzzled. "He was very ordinary, sir. A trifle portly around the middle. A sort of a . . . blunt kind of face."

"Was he dark or fair?" Brancaster asked.

"I . . . don't recall. Medium. Sort of brownish, I think."

Pryor waved his arms. "My lord!"

Brancaster ignored him. "And what sort of age?"

"Between thirty-five and fifty," Rivers replied.

"Clean-shaven, or bearded?" Brancaster persisted.

"I don't recall," Rivers said hotly. "But he was a good witness, clean and well-spoken."

Pryor stiffened.

Brancaster smiled. "But you, a trained police officer, who stood opposite him in the daylight, cannot recall anything specific about him, not the color of his hair, his age except within fifteen years, or whether he was clean-shaven or had a mustache!"

Now he had the jury's total attention.

"I was trying to judge his honesty, not remember his appearance!" Rivers protested.

"Of course," Brancaster agreed. "I imagine your witness was minding his own business rather than trying to recall the face of the man he saw boarding the *Princess Mary*." He smiled. "He, too, was an honest man, doing his best to help after an appalling act. And, just like you, Sergeant Rivers, his memory is fuzzy. He does not know the details, because at the time they did not matter. Thank you. That is all I have for you."

Pryor hesitated, briefly scanning the jurors' faces. Then he gave a slight, dismissive wave of his hand and declined to pursue the issue.

Brancaster called a lighterman who worked strings of barges frequently passing the places of main concern on the last voyage of the *Princess Mary*. His name was Spiller. He was grizzle-headed and strong, and he climbed the steps up to the witness box with some grace. He looked like a man who was used to keeping his balance on a moving deck.

Brancaster asked him about his job, the places it took him on the length of the river, and the sort of sights he was accustomed to pass every day. This time the jury was not bored, and Pryor paid attention to each question and answer.

Brancaster had to be more careful. Rathbone knew that all he expected was to show that Spiller was experienced, observant, and familiar with all the workings of the river and its people. He had noticed few of the things the witnesses against Beshara claimed to have seen. Those he had seen he said happened almost every day, and he attached no significance to them.

"Did you explain this to the police when they asked you?" Brancaster said curiously.

"They didn't ask me," Spiller replied. There was a gleam of both humor and contempt in his eyes.

Rathbone saw that this remark was not lost on the jury.

"But you were there?" Brancaster said, investing his tone with confusion.

"'Course I was," Spiller answered. "I suppose the police had what they needed already."

"But your answer would have changed their understanding of what they were told," Brancaster pointed out.

Pryor rose to his feet, burning for the chance to attack.

"My lord, Mr. Brancaster cannot know why the police did not ask Mr. Spiller, or what difference his answer might have made, if any at all. He is deliberately misleading the court."

"Ah, Mr. Pryor," Antrobus said with no inflexion in his voice, "I am glad you are awake." He turned to Brancaster. "You know better than that. You may give us facts, sir, and allow the jury to draw their own conclusion as to their importance or their meaning. Please do not oblige me to tell you that again."

"No, my lord," Brancaster apologized. "I'm sorry." Then he turned back to the witness stand. "Mr. Spiller, when the case was handed back to the Thames River Police, did anyone approach you then?"

"Yes, sir, Mr. Hooper. I told him what I told you."

"Thank you." Brancaster turned to Pryor.

Pryor rose and immediately attacked Spiller, even as he was walking across the open area toward the witness stand.

"You are known to the River Police?" he asked, his voice derisive.

"'Course I am," Spiller replied, but his body stiffened. "I work the river. It's their job to know everyone on it."

"This is not a time for humor, Mr. Spiller," Pryor snapped. " 'Known to the police' is not a phrase meaning 'acquainted with them socially.' You have been a police informer on criminal matters, haven't you?" He did not wait for Spiller to answer. "And one wonders how many criminal matters you did not inform them of!"

"No, I haven't!" Spiller said vehemently.

"Indeed? So you know of criminal matters and did not inform the police?"

Spiller was confused. "Yes . . ."

"Yes or no?" Pryor demanded. "Make up your mind, sir!"

Brancaster shot to his feet. "My lord! Every decent citizen reports criminal offences to the police. My learned friend is making it sound as if the witness is lying when the question is unclear. I myself no longer know what he means. There is a world of difference between a police informer and a citizen who reports a crime, and he is deliberately obscuring it."

Pryor turned back to Spiller. "Perhaps you can explain yourself so we can all understand?" he challenged him.

"Only a fool works the river and don't keep on the right side of the police," Spiller replied, his face tight and angry.

"My conclusion exactly," Pryor said with a sneer. "And was helping them get their revenge on the Metropolitan Police for taking their case from them part of 'keeping on the right side,' Mr. Spiller?" He held up his hand as if to silence Brancaster, and even prevent Spiller replying. "I withdraw the question. I don't wish to confuse you any further." It was an insult, an implication that Spiller was lacking intelligence.

Spiller flushed with humiliation, but he did not speak.

The afternoon and the following day continued in the same vein. Brancaster called another ferryman who had been working the night of the explosion. He had not been questioned by Lydiate's men either. He was a good witness, but Pryor attacked him also, and ended by leaving the man angry, which destroyed his value with at least some of the jurors.

Rathbone could see it, and feel the advantage of Brancaster's argument slipping away. Pryor had not disproved any facts, but he had managed to make it seem as if the new evidence was born of troublemaking, invented by men with their own grudges to exercise.

"You live and work on the river, don't you, Mr. Barker?" he said to the last witness Brancaster called.

"Yes, sir," Barker answered.

"And to do that successfully, as you told us, you know the River Police and stay in their good books?"

"Yes, sir. It's natural."

"Of course it is. I'm sure the gentlemen of the jury will well understand the need to have the favor of the police, their help, from time to time, even their protection. Life on the water can be dangerous. As we know only too tragically, a man who falls into the Thames will be lucky to come out alive. It's deep, its tides can be swift and erratic, its mud can hold a man fast. Its waters are enough to poison you, even if you can swim. And that does not take into account the thieves and pirates who infest the worse parts of it, the rotting slums, the wrecks, the marshes, places like Jacob's Island. Of course you need the River Police as your friends. They are hard, skilled, and brave men, suited to their jobs. I imagine the weak don't even survive! Thank you, Mr. Barker."

Rathbone looked at the jury's faces. He saw the fear in them, the understanding of all that Pryor implied without ever crossing the line of propriety so Brancaster could interrupt him and break the spell.

Rathbone stood up slowly as the court was adjourned. He found he was stiff, as though he had been sitting uncomfortably for a long time and he realized his body was aching from clenched muscles, and the inner effort to hold onto a victory that was sliding out of his grip.

He glanced across at Pryor, and knew with bitter certainty that it was going to get worse.

CHAPTER

18

Hester was in court the following day when Pryor began his defense of Gamal Sabri. The courtroom was respectfully silent. The jurors were wide awake and intensely interested. From her place in the gallery, Hester could see that many of them had now lost all certainty as to who was lying, mistaken, or driven by motives one could only guess at. Looking at them, studying their faces, she could see that this was not a situation that sat well with them. There were unanswered questions regarding the first trial. How could so many mistakes have been made, and then compounded? It was anxiety she saw, and rising fear. They glanced at one another and then away again hastily. They moved minutely as if unable to find a comfortable position.

Hester had deliberately chosen a place from where she could see the accused man, though it was not a good view. She had to twist round and stare upward at the dock, which was at a considerable height above the main courtroom floor. She saw a dark, somber man with a narrow face. He was clean-shaven and smartly dressed. From her sideways view it seemed as if his eyes moved along the faces of the jurors, studying them, as she had been doing.

Pryor stood up and also looked at the jury. He had been handsome in his youth, and now was slightly corpulent, but his white wig became him and he was immaculately dressed. His voice was excellent, an instrument to be played with skill.

"Gentlemen," he began gravely. "You are faced with some terrible decisions, and I am going to add to them. I am going to confirm to you just how muddled this whole case really is, how many mistakes have been made by men who may well have believed passionately that they were right—when in truth, they were not. So much you may already have gathered. I regret that not all errors were innocently made. There are rage, fear, self-preservation, and revenge, too.

"No one here will suggest for an instant that the sinking of the *Princess Mary* was not a crime, in fact an atrocity the like of which we have not seen within our lifetime. Such horror can frighten people, warp judgment, and tear at the emotions until wisdom is lost. Men may think they are seeking justice, when in truth it is vengeance they want.

"Is that understandable? Of course it is. It is only human to wish to see such brutal violence punished. Is it right? No, it is not. It is a blind reaction, born of pity and outrage: two very human passions that we all feel—indeed, we need them. It is part of our humanity that we should be racked with horror when such a nightmare occurs. What would you think of a man who felt no pity for the maimed and the drowning? You would judge him less than human!

"What would you think of a society that was not outraged by such an act of barbarity? You would not want to own yourselves part of it.

"Is it justice?"

He gave a very slight shrug: a small gesture of his hands. "No. Justice requires understanding, and above all it requires truth. Listen to the case I will present to you, and judge the truth. That is what you are sworn to do, and that is what people require of you. It is in your hands alone. You speak for all of us: the survivors, the bereaved, all men and women who hope for justice in the future."

Watching the jury, Hester saw the interest sharpen in their faces, the attitude of their bodies alter. They were leaning forward a little, keen, both frightened and proud to have such a burden placed upon them.

She glanced up at Sabri and saw on his face what might have been a smile. Pryor had begun well. Who was paying him? He would be very expensive indeed. Unless, of course, he had some interest of his own in winning. Reputation? Old favor to repay, or new ones to earn? That might be worth someone's investigation. Would Brancaster be able to find out? She must ask him. Or Oliver might know more.

Pryor called his first witness. It was John Lydiate. He looked quiet and grave as he mounted the steps to the witness stand. There was apprehension in his face, and he gripped the rail so tightly the pale ridges of bone in his knuckles shone white. He swore to his name and occupation as commissioner of the Metropolitan Police. He promised to tell the truth, and the whole truth, and then faced Pryor as he would an execution squad.

Hester felt profoundly sorry for him. He was about to have his most public failure examined in detail in front of the court. The fact that he must have expected it would be no comfort at all.

"Sir John," Pryor began courteously, "like all of us in London, possibly in all of England, you were aware of the atrocity against the *Princess Mary* and her crew and passengers right from the morning after the event. But since it occurred on the river, the investigation fell first to the Thames River Police to handle. When were you called to take over command of the investigation?"

"Later that day," Lydiate replied, his voice rasping a little as though his mouth were dry.

"By whom?" Pryor asked.

"Lord Ossett."

"Who had command of it up to that point?"

"Commander William Monk, of the Thames River Police."

"I see. And did he yield this to you willingly? Perhaps he realized that this was beyond his power or experience?" Pryor suggested.

Lydiate hesitated. The question had been phrased so that it was impossible to answer without seeming to condemn Monk.

"Sir John?" Pryor raised his eyebrows.

"He did not ask my help." Lydiate chose his words. "The command was taken from him and given to the Metropolitan Police because of the delicacy of the situation. It was felt that the relatives of the foreign dignitaries who were killed might not appreciate the skill or experience of the River Police, and believe that we were taking the matter less seriously than we should. There was a degree of diplomacy required."

"So his command was removed from him without consultation?" Pryor concluded.

Brancaster shifted uncomfortably in his seat, but there was nothing to which he could object without making the matter worse.

Hester looked at Rathbone sitting behind Brancaster, and saw him stiffen. She wished she could see his face.

Lydiate stared at Pryor.

"I have no idea," Lydiate replied. "I was not consulted. If I had been, I would have asked for the River Police's cooperation."

"Indeed?" Pryor looked taken aback. "Would you not automatically have expected that? In view of the tragedy and horror of the event, the loss of life, I had imagined their cooperation would come as a matter of course."

Lydiate had stepped neatly into the trap prepared for him. He flushed hotly. "Commander Monk had already been into the wreck while it was still submerged, and gave us his report," he said tartly. "Your suggestion that he in any way failed to cooperate is misinformed, sir, and does you no credit."

There was a rustle in the gallery, and one or two jurors nodded.

"Very loyal of you," Pryor said with approval, as if he had foreseen the reply. "Did you consult Mr. Monk again after that?"

"He gave me his notes," Lydiate answered. "They were sufficiently clear that contacting him again was unnecessary."

Pryor smiled, but his lips were tight across his teeth. "Loyal again. Or, on the other hand, a very gracious way of saying that you assumed complete command yourself and consulted no one else."

Hester saw that Brancaster was scribbling notes to himself. She had expected Pryor to attack Monk, but she still seethed with anger at the way he did it.

"It is not!" Lydiate said sharply. "I consulted many other people, experts in several fields. Your suggestion is not only unfair, sir, it is incompetent."

There was a rustle of movement in the gallery, an awakening air of curiosity. The tone had become outright combative.

Hester saw the judge look from Pryor to Lydiate, and back again. Was that a flicker of humor in his face? She looked up momentarily at Sabri and saw a smile of satisfaction cross his lips and then vanish.

Pryor swallowed his temper with some difficulty.

"Did these 'other people' that you say you consulted include members of the Thames River Police?"

"Of course. The *Princess Mary* was sunk in the river," Lydiate responded.

There was a ripple of nervous laughter around the room but it died almost immediately.

Antrobus leaned forward. "Mr. Pryor, if you have a purpose in all this, perhaps you would be good enough to reach it? Entertaining as it is, I do not feel this is the right setting for verbal wit, or the scoring of irrelevant points. We are all perfectly aware that the case was taken from the River Police and given to the Metropolitan Police. Then, after the trial and conviction of Mr. Habib Beshara, Commander Monk found evidence that threw another light on the subject, and was given the case back again. I imagine Mr. Brancaster will raise no objection to us all accepting that to be true?"

Brancaster rose to his feet.

"Thank you, my lord. That is indeed so."

Pryor flushed red, but he had no grounds to object, other than that he had been made to look as if he were using the trial as a grandstand for his own skills, rather than a solemn search for justice.

He returned to questioning John Lydiate, but Hester knew that he would neither forgive nor forget the incident. He was calling Monk to the stand after Lydiate, and she found herself knotted up in tension in anticipation of it.

"Sir John," Pryor began, walking a little farther out into the open space of the courtroom, as if it were an arena, and he a gladiator facing barbarians, "many of us attended the trial of Habib Beshara, and we are aware of the evidence against him. Much of it rested on eyewitness accounts. Did you consider it valid at the time?"

There was only one possible answer. To deny it would condemn his own skills and even his honesty.

"I did. I know since—"

"Thank you," Pryor cut him off, holding up his hand as if to stop traffic. "Did you believe the lawyers and the judge in the court that tried Beshara to be honest men, and skilled in the law?"

"Of course—" Lydiate made as if to continue.

"Of course," Pryor interrupted him. "If not, you would have said so at the time. Did you yourself believe Beshara to be guilty?"

"Yes." Lydiate's face was also flushed. "If not, then I would not have charged him."

Pryor bit his lip. "Regardless of the newspapers crying out for action, and the pressure from the government, particularly the ministers most closely involved?"

"Of course!" Lydiate's answer was stiff, even angry.

"Of course," Pryor repeated in a tone so clear as to be almost mimicking. "I can take you through your evidence point by point, if the court believes it necessary—"

"No, thank you, my lord," Brancaster interrupted.

"Just so," Pryor nodded, and then turned back to Lydiate. "It was eyewitness testimony, you said, and less reliable than you had previously believed?"

"Yes."

"And what kind of evidence was it that Mr. Monk found, and upon which we are now prosecuting Gamal Sabri?" Pryor asked gently.

Lydiate's face flushed so red it was hot even to look at.

Hester felt for him. He had been maneuvered into an impossible situation. Even had he seen it coming, he had no room to evade it.

"Eyewitness," he said, his voice grating. "But of many people . . ."

Pryor's eyebrows rose. "Was not Habib Beshara also seen by many people? Did I misunderstand?"

Lydiate must see his way was blocked in all directions. If he claimed they were expert, unbiased, not personally involved, not bereaved, then he implied that the victims were somehow less worthy or less honest. If he mentioned the physical evidence of the seahorse on the stern of the boat that both rescued the jumper from the *Princess Mary*, and tried to plow down, and thus kill, Monk and the ferryman, he seemed to be making excuses, and perhaps sabotaging Brancaster's return cross-examination. He stood silent and miserable.

Up in the dock, Sabri leaned forward a fraction, just a tiny movement, but to Hester it betrayed eagerness, even satisfaction.

"Did I misunderstand, sir?" Pryor repeated insistently.

Lydiate lifted his chin and stared back. "If you think that Beshara was in the *Princess Mary* just before it blew up, and that Gamal Sabri is innocent in this atrocity, then yes, I believe you did," Lydiate replied. "At least I hope you did. I would prefer not to believe that you are knowingly trying to free the man who murdered almost two hundred people."

There was an instant's absolute silence, and then a rush of sound from the gallery as Pryor swung around to the judge.

"My lord!"

His voice was drowned.

Antrobus spoke above the roar. "I will have order! If there is not order restored immediately I will clear the court. You will not attend the rest of this trial! Is that understood?"

The gallery held its peace, angry, rumbling, but too fascinated to risk being banished.

Pryor was shaking with fury, either real or very well assumed. "My lord, this is outrageous!" he said furiously. "Sir John knows better than to make such an—an appalling breach of all etiquette and . . ."

"Yes, yes, I know," Antrobus agreed. "But you did rather open the door for him, Mr. Pryor, by asking if you had misunderstood. Perhaps you might find a more fortunate question for him? Unless, of course, you have no more to say?" A faint flicker of hope crossed his face, heavily laced with amusement.

Hester found herself liking Antrobus. He reminded her of Henry Rathbone.

"I do not wish to further embarrass him," Pryor said a little waspishly. "We cannot afford to have our police and judicial authorities held in less than the highest respect. Justice and the rule of law that all men may equally rely on is the cornerstone of our civilization." He turned to Brancaster, frowning heavily. "Your witness."

Brancaster rose to his feet. "Thank you," he said politely. "May I echo your sentiment? We must both be right, and be seen to be right." He looked at the jury, and then briefly at the crowded gallery where men and women were sitting so tightly packed many seemed barely able to move.

"We all are fallible," Brancaster observed. "Sometimes we make mistakes, even though we believe we have been meticulously careful. When emotions are deep and grief is numbing us, fear waits in the darkness, then—"

Pryor rose to his feet. "My lord, my learned friend seems to have the misimpression that I have concluded my case for the defense, whereas in truth I have barely begun! If—"

Antrobus nodded. "Mr. Brancaster, we are all aware that you are attempting to show that there has been a previous error that you are now able to correct. You do not need to explain that again. Please allow Mr. Pryor to do his best in assuring us that we were, in fact, correct the first time. If he has concluded his questions for Sir John Lydiate, then you may cross-examine him . . . without speeches, if you please."

Pryor sat down, his dislike for Antrobus sour in his expression.

"I apologize, my lord," Brancaster said humbly.

Hester wished she could tell him to be careful. Antrobus might have a degree of tolerance toward him, but if he strained it, the result would come back on him very harshly. Had Rathbone not warned him of that?

Brancaster turned to Lydiate. A complete hush fell over the courtroom again.

"If I understand you correctly, Commissioner, you were given the case urgently, for political or diplomatic reasons. You did not request it?"

"That is correct," Lydiate agreed.

"You believed you had the guilty man when you charged Habib Beshara?"

Again Lydiate agreed.

"Beshara was tried and convicted. Then some time later, further evidence emerged that brought that verdict into question, at which point the case was reopened and placed with the Thames River Police."

"Yes."

"With whom you cooperated fully?"

"Of course."

Hester was sitting forward, her hands clenched in her lap. Please heaven, Brancaster would have the sense to stop now! Don't open the door for Pryor! Rathbone must be aching to pull on his coattails and warn him!

Brancaster smiled charmingly. It lit his dark face.

"Thank you, Sir John."

A rustle of relief sighed through the whole room.

Hester relaxed and found herself smiling widely.

Her relief did not last long. Immediately after the luncheon adjournment, Pryor called his next witness—William Monk of the Thames River Police.

Hester watched as Monk walked across the open space of the court and climbed the steps to the witness stand. He was sworn in, and faced Pryor. It was immediately obvious to everyone that there was considerable hostility between them.

Pryor was punctiliously polite.

"Commander Monk, you were on the river in a small boat on the night of the sinking of the *Princess Mary*. In fact I believe you saw the whole tragedy, right from the explosion to rescuing the last of the survivors from the water. Is that correct?"

"Yes, it is. And I returned the next—"

"Thank you," Pryor cut him off. "I did not ask that. We will please take events in the order in which they occurred."

Anger flushed up Monk's face, but he did not respond.

"You saw the explosion, which tore the ship apart and sank it within four minutes?" Pryor continued.

"I saw it, yes," Monk agreed between his teeth. "I cannot swear as to the time she took to sink."

"It was approximately four minutes," Pryor assured him.

Brancaster rose to his feet.

"Yes, yes," Antrobus agreed. "If the time is important, Mr. Pryor, then you had better establish it other than through Mr. Monk."

Pryor was annoyed. "It was extremely fast, was it not?" he said to Monk.

"Yes," Monk accepted.

"And yet you had time to notice a man leaping from the deck into the water, and being rescued by someone on a boat with a distinctive emblem on the stern?" His tone was heavily laced with disbelief. "You were not momentarily blinded by the flash? You were not frozen in horror at the devastation? You did not leap to the oars to begin the rescue of the drowning men and women in the water around you?" There was not only incredulity now but also disgust in his voice.

"It was a pleasure boat," Monk said quietly, staring at Pryor as if there were no one else in the room. "All the lights were on. They were having a party. The man leaped off the deck into the water before the explosion, not after it. To jump afterward wouldn't have done much good. That was the point. It was in the flash of the explosion moments later that I saw him picked up by the boat with the seahorse on the stern."

"Which you conveniently remembered several days later, even weeks," Pryor said sarcastically.

"Inconveniently," Monk corrected him. "The thing nearly killed me when it rammed the ferry I was in. Which I believe you know from the poor ferryman who was injured in the event. But are you not ahead of yourself? You told me to keep it in the order in which things occurred!"

Pryor's face reddened with anger. He glanced up at Antrobus, and saw the amusement flash in his eyes, before he leaned forward and addressed Monk.

"Your observation is out of order, Commander, even if it is correct. You had best allow Mr. Pryor to proceed in whatever order he wishes, or we shall be here for even longer than is necessary."

"Yes, my lord," Monk said meekly.

Pryor's face was tight with arrogance.

"The case was given back to you after you so fortuitously discovered the witness, the eyewitness, whose testimony made you question the conviction of Habib Beshara, is that right?" he asked.

Monk hesitated, and decided not to argue.

"Yes."

"The case was restored to you?" Pryor emphasized.

"The police deal with whatever cases arise," Monk answered him. "We do not own them."

"You are very sensitive about it, Mr. Monk," Pryor challenged him.

Monk glared at him. "Nearly two hundred people drowned, sir. It is not something about which I can be indifferent!"

There was a murmur of approval around the gallery. Several of the jurors nodded and turned to one another.

Pryor leaped on the answer. "Far from it! You have a history of very personal involvement with some of your cases in the past. So much so that you have been dismissed from the Metropolitan Police force, is that not true?"

Brancaster was instantly on his feet. "My lord! That is totally improper and Mr. Pryor knows it! Mr. Monk left the Metropolitan Police of his own accord, many years ago, and the matter should be either addressed properly, or omitted altogether. This is innuendo and an attempt at slander. If that is the best that the defense can do, it is as good as an admission of guilt!"

Rathbone leaned forward, but he could not attract Brancaster's attention.

Pryor faced Antrobus. "My lord, Sir John Lydiate came to his conclusion regarding this case, Commander Monk to another, quite different conclusion. Surely the jury is entitled to question the reputations of each of these men so as to judge which one they will believe."

"Have you considered questioning the evidence?" Brancaster shot back. "The case was given back to Commander Monk once it was thoroughly compromised. We all know that! The only way to find the truth is to look at it issue by issue. If my learned friend would like to tear apart the reputation of everyone involved in it, he may find himself in very much deeper water than he can manage!"

"We have more than enough people drowned in this already," Antrobus said with distaste. "Mr. Pryor, is it really your intention to open the door to questioning the characters and the motives of all the men concerned in this unhappy business?"

That was the last thing Pryor wished, and he was obliged to withdraw, angry and longing to have his revenge.

Hester wondered more urgently why Pryor seemed to care so much about this case. Watching him, hearing the emotion in his voice, she was convinced he fully intended to win. Even looking up at Sabri now and then, she had the same powerful feeling that he also expected Pryor to win. There was anger in his expression, contempt, jubilation when Pryor won a point, but very little fear.

The question and answer, attack and evasion continued all afternoon and into the next day, first with Monk, and then with other witnesses.

Pryor was willing, reluctantly, to grant that there had been errors of identification, but insisted they were honestly made. Ordinary, decent people were shattered and eager to identify those guilty.

"Of course they are not infallible," he said passionately. "Which of us would be, in such circumstances? Please God, we will never have to find out. Do I have to paint the scene for you again?" He swung round from the jury to the gallery, imploring their comprehension, doing all he could to force them back into remembering all they had heard and imagined. He knew he dared not tell the story another time. He would lose them.

"They are good men," he insisted. "Seeking not only some form of justice, but—perhaps even more importantly—to catch those who were responsible for this monstrous evil, and see that they can never do such a thing again." Now he spoke specifically to the jury. "Would you not do the same? And could you swear that you would make no errors?"

Hester watched the jurors' faces, and was overtaken with the cold fear that Pryor would win.

They needed more time. Could Rathbone think of some way in which Brancaster could drag out his cross-questioning of Pryor's witnesses? At the very worst, if Pryor saw what he was doing, he would simply declare his case closed, and then there would be nothing anyone could do. The jury would deliberate, and that would be the end.

What would they conclude, as it stood now? Just what Pryor had implied: Good men had been fallible, overzealous, but not corrupt at heart. They had used desperate means, at times incorrect, but in order to convict the right man of a hideous crime. If Sabri were guilty as well, then they should punish him too. Mistakes have been made, but the right and just end had been achieved.

The law was safe after all.

And Pryor would be rewarded for that for the rest of his life. The sheen of victory was already in his face.

Brancaster had still established no motive for Sabri, just as Camborne had not for Beshara. The suggestion of revenge—nonspecific, unsubstantiated—was not enough this time around.

In defending Sabri, Pryor was also defending England, and the justice they believed had already been dispensed. How did you tell people something they did not want to know? What did you need to say to have them question the bedrock on which their beliefs of themselves were built?

Why the *Princess Mary*? And—possibly even more importantly—why that night?

The next time there was a pause, Hester stood up and inched her way out of the row of seats where she had been. There was a sigh of relief as people eased a little, each taking a fraction more room, straightening a skirt.

As soon as she was in the hallway, she walked toward the entrance and out into the street. Her mind was already busy with the idea Monk had mentioned briefly the night the ferry was rammed and he so nearly drowned: the possibility that the whole ship had been sunk to be certain of killing one specific person.

Why would anyone do that? It was dangerous and terrible. There would be no excusing it. The reason must have been equally powerful. Especially if no one knew who had done it or why.

Where was the passenger list that Monk had obtained? He must have looked at it, stretched all the possible connections. But what had he been looking for? There had been plenty of wealthy people celebrating some private event, or simply having a highly enjoyable evening with friends, good food, and good wine.

Who should she ask?

She stepped to the curb and hailed the next hansom. She gave the driver the address of the Wapping Police Station. Orme would have the list, and he knew the situation was desperate.

CHAPTER

19

Hester found Orme very willing to show her the guest list for the party on the *Princess Mary*, and also the rest of the passenger manifest. It had been a long trip, all the way from Westminster Bridge to Gravesend and back again; so all places had been reserved, and names written down.

A great deal of work had already been done to identify most of the passengers and eliminate them from suspicion.

"What are you looking for, ma'am, exactly?" Orme asked as they sat together in Monk's office. Monk was still in court, as she had known he would be, so at least for the moment, they were uninterrupted.

"I'm not sure," she admitted. "I think it is possible that the *Princess Mary* was sunk not to have some kind of revenge, or create a political horror, but to kill one person . . ."

Orme could not conceal the look of disbelief on his face. "Who'd do a thing like that?" he asked, shaking his head.

"I don't know. It's just an idea William had, after he was hit by Sabri's boat when he was on the ferry. It's possible, isn't it?"

"I suppose it is," Orme agreed reluctantly. "But how would we find such a person? It could be anybody."

She had been thinking about it on the omnibus while coming here.

"If you needed to get rid of someone, you would pick the best way you could to do it. One that was certain, and that did not make you a suspect. One that looked like an accident would be best, but if that were not possible, then at least one that hid your involvement in it."

He pursed his lips, but nodded agreement. "This was no accident, but I see what you mean. With near two hundred dead, we don't look for one that matters more than the others."

"Exactly. We look for a really big motive, probably political, or with a lot of money involved, fortunes made or lost."

"So how do we look for one?" he said grimly.

She had given that some thought also. "Someone who had to be killed this way because no better way was possible. And perhaps someone who had to be killed urgently, and was vulnerable right there and then."

Orme began to smile. "I see. And it needed to be certain; so the person would have been at the party below deck. That must exclude a lot of people."

"Also anyone who went as a last-minute decision," she added.

He nodded his head. "The sinking must've taken planning. That dynamite stuff isn't that easy to get hold of."

"Where did it come from?" she asked quickly.

"Stolen from a quarry twenty miles away, we reckon."

"Reckon?"

"You can't tell one lot of dynamite from another. But there isn't that much of it around."

"So we can narrow it down by taking out all the people who were not at the party below deck because they wouldn't be certain victims." She winced a little at the thought. She was doing it logically, deducing the one intended victim as if she were speaking of something quite casual, not mass and indiscriminate death.

"We must think of who was vulnerable only this way," she continued. "It was dangerous. Either Sabri was paid a lot, or else he cared about it enough to take the risk for his own reasons."

"We looked at that," Orme told her. "We couldn't find any connection between Sabri and anyone on the *Princess Mary*."

"I know," she said quietly. "I'm only doing this because if we don't find a motive I think Pryor's going to win. Sabri will get off and the verdict against Beshara will stand. And, maybe even worse, whatever corruption or incompetence there was will be covered up, and for all we know, could happen again. And the very worst of it is that most other people will know it too. And when the law is held in disrespect, we don't know what other things we trust may also fail."

Orme's wind-burned face was pale beneath the superficial color. "Then we'd better be getting on with it," he said quietly. "We're looking for a victim who couldn't be killed any other way without it being obvious who did it. In fact someone who had to be killed then and there. Maybe this was the only way the killer could eliminate his victim without casting suspicion on himself. That cuts it down a lot. Let's go through that list again."

An hour later they had reduced it to a dozen people, excluding anyone who had booked passage after the dynamite was stolen, or who would have been just as vulnerable in a less dramatic and dangerous way.

"Soldiers," Orme said, looking at her carefully. "Men on their way home on leave, celebrating with a party on the river. An' most of them were here anyway. Could've been got at other ways."

"I know. I've got six names to follow up. Thank you very much, Mr. Orme." She rose to her feet, realizing how long she had been there only when she felt the stiffness in her back. "I'll start tomorrow morning."

He stood also. "You're welcome, ma'am. If I can do anything more, please tell me."

"I will," she promised, then turned and walked out onto the dockside, and the steps to catch a ferry home.

She did not tell Monk about her intention. She arrived home late, but he did not know that, being even later himself, and Scuff was too tactful to comment. They sat talking in the parlor. She tried to sound positive as he told her of the rest of his day in court. She wanted to be encouraging, but she knew meaningless comfort was worse than none at all. In the face of what he told her, and Pryor's extraordinary confidence, her own ideas sounded foolish and she did not mention them.

Next day she began by visiting an old commanding officer she had nursed on the battlefield in the Crimea. He seemed frail now, aged before his time by pain. He was delighted to see her, pleased to recall the past, although it was filled with loss. Even the concept of that war far away on the Black Sea looked in hindsight to be purposeless. So many men had died or been maimed, health lost forever; the memories they shared were full of sadness.

She had no time to spare recalling the cold and the endless journeys with cartloads of wounded, the sound of gunfire in the distance, the makeshift field surgeries where she had worked to exhaustion. But she could not find the heart to tell him that she needed to go. Each time she drew in her breath to say it, the loneliness in his eyes stopped her from being blunt. Another memory came back to him, another face filled with courage, laughter, and pain. So many of them would be dead now it seemed like another life.

"Egypt?" he said at last, returning to the subject she had raised initially. "You should see young Kittering. Good man. On leave at the moment. Injury. Not critical, but enough to need several months to recover. He could tell you about the forces in Egypt. Served with them for a while. Lives just around the corner. See him now and then, if it's a decent day and I'm sitting outside." He smiled. "I'll give you his address. Tell him I asked after him, will you?"

She met Kittering at lunchtime, after not finding him at home and having to make several enquiries. He was walking slowly back from the local inn, limping badly and stopping every now and then to catch his breath. He was nice-looking, with a trim mustache, and square shoulders—even if they were a little lopsided right now.

"Major Kittering?" she asked, meeting his eyes.

"Yes, ma'am," he said with surprise. He was clearly embarrassed because he could not place her, and thought that he should.

"Mrs. Monk," she introduced herself. "I've just been calling on Colonel Haydon, and he mentioned your name as someone who might be able to assist me."

"Ah . . . yes. I mean to call on him myself, as soon as I'm a little more . . . mobile." It was an excuse, and he did not like making it. "Fine man."

She smiled. "He said as much of you."

"You know him . . . well? You are family, perhaps?"

"No. Before I was married I nursed, in the Crimea," she began, and saw the sudden light in his face. She judged him to be of an age when he might have been just beginning his career then. "I need your help, Major Kittering. May I walk with you?" she asked as a matter of courtesy. She had no intention whatever of accepting a refusal.

He was puzzled, but he began moving again, as if to oblige her. Actually she guessed he had no wish to stand any longer than was necessary.

"Of course. What can I do to assist you?" he asked.

He probably imagined it was something to do with nursing. She should tell him the truth quickly.

"My husband is Commander Monk of the Thames River Police," she explained. Then she went on to tell him first about Beshara, and now Gamal Sabri, and why it mattered so much that the police find the truth. When she at last finished they were sitting in the sun in his small parlor. His sister, who cared for him, had made them tea, even though it was far too early in the afternoon for it to be customary. He had introduced Hester proudly as one of Miss Nightingale's nurses. It was something Hester never boasted of, but it was true, and she could not afford to refuse any help she might receive.

"And you are sure this man, Gamal Sabri, is guilty?" he asked very quietly, as if he did not wish his sister, now in the kitchen, to overhear him.

"Yes."

"May I ask you why you now have no doubt, when earlier everyone was equally sure it was Habib Beshara? I don't wish to be offensive, but a great deal hangs in the balance."

She looked at the fear and the grief in his face, now more powerful than the weariness of constant physical pain.

She told him the evidence as she was aware of it, and the fact that none of it rested on the accuracy of eyewitnesses, frightened, confused, and too willing to help, too eager to see justice, to separate wish from memory.

"Why do you feel that Sabri will not be convicted?" he asked.

"Pryor is very skilled. We don't want to accept that we could have been wrong in convicting Beshara and sentencing him to death. If we could make that terrible mistake so easily, who may be next? It seems inescapable that it included not only bad police work, bad conduct of the law, but also deliberate corruption. If that is so, is anyone safe?"

"But Beshara was murdered in prison," Kittering pointed out. "If he was innocent, and knew nothing, was that no more than a coincidence?"

"I don't know," she admitted. "It seems he was an unpleasant man, quite apart from the sinking of the *Princess Mary*. But it was wrong, regardless of his nature. And I did not say he had nothing to do with the sinking. He may have helped, but he did not place the dynamite or light the fuse."

Kittering appeared to be deep in thought, struggling with some awful conflict in his mind.

"And we can find no reason why Sabri should have done such a terrible thing," she added. "Nearly two hundred completely innocent people were killed. Why would anyone do that?"

He was silent for so long she thought perhaps he was not going to answer. She was about to make her argument stronger when finally he spoke.

"Revenge," he said huskily, his eyes full of pain. "For the destruction of Shaluf et Terrabeh. It was a small village that was wiped out in a raid by mercenaries, just about a year ago." His face was pale. "A small band of mercenaries, four dozen or so, fell on it at night. It was just a village, a couple of hundred men, women, and children. But if they had sentries, they were picked off first, before they could raise an alarm."

Hester did not interrupt him. There was nothing useful to say about such a horror as he went on to describe in halting sentences, short, simple words broken as he struggled for breath. She thought of the terror, the darkness, women desperate to protect their children, the old and the frightened stumbling over one another, the screaming, the smell of blood.

"They counted over two hundred bodies," he said softly, his voice cracking a little. "Including babes in arms."

"For the two hundred on the *Princess Mary*," she answered. "Equally innocent. Did Sabri come from that village? Or was he paid to do it, do you think?" She tried to hold in the grief that all but suffocated her. "Why did no one say anything? What sort of revenge is it if the guilty don't know?" She gave a tiny shrug. "My husband had an idea that perhaps it was to kill one person on the ship. The rest were just . . . part of the plan. Expendable. If you are right, then he was mistaken. Perhaps this isn't as terrible, as frighteningly insane." Then she asked the question she had to, no matter how much it hurt. "Were they British mercenaries?"

"Not specifically," the major replied, his voice grating with the effort of controlling it. "A bit of all sorts. But the commander was British. That's what counts."

"Who?"

"A man named Wilbraham. I don't know much more about him. Don't look at me like that, Mrs. Monk. I really don't."

"How do you know any of it?"

"From a man who was there and tried to stop it."

"Obviously he failed . . ."

"He was badly injured trying to prevent it, and was left for dead by the man in command." His voice dropped a little lower, but his eyes never left hers. "He was rescued by the great courage of one of his own men, an Egyptian who saw it all."

"But he didn't testify to any of it?" She would rather not have said it, but it hung in the air between them like a tangible thing.

"I don't know why," Kittering admitted. "But I imagine it was to protect his family. If he had done, vengeance on them would have been swift, and complete. Would you?"

She thought of Monk, then of Scuff. "No." She took the paper out of her pocket that had the six names on it and passed it over to him. "Is he one of these?"

"Yes," he said quietly. "Who are they?"

"Among the dead," she replied.

"Then your husband was right," Kittering said quietly. "The *Princess Mary* was sunk to be sure of silencing one man."

CHAPTER

20

After the court was adjourned, Rathbone spread out on his dining room table all the documents he had regarding the trial of Habib Beshara. It was the best way he could think of to help Brancaster. They were drawing near to the final stage of the battle, and it was far more evenly balanced than he wished. There was a difficult judgment call to make. If they allowed the jury to be complacent, to believe that all was well with the justice system, then they would lose. It was always harder to defy or overturn a verdict than it was to reach one in the first place.

And yet if they used fear, either of the atrocity happening again because the guilty man had gone free, or of an innocent man being convicted and hanged in the future, they might panic the jury, and all its vision and balance would be lost.

That was the trouble: The whole case rested on emotion. Therefore none of the usual rules could be relied on.

Rathbone started reading the transcript of the trial of Habib Beshara, presided over by York. He smiled to himself. Here he was searching for emotional bias in York's rulings, and he was so emotionally involved himself that he was overcompensating in every direction in order to try to be fair. He should not be the one doing this, but it was his skill, his experience, that was needed.

He understood the law and most of the idiosyncrasies, particularly those that opened either traps or opportunities for men who made their money and their fame in its practice.

Brancaster had to use this all-too-short weekend in order to think of a strategy to keep Pryor from simply closing the case and relying on the jury to return a decision that Sabri was not guilty beyond a reasonable doubt.

Rathbone had been reading for nearly two hours, unaware of the evening drawing in, when he found the first serious error. York had upheld Camborne's objection when the grounds were insufficient. Over and over again Camborne had interrupted unnecessarily, played on the emotions of grief, even suggested that failure to convict Beshara was a blasphemy against the memory of the dead. Twice Juniver had argued vehemently and been overruled for questioning York's decision. He had wisely refrained from trying a third time, but Rathbone could imagine his frustration. Had it been Rathbone in his place, he would have taken it as a warning that he had a deeply unfriendly judge, maybe even a prejudiced one.

Of course, it was always possible that the horror of the case had affected York. The authorities would have made certain that he had no immediate family bereaved by the atrocity, but many people would've had friends or neighbors or associates who had lost someone, or knew someone who had lost someone.

Rathbone requested a pot of tea, and read on. Camborne was good: In fact, he was excellent. Not only that, but of course the crowd had been with him, and he had taken advantage of it. The rulings had leaned more and more his way.

Would Rathbone have done that, in his place? If he were honest, he was obliged to admit that he probably would.

Dover brought the tea and Rathbone accepted it gratefully. He had not realized he was so thirsty.

He went back to the transcript and studied it further. Very few of York's decisions were in favor of the defense. Had Juniver been so often wrong? Had he been so desperate that he'd been grasping at straws that would not bear the weight of his argument?

Or was Camborne simply the better lawyer? The fact that he was actually wrong could not have been known then.

Rathbone reached the end and went back to the beginning again. By that time it was midnight—the clock on the mantelshelf struck the hour. He ignored it. He made notes of every single one of York's decisions, and slowly a pattern emerged. York had favored the prosecution, and then favored them again to avoid reversing the earlier decision, compounding the error.

Singly, each decision was just about acceptable. Only when viewed cumulatively, and apart from the emotion of the case, did they amount to prejudice.

He finally put the papers away and went to bed at just after two in the morning. He was determined to go to visit Alan Juniver the following morning, regardless of the fact that it was Saturday. They had no time to spare.

JUNIVER WAS STARTLED TO see him. He was sitting in his home glancing at the morning newspapers before preparing to go out for the day with his fiancée's family.

"I'm sorry," Rathbone said. "I wouldn't call now if any other time would do. In fact I am concerned that I may already be too late."

Juniver looked worried. "It will not be viewed well if I don't turn up on time," he said anxiously. "Mr. Barrymore is already of the opinion that I am not the best choice his daughter could make."

Rathbone smiled ruefully. "I am not in a position to argue that particular case," he admitted. "If she wishes you at her beck and call for social occasions she might do better with a banker, or a stockbroker in the City. Of course she might then be bored to death, but one has to pick and choose which virtues or advantages one counts most important." The moment he had said it he could have bitten the words back, but it was too late. Apologizing might only make it worse.

"I suppose it is better he find out now." Juniver pulled his mouth into a tight line. "I assume this is about the Beshara case? You must normally have something better to do on a fine summer Saturday."

"I'm sorry," Rathbone said again. "We resume the trial on Monday, and I don't know how to stretch it out much further. If I were in Pryor's place, I'd close as soon as possible, while emotions are high and there's still reasonable doubt. We've no motive yet. It's a mess . . ."

"What do you want from me? I didn't get Beshara off."

Only in that moment did Rathbone perceive how deeply that still wounded Juniver. It was not his own failure that hurt—no lawyer always won—it was the fact that he now knew his client had been innocent, and was already dead, however long he might or might not have lived otherwise. It was not advisable to use that guilt against Juniver, but done well, it would be effective, and Rathbone dared not lose.

He put his leather attaché case on the floor. "I have the trial transcripts here. I spent a good deal of the night going over them several times. I would like very much to go over them again with you, because there are instances that trouble me. I would like your recollection, in case I am reading errors into them that, had I been present, I would realize were not as they seem."

Juniver frowned. "I was overruled a lot, but I was pretty desperate, and I knew it. I thought the man was guilty."

"I think everyone did," Rathbone conceded.

"You didn't?"

"I was out of the country. I didn't have an opinion at all. I'm sorry about your day, but a great deal hangs in the balance. It's the devil of a lot more than simply proving Sabri guilty."

"I know. Excuse me while I send a message that I cannot come."

"Of course. Juniver . . . I'm sorry!"

Juniver smiled. "I'd do the same . . . I hope."

A few minutes later he was back again. They went through the entire transcript, Rathbone making notes where York's judgments could have gone either way. Some of them were above question, some he had ruled for Juniver anyway, but precious few.

With increasing anxiety, Rathbone asked Juniver about each ruling that was against him. He had him look at the transcript and see if it was absolutely accurate, and if he could to recall anything more about the circumstances.

Juniver's memory was excellent. Very often he could recite what his objection had been and, word for word, what York had ruled. He also remembered the objections Camborne had made, and almost all of them had been upheld.

"There's a pattern," Rathbone said finally, rubbing his hands over his eyes. "Taken one by one they all seem reasonable, except the last two. But put together, and including your memory of small remarks not noted, expressions and silences, it amounts to bias, at the very least."

"It's only my memory," Juniver pointed out unhappily. "And when I look at it now, honestly, I didn't fight as hard as I could have, or would have if I hadn't believed Beshara was guilty. I'm not proud of that."

"None of us is proud of our losses," Rathbone said gently. "Whatever the reason."

Juniver's face was pale. "The reason was that I didn't fight with everything I could think of. I believed he deserved it. He was a nasty man and I disliked him from the beginning. I couldn't get the vision of those people in the water out of my mind, even though I didn't see it myself . . ."

"I imagine the jurors couldn't either," Rathbone agreed. "And Beshara may have been involved, on the periphery. The law is the question, and what pressures were brought to bear." He smiled, but his eyes did not waver from Juniver's, and it was the younger man who lowered his gaze first.

Juniver breathed in and out slowly. "Are you speaking of York?" he asked.

"Do you know if I'm right?" Rathbone countered. "Or suspect it?"

"Suspect," Juniver said immediately. Then, quite clearly, he regretted having not been more evasive. "At least . . . I wondered. It may have been no more than an emotional revulsion to the crime. It would be natural to be outraged. In fact, how could you not be?"

"We are all offended by crime," Rathbone answered. "Some more than others, of course. Violence is frightening; extreme violence is extremely frightening. We appoint judges because we believe they have the strength and the wisdom to separate their personal fears or weaknesses from the facts of the case. Lawyers who prosecute or defend are allowed to be as passionate as they wish. Judges are not . . . as I know, to my cost." He saw Juniver's face and immediately wondered if he had been wise to make the remark. Perhaps he had temporarily forgotten Rathbone's fall from grace. It could have been profoundly inopportune to remind him.

"We are all vulnerable," Juniver replied, lowering his eyes. "We want justice as we see it. We want to be heroes. We want to be on the side of right. And a good few of us want to climb on up the ladder as well . . ." He stopped. Then he added as if it were an afterthought, "And some of us want to earn favors of certain people."

That was what he had been meaning to say. Rathbone knew it as surely as if he had spoken of nothing else. He did not need to ask if he were referring to York. What did York want? To rise to the Supreme Court or the House of Lords? Not lord chief justice, surely? He had neither the brilliance nor the reputation among his peers for that.

Rathbone looked at Juniver again. Had the Beshara case really been big enough to build a reputation from which to reach for that? Or was York deluding himself? Perhaps Rathbone should have read more of the newspapers from the time of the sinking; then he would have understood the mood better.

"Is York in line for the next high office vacant?" he asked Juniver. Answers winged through his mind: York as lord chief justice, smiling under his white wig, nodding as he spoke with the prime minister, bowing before the queen. He saw Beata behind him, watching. Even if she just affected to be proud to be his wife, his heart ached for her. If she really was proud, because she had no idea the price York had paid for the honor, Rathbone was hurt as if with a raw wound. And if she knew the price, and did not care, then the pain within him was intolerable.

Had his tragedy with Margaret so warped his belief in people, and in his own judgment, that he trusted nothing anymore? He should not allow her to do that to him! No, that was not strictly fair: He was doing it to himself. Blaming others was what had driven them apart, the refusal to accept the truth because it hurt.

He forced himself back to the issue.

"It began as minor error," he said to Juniver. "But it looks to me as if he compounded it until it moved into the realm of something that would be cause for reversal in an ordinary trial for theft or assault. No one is going to reverse Beshara's conviction, because of the horror of the crime. York will have known that, as will Camborne. But is there anything here, looking at it now with the knowledge that Beshara was innocent, that could be viewed as corruption?"

Juniver's eyes widened. "You'd accuse York of corruption?"

"If there are grounds," Rathbone replied. "Wouldn't you?" Then instantly he changed his mind. He had been willfully insensitive. "If it is necessary, I will. I have nothing to lose anyway, and more chance of presenting it successfully. If it came to that."

"Bring down York?" Juniver said in little more than a whisper. "Because of the Beshara trial?" There was more than doubt in his voice; there was the weight of all he must know about Rathbone's own trial over which York had presided, and he might even guess what else lay between them.

"Do you think I should ignore it?" Rathbone asked quietly. He did not mean it, or like the sound of it on his lips. "Or give the information to someone else to use? Would you like it?"

"I should have done it at the time of Beshara's trial," Juniver replied unhappily. "I should have gone over it all, and I should have appealed then. Not that I imagine it would have done much good." He bit his lip. "But it wasn't fear for myself that stopped me, I swear. I thought the man was guilty, and the sooner they hanged him the better."

"And now?"

"I'll help you prepare an exact statement of the facts, all York's rulings on the Beshara case. If they amount to corruption, I'll do whatever I can to help you bring it to the right attention. A corrupt judge damages every person in England."

Rathbone thought about it all the rest of the day after he got home, and for far too much of the night. When he and Juniver had assembled all their notes and references, there was no doubt left. York's bias had come through in his rulings, and then his summing up. It had probably not been noticed by anyone else because the heat of emotion had been so high, and a conclusion was greeted with a wave of relief.

Rathbone turned it over and over in his mind, rereading the conclusions that he and Juniver had reached. The answer was inescapable. Either he must have Brancaster raise the issue in court, with reference to Beshara's conviction, which so closely reflected on the trial of Sabri, or he must face York with it himself.

Both possibilities were extremely unpleasant, but also unavoidable. What was the right thing to do? His first instinct was to ask Henry's advice, then he realized how feeble that was, how selfish. Of course Henry would give his counsel. He would do it gently. But would he not also wonder when Oliver was going to become adult enough to trust his own judgment and carry his own responsibility? He had always done so professionally, on occasions with too much self-assurance. But on the moral questions, and those of deep emotion and the possibility of hurt, he had sought strength from Henry.

During their tour of Europe and the Near East they had been as equals. Oliver had tried very hard to carry extra luggage, and take care of details to relieve his father of the necessity, but he had done it so carefully it had not shown. At least he thought it had not!

Now he should make the decision about facing York without expecting anyone else to examine the details with him, or bear the brunt afterward for whatever pain it caused.

Facing York would be excruciating. But it was a lot less dishonorable than reporting him behind his back. He must do it, prepare exactly what facts he would cite, with the proof, and do it this evening. The trial of Gamal Sabri continued tomorrow morning.

He had not even weighed up what might be York's reasons for his bias. It could be as simple as revulsion at the crime. Anyone would understand that.

But there was also the far darker possibility that someone had brought pressure to bear on him, threats or promises, to protect their own interests. Or worse even than that, to hide their guilt.

He took a hansom to York's house. There was no way to determine in advance whether he would be at home or not. Traveling at a fast clip through the darkening streets, the summer evenings already significantly drawing in, he half wished he would find York out and not expected back within hours.

And yet it was like going to have a tooth pulled. If it was infected it would have to be taken. Better to get it done without delay.

He alighted at the end of the block where York's house was, and paid the driver. He would look for another cab in which to return. He had no idea how long it would be. He might even be refused at the door!

Would it really be so ugly a meeting?

Yes. Yes, of course it would.

He turned and walked up the short path to York's front step, and before he could let thought weaken him, he grasped the bellpull.

The door was answered within a few moments.

"Good evening, sir," the footman said courteously, his blank face inviting some explanation.

Rathbone put his card on the silver tray that the man held out.

"Oliver Rathbone." He did not give his title. "I apologize for calling without previous arrangement, and at such an hour, but it concerns business taking place tomorrow, and therefore it cannot wait."

The footman blinked. "If you will come inside, Sir Oliver, I will see if Sir Ingram can see you. May I tell him what manner of business it is?"

"It concerns a trial that is of national importance," Rathbone replied, following the man into the vestibule and then the hall. The evening was too warm for him to have worn a coat, but the footman took his hat.

"Would you care to wait in the morning room, sir?" the footman asked.

Rathbone smiled. "I would prefer to wait here, thank you."

The footman did not argue but disappeared toward the withdrawing room, closing the door behind him. He returned a few moments later and showed Rathbone in.

York was sitting in the large armchair nearest the fireplace. He was possibly a little heavier than when Rathbone had last seen him, but his white hair was as gleaming and as thick. His complexion was flushed as if even the expectation of seeing Rathbone irritated him.

Rathbone glanced at Beata, who was on the sofa to his right. Not to have acknowledged her would have been appallingly rude. When he did, he felt a jolt of electricity. She was more than beautiful. There was a passion for life in her face, laughter, and tenderness. He looked away quickly, even before he spoke, afraid his own eyes would give him away.

"Good evening, Mrs. York. I am sorry to intrude—"

"What is it you want, Rathbone?" York interrupted. "If you've come to plead with me for some leniency on your bar from practice of the law, don't embarrass yourself. I have neither the power nor the will to do anything of the sort. Your punishment was deserved. For God's sake stop whining and take it like a man!"

"Ingram!" Beata said sharply, horrified at his bluntness. She turned to Rathbone, but before she could speak, York cut across her.

"Beata! This is not your concern. Your compassion speaks well for you, but please do not interfere. You can only make it worse." He looked at Rathbone again, leaning forward a little in the big chair. "I am quite aware of the current, farcical trial of Gamal Sabri, for a crime of which Habib Beshara is already convicted. I am also aware of your part in it, and I can imagine the desperation you must feel that you can only sit silently and watch it crumble. Were your friend William Monk not such an ambitious fool, you would not be placed in such elegant torture. But there is nothing whatever that I could, or should do about it. Now please leave my house without giving me the necessity of calling extra staff to remove you by force. Good night, sir."

This was the moment. Oddly enough, Rathbone did not feel a surge of anger boil up inside him; it was rather more pity, a regret that this could not be avoided, only pointlessly delayed.

"You are perfectly correct, sir," he said quietly. "It is a deserved punishment. Those who transgress the law must be removed from the practice of it, in the interests of us all." He moved his attaché case a little farther into view.

"Then why the devil are you intruding on my evening, and into my home?" York demanded.

"Would you not prefer to discuss this in private, sir?" Rathbone asked.

"No, I would not! If you want to make a fool of yourself in my home, then you will do it in front of my wife!" York retorted.

There was no escape.

Rathbone remained standing.

"I have studied the transcripts of Beshara's trial very carefully, and with legal colleagues, in case I should misinterpret anything in them," he began. "I have studied your rulings and your summation."

"For what purpose?" York snapped.

"To see if there are any grounds for reversal . . ."

York started to his feet, his left hand grasping for the cane that leaned against his chair.

"How dare you, sir?"

Beata rose also, her face creased with anxiety. "Ingram!"

"Don't you dare protect him!" he snarled, then swung back to face Rathbone. "I know you want to make a spectacle of yourself, one way or another, but this is beyond disgraceful! You dare to question the rulings of one of Her Majesty's judges, and a verdict that every sane man in England knows was fair and true?"

"Yes, I do," Rathbone answered him. "Some of your rulings were arbitrary and in error. At least two of them seriously so, and—had the case not been so deeply emotional and the verdict desperately desired—they would have been questioned at the time. Your summation was biased to the point of, politely, serious error; less politely, corruption."

York lurched fully to his feet. At first he leaned his weight on his cane, and then, ashen-faced, he raised it in the air.

"How dare you, of all people, question the law?" His voice was raised and shrill. "You took the law into your own hands and smashed it to pieces when you were on the bench. I backed you! I recommended you, and you thanked me by perverting the course of justice, blackmailing a witness with obscene photographs and very justly getting yourself disbarred. And now you come into my home, under false pretenses, and in front of my wife you accuse me of corruption in a case you weren't even in the country to see."

"And I paid for my mistake," Rathbone kept his voice level. "I am no longer practicing law. I am doing no more than giving Brancaster my advice . . ."

York gave a loud, derisive laugh. "The more fool he!"

"Your rulings were biased in favor of the prosecution against Habib Beshara," Rathbone continued. "The case is going to be overturned . . ."

"The hell it is!" York shouted, his face twisted with rage, spittle on his lips. "The man was as guilty as sin. If Sabri is guilty too, then they were in it together." His knuckles were white where he clutched the cane. His whole body shook.

"Ingram . . ." Beata tried again, moving a step toward him.

"Be quiet!" he said furiously, brushing her aside so hard he actually knocked her off balance. Only her closeness to the side of the armchair saved her from falling.

Suddenly the tone in the room changed. Rathbone struggled to regain control of the situation, and then he saw York's eyes and knew he had already failed.

"Beshara is dead, as he needed to be," York went on. "If you can hang Sabri as well, so be it. But you will not question my rulings or my conduct of one of the most important cases in British jurisprudence. It was my last great case, and I will not have a disbarred hack like you smear my legacy with your pathetic whining. Do you hear me?"

His voice was so loud they must have heard him in the kitchens.

"Only one man laid the dynamite on the *Princess Mary*, then lit the fuse and jumped overboard," Rathbone said as levelly as he could, but his voice was shaking. "Your ruling said it was Beshara, and he is dead. It was not Beshara, it was Gamal Sabri, and he is very much alive. We cannot convict two men of the same, single act. And apart from that, Beshara may be guilty of many things, but he was not guilty of this."

York lifted his cane and raised it to the side of him.

Beata jerked backward.

"Don't you dare tell me how to judge the law, you prancing jackass!" York shouted. "You are disbarred!" He swung the cane through the air with a sharp hiss of sound. "You are a suborner of perjury!" He swung the cane again. "A dealer in filthy pictures, a blackmailer . . . a lecher!"

"Ingram!" Beata shouted at him. "Stop it! That is untrue!"

York ignored her. He was moving toward Rathbone now, his cane lifted in the air. His face was scarlet. "I've seen you looking at my wife! Sniffing around her like a dog . . ." He lashed out with the cane, swinging it sideways until it struck Rathbone across the shoulder and sent him crashing to the floor with the force of the blow.

York took another step forward, his cane raised to strike again.

Beata picked up the coffeepot off the side table and smashed it over the back of his head. He stood swaying for a moment as coffee and blood trickled down his face and over his shoulders. Then he crumpled up and pitched forward to collapse on the floor in front of the couch.

Rathbone climbed to his feet, bruised, feeling shocked and ridiculous, but above all concerned for Beata.

She was shuddering, her face ashen, her eyes wide.

"I'm so sorry," she said huskily. "I—I think he has lost his mind. I must call his valet . . . and the doctor. Are you . . . hurt?" She looked stricken.

He took a deep breath. His well-being, and York's mistakes in the Beshara case, seemed insignificant now. This was the end of Beata's life in the way she knew it. It had to be a disastrous end to her husband's career.

The thoughts raced in Rathbone's mind.

"Yes," he agreed. "You must call the doctor immediately. There has been a most unfortunate accident and I fear Mr. York may have had some kind of seizure."

"He attacked you . . ." There were tears in her eyes; he thought they were of shame.

"Not as I remember it," he replied. "He stumbled and fell backward, grasping the cane to save himself, and regrettably caught me with the end of it as I lunged forward to help him. May I stay with you until you have assistance? Perhaps you should sit down and I will fetch the butler . . ."

She straightened her shoulders. "I will fetch him, thank you, Oliver. As . . . as you say, my husband is ill. I think perhaps he has been so for some time, and I did not realize how serious it was."

"Exactly," he agreed.

The butler was at the door. He must have heard the crash of York's fall. He regarded his master, who was still senseless on the floor, with some pity, but his concern was for Beata.

"I shall send Duggan for Dr. Melrose, ma'am," he told her. "Immediately. Perhaps, Sir Oliver, you would be good enough to remain here until we can get the appropriate assistance, and give Mrs. York what comfort you can? I don't believe we shall be able to resume . . . things as they were."

York was still lying insensible on the floor, coffee and blood on his head and face, spittle on his lips.

Rathbone said nothing, but bent to straighten out the fallen man's legs, before guiding Beata to one of the other chairs. Then he sat in silence opposite her until the servants returned.

CHAPTER

21

Rathbone was at Brancaster's chambers by eight o'clock the next morning, carrying the papers he had regarding York's conduct of the Beshara trial. He was too tired and too confused in his emotions to feel any sense of triumph in the fact that he almost certainly had enough material to gain Beshara a new trial, were he alive, or—since he was not—to overthrow a highly questionable verdict. But the victory over Ingram York gave him no sense of triumph. The man had abused his position. Perhaps Rathbone would never know all the small reasons that had brought it about, but he would not have had Beata suffer the distress of seeing him collapse in such a way, stripped of dignity and reason.

The doctor had come immediately. On seeing York still lying on the sitting-room floor, apparently in some sort of coma, the doctor had had him carried gently and carefully to his own room. When the doctor had heard more of the story, York had been taken to a private clinic.

Rathbone had stayed to be of whatever assistance he could. He felt foolish, perhaps intrusive, but he could not leave Beata alone to watch over what might very well be York's last journey from his own home to a place where he could be cared for, and perhaps from which he might never emerge.

Dr. Melrose could offer no prognosis. He was at a loss, and he had more dignity than to lie about it. Beata seemed to be grateful for that. At her insistence, he also looked at the angry red weal on Rathbone's shoulder and across his cheek. He glanced at the cane still lying on the floor but he did not ask Rathbone what had occurred. Perhaps York had lost his temper before and Melrose already knew it.

Rathbone was cold at the thought of what Beata might have endured, and forced the imaginings from his mind—not for his own sake, but for hers. If York had indeed struck her, she should be able to believe that Rathbone had no idea.

There was nothing to say beyond the formal words that filled the awkward silence. He had met her eyes once, and knew that she understood at least something of his feelings.

She answered with a tiny smile. It was not yet time for anything else.

It was after midnight when he left. He wished he could do something to help, but was certain that there was nothing yet, except to be discreet. He would speak to no one, not even Monk or Hester, about the blow York had struck him, or the convulsion of rage he had seen. But he could not remove from York's memory, and also Beata's, the knowledge of York's misconduct in the trial of Beshara. That was an abuse of the law, even if they attributed it to York's ill-health, and it must be faced.

Accordingly he was at Brancaster's chambers before Brancaster was there himself, and was waiting for him as he arrived. The morning was warm with the still, faintly dusty tiredness of late summer, when the air longs for the cleanness of autumn, the edge of frost, crisp leaves underfoot and the sharp tang of woodsmoke on the wind. The gardens would be bright again with the purple of Michaelmas daisies and the gold of late-blooming chrysanthemums.

Brancaster looked at Rathbone's face, started to speak, then sensed the gravity in him and waited.

Rathbone followed him inside and set his case of documents down on the floor. "We have sufficient for a reversal, I believe," he said very quietly. "If we cannot be sure of a conviction then we may have to use it. If we lose, Sabri cannot be charged again."

An expression of relief crossed Brancaster's face, and yet none of the tension slipped away from the body. His shoulders were still tight as if he could hardly draw a full breath, and his eyes did not leave Rathbone's face.

"York will fight hard," he said grimly.

"He won't fight at all," Rathbone answered, and the words sounded odd to his own ears. "He has had a seizure and I'm not sure he will recover. Certainly he will not be in a position to defend himself." Briefly he gave Brancaster the details of the errors he had found in the rulings. He gave only the facts, as if he were presenting a case to a jury. He said nothing of mercy, professional honor, the reputation of justice or the law. He trusted that Brancaster would know it all without the necessity of words. No discipline under the law could equal in darkness, confusion, and disgrace what York's own raging mind had done to him already.

For several seconds Brancaster said nothing. His face reflected many emotions. Then anger and pity gave way to a kind of desperation.

"Even if we overturn the verdict against Beshara, we still have to prove Sabri guilty," he pointed out. "How can I give the jury any confidence that we have the faintest idea what we are doing?" He clenched his fist as if he wished to strike at something, but there was nothing deserving of his anger, nothing to direct it against, so he was left standing there helplessly. "Why?" he demanded, suddenly.

"Why what? Why York?" Rathbone asked.

"Why any of them?" Brancaster replied, his voice rasping. "Why was Camborne so diligent in prosecuting a case he must have known was flawed? He's a damn good lawyer. He can't have missed the holes in it, even if Juniver did." His eyes searched Rathbone's, as if he should have the answer.

Rathbone had heard from Hester how passionate Camborne had been. At the time he had considered that the horror of the case fueled a natural outrage. Now he wondered, reading York's decisions and how harsh they had been against Juniver, if there had been more to it than that. Was it possible Camborne had also had some personal interest in it, a gain or a loss?

"And why is Pryor so dedicated to preserving the first verdict?" he said to Brancaster. "What stake has he in it? It's gone far beyond trying to defend the reputation of the law. Is he trying to gain higher office? To be a judge? He loves the battle too much merely to preside, for all its apparent power."

"Apparent?" Brancaster asked wryly.

Rathbone shrugged, yielding the point. "Then what?"

Brancaster let out his breath slowly. "Hatred."

Rathbone was startled and then seized with a coldness inside. "Of whom?"

"Of you," Brancaster replied. "There may be other incentives. I still have no idea what's really behind this whole thing. As we keep saying, we can only conclude he was paid, but we have no idea why, or by whom."

"We shouldn't have to prove that to get a verdict," Rathbone answered, but he wished he felt more certain of it. He did not argue that Pryor had no personal hatred of him. He simply had not realized it was so deep. The man's vanity was more easily wounded than he thought, his visions of glory too bright.

"And Lydiate," Brancaster continued. "He was forced into taking the investigation in the beginning, and perhaps also into conducting it a certain way. But he's not a fool. He couldn't have missed so much."

Rathbone felt the weight of this case settle even more heavily on him, as if he were hemmed in on every side. He looked at Brancaster, seeing in him also the signs of weariness, fear, even surrender.

Brancaster smiled bleakly, as if Rathbone had spoken it aloud. "It could cost us dear," he said softly.

"Cost you," Rathbone pointed out. "I have no office, and I'm honestly not sure what chances I have of being allowed back in the future. I wish I could take the risks for you, but I've denied myself that."

Brancaster gave a short bark of laughter. "I've always admired you. I even wanted to be like you. It rather looks as if I still do. I'm following this to the end. Give me the papers on York." He put out his hand.

Rathbone passed the case to him, yielding it reluctantly, even though it was what he had come to do. He was giving control of it to someone else, along with what was left of York's reputation, and the silence that might save at least something of it for Beata.

WHEN THE TRIAL RESUMED about two hours later, Brancaster rose to his feet. His body was tense. He looked utterly different from the man Rathbone had left in his chambers a little after eight.

"My lord," Brancaster began before Pryor had a chance to call his first witness of the day.

Rathbone stiffened also, feeling his breath catch in his throat. Why was Brancaster speaking already? It was inappropriate to introduce the evidence on York in this way. He should have spoken to Antrobus first, privately. What was the matter with him?

Antrobus raised his eyebrows and held up his hand to silence Pryor, who was now also on his feet, his face set in anger.

"This had better be important, Mr. Brancaster," Antrobus warned.

Rathbone even considered standing as well, then realized with a sick knot in his stomach that he had no more right or power here than any other person sitting in the gallery. This was the real bitter cost of his action in the Taft case, and he had brought it upon himself. Now all he could do was sit here in silence and watch Brancaster lose the biggest case of his life. He had given away his own weapons, and lost all the good he could have done.

"It is, my lord," Brancaster said quietly. "And I apologize for doing this at such short notice, but I received vital news only this morning, or I would have presented it to you, and to the defense, at a more fortunate time."

"My lord," Pryor protested, "this is preposterous! The prosecution is desperate and is putting on an ill-considered and—"

"Mr. Pryor!" Antrobus said sharply. "Am I the only one here who is unaware of what Mr. Brancaster is going to say?"

Pryor was caught on the wrong foot. "No, my lord . . . I . . . I am speaking of his melodramatic . . ." He stopped. Antrobus's stare would have turned a glass of water to ice.

Rathbone buried his face in his hands, and no one took the slightest notice of him.

"Mr. Brancaster?" Antrobus's voice was polite and knife-edged.

Brancaster swallowed. "Yes, my lord. I have a new witness who has just come forward. Unfortunately illness prevented his being aware of the value of his information, but his testimony explains all those aspects of the tragic sinking of the *Princess Mary* that have confused the issue until now."

Pryor threw his hands up in disgust. "For heaven's sake! This exhibition of—of gamesmanship is absurd, and offensive! Two hundred people died in—"

"Four hundred people were murdered!" Brancaster shot back at him. "And British justice was held up to ridicule, like blind men chasing each other in the dark!"

"Two hundred!" Pryor snapped. "For God's sake, man, sober up! You are behaving like something out of a seaside farce!"

Antrobus glared at him. "I know you are an ambitious man, Mr. Pryor, but you will not yet usurp my place in this court. I decide what is evidence and what is not."

The scarlet blood washed up Pryor's face, but he was wise enough not to argue this time.

Antrobus looked gravely at Brancaster. "Was that a highly unfortunate slip of the tongue, sir? Or are you aware of something that we are not?"

"I am aware, my lord, of something that the rest of the court is not," Brancaster replied respectfully. "And I would like to call Major Richard Kittering to the stand to testify of it. I have his particulars here, which I will pass to your lordship, with your permission. And a copy for Mr. Pryor. If you would prefer to adjourn while . . ."

Antrobus held out his hand.

Brancaster picked up the papers on the table and gave them to the waiting usher.

Rathbone held his breath. What on earth was Brancaster playing at? Who was Kittering? And why now? He turned in his seat to look around the gallery. Was Monk here? He could not see him, but Hester caught his eye almost immediately. She was sitting in a seat next to the aisle, and she watched Brancaster as if he were the only man in the room.

There was utter silence while Antrobus read the papers, then looked up.

"You say this witness was unavailable earlier, at the time you were presenting the case against the accused?"

"Yes, my lord. He was injured in the Middle East, and invalided home. He has come, at some cost to himself, and with the assistance of an ex-army nurse who served in the Crimea with Miss Nightingale. It was she who sought him out and made him aware of the value of his knowledge. His testimony will explain the whole, terrible tragedy. I cannot believe that there is any honest person in this room who would not wish that, my lord."

"We will adjourn for one hour, and give Mr. Pryor the opportunity to prepare such rebuttal as he can," Antrobus declared.

"That will not be sufficient," Pryor said immediately. "I have no idea who this Kittering is or what he may say. I object to his testimony altogether." He swiveled round to face Brancaster, his lips drawn back in a snarl. "But I can take an educated guess as to who the nurse is who went searching for him, and now suddenly presents him to the court, without warning. That will be Mrs. Monk, wife of Commander Monk from whom the case was taken in the beginning. She is well known, very well known indeed, to Sir Oliver Rathbone!" He let the words hang in the air as if they were some withering, poisonous fumes.

Rathbone's hands were clenched so tightly he was shaking. He felt the breath rasp in his chest. Pryor had to be right: It was beyond coincidence. Had Hester brought Kittering to Brancaster this morning, between the time Rathbone had left and the beginning of today's hearing?

"Mr. Brancaster?" Antrobus's temper was wearing thin. "Mr. Pryor has a degree of right on his side."

Brancaster drew in his breath, held it a second, then let it out slowly.

"Yes, my lord. It was Mrs. Monk who brought me word of the information Major Kittering possessed. I have checked it as far as I am able, and I believe it to be accurate, and extremely relevant. And of course I checked that Major Kittering is exactly who he says he is, and of an office of high standing and exemplary record."

Rathbone stared at him in disbelief. What on earth was he thinking he could achieve, at this late date?

"My lord, Major Kittering served in Egypt," Brancaster continued. "In the area of the new canal from Suez to the Mediterranean. He has personal knowledge of an incident that may be the beginning of this story. I do not believe Mr. Pryor will find anything he wishes to rebut." He stopped abruptly.

Pryor was on his feet again, his face twisted in fury. "My lord, this is a last-minute trick of Sir Oliver Rathbone and Commander Monk to try to take control of the case and set the law at mockery and disrepute! A court has already found another man guilty of this monstrous crime, and sentenced him to death for it. The conduct of the case was taken from Commander Monk and the River Police because of its magnitude, and out of vanity Monk is now seeking revenge, even at the cost of the honor of the law."

Antrobus's face darkened, but Pryor would not be stopped.

"I can call many witnesses, my lord, who will testify to Commander Monk's past reputation for arrogance and disregard for his superiors. He was dismissed from the Metropolitan Police and is now seeking revenge on them. He has no compunction in trying to destroy the reputation of Sir John Lydiate because he is a man who does not forget a grudge, and is bitterly jealous of a dignity and office he cannot attain himself."

"That is a door you would be very ill-advised to open, Mr. Pryor," Antrobus said curtly. "It is wide enough to allow all through it, yourself included. The privilege of seeking for the defense does not allow you to slander officers of the law. Do I have to remind you that your evidence must be not only provable, but also relevant? Do you wish to call Mrs. Monk regarding her acquaintance with Major Kittering?"

"I have no knowledge of it," Pryor said bitterly. "It could be anything at all!" He spread his hands wide in a hopeless gesture. "She was an army nurse, I am told. For God's sake, that could mean anything! She is no doubt acquainted with scores of soldiers—even hundreds!"

Rathbone nearly shot to his feet, but Brancaster did so first.

"My lord, if Mr. Pryor wishes me to call Mrs. Monk then I will do so. But he would do well to take heed of your lordship's warning. Slander is a very wide door indeed—but not wide enough to wreck the reputation and honor, indeed the nation's gratitude, to the women who served with Miss Nightingale in the Crimea, sharing the desperate hardships of our men there and caring for the sick and the wounded . . ."

Pryor made a choking sound in his throat, but swallowed back the protest as he gagged on it. The jurors were staring at him, eyes wide, and there was a sharp rustle in the gallery as people stiffened to attention.

"Very well. Call your witness now, Mr. Brancaster," Antrobus ordered. "But if you abuse your privilege I shall rule against you."

"Yes, my lord. Thank you." Brancaster relaxed visibly, relief flooding up his face.

Pryor returned to his seat with an ill grace, biding his time.

There was a buzz of excitement as Brancaster called Major Richard Kittering. The doors opened and Kittering, lean, gaunt, walking slowly and with the aid of crutches, made his way to the witness stand.

Antrobus leaned forward. "Major Kittering, would you prefer to give your evidence from the floor, sir? There is no need for you to climb up to the witness stand. The steps are somewhat awkward. If you care to sit, a chair can be brought."

"Thank you, my lord," Kittering replied. "I shall stand as long as I am able."

Antrobus nodded. "Mr. Brancaster, perhaps you will keep your examination as brief as you may, and still serve your purpose."

"My lord."

Kittering was sworn in and Brancaster came into the body of the floor, speaking respectfully as to a man who had earned the right to it. He established Kittering's military record and the regiment in which he had served, that he had been wounded in Egypt and had returned to England earlier in the year.

"Are you acquainted with the accused, Gamal Sabri?" Brancaster asked.

"No, sir, not personally."

"His family?" Brancaster enquired.

Kittering's face was stiff, as if he were controlling his inner pain only with difficulty. "No, sir, only by repute."

"Repute?"

There was not a sound in the courtroom except for a woman coughing and instantly stifling it.

"Yes, sir. My friend Captain John Stanley knew Sabri's family . . ." Kittering's voice faltered and he struggled to maintain his composure. His emotion was palpable in the room.

"You use the past tense, Major Kittering," Brancaster said gently. "He does not know them anymore?"

Kittering lifted his chin and swallowed hard. "I regret to say that all Mr. Sabri's family perished in the massacre at Shaluf et Terrabeh."

"All of them?" Brancaster said incredulously.

"Yes, sir. There were two hundred people who died that night. Every man, woman, and child in the village." His voice broke and his face was ashen.

Brancaster's question was little more than a whisper, but the room was motionless; every word was audible.

"You used the word 'massacre.' Do I take it that they were murdered . . . two hundred of them?"

Kittering, standing ramrod stiff, swayed a little.

"Yes, sir. By marauding mercenaries who mistook where they were."

Brancaster moved forward a step, as if he were afraid Kittering might fall.

"Were you there, Major?"

"No, sir, I was not. I heard of it from Captain Stanley."

"He was there?"

"Yes, sir. He tried to prevent it, but the officer in command wouldn't listen. Mercenaries, all nationalities . . ." His voice tailed off. His skin was ashen. "But the man in charge was British . . ."

"Captain Stanley told you this?"

"Yes, sir. The man in charge was arrogant, brave, a good soldier spoiled by a filthy temper."

Kittering looked so fragile Brancaster began a sentence and changed his mind, afraid to draw the questioning out any further than he had to. "Stanley was there, and saw it all?"

"Yes, sir, almost all. In trying to stop the massacre, he was knocked senseless. That may have saved his life."

"Then why are you here testifying, and not Stanley?" Brancaster asked, moving another step forward.

"He was injured and had only just returned to England, sir. He went down on the *Princess Mary*."

There were sighs around the room. A woman sobbed.

On the bench Antrobus leaned forward and ordered the usher to fetch a chair for Kittering. Brancaster helped him onto it, propping the crutches beside him where he could reach them.

"Thank you, Major Kittering," Brancaster said gravely. "We mourn the loss of Captain Stanley, and all the other nearly two hundred men and women who drowned in the Thames that night. We also mourn those innocent people who lost their lives in Egypt, due to the arrogance and ill-temper of a British renegade officer who would not be counseled." He turned to Pryor. "Your witness, sir."

Pryor stood up. Perhaps he was at last aware that the entire room was against him. They were numb with horror at the tragedy, and the mindless evil of it all. They looked at Kittering, his pain and his shame for his brother officers written indelibly in his face. They waited for Pryor to attack him.

Pryor was too wise and, Rathbone thought, also too self-serving, to make such an error.

"I will not keep you long, Major Kittering. I regret having to trouble you at all."

Kittering nodded.

"When and where did Captain Stanley tell you about this appalling event?"

"When he came to see me, on returning home," Kittering answered. "It was at the beginning of May. Two days before the sailing of the *Princess Mary*."

"And you believed his account, word for word?" Pryor did not invest his voice with doubt; he knew better than that.

"Yes. I knew Stanley, and I know of the officer in command, a man called Wilbraham, by repute. I knew the massacre had occurred because I knew men who saw the place two or three days after. Many bodies were unburned and the stench of blood was still in the air."

"Perhaps you are fortunate you were not able to be on the *Princess Mary*?" Pryor left only a suggestion of disbelief in the air.

"Why?" Kittering said, twisting his mouth in a grimace of misery. "I wasn't actually there, after all."

"Indeed you were not," Pryor agreed. "It seems you have a very partial knowledge of a horrific incident, and a great deal of loyalty to a dead friend who may well have been to blame for it."

Kittering was so white that Brancaster rose to his feet, not to object but to help him physically if he should faint in the chair and fall sideways onto the floor. Even Rathbone was poised to rush forward if that should happen.

Everyone else in the room was motionless.

Pryor broke the spell.

"It seems from your story, Major Kittering, that you believe Gamal Sabri took a fearful vengeance on the man who destroyed his village, and some two hundred of his fellow countrymen. An appalling act, but one I dare say many of us here would at least understand. If someone hacked to death every man, woman, and child in the village where I grew up, I cannot swear that I would forgive, or trust in a powerless law to avenge such an act. What I do not understand is why you appear to defend Stanley. If your story is true, perhaps you will explain that to us?" He stood with a helpless, confused expression, waiting for Kittering to answer.

Kittering took several long, deep breaths. Clearly he was exhausted and in some considerable physical pain.

Brancaster remained standing.

Antrobus looked at Kittering with some concern, but he did not intervene.

Rathbone felt as if each second dragged by, but there was nothing he could do to help.

"You have misunderstood, sir," Kittering said at last. "Perhaps that is your job. It appears to be. Stanley did not commit the massacre at Shaluf et Terrabeh. He tried to stop it and was nearly killed for his efforts." He stopped, struggling to keep his composure.

Pryor seized the chance to interrupt. "That makes no sense, sir. If Stanley was not guilty, why on earth would Gamal Sabri sink an entire ship of people just to be sure of killing him? It is absurd! You cannot expect this court to believe that. Perhaps your own injury has . . . affected your memory." He said it in a conciliatory tone, but it did not disguise his contempt. "May I put it to you, Major Kittering, that it was Stanley who led the atrocity against the village, and you yourself who were severely injured in trying to prevent it?"

There was a stirring in the gallery; whether out of pity, disgust, or fear, it was hard to tell.

"They were mercenaries," Kittering said with weary patience, as if speaking to someone slow of wits. "There will be no military record of them. But I am a regular soldier. It would be perfectly simple to check that I was nowhere near Shaluf et Terrabeh at this time, if you were interested in the truth. And I did not say that Sabri sank the *Princess Mary* to kill anyone in revenge, although I dare say he was willing enough. God knows what we have done to his people. Of course it makes no sense to kill Stanley. I don't suppose he knew Stanley was on board . . ."

Pryor rolled his eyes.

Kittering kept his patience with an effort. "He was paid to sink the ship," he said quietly, his voice fading as his strength drained away. "Stanley was the one man who could have testified against Wilbraham, and would have if he could be brought to trial."

The court was silent. No one moved in the jury box, or in the body of the gallery. Even Antrobus was momentarily lost for words.

Pryor turned one way, then the other, but for once he could think of nothing wise or clever to say.

Brancaster looked around, then moved forward and offered his arm to Kittering.

"Thank you, sir. May I take you back to a more comfortable place, and perhaps fetch you a glass of water?"

Kittering rose with difficulty and accepted Brancaster's arm.

Antrobus nodded slowly. He looked at Pryor, then at Brancaster's back as he walked all the way to the doors with Kittering. He glanced at Rathbone and smiled very slightly before adjourning the court. They would check the military records Brancaster had given them, perhaps even check with the Egyptian embassy that the massacre at Shaluf et Terrabeh had been as reported, but no one doubted it.

Outside Monk joined Hester.

"God, what an awful crime," he said with emotion all but choking him. He put his arm around her, drawing her closer to him. "I must tell Ossett that it's over, at least the legal part. Whether Pryor loses anything, except the case, time will tell. York's finished. The decision on Beshara will obviously be reversed, so Camborne will lose, maybe more than just that decision. I hope Lydiate won't lose his job, but he might." He did not add that possibly he deserved to. He was not sufficiently sure he could not have been manipulated, were his family's lives at stake.

"Come with me," he added. "You can tell Ossett about Kittering better than I can. And it was you who found him. He'll be relieved that we've found the truth at last."

She nodded silently, linking her arm in his as they went down the steps toward the busy street.

Ossett received them almost immediately, putting all other business aside. They were shown into his gracious and comfortable office with its striking portrait above the mantelpiece.

"It is over, sir," Monk said without preamble. Ossett looked drained of color, as if he had neither eaten nor slept well in days, possibly weeks, and Monk felt a surge of pity for him. Perhaps he was guilty of having pressured Lydiate into a fatal haste where Beshara was concerned, but if so he had done all he could since then to support Monk in his pursuit of the truth, and then the trial of Gamal Sabri.

"There is no question that Sabri is guilty," Monk said with certainty. "Kittering's evidence makes sense of it all."

Ossett was very pale, but there was a tension within him as if he were unable to remain seated.

"How did you find him, Mrs. Monk?" he asked.

Was it politeness to make her feel included, or did he really wish to know? Monk himself was uncertain. But now that it was all but over, he felt the man deserved any information he asked for. He was the one who would have to deal with the political consequences, and advise on the legal ones, should there be any.

Briefly, Hester told him of her service in the Crimea, and that she still knew several men with military careers. As she did so, she glanced up at the portrait, and smiled.

"I see," Ossett said hoarsely. "And what does this Major Kittering have to say about the sinking of the *Princess Mary?*"

Quietly and in the simplest of words, Monk told him of the atrocity in the village of Shaluf et Terrabeh, and how the raid had been a hideous error by an arrogant mercenary commander. One man had stood out against him, and all but lost his life for his temerity.

Ossett looked as if he himself had been struck. He was shaking, and as pale as the white paper on the desk in front of him.

"Are you . . . certain of this?" he said falteringly. "Does this man, Kittering, know beyond doubt?"

"I believe he does," Monk answered. "His friend, Stanley, was there and all but lost his life trying to prevent it."

"Stanley?" Ossett repeated the name as if it had some terrible meaning for him. "Captain John Stanley?"

Monk was puzzled. "Yes, sir. Do you know of him?"

"Could he not be guilty of leading this . . . abomination?"

"Kittering says not," Monk answered, recalling Kittering's vehement denial. "He said it was a man named Wilbraham, apparently known for his violent temper."

Without warning Monk felt the pressure of Hester's fingers digging into his arm with sudden extraordinary strength, as if she meant to hurt him.

He gasped, confused by the violence of it. She was smiling, but at Ossett, not at him.

"That is what Kittering said, sir," she said to Ossett, ignoring Monk. "But he appeared to have a deep regard for Stanley. They had been personal friends for years, brothers-in-arms, as it were."

"But . . ." Monk began. Then he felt her fingers dig into him again, as if she would puncture his flesh with her nails.

She was still smiling at Ossett, her eyes brilliant, her breath a little ragged.

"What is important is that Sabri is unquestionably guilty of sinking the *Princess Mary,* and therefore of the deaths of all on board her. Mr. Pryor seems to have had some personal stake in fighting so hard to defend him. From what was said, it was not pressure from anyone in high office, rather more a personal rivalry with Sir Oliver Rathbone that got out of hand. I dare say it will damage his reputation somewhat, but it is not an injury to the law."

Ossett was staring at her, fighting to find words.

Hester's smile faded a little.

"Mr. Justice York has been taken seriously ill, so his rather eccentric rulings can be easily understood. Sir John Lydiate may have lost something of the confidence of his superiors, but no doubt they will act as they see fit. Altogether, it is a better ending than one might have received." She turned to Monk. "I'm sure you will be sending a written report in due course. That is all we need to tell his lordship in the meantime." Again her fingers dug into his arm.

"Thank you," Ossett said. His voice cracked as he rose to his feet, leaning a little forward on the desk as if to steady himself. "I am most grateful that you took the time to let me know so quickly of the result. Now, I—I have certain other people I would like to inform. Thank you again, thank you, Mrs. Monk."

As soon as they were outside on the street Monk stopped and caught hold of Hester's shoulder, swinging her around to face him.

"What the devil was that about?"

"The portrait," she said almost under her breath. "Above the fireplace."

"Yes. It's him as a young man. What about it?"

"No, William. It's not!"

"Yes it is. He hasn't even changed all that much! Anyway, what does it matter?"

"It's not him," she insisted. "It's current, not more than a couple of years old."

"Hester, he's in his mid-fifties!"

"The campaign medals, William. They're from three years ago."

"They can't be! Are you sure?" He began to have an awful glimpse of what she meant.

"Yes. I still have military friends. They're Egyptian, like the group in the background of the painting. And his eyes are not really the same color."

"Artist's mistake . . ." But he knew he was wrong. "You are sure about the campaign medals?"

"Yes. It has to be his son . . ." She took a deep, shaky breath. "What is his family name?"

"Family name?" He started to walk along the pavement, to be away from Ossett's doorstep. "I don't know . . ."

"He has a monogram on his cigar box on the table. RW. Are you certain he doesn't look like a man who has looked into hell because Robert Wilbraham, who led the massacre at Shaluf et Terrabeh, and then paid Sabri to sink the *Princess Mary* and get rid of the only witness, is his son?"

Monk closed his eyes, as if refusing to look at the busy London street could somehow wipe away the knowledge, finally, of the truth.

It all made sense. The pieces fitted together.

Now the touch of her hand on his arm was gentle.

"We believe of people what we need to," she said. "As long as we possibly can."

"You believed I didn't kill Joscelyn Grey," he said, remembering back to when they had first met, soon after she had returned from the Crimea and the horror of that appalling war. "You didn't even know me!"

"And I would believe you now," she said firmly. "Perhaps I know you better than he knows his son. Sometimes sin is the hardest to accept when it is in someone we have known always, for whose birth and life we are responsible. Everyone is somebody's child."

"I know." He put his hand over hers. "I know."

She did not answer him. She was staring over his shoulder at something beyond, something on the pavement behind him.

"What is it?"

"No!" she said urgently. "Don't turn yet. It's Lord Ossett. He's left his office and he's going toward the main road. Do you suppose he knows where Wilbraham is?"

Monk did not bother to answer. There was no time to call anyone else. They were miles from Wapping and any of his own men. He could hardly stop a constable, even if he could see one, and order them to follow a government minister of Ossett's standing. He would be more likely to find himself arrested.

He turned and started to walk along the footpath after Ossett, Hester at his side. He felt miserable, and yet compelled. Ossett was almost certainly going to try to save his son. Monk was going to arrest a man responsible for four hundred innocent deaths, men, women, and children who died by mischance, because they served his purpose.

A long hansom ride, two stops and an hour later, Monk finally knew where Ossett was going.

"Wilbraham must be at the wharf where the damaged *Seahorse* is kept," he said. He and Hester were standing on the dockside, twenty yards behind Ossett and half sheltered by a stack of timber. The low sun was dazzling. A laborer with a loaded barrow traveled past them, sending up a cloud of dust.

"I'm going after him," Monk said quietly. "I have to."

"I know," she agreed.

He nodded. "Go back to the main street. We passed a omnibus stop. There are plenty of people around. I have to go down to the mud flats and if Wilbraham is there I must stop him. Once he's on the water he could escape on any seagoing freighter. He could be in France by tonight."

She did not move. "You can't go alone. There are two of them; Ossett will fight you."

"I know that," he admitted. "He can't bear what his son is, but neither can he give him up. I don't know what I would do, if it were someone I loved." He stopped because the thought was too dark to give shape to. "Go back to the street, please, so I know you are safe."

She hesitated, the decision to leave him, to walk away, too big to take.

"Hester . . . please . . ."

White-faced, tears on her cheeks, she turned to obey.

Monk watched her for barely a moment before he was aware of someone behind him. He swung around and thought for an instant that somehow Ossett had doubled back, and then he realized it was a younger man. He had the same features, the same fair hair falling forward a little, but there was an ugliness in his face, about his lips, that was different.

For one second, two, three, they stared at each other. Monk knew that there was no purpose whatever in trying to plead with this man. He had led a massacre, and then paid to have someone drown two hundred innocent people in order to be certain of killing the one witness against him.

Wilbraham lunged forward, knocking Monk aside, but he did not stop and strike at him with the knife in his hand. Instead he ran onward toward Hester, knife blade gleaming for an instant in the sun.

A gunshot rang out.

Wilbraham froze.

Monk turned to see Ossett standing with a pistol raised in his hands, pointing toward Monk's chest. He had his back to the sun and the burnished river mud of slack tide. Wilbraham was balanced on the edge of the shingle, yards from Hester.

There was no sound but the faint ripple of the water.

Wilbraham took a step toward Hester, the knife blade raised again.

"Take him," he said to his father. "I'll take her."

Very steadily, Ossett raised the barrel of the pistol as if it were of immense weight, and moved his aim from Monk to Wilbraham.

Wilbraham stood smiling. He barely had time to register surprise when the bullet hit him between the eyes. He crumpled into the slick, shining mud, which almost immediately, as if it had been waiting for him, began to suck him down.

Monk lurched forward and struck the gun from Ossett's hands. Then he hesitated, filled with a scorching pity, not knowing what to do. How could he attack a man in such agony?

Hester was running toward him, tears of relief streaming down her face.

Ossett shook his head. "You don't need to shackle me. I have a debt to pay. I shall not evade it. I have lied to myself far too long. It is the end." He began to walk blindly up the shingle toward the edge of the road.

Monk stood on the shore in the waning light and held Hester so close, at any other time he might have feared hurting her. Now, at this moment, nothing could be close enough.

ABOUT THE AUTHOR

ANNE PERRY is the bestselling author of two acclaimed series set in Victorian England: the William Monk novels, including *Blind Justice* and *A Sunless Sea*, and the Charlotte and Thomas Pitt novels, including *Death on Blackheath* and *Midnight at Marble Arch*. She is also the author of five World War I novels, as well as twelve Christmas novels, including the upcoming *A New York Christmas*. She lives in Scotland.

WWW.ANNEPERRY.CO.UK